THE

BISHOP'S MANTLE

THE
BISHOP'S MANTLE

BY

AGNES SLIGH TURNBULL

THE MACMILLAN COMPANY · NEW YORK

1948

TO MY DAUGHTER
MARTHA LYALL TURNBULL

CHAPTER I

THE YOUNG MAN in the taxi leaned forward.

"Can you go faster?" he said to the driver. "It's a matter of life and death."

The grubby man on the front seat turned, glimpsing again as he had done when he first picked up the fare a white set face above a clerical vest.

"Do my best, Father," he answered respectfully.

The young man half smiled. No need to disillusion him, he thought. The fact that he had not had time to change clothes might serve him to some advantage now.

"Straight out Forest Avenue when you get to it, for about a mile," he added, "then left on Letheridge. I'll tell you the house."

"Right, Father. I'll step on it."

The car seemed to gather a new power from its deep mechanical subconscious. With a surprising spurt it escaped the downtown traffic and headed for the residential section. The young man, his face tense, kept watching the passing landmarks. When the car at last made the turn on Letheridge, he had already grasped the door handle. The houses were all large here, mostly of stone, standing well back in spacious grounds. As they neared one of the largest he spoke quickly.

"Here, on the right. This next one. Go up to the drive. Thanks. That was good work!"

The car was not yet out of motion when he sprang from it with his bag, leaving a bill on the seat by the driver. He took the stone steps at a bound. As he reached the great front door, it opened, as he felt sure it would, without his ring. Morris would be watching for him.

He faced the old man servant in the wide hall.

"Is he still . . ."

Morris nodded. His eyes were red and his voice very husky.

"Hurry on up, Mist' Hilary. There isn't much—time."

Hilary started to run up the long stairway. At the landing he paused, not for breath, for his lungs were strong from many an obstacle race of college days. Rather it was a sudden sense of unseemliness that made him walk the rest of the way. He was approaching a chamber of death. Before the vast dignity of a soul on the eve of departure, he must not, even in his desperate eagerness, burst with the outward appearance of hurry into the room. So when he reached the door he turned the knob slowly and quietly stepped inside.

The bed had been moved, he noticed at once, out of its recessed corner, and a nurse was standing, watchful, beside it. She raised her eyes now, and then signed to Hilary to come forward. As he did so, the Bishop opened his eyes, and smiled incredulously.

"I never thought you'd make it," he said, with slow effort. "They're hurrying me a bit on this business."

"Grandy!" The childish name always slipped out. He caught the old man's hand. "I flew. Now who says airplanes are a curse?"

"I do," said the Bishop.

Then upon them both fell the bitter and imminent necessity of separation. The old familiar banter must be put aside.

"There are a few things to say, Hilary. Not many."

The young man's grasp on the thin hand tightened. His eyes were wet. The nurse withdrew.

"Yes, Grandy."

"You're executor, as eldest. All I have is for you and Dick. Do as you please with the personal things. This scrap-book on the stand is for you. I hope it may be of some help. Any word yet?"

"Yes. I was just going to phone you before I got—your message. I'm called to St. Matthews."

"Good!" The Bishop closed his eyes a moment as though in pain, and then freed from the seizure pressed his grandson's hand with surprising strength.

"Nunc dimittis. I'm glad, my boy. I'm proud. 'Good luck in the name of the Lord.'"

"Thanks, Grandy. But it looks like a big order for me."

"You can do it. What about—the girl?"

Hilary flushed.

"I still want to marry her, if she'll have me."

Something like a shadow passed over the Bishop's face.

"She has beauty. Great beauty."

"Yes, sir."

"And the flesh is far from negligible. Only—be sure, Hilary. Take time to weigh everything."

"I will, Grandy."

The nurse came back and took the Bishop's other hand in hers. As her

2

finger touched the pulse her eyes met Hilary's. The old man intercepted the look.

"About time for me to be leaving, Nurse?" he asked.

She made an effort to return his smile.

"I wondered just how—you felt."

"I can't tell," the old man said whimsically. "I've never done this before, you know."

The nurse looked faintly shocked. "I'm going to call the doctor," she said.

When she had left the room the Bishop turned his head again toward his grandson.

"About the service. Bronson will have to have it of course. But hold him down if you can. No fuss. You know my tastes."

"I'll see to everything."

"Give my love to Dick when he gets here. I had them send a wire to his room address as soon as I knew. Dear knows where he may be, though. Keep an eye on him, Hilary."

"I will."

There was a little pause in which Hilary felt his throat too tight for speech.

"You might say a prayer, if it isn't too much for you. 'Support us all the day long,' I think is my favorite."

Suddenly he raised himself on his elbow.

"Remember, Hilary, there will be times . . . Just hang on even when you feel there's No One or Nothing there. Hang on, anyway."

"I promise, Grandy."

He knelt down and took both the frail hands into his grasp. His voice was unsteady but he managed the words.

". . . until the shadows lengthen and the evening comes and the busy world is hushed, the fever of life is over and our work is done. Then in Thy mercy grant us a safe lodging and a holy rest and peace at the last."

Their voices joined in the Amen.

The nurse returned and before long the doctor. But the Bishop made no sign when they spoke to him. He lay with his eyes closed, a faint smile upon his chiselled lips. Hilary, by the window, felt an outrageous twinge of mirth. His grandfather was practicing an old device.

"When you're stuck with a caller who has his sittin' britches on, Hilary, I'll tell you how to get rid of him. Just sit. Wear an expression of ineffable benediction, but don't say a word. It always wears them out."

He could hear the old chuckle which had accompanied the advice. Now, the Bishop was applying it again for the last time. He had said his say. He was through. He wished to be alone.

3

By sunset he had taken his departure with the same simplicity and dispatch which had marked all the actions of his life. Hilary knelt again for a few moments beside the bed and then, shaken with a terrible desolation, he opened the door and went down the hall to his own old room.

The window overlooking the garden was raised and the fresh spring air blew in. He dropped into a chair and sat with his head in his hands. Very soon he must become involved with that ironic busyness which follows hard upon the silent detachment of death. For a few short minutes, however, he could look his personal grief in the face and try to get control of himself.

Grandy was dead. The man who had been father to him since childhood, who had been both mentor and comrade through all the years, was gone. And now in the first great crisis of his life he was to be left without the wisdom, the tolerance, the saving humor as well as the unshakable love upon which he had always depended. A blackness settled upon him; a sense of intolerable loneliness and insufficiency.

There was a hesitant knock on the door. When he opened it the nurse stood there with the brown scrapbook in her hands.

"I thought I should give you this for fear it might get mislaid. He seemed so anxious about it. 'That book,' he kept saying, 'is for my grandson, Hilary. Please be sure to see that he gets it.' He made me promise, so here it is."

"Thank you," Hilary said. "You've been very kind."

The woman waited a moment. She had difficulty in speaking.

"He was different from anyone I have ever nursed. So different from what I thought a Bishop would be like. I wish I could have known him better."

"He was worth knowing."

"I could see that," she said. Then more slowly: "There was something else he kept telling me last night. I don't think his mind was perfectly clear at the time, for we had to give him drugs. But he kept saying this over and over and I felt perhaps I should tell you even though you had seen him."

She stopped, embarrassed, and Hilary regarded her gravely.

"I think you should. Please go on."

"He kept saying, 'If Hilary doesn't get here in time tell him I said to go slow, to be sure.' There was a little more but perhaps you will understand from that—"

"I think so," Hilary said, coloring, hoping no name had been spoken, "and thank you again."

With a sigh as of relief at a difficult thing done, the nurse turned back to her remaining duties and Hilary closed his door. He did not open the book, but the very feel of it in his hands brought him strange comfort. It was something tangible, concrete, to be touched and used. In all the years he had never seen the volume before. It must be deeply personal then and precious, containing some crystallization of the spirit, some residuum of the life now gone.

He sat on, holding it, mastering his shaken nerves as a child alone in the dark clasps some object of daytime reality to its breast and ceases to weep.

At last he got up and laid the book on the table.

"Morris!" he muttered. "Poor old cuss! I'll have to see to him. Then Bronson and the rest."

He went downstairs. There was as yet, of course, no change in the familiar rooms. The Bishop's pipe lay on the library table just as he had put it down, half smoked, the day before.

"You may mislay my Bible or my Prayer-book, Morris," he had often remarked, "but never my pipe! Don't ever touch that!"

So there it was now just as he had left it with the book he had been reading lying open at the page. So suddenly had he been stopped in the usual routine of his days. On the desk a neat stack of letters lay ready to be mailed. The one on top, Hilary saw with a pang, was addressed to himself.

He went on through the dining-room guided by a faint, breathy sound. In the butler's pantry the old negro stood, sobbing. Hilary went up to him and patted the thin, bony shoulders. He remembered once that Morris had found *him* here, a small boy, frightened by Katy, the cook, and had comforted him the same way.

"He's—he's gone, Mist' Hilary?"

"Yes, Morris."

The old man trembled.

"He was a good friend to me, Mist' Hilary."

"He was a good friend to everybody."

"I got nothin' to live for now. If I could jus' die an' go 'long with him! You know how he always losin' his glasses? Jus' yesterday he couldn't find them an' when I fetched them he say, 'If I lose my soul some day, Morris, I know you'll be on hand to find it for me.' Jus' yesterday, Mist' Hilary."

"I know, Morris. I know. But we've got to stiffen. I'm going to take you back with me. I've got a church of my own now and a house. I'll need you very badly. And right this minute I want a good strong cup of tea and some sandwiches. I had no lunch and I've hard work ahead of me."

5

The old man straightened and controlled himself at once. His reaction was pathetically instinctive.

"Will you have tea in the library, Mist' Hilary?"

"Yes, please. And hurry, will you, Morris?"

He went back to the desk and picked up the phone. The nurse had taken care of the most essential and painful calls. As to his own list, it would have to be Bronson first. He would consider it irregular that he had not been called before. His sense of the dramatic was strong. He would feel that at the deathbed of a Bishop, as of a king, there should be present the next in line, Hilary thought wryly. He would be equally sure, with his growing High Church predilection, that a simple prayer was insufficient for the occasion. Extreme unction or the nearest thing to it would be his idea. But the news itself would elate him beyond words. Hilary hated himself for the thought even as he hated the truth of it. In view of his new eminence Bronson would probably be gracious now even to him, though there had never been any love lost between them.

He swallowed, drew a deep breath and dialed the Coadjutor's number. When he heard Bronson's voice he spoke quickly.

"This is Hilary Laurens, Bishop. I have to tell you that my Grandfather died within the hour."

There was the sound of a muffled exclamation at the other end of the wire.

"My dear boy, did you say—*died?*"

"Yes. It was very sudden. His heart."

"But—I can't believe it. Only yesterday morning he was in his office. We discussed together the . . . I'll come out at once."

Hilary managed a faint thanks and hung up. Then he sat with his head in his hands. It was going to be hard to face Bronson. It was not only that he personally disliked the man, but he knew only too well that his grandfather's last years had been disturbed and harassed by him. He remembered the last night he had been home; he and the Bishop had sat here before the fire discussing the Coadjutor.

"Bronson's nothing but a stuffed shirt, Grandy," Hilary had said.

"He's becoming a *hair* shirt to me," his grandfather had replied with a wry smile.

Hilary turned now as Morris set the tea tray beside him. He *was* hungry, even at such a time as this. He ate the food quickly, allowing Morris to hover over him—refilling the cup, bringing more hot water, and more sandwiches. Anything to keep the old man busy. When he had finished he took from an inner drawer of the desk a small black address book. Grandy had told him once a long time ago that a certain list was on the back page. He kept reminding him through the years. And now the time

6

had come to use it. In the Bishop's small, precise hand, he read the names.

The church officials he would leave to Bronson. That would please him. There were then the personal friends and the few remaining members of the family to be notified. He composed the same telegram to each of the first group and sent them. Then he sat, thoughtful. What about the Maryville people? Should he telegraph or write them? Grandfather had been born there eighty-two years ago. He himself had been there once when he was a small boy. He could remember the sleepy old village, the droning of cicadas in the August heat, the unfamiliar plain church service on Sunday when Grandy, strangely enough, sat in the pew with the others, the good dinners during which a kindly woman kept refilling his plate as she remarked, "This child needs to be nourished up." There had been a trip to a farm too, and a night spent there in a low room under the eaves. It had rained, Hilary remembered, and he had lain awake listening to the gentle closeness of the sound.

It was all a vague memory but a pleasant one. There had been only letter contacts now for years, so Hilary decided he would write to the Miss Mattie Laurens, and the Mr. David Guthrie of the list. He knew, when he stopped to consider, that Miss Mattie was the Bishop's first cousin, and David Guthrie his grandnephew. It was he who had the old farm.

He scanned the other names on the list. The same message could go to all. He called Western Union and heard his voice mechanically giving out the statement—so unreal and bitter in its finality.

Better send another wire to Dick too, he thought. Heaven only knew where he might be. The last he had heard was from Arizona but he could be back by now. Or anywhere else, for that matter. He wired the hotel where Dick always kept a room and asked them to forward the telegram. Of course Grandy's own wire might have reached him, and with Dick's uncanny good luck in matters of timing, he might be already near at hand.

As Hilary finished he heard Bronson in the hall and rose to greet him.

The new Bishop was a large man, tall and heavy, with massive shoulders, a florid face and an unusually round bald spot on the top of his head. Hilary had always wickedly blamed him for aiding the tonsure-like effect. He was continually clothed with an ecclesiastical unction of manner which contrasted with the late Bishop's simple naturalness. Hilary recalled his grandfather's remark once that "Bronson would make a pontifical ceremony over burying a dead mouse." To Hilary's surprise and relief now, he came forward with less assurance and manner than usual. Maybe after all Grandy had gotten through to him.

"This is a great shock, Hilary."

"Yes, I'm pretty dazed. I guess you know how I felt about him. In spite of his age I somehow never pictured just how it would be to have him go."

"How did you happen to be here?"

"He wired me this morning. I caught a plane."

The new Bishop coughed. "It would have given me pleasure to serve him in some way at the last, if I had only known—"

"There was so little time," Hilary said, rather lamely he feared. Then he hurried on. "You're very kind to help me now. The church people whom he wanted notified are set down here in this little book. I wondered if you would see to them and also the newspapers. I'll look up a photograph and write out the main facts, but maybe you'll be so good as to handle it. The reporters will be wanting to interview you anyway."

"I'll be glad to take care of it. And the service?"

"Very simple. It was his last request. You'll have charge, of course. We can't set the time until we hear from my brother. We don't know exactly where he is, but we've wired."

"Ah—Dick."

There was an accent of disapproval in the Bishop's voice which annoyed Hilary.

"There's a private wire upstairs. I'll use that now for a few more calls and you can have the phone here. Will you stay to dinner, Bishop?"

"Thank you, no. I'm afraid I can't unless you actually need me. We have an engagement. But I'll hold myself completely at your service tomorrow."

Hilary felt relieved. He started up to his own room and then turned suddenly back. The new Bishop was already busy at the desk. Hilary took the letter addressed to himself and then picked up the pipe from the table. Morris, he knew, would never touch it, but someone else might.

Once in his own room he read the letter:

DEAR HILARY:

Nothing new here except a curious twinge in my big toe. I suspect in England it would be called gout. In old novels, Bishops and country squires all had it. Morris put me to bed last night with a hot-water bottle which offended my dignity. It detracted from the picture of strong, gouty, hard-living masculinity I had just built up of myself!

No word of Dick for some time. I hope the Arizona job will work out. Do you suppose marriage would help him to settle? It would have to be a very unusual girl, though, and naturally that is entirely his own business. Send him plenty of advice. Yours is likely to be better than mine. He's much on my mind.

Bronson is off to a rampageous start on the Cathedral. I've ceased to oppose it. I've felt all along that this Diocese

8

needs one about as much as a dog needs a second tail, but I'm beginning to scrutinize my motives. I may have been *too* indifferent all my life to form and pageantry. It has its place. If Bronson is a pompous ass, as I say frequently to myself, maybe *I* am pretty smug at that. In other words one can make an affectation of simplicity as well as of ostentation. In the eyes of the Lord I may be as prideful in my way as Bronson in his. This thought just came to me and it's quite a shock. At heart B. is a good fellow and a very much better executive than I have ever been. At all events, I'm now backing the Cathedral project.

Still anxious to know about St. Matthews, but as you requested, I've kept my nose strictly out of it.

I have taken a sudden notion to go back to Maryville this summer. I feel a great desire to look at the old farm once again. How about joining me there for a few days, perhaps in June? Do you good.

Have just been reading Browning. Too bad you young folks don't take to him.

> I've grown peaceful as old age tonight.
> I regret little. I would change still less—

except the gout.

God bless you, my boy,

GRANDY

He folded the paper and put it in his inner pocket. It was borne sharply in upon him that these characteristic messages would now come to him no longer. Even with the new and thrilling prospects which he felt were opening up before him there would be one desolated and empty corner in his heart.

With a conscientiousness which was an integral part of his nature he completed all the calls on his list, and then turned to the arrangement of other matters which could be settled before Dick got there. Then, and not till then, did he put in the call for Lexa. His cheeks flushed as he gave the name and number to the operator. Such was her power over him.

When her voice actually came, he felt the sudden trembling of his limbs which he often did in her presence.

"Lexa!"

"Hilary, is it you? I couldn't imagine when the operator said—I didn't know you planned to go home."

"I didn't. It's all been very sudden. Lex, my grandfather has just died."

"The Bishop!"

"Yes. I'm pretty well shot. I wanted you to know. I'll have to be here for at least a week, I imagine, seeing to things."

"Oh, I *am* sorry. You were so devoted to him. I'll tell Father. He was one of the Bishop's great admirers."

"Please do. I—what are you doing tonight, Lex?"

He hadn't meant to say such a gauche thing. It slipped out, driven by that racking feeling to which he would not give the name jealousy.

"Not anything really. Mother has some people in to supper. Hilary, I can't say it well, but I feel terribly for you. Truly."

"I know. I felt if I could just hear your voice it would help. I have some other news. I had hoped to go to see you and tell you in person before you heard it there. I've received a call to St. Matthews."

There was a quick sound as though from a breath of amazement.

"St. Matthews! *Here?* Why Hilary, I can't believe it! That would be momentous! They've always had someone quite elderly and awfully distinguished! Do you really mean *St. Matthews, here?*"

"That's it. I'm glad you're pleased. Your father knew it was in the wind but I asked him not to mention it to you. I felt it might fall through, but if it really did come to a call I wanted to tell you myself."

"Hilary, I'm so proud of you, I can't bear it!"

"That sounds sweet to me. Nothing else will ever mean as much, as you know."

"Was—did your grandfather hear of it?"

"Yes. He was conscious when I got here. I had time to tell him."

"I'm glad. As to myself, I can't believe it yet."

"Lex, are you still weighing things?"

"Yes."

"How long will it be?"

"I—I don't know."

"I love you. More than a man ever loved a girl before, I think."

"I wish I could be sure."

"I'll call up every night. What's the best hour?"

"This time is good. I'll be here."

"Good-bye, darling."

"Good-bye, Hilary." He hung up.

There was the sudden sound of voices in the hall below. He opened his door quickly. Even as he did so, he saw Dick at the top of the stairs. His long, lean face under his blond hair looked white. The astonishing dark eyes were sunk in his head. Hilary grasped his hands and drew him into the room.

"My word, Dick, I'm glad to see you!"

"Bronson says it's all over."

"Yes. About four. When you want to hear, I'll tell you everything. He told me to give you his love."

Dick walked to the window and stood looking out over the garden. There was no outward sound, just the quiet beating of the grief in their hearts. At last Dick straightened his shoulders and turned.

"Well," he said, "that's that. But I didn't know it could hit me so hard."

"Neither did I," Hilary echoed heavily.

Dick picked up the desk chair with a quick movement and sat down astride it, resting his arms along the back.

"I suppose Bronson's already spreading himself." His voice was bitter.

"He's been very decent," Hilary answered. "We mustn't be too hard on him. After all he *has* carried the physical burden of the diocese for five years. Grandy had a letter addressed to me on the desk. I just read it. He says maybe he was as smug in his simplicity as Bronson was in his ponderosity. Who but Grandy would ever have worked that one out!"

"I had a letter myself day before yesterday. Kidding me along as usual. Thought maybe I ought to get married."

Dick lighted a cigarette. All his motions were swift and nervous.

"I don't mean to pry, Hil, but how about you and Lex?"

"Status quo. I'm hoping though."

"Up to the hilt, eh?"

Hilary nodded. He was drawing slowly on his pipe.

"Good luck, old man. I don't see how she can resist you. The only thing . . ." He stopped.

"Well, come on with it."

"I can't somehow ever picture Lex as a clergyman's wife!"

"She wouldn't be marrying the parish," Hilary said sharply.

Dick tossed his cigarette into the fireplace. With characteristic abruptness he changed the subject.

"Remember the time we ran off from school—Foster Hall, wasn't it? Thought we'd go West and see the world. Remember?"

"I certainly do. You were the brains of the expedition all right."

"Funny I can't recall where we went before they caught up with us. The thing I see plain as day is Grandy when they brought us home. We sat round the fire in the library and he treated us like princes. Nothing was too good for us!"

"I know. And we looked like two gutter snipes. You said, 'Aren't you going to punish us, Grandy?' and he said—"

Dick's head suddenly went down on his arms. Hilary's voice broke on the words.

"He said: 'Why should I? I'm too happy. These my children were lost and are found.'"

At last Dick looked up. His eyes were wet.

"As man to man, Hil, what do you honestly think about an after life? This has got me. Grandy's going out of the picture. As you see it, what are the chances?"

Hilary hesitated. "It's so hard to—"

"Don't hedge," Dick cut in sharply, "just because you're a damned parson."

"I'm not hedging," Hilary said, his own voice irritable. It eased the pain somehow to be arguing with Dick in their old fashion. "What I'm trying to say is that it's hard to evaluate one's own beliefs. As a rule I'm dead sure, though once in a while I have doubts."

"But you feel it's at least an even break?"

"Oh, infinitely better than that."

Dick drew a long breath, got up and shoved the chair back in its place.

"I hope Grandy gets the breaks then," he said. "Now I'd better go and see Morris. Poor old sinner! He'll be sunk."

"And we must talk over details with Bronson while he's here. Let's be pretty civil to him, Dick. There may be more to him than meets the eye."

"God forbid," Dick muttered.

Hilary was thinking, I'll not say anything yet about my call. Dick would never be jealous of any success of mine but still—I'll wait till it comes up naturally.

They went slowly along the wide hall. Already, subtly, the odor of death had invaded the house. Before the Bishop's door they paused.

"Do you want to go in now?" Hilary asked.

Dick shook his head.

Then their eyes met. They could hear Bronson still on the telephone. No one was in sight. Each knew what was in the mind of the other. The old bedtime ritual. They had started it of their own accord long ago when they had first read how young royalty said good night to their sires. Now with one accord they faced the door, straightened, clicked their heels, and saluted.

Then, shoulder to shoulder, the two young men started down the stairs.

CHAPTER II

THE CHURCH OF ST. MATTHEWS lifted its heaven-pointing spire from the heart of a great eastern city. Its pile of gray stone masonry had stood there since the street had been a quiet thoroughfare where horse-drawn carriages paused to allow ladies in crinolines and gentlemen in stocks to alight for Sunday service. Fashionable residences had once flanked it on every side, edging close, as though proud to exist in its shadow. There had indeed been a social prestige even in this proximity. As to membership, one wag of the older generation had been wont to state that to be a pew holder in St. Matthews one must also be eligible to the annual Assembly Ball!

Through the moving years, however, industrial development had worked its will upon the surrounding neighborhood. Slowly but surely the old brownstone fronts were vacated. Where there had once been great dinners under glittering chandeliers and elegant soirées behind thick velvet curtains there were now only office buildings, storerooms and lofts. The membership of St. Matthews with quiet dignity had withdrawn first uptown and eventually to the wide suburban section which had grown practical as well as fashionable.

But while other downtown churches had suffered from this same hegira of their members through the years; while their buildings had grown gradually seedy in appearance and their congregations dwindled to a miscellaneous handful, old St. Matthews had never given ground. Perhaps because its traditions were too deeply rooted. Perhaps because its tenacity upon life was founded upon a curious intermingling of spiritual and temporal distinction. In any case it had remained a bulwark both of religion and fashion in the city. Its pews were still filled Sunday after Sunday, many of them with the children and grandchildren of former parishioners. Its vestrymen still held great corporations in the hollow of their hands; its dowagers still dominated society.

People in the city felt this as they passed the great stone edifice by. "That's *St. Matthews*," they said to each other, whether they had ever crossed its portals or not. Even the most ordinary man of the street knew the name. This was where the great financiers, the "big bugs" went to church; this was where the most important weddings took place; this was where visiting dignitaries were brought to worship.

To those who passed through the heavy bronze outer doors, and then the tall carved inner ones, however, there came a startling moment of revelation. It was as though the old church, like a beautiful woman born to the purple, wore its pride of position on the outside only. Within was a heart of gentleness and mystery. At first the soft gloom left the eye, conditioned to sunlight, almost in darkness. Then gradually, as the deepest beauty should ever be revealed, the tender radiance of windows and altar stole upon the senses and the soul.

At nine o'clock on a bright March morning a young man in his first thirties walked slowly along High Street. He was tall with the shoulders and waist of an athlete. His gray eyes under unusually fine brows were thoughtful, but his wide mouth held a quirk of humor as though it smiled easily. His clothes were distinctly well tailored and he wore them with an easy nonchalance. A stranger if interested enough to hazard a guess might have set him down as a handsome young lawyer or business man with his feet well set upon the ladder of success. They would probably not have surmised that he was a clergyman coming to assume the duties of his first large parish.

Hilary walked slowly, for he was conscious of a strange reluctance. The events of the last years were flowing through his mind. They had all apparently been leading up to this day which he now felt inadequate to meet. He remembered the evening when he had told Grandy he meant to take the church as his profession. The Bishop had looked surprised and then severe.

"It's hard work, Hilary. In other professions a man works his body and his mind. In the ministry you have to wear your heart and soul to tatters too. What made you decide on this?"

Hilary smiled. "Well, you, for one thing."

The Bishop had been all but angry. "I never said a word! I never influenced you in any way! I never lifted a finger to bring this about!"

Hilary grew serious. "Of course you didn't. What I mean is I've lived with you for twenty-odd years, and it's had its effect."

The Bishop had still seemed upset.

"You have an extraordinarily fine mind, Hilary. You have a compelling personality. You have the gift of words. What about the bar? I can picture you one day as Judge in the Supreme Court. Have you thought sufficiently of the law?"

Hilary had felt desperately hurt. He stood up.

14

"I have weighed everything. I've thought this over for a long time. My decision is made and I naturally thought it would please you."

He was heading for the door when he heard the Bishop blowing his nose.

"Pleased?" he was saying, as he wiped his eyes. "Pleased? Why, my boy, nothing this side of heaven could make me so happy. It's only that I had to be sure you knew your own mind."

They had talked then long into the night, and settled the first steps. The next fall Hilary had entered Union Theological in New York, and from the first, things had gone smoothly and well with him.

Immediately upon his ordination he had accepted a call to Chicago as curate and there had followed six full and, in the main, satisfying years. He knew himself that he had grown in stature. The faults of inexperience had been somewhat overcome. While still conscious of ineptitudes he did not fumble. He had begun to want a church of his own. Then had come the overtures leading up to the incredible call to St. Matthews back East. Back in Lexa's own city.

It was this proximity to Lex which he had thought of day and night while the call was pending. It was this physical nearness to her now, however, which he must on this morning thrust from his mind as he neared the church lest the torture of his uncertainty over her might distract him from the duties of the day.

He had reached the edifice at last, and stood for a minute looking up at it. The stone was weathered dark and there was a slightly forbidding look to the heavy bronze doors. There was the usual sign, *Come in. Rest and Pray,* but the words were dim. At the left of the door a long tablet gave the designation of St. Matthews Protestant Episcopal Church and the hours of service. The name of the former rector, Dr. Partridge, was still upon it. Soon, Hilary thought with a feeling of surprise, his own name would be there for all who passed to read.

He went up the wide stone steps, pushed open the doors, crossed the vestibule, and then stood, hat in hand, at the back of the church.

He waited there, allowing his eyes to accustom themselves to the dim light, and looked slowly around him. Although he had been in the church once before, he had not realized until this moment that it was so large. From where he stood the pews stretched forward endlessly; the chancel seemed miles in the distance. Far away, too, yet almost unpleasantly distinct under its panoply of heavily carved wood, was the pulpit, where Sunday after Sunday now he must preach. It looked ominous, terrifying, and most remotely superior, as though all the ecclesiastical eloquence of years still clung to it; an eloquence which he felt he could not even hope to approach. The names of past rectors flashed through his mind: Brainerd,

Haverstraw, Stokes, Partridge. Giants in the church. And now he was to follow them! There was neither exaltation nor pride in this present thought; he felt only a sudden mad impulse to turn and flee from a responsibility that loomed too great.

Instead of turning, however, he started to walk slowly up the aisle, his footsteps making only a faint echo in the stillness. He became conscious as he moved forward of the mellow beauty enfolding him: the window colors which melted into the soul like music; the lift of the Gothic arches, delicate as lace, strong as the riven stone; the far gold and white mystery of the altar itself. The heart of the old church began gently to commune with his own.

He entered the chancel hesitantly, as might a first young communicant, and advanced to the altar rail where he knelt down. Dimly, far behind him, as the sounds of earth might conceivably be borne upward to the spheres, came the muted roar of the city. Here in the sanctuary was the strange, penetrating voice of silence. As he listened he became aware of overtones. The pulpit and a possibly critical congregation were receding, were at this moment making no claim upon him. What he seemed to hear within him were the prayers of sorrow and joy, of penitence and of dedication, which for a hundred years had risen from worshippers kneeling here where he now knelt as one of them.

And through it all came Grandy's voice with surprising distinctness, "You can do it, my boy."

He rose at last and made his way through to the Parish House where he must look up Hastings, the sexton, and then find his study and prepare to settle down. He had heard plenty of rumors about Hastings but had not yet met him since he had been ill when Hilary had been on to look over the church and discuss plans with the vestry earlier. He knew, however, that Hastings was an institution in himself. Been there for forty years. Ruled everything and everybody with a rod of iron. Hilary drew an anxious sigh and went on.

Suddenly in the doorway opposite him appeared an old man. He was long and lean and possessed of a vast dignity. His head was bald, his face as Anglo-Saxon as though it had been carved from the Cliffs of Dover, his expression melancholy. He was clad in a rusty black suit, possibly a clerical bequest, and carried a feather duster as though it were a mace.

"Mr. Laurens?" he asked with condescension.

"That's right, and you must be Hastings."

"I am."

"I'm looking things over preparatory to getting to work. Perhaps you'll show me round. I've really had a very hasty survey before and I'm not sure I could even find the study now."

16

"Just come this way," Hastings returned, his solemnity unbroken.

"He takes to me like poison," Hilary thought uncomfortably to himself as he followed his guide.

Hastings led the way upstairs, opened a door and stepped aside. "The study, sir," he intoned.

Hilary went in, with a strange feeling of standing in another man's shoes which were too big for him. For thirty years this room had belonged to Dr. Partridge. Hilary had met him a few times at church conventions. He had been a man of brilliant mind and ready wit. A man who quickly invested a group or a place with his own personality. Blue-blooded, conservative, an able preacher, capable of politic compromise when necessary, but devout and kindly, he had suited St. Matthews in every particular. Now at seventy-odd he had been gathered to his fathers. "And I reign in his stead," Hilary muttered grimly.

He moved about the long room. Mullioned windows opened along one side toward the court; high, walnut bookcases, now empty, ranged along the other. There was a fireplace, the usual assortment of miscellaneous chairs, and a large desk in the middle.

Hilary stopped and regarded it, feeling upon him increasingly the chill of Hastings' presence.

"I believe," he said, considering, "that if you'll give me a hand we'll push this desk over in front of the windows. I like to work with the light at my back."

Hastings did not budge.

"That desk has stood where it is for as long as I've been here, sir." The tone was final. The cliff-face adamant.

Hilary sat down in the desk chair and looked at the old man. He would have to win him over or get rid of him, that was sure, and the latter course was impossible. The tradition of Hastings, he knew, was one of the pet ones of the parish. Stories of him grew and multiplied and were passed with relish from one dinner table to another throughout the city. Hastings had held up funerals and hurried up weddings; he had told the Bishop how long he should preach and had even switched sermon notes once on Dr. Partridge when his eagle eye had spotted what looked like a threatening committee of visiting vestrymen in the congregation. No, rectors might come and go, but Hastings would remain.

Suddenly Hilary spoke. The confession was not studied. The words came involuntarily to his lips.

"I might as well tell you, Hastings, for you'll probably discover it for yourself. I'm scared. I'm scared to death. I'd like to cut and run."

The old sexton fixed his eyes sharply on the young man before him while in them grew an expression of profound amazement. Then, with affected briskness he began to wield his feather brush on the book shelves which Hilary could see were already free from dust.

"When you get some pictures up here, it'll look better," he remarked. "The Doctor had his own and the family wanted them. This here spot on the wall was where a big Cathedral one hung. If you'd happen to have the same-sized one it would help. Never thought this paper would fade when we put it on, but it has a little. What about Miss Mowbray? Are you keepin' her on?"

"Oh, she's the secretary, isn't she? I'll talk with her."

"She's pretty good. Better hang on to her. She can keep her mouth shut and she's homely. Good things, round a church. Keeps talk down. When are your books comin'?"

"Tomorrow, I hope. I'll feel better when they're here. More as if I belonged."

"About this desk." The old man looked at it as though seeing it for the first time. Then with utter gravity he went on. "I was thinkin' if we moved it over in front of the windows, it might give us more room when we're tusslin' round with all your book boxes."

Hilary choked slightly, but he too stared at the desk as though pondering a new suggestion.

"Do you think so?" he asked at last.

"Believe we'll try it," Hastings replied.

Together they turned the desk. With a little skilful guidance Hilary succeeded in placing it in the exact spot he wanted.

"You're right, Hastings," he said. "This will certainly give us more floor space and I've seven boxes coming. Another thing. When I sit behind the desk now, I'll be facing the door and get the first glance at anyone who comes in. That's an advantage, don't you think?"

The old man didn't reply at once. But in a moment he came over and touched Hilary's arm.

"Now don't you fret yourself," he said, "you and me can run this place. If you come I'll show you over the Parish House."

At five o'clock that afternoon Hilary returned to the Rectory, which stood next the church, separated from it only by a small courtyard with a fountain. It was a large house of graystone Victorian angles on the outside but, within, comfortable as only old city houses know how to be. The window sills were deep, the fireplaces wide, the rooms high. Even the partial emptiness now as he walked through the long drawing room, the dining room facing the little fountain, and the paneled library in the rear, did not completely remove the feeling of pleasant living which clung to the very walls.

He had brought most of the pieces from the old house, since Dick had wanted nothing, and Morris had disposed them about, but there could be no attempt at complete furnishing until he knew . . .

That night he was to dine alone with Lex at her house. Her father and mother were going out, she had said when he phoned. Could he be there by seven-thirty? It would give them a long evening to talk everything over.

He did not know whether to hope or to despair. When he had asked if he was to receive his answer, she had seemed nervously evasive. The invitation might mean that she was about to tell him she would marry him, or give him gently and at length the reasons why she could not. Somehow he felt sure that he would know either way that night; and the imminence of this certainty made his heart pound in his chest and his knees feel weak as water.

During the three months since the Bishop's death, Hilary had honestly tried to weigh his own feelings in the balances of reason. His grandfather's advice, as the nurse had repeated it to him, had been more disturbing than he realized at the moment. But all his attempts at prudent deliberation, at cautious delay were futile. There ran through him hotly, passionately, too passionately he felt for a priest, a love that he was powerless to subdue even if he had wished it. He marveled at himself. If this tempestuous up-surging of desire had been Dick's it would not have been so surprising. It would have seemed in keeping with his brother's heated impulsiveness of character. From boarding school days on Dick had gone off the deep end regularly over a dozen girls. True the emotion had always been transient, and after a few months, or even weeks, he had emerged apparently un-scathed. Yet it was Dick who was unquestionably cast for the role of the great lover, and he, Hilary, for that of the quiet, steady-going husband. They had somehow mixed their cues.

He had first met Lex two years ago when he had gone one summer to join Dick for a short vacation in northern Maine. Dick had introduced them characteristically.

"Lex, this large, benevolent looking creature is my brother, Hilary. He appears innocent but he has fatal charm. Hil, this young lady is dynamite and not suited to the clergy. Now don't say I didn't warn you both."

Hilary had found himself face to face with a slight thing of twenty with Irish blue eyes under smoky lashes, a patrician nose, full red lips and curly hair with a bronze fire in it.

But these physical marks of beauty were all heightened and intensified by a tremendous inner vitality which in a man might have been called power. In this slight girl it was to Hilary a fire, a flame, which struck him and set him aglow as when the dull cold wood leaps to living warmth.

19

The impact was at once so violent and irrevocable that his tongue had stammered on the conventional words of greeting. She in her turn had regarded him with genuine amazement.

"Are you honestly a clergyman? All the ones I know are doddering along in their seventies. I thought parsons were old from the cradle. Come on, I must investigate you. You're a novelty."

They had sat all that afternoon, forgetful of the tennis matches, on the grass under a big elm. Dick passed them occasionally with a raised eyebrow but they had scarcely seen him.

Hilary had taken her to a party at one of the neighboring houses that night, but they had left the crowd soon and sauntered off toward the lake. The tumult in his heart increased. Before the evening was over he had kissed her. And it was far from being a light kiss. It had left them both trembling. What the girl felt, he did not know; but he knew that he could never rest until she was his wife.

The next morning early a note had been brought to his room. The handwriting was small, firm, and distinctive. He opened it quickly. It read:

> Look, Preacher Man, this chit is to tell you I'm not in the habit of doing what I did last night on first meetings with strange young men. In retrospect I don't like it. Go on back to your sermons. I'm going fishing and we'd better both forget it.
>
> LEX

He had jumped into his clothes and driven like mad over to where Lex was staying. The information there confirmed the letter. Miss McColly had left very suddenly early that morning for Canada. There was no address forthcoming.

Dick had been worse than no help. He had been merely amused.

"I told you," he kept repeating cheerfully. "She's not for the likes of you, Hil. Don't be an ass at your age. The girl's dynamite for anybody. Let alone a gentleman of the cloth."

"I'll make my own decisions, thank you," Hilary had snapped. "Tell me all you know of her. I'm dead serious and I'm no fool."

"Well, here's what I know. She's the daughter of Alexander McColly. You know who he is. McColly Ironworks. Lousy with money, but up from the ranks. Shanty Irish. His wife is the old Breckenridge stock. Blood so blue you could rinse clothes in it. But she fell for the old boy when he was a rough diamond and eloped with him. Family disowned her. McColly made so much money he could thumb his nose at the lot of them. Grandy knows him."

"He does?"

"Sure. Who doesn't Grandy know? He told me once McColly was the hardest headed man in the state and in some respects the most lovable. That ought to warn you."

"What has that to do with Lex?" Hilary asked.

"Well they call them Old Alex and Young Alex," Dick had answered, grinning.

The courtship had been a strange one. Everything had been against it, even distance, but Hilary had persevered. He was not a stripling; he was a man in his late twenties. He had known many girls; known them pleasantly, calmly, appraisingly. He had always felt that in good time he would meet the suitable one, the perfect help-meet, would fall in love deeply, decorously, marry and live contentedly thereafter. He had not reckoned upon this sudden, mad fire in his bones.

There had been plenty of competition. So much and of such character that a weaker man than Hilary would have given up long ago in the face of it. But in addition to his unshakable determination to possess her as his wife, there was also the inherent consciousness of his own worth. This, entirely removed from vanity, was a deep realization of his strong, clean manhood and the quality of his love.

He had had a long talk with Alex McColly himself one night. He had stated his case simply and with complete honesty. He loved Lex and would make every effort to win her. Whether he had a chance or not he did not know but wanted her father to understand his position. The older man, huge of body, with a ruddy face and grizzled, curly hair, had the very smile he had passed on to his daughter. Not even his brusque voice with the far echo of Shantytown in it, could dispel the charm of that smile. So he must have looked once at young Eunice Breckenridge to make her steal off in the night to marry him. There was in him the same inner burning vitality that Hilary had felt in Lexa's slender frame. A man of power. A man to fear or to hate or to love.

"I've been watching you," he had said to Hilary. "I watch every young fellah that comes round Lex. Always have. Since she was twelve. I find out all about them. There's been plenty of them, too, through the years, I'm telling you, but you're the first one I'd feel safe to give her to. I know all about you. I know your grandfather. I like you. Go ahead as hard as you can and I hope to God she'll marry you."

"And her mother?" Hilary had asked, somewhat breathless.

It was then he had felt the full weight of the older man's charm. McColly smiled and his voice was low.

"Her mother," he said, "usually thinks the way I do."

During those first months Lex had held him playfully at bay. Later, she had been more serious but frequently irritable. She had told him flatly that the last thing in the world she would ever do was to marry a parson; that he was wasting his time and upsetting them both for nothing. More recently she had softened a little, admitted she was beginning to be afraid of weakening and eventually promised to reconsider the whole matter over a period of time and give him a final answer. Would it be tonight?

Hilary went on through the rectory now to the big kitchen where he found Morris polishing silver. He had noticed that whenever the old man could think of nothing else to do, he recleaned the service. Hilary perched on a high stool as he used to do as a boy, to watch him. He knew Morris was lonely for the Bishop even as he himself was, and homesick for the old surroundings.

"Well, I've been all over the Parish House, Morris. It's quite a place."

"Yes, Mist' Hilary. That's fine."

"I feel pretty small about trying to run it all."

Morris raised worshipful eyes.

"You're a big man, Mr. Hilary."

"In inches," Hilary said. "You remember I'm going out to dinner? Be sure to cook yourself something good. You're thin as a snake, Morris. We've got to fatten you up."

The old man stopped his work.

"We need more folks here, Mist' Hilary. We needs a nice young madam here an' lunchin' parties an' dinner parties an' a whole tableful of little boys an' girls growin' up."

Hilary laughed. "Nothing wrong with that picture, Morris. I like it myself. What about making a wish?"

For the first time in weeks the old man's eyes twinkled. His brown wrinkled face broke into smiles. He put down his polishing cloth and began to fumble in an inner pocket.

"You don't never forget, you an' Mist' Dick. From the time you was little fellahs an' we wished for them velocipedes."

He produced a dirty, moth-eaten rabbit's foot, waved it three times in the air, muttering as he did so, then kissed it and put it on the table. Hilary laid his finger upon it and Morris placed his atop.

"If my parish could see me now!" Hilary said gleefully.

"Sh!" Morris warned. "Think fast while the charm's workin'!"

When the rite was completed, Morris was still cheerful.

"That ought to do it, Mist' Hilary. I wishen you a nice wife an' six chil'ren, three of each."

Hilary laughed and slapped the negro's back.

"Pretty generous, Morris. Now I've got to go upstairs. Listen for the phone tonight, will you? There may be no calls but on the other hand, people know I'm here. I'll be at the McCollys' and I'll leave you that number but don't disturb me there unless you need me personally, understand?"

He went on up to the room he had furnished for himself. It was at the back of the house, next the church. From the one window he could look down on the little court and across to the church itself. He had loved this outlook from the moment he had entered the room and had determined to establish himself here. The other room at the back was much larger and had a connecting door through to this one. If he and Lex were married that would doubtless be the one she would like. He would still keep the smaller one for his dressing room . . .

He pulled himself up sharply. Morris and his old rabbit's foot foolery had for the moment lightened his spirits. But he must rigidly hold himself against real expectation of happiness. Lex had been unflinchingly honest all along. She had never given him much hope.

The blackness, the desolation of his life if she finally refused him, swept over him now like a drowning surge. He paced nervously up and down, started a letter to Dick, then tore it up, finally took a shower and forced himself to dress slowly, stretching out the time. His hands were unsteady, he noted, as he put on his tie.

At seven he left the house. The McCollys lived in Wynbrook, the most fashionable suburb of the city. It should take him just about half an hour to reach there if he drove with care.

It was a beautiful evening for March. The first warmth had been in the air all day along with a faint smell of spring. Even the city held it, but as Hilary reached the streets of wide acred lawns and gardens he felt the uncertain essence intensify. It became here the breathing of the patient, waking earth and the punctual quickening of leaf and blossom. The last threads of red and gold showed now to the west behind the great beech trees on the McCollys' lawn and the first star looked out of the dusk.

Hilary parked his car at the back of the house and walked slowly around to the pillared porch, trying to let the outward beauty quiet the nervous beating of his heart. Moffet, Lex's old Scotch nurse, familiarly known as "Muffet" or "Muff," met him in the hall. He had often noticed that she was always on hand when the elder McCollys were absent. The very sight of her, he thought once again as she was showing him into the library, would lend decorum to any occasion. She was tall and spare with the strong prominent facial bones of her race. She might have been either forty or sixty, though in point of fact he knew she was fifty. She would probably look the same at ninety. Her eyes were shrewd and wise, her mouth homely but kind.

"Miss Lexa thought you might like dinner in here before the fire when there's just the two of you. There's a bit of chill still in the air come night though the day's been fine."

Hilary felt a sudden outrageous hope as Muff lingered. He had always known she approved of him as a suitor even as he had suspected Mrs. McColly's disappointment when Lex refused an English title.

"Miss Lexa will be down shortly," Muffet went on. "Just make yourself comfortable. I told her the time was passing. But—you know how she is!"

For a moment, their guards down, she and Hilary looked into each other's eyes. It was a tender, intimate, smiling glance, during which each read the love the other bore to Lex.

"I'll hurry her along—and the dinner too," Muff added, returning to her usual manner.

Hilary, still strangely cheered, remained standing by the small table laid for two, his back to the fire. He admired this room more than any other he had ever been in. To him it represented the best of the McColly wealth plus the Breckenridge culture. Although the rug must have cost a king's ransom and one painting at least would have been welcomed in the Louvre, there was a quietness about it all which could easily have deceived the uninitiate. It was a comfortable room of deep chairs and couches, with one wall of books rising to the ceiling and Lex's small grand piano by the south casements. There was dignity and elegance but withal an easy grace of daily living. Mrs. McColly's knitting bag hung over the post of a rare old chair; Mr. McColly's tobacco jar and pipes stood alongside a fine bit of sculpture; Lex's red beret lay on the farthest couch where she had evidently flung it in haste, and forgotten it.

"A good, sound, beautiful room," Hilary was thinking. His own roses which he had ordered sent that morning were arranged on the low table and on the mantel, reflecting in the high mirror. How perfect was the stage! If only the play had a happy ending.

There was a familiar little rush in the hallway, a quick call to Muff, and Alexa had entered the room. For once as she came toward him he did not move to meet her. He stood, his face flushed, his eyes deep, overcome as always by her beauty. Her dress was green, a color he had never seen her wear before, and her curls were brushed back and tied like a child's with a ribbon around her head. She was smiling up at him under her dark lashes.

"Hello," she said. "How's the new rector?"

"Will it be tonight, Lex? I can't wait much longer. I must know." The words rushed from him uncontrollably.

She motioned him to sit down. "Muff's sending dinner right in. Let's eat, then we'll talk. And don't look so desperate," she added. "I'm not worth it, Hil."

24

"You are to me."

"Time will tell," she laughed. "Come on, I'm starved."

She was very gay during the meal and Hilary forced himself to respond in so far as he could. But the food all but choked him. He was conscious of a tremulous relief when the maid removed the table at last and they changed to the couch facing the fire, with their coffee.

"And now," he began, "we have to settle things between us, Lex. I've waited for your final answer for six months. I'm at the end of my tether. I've got to put an undivided mind upon my new work. That's why I have to know the truth even if it kills me."

She set the fragile cup down beside her.

"I'm going to tell you everything, Hil. I'm putting all my cards on the table. After that, it's for you to decide."

There was a forthrightness about her tone, a brusque strength with none of the usual bewitching raillery which drove him mad with longing. It was Old Alex who was speaking in his daughter.

"It's like this. I've fought you off for two years. I guess I really knew that first night by the lake. I do love you."

"Lex! My darling . . ."

"Wait till you hear it all. Yes, I love you in this sense. I've never wanted to belong to any other man. I do want to marry you. But if you hadn't been called to St. Matthews I wouldn't have done it. I was perfectly honest when I said all along I wouldn't marry a parson. I had planned to take a trip round the world and deliberately put you out of my mind."

"But why, dearest, if you love me?"

"Because I like a good time. I like excitement. I can't live without it. I'd break over the traces. To go to some poky city where I didn't know a soul and everybody just thought of me as the rector's wife—I couldn't do it, Hil."

She smiled into his eyes.

"But when you were called here to St. Matthews, that was something different. Everybody knows me. Most of our crowd belong there—even if they never go. I could do about as I please and nobody would mind. At least I think not. That was Mother's old church, you know, before she married Dad. Then they switched to Christ Church. Family row, you know. So . . ."

"Dearest, none of this really matters. Say the final word. Will you marry me?"

"That last word I can't say just yet. I want to be perfectly honest with you, Hilary. You're a bright boy. You ought to see for yourself that I'm not really the wife for you. I know that. I'm different. I'm not . . ."

Hilary suddenly caught her to him and kissed her as he had not done since that first strange night by the lake. Their whole bodies seemed to fuse in it and become one.

When she finally drew away there were tears in her eyes.

"You see?" she whispered. "That's what you do to me. But I'm not sure it's right for us. It's taking a big chance."

"Right?" Hilary's tone held the triumph of a man whose heart is bursting with happiness. "It is eternally right. We were made for each other! Oh darling, I love you so! I said I wanted an undivided mind for my work. But how am I going to do anything now? I'll want to stop every man on the street and say, 'Lex is going to marry me!'"

"But I haven't actually promised that!"

"It's the same thing. You've told me you love me. That's enough for now. It was the uncertainty that was killing me. I won't hurry you about the rest. Only . . ."

Lex laughed. "Only you will!"

"I'll try not to. Honestly. Are you still really unsure, Lex?"

She sobered and sat quiet for a little, pulling a curl that glistened in the light.

"I wish you were anything else but a clergyman. That's why I'm holding back about an actual engagement. I want to see how things work out for a few months more."

"But you do love me."

She nodded, the color rising sweetly in her cheeks.

"How much?"

"So much that I'm afraid. It gives you too much power over me and I like to be a very free agent." She looked up roguishly. "Maybe it's a good thing you are such an exemplary young man—a parson, no less."

"I never felt less like one than at the moment, so don't trust me too far!"

They laughed then, all at once carefree and gay and happy in the moment; and through the long evening closer than they had ever been.

"If I get rightly settled in my work during the summer and can convince you that the lot of a parson's wife is not an unhappy one, couldn't we be married in the fall?" Hilary begged.

"Maybe. The engagement could be announced in September as soon as we're back from Maine and then . . ."

"The wedding!" Hilary prompted joyously.

"In late October, perhaps. I don't like long engagements. *If* we ever do marry, Hil, I'd like a marvellous wedding. Should it be in St. Matthews since it's your own church?"

"Why, I never thought of that. I like the idea enormously. Would your father and mother mind?"

A curious expression came into Lexa's eyes.

"I think they'd rather like it."

"The fall then and in St. Matthews. I suppose I'll live through the summer but it's going to be tough."

"Silly. Remember I haven't said for sure I'll marry you then, but if I do, you'll have me all the rest of your life."

"It will never be long enough."

Just before he left, Lex stood fingering the lapel of his coat. He towered over her.

"Just as high as my heart," he said, his eyes warm and shining.

"Another thing, Hil. I do want to be honest with you. If we *should* marry in the fall, for instance, I would like to be free for a while. Not tied down right away. You know. I don't think I'm a terribly maternal person."

He was watching the way her dark lashes shadowed her cheek. He started and colored slightly.

"All that shall be just as you wish. You should know that,"—and then was lost in their final embrace.

"I'll call you up the minute I get back to the rectory for a last goodnight."

"I'd love that. I'll be waiting. Don't forget!"

"As if I could! And tomorrow I'll call for you early. About eleven? I want to see your mother, you know. Then we'll go buy the biggest bunch of violets in the city and end up at Moxam's for lunch."

"Wonderful, Hil, only please remember we aren't really engaged yet."

"It's all wonderful. And I refuse to admit a doubt!"

He drove home crazily. He had never been drunk but he knew his reactions now were much the same as though he were. There was a lightness in his head and an unsteadiness about his hands. He felt outrageously daring as though the world and all within it was his own. And was it not? Lexa was his world. After all the extremity of his fears he was returning now with the knowledge that she loved him. Greatly, as she herself had confessed. He was returning to the rectory which would one day be their home together. He could plan now. He could picture the rooms with Lex as their mistress down to the last intimate detail without having to check himself. For with her love freely admitted, the marriage could not fail to follow. The knowledge of this would give him power to break down the last barrier of uncertainty on Lexa's part and bring about speedily his heart's desire.

A vast elation filled him. All the natural gratification in his new position which during the day had been submerged by his feeling of inadequacy now rose to the surface. Married to Lex and rector of one of the most important old churches in the country at thirty-one! He would be a greater preacher than either Partridge or Brainerd! He would build up the church until it had twice the present membership. He would become active in the diocese, take a prominent place at conventions, maybe even as the years passed, attain a bishopric! Who knew? And always, always there would be Lex! His. His to possess. His to have and to hold!

He drove on recklessly, missing cars by the breadth of a hair. He was free, immune, untouchable in the immensity of his joy.

He put the car in the garage next the Parish House and went up the stone steps at two leaps. The door unexpectedly opened and Morris faced him.

"What are you doing up?" Hilary began.

"Mist' Hilary, I didn't call you like you said I wasn't to lessen it was for me, but a man's tryin' to get you. Sounds like there's something wrong someway."

"What is it, Morris?" Hilary's voice was quickly grave. "Tell me the message carefully. Did you write it down?"

"Yes, Mist' Hilary. I got it all here by the phone. This here Mistah Anderson's the man that called 'bout five minutes ago, but it's this Mistah Cole that's in trouble. That's what he said to tell you, 'Mistah Cole's in trouble and to please call this number soon as you come in.'"

Hilary sat down and dialed at once. Stephen Cole was one of his vestrymen. The one he had particularly liked when the small group came out to Chicago to see him and make arrangements about his coming to St. Matthews. He had looked forward to knowing him better. What had happened to make this call necessary at one-thirty in the morning?

A voice answered. A low, guarded voice.

"This is Hilary Laurens. I found a message here when I got home, asking me to call."

"Mr. Laurens, this is Miles Anderson, Stephen Cole's brother-in-law. I'm at his home now. There has been a tragedy. I thought maybe you could help us. Could you possibly come over at once?"

"Of course. I'll go immediately. Is it—Mr. Cole?"

Anderson's voice sank lower. "His only son shot himself this evening. Cole himself is— We need your help."

"I'll come. Is there a short cut from here? I'll be driving."

"Out High to Walnut and Sixth, then turn into the avenue and come straight out. The number is 1065. I'll be watching for you. There'll be a light over the door."

"At once, then. Good-bye."

Hilary ran up the stairs wondering if he should change to his clerical vest and black suit. He decided he would not wait. He picked up the

Prayer-book which he used for home visits and hurried down with a word for Morris. He got the car and once again, but this time in a steely calm, drove as fast as he dared. Mr. Cole had mentioned his son still at college, his whole face lighting as he did so. That boy tonight had taken his own life. And he, Hilary, must face this thing, must stand somehow, by what incredible and awful mutation of fate, in the place of God. God's minister. His mouthpiece to men. What could he say? What could any human being say, confronted by such catastrophe?

He sped up the long avenue, watching for the lighted door. He saw it and the number below. The great city house looked impregnable even to death itself. But death had entered.

Anderson met him in the hall, a tall, thin man, his face haggard:

"Mr. Laurens. This is good of you. Come into the library here. I must tell you the situation, as quickly as possible."

He did not offer to sit down, but went on speaking.

"Steve is—was—the Coles' only child, a senior at college. He came home late this afternoon for spring vacation, ate dinner apparently as usual and then went up to his room. The Coles went to a concert. I was here in the library reading. I live here. An hour ago I heard a shot. I went up to Steve's room . . ."

Anderson suddenly went white and swayed a little. Hilary saw a decanter on the low table by the fireplace. He hurried over and poured some of the contents into the glass, hoping it was brandy.

"Here," he said to Anderson. "You've had about all you can stand. Drink this. It may help."

The man took it with a shaking hand.

"Thanks," he said. "I guess I can do with something."

In a moment he went on. "He was dead. I called the doctor at once. He was here when the Coles came in. We told them as best we could. My sister collapsed and the doctor is with her now. But Cole won't leave the boy's room. He sits by the bed with the gun in his hand. He seems beside himself. He threatens to shoot anyone that goes in. He says no one must know about it. And the coroner and the police will be here any minute. We don't want more tragedy. He's just crazed for the moment—doesn't know what he's doing."

"I can understand that," Hilary said. His own face had paled.

"So I thought of you. He's talked so much about you. I wondered if you could do anything with him. There may be real danger involved, I just don't know. But I've got to warn you."

For reply Hilary said, "Shall we go on up?"

They climbed the beautiful stairway, velvet-soft to the foot, and followed the wide upper hall to the end. Here Anderson stopped.

"I feel guilty getting you into this," he said. "There may be danger . . ."

"This," said Hilary quietly, "is part of my business."

He opened the door and stepped inside. The figure sitting beside the bed straightened. The revolver in the man's hand seemed to point directly toward him.

"Don't come in here," Cole said in a hoarse voice.

"I'm Hilary Laurens, Mr. Cole—your rector. I had to come to you."

Without hesitation he walked over to the bed and knelt down beside it. With an effort of self-control greater than any he had ever known, he forced himself to put out of his mind the menace so near him. He prayed silently for the soul of the boy who lay there; for the young, troubled soul who had found some burden too great for his years. Then with all the intensity of concentration of which he was capable he prayed for the man beside him.

When he got up, Cole had lowered the gun and was staring dully at him. Hilary took the revolver gently and laid it on the table.

"Could we go to another room where we can be alone? Where we can talk?"

Cole stood up weakly. Hilary led him as one would lead a child out of the room into the hall where Anderson and the doctor were standing.

"Which way?" he asked.

Cole indicated the right and stopped at last before a half open door. It was evidently his study. There was a light on the desk. Hilary helped the older man to a chair and sat down close to him, still gripping his hand.

For several minutes neither spoke. Then with something like a sob Cole began. As he talked the tears ran unchecked down his cheeks. His voice broke on the words but at least Hilary realized the man was once more himself. The wild look was gone from his eyes.

"It must have been about a girl. I can't think of anything else. He was doing brilliantly at college. He has never given us a moment's anxiety. Oh, if he had only told us! No matter what he had done . . ."

Hilary felt a strange intuition, born of his own consuming love and the brink of misery on which he had himself so recently stood, wondering, fearing.

"Mr. Cole, I feel somehow that Steve did nothing wrong. He may, though, have had some great disappointment and for one tragic moment felt he could not bear it."

The man looked up with tortured eyes. He shuddered.

"But this—this terrible act . . ."

Hilary kept his firm hand on the other's shaking one.

"You would forgive Steve anything, even this, wouldn't you?"

"Of course."

"Then remember, 'Like as a father pitieth his children, so the Lord ...'"

"Say that again, please."

Hilary repeated it slowly, then waited. He felt he should say more but the weight of the catastrophe seemed too great for any words of his own. He could only sit close to this man and suffer with him.

At last Cole spoke quietly.

"My wife," he said. "I must go to her at once. And poor Anderson. He's a bachelor. He loved Steve like a son. I haven't really talked to him yet. After I got home I think I was completely beside myself for a while. I can scarcely remember what I did. Strange, I never lost control before."

"You won't again," Hilary said. "You'll be a tower of strength for the others. I'll come to see Mrs. Cole tomorrow as soon as she would care to have me. Call me at any moment and count upon me for anything. My heart bleeds for you all."

They rose and went toward the hall. Mr. Cole clung for a moment to Hilary's arm.

"You've helped me. Thank you for coming. I'll hang on to that verse."

Hilary walked with him to his wife's room, then went on down the stairs. Anderson was in the lower hall.

"I think he'll be all right now," Hilary said quietly.

"There are no words," Anderson answered, "but we'll never forget you for this."

"I'll stay with you," Hilary said. "There are some hard hours ahead. Maybe I can help."

"If you could," Anderson said, the relief showing in the white lines of his face. "If it isn't too much! I don't want to bring anyone else in tonight if we can help it, and Cole must be kept away. The servants of course are terrified. I feel terribly alone. If you could stay—"

"I'm staying," said Hilary.

"There!" Anderson said suddenly as the doorbell rang. "The hard work is beginning."

It was daylight when the last heavy, stranger foot had gone up and then down the velvet stairs. The law had been satisfied. The professional inspectors of tragedy as well as the routine ministrants of death had been there, had done their work and departed. A great quiet, more painful even than the subdued confusion, had settled upon the house. Anderson wrung Hilary's hand but his voice failed him.

"Try to get some rest," Hilary told him, his own face white and drawn. "Call me for anything, day or night. I'll come to Mrs. Cole whenever she wants to see me."

Anderson still could not speak. Hilary waited until he saw him begin slowly to climb the stairs, then he opened the heavy front door and went out into the early light. As he drove home he wondered if, as a priest, he had done or said enough. It came to him as a shock that he had uttered no prayer aloud. Should he have done so? Of course he had kept up his own unceasing inner petitions for them all. Of one thing he was sure: he had felt the tragedy in his very flesh. It was as though his own heart's blood had been drained out of him.

He went into the rectory, this time slowly, every step weighted with exhaustion. He put out the hall light, climbed the stairs, undressed, and flung himself upon the bed.

Just as he was dropping heavily to sleep he roused with a sharpness which made him sit bolt upright. Lex! He had forgotten his promise to call her as soon as he got home from her house! But of course she would understand. She would know he couldn't think of anything then but the tragedy he had to face. Of course she would understand.

He sank back again into sleep.

CHAPTER III

THE NEXT MORNING Hilary did not waken till he heard Morris' discreet tap on the door. He looked at his watch. It was nearly ten!

"Come in," he called, and the old man entered with a breakfast tray.

"Look here," Hilary said, "you can't do this to me, Morris. Good heavens, man, I'm not a debutante. Take that tray away. I'll be down in ten minutes."

"The Bishop always taken breakfast in bed once in a while. Said it was to rest up his conscience," Morris replied firmly.

Hilary laughed. "All right, set it here. It may save me some time anyway. Any messages?"

"Yes suh. That Mistah Anderson called up a few minutes ago an' last night, good while after you left, there was the young lady. Miss McColly. I told her you'd gone out."

Hilary was grave again. "Yes. What did Mr. Anderson say?"

"Just would you please call him back soon as you was up."

"Right, Morris. Hand me that robe, will you? I'll answer the calls at once before I eat. I never even heard the telephone ring here this morning."

"I caught it mighty quick downstairs, Mist' Hilary. Now don't you let your coffee get cold."

"I won't. Run along and thanks."

He sat down at his desk, hesitating with his hand at the dial. He was to have stopped for Lex at eleven—but what if the Coles needed him this morning? That was clearly his first duty. After all, life and its joy could wait a little, death and its claims could not. He would call the Coles first and then he would know what to say to Lex. It might only be the matter of an hour's postponement of their appointment. As he dialed his heart felt strangely heavy. It seemed so like putting Lex and their happiness in second place, yet, what could he do? The lines kept running through his head:

> I could not love thee, dear, so much,
> Loved I not honor more.

I doubt, he thought to himself, if that sentiment was ever much comfort to a woman!

Anderson answered.

"How are you all this morning, Mr. Anderson?"

"Cole has just now fallen asleep. He has been calm though, ever since you left. But my sister is prostrated. She would like very much to see you. There are arrangements that must be made at once, and she would like to consult you. Could you come over about eleven-thirty? She insists that by then she will try to get up."

"I'll come, of course," Hilary said.

His heart beat fast as he called Lex. To hear her voice would be heaven, and it would relieve him not only to explain it all, but to talk over with her what lay so heavily upon him.

It was Muff who answered. Hilary thought she sounded a bit flustered. There was a long interval and then Lex's voice.

"Yes?"

"Lex, dearest! I haven't been able to call you sooner. I ran right into tragedy last night. Terrible tragedy. The message was waiting for me when I got home. Young Steven Cole is dead."

"*Young* Steve!" He felt her startled out of the reserve of her first response.

"I'll tell you all about it when I see you. It's desperately sad. I was there till four this morning and I have to go back at eleven-thirty. I'm just awake now. Can you forgive me for not calling last night?"

She did not answer that. Instead she said, "I was under the impression we had an engagement at eleven."

His heart felt sore.

"I know, sweet. But you understand, don't you, how it is? This other is my work, my job, my duty. I must help these people if I can. I'm sure I can call for you by one at the latest. If your mother is busy then I'll come back again to see her. Tell me you understand."

"I understand perfectly. Better even than you do." But the tone was not right.

Hilary felt helpless and lost.

"Lex!" He was pleading.

"I'll be ready at one."

Her good-bye was hardly audible.

Hilary sat very still. There was in his nature a curious capacity for putting himself completely in another's place. This quality had many times kept him from the sharp, definite judgments of his fellows. Where presumably wiser men saw human conduct in terms of black or white,

34

he, because of his ability to project his personality into that of another, saw also the soft gray nuances which altered the outline.

On the face of it now he was hurt that Lex did not at once accept the demands of his office; but he saw clearly how it must seem to her. On that night she had first told him she loved him he had failed to keep a promise to her.

He pictured her there in the library, glowing as he had left her, breathlessly waiting for the ring which would bring them close once more. When the half-hour passed and the telephone was silent, there must have ensued a time of anxiety. She would consult with Muffet. Could there have been an accident? At last her own nervous call to the Rectory and the receipt of the cold news that Hilary had gone out! No wonder she was mystified and angry. And would it make her any happier to know the incredible truth that in the tense moment when the dark message came from the Coles he had completely forgotten her?

Then too, there was the matter of this day's change of plan. A small thing in a way and yet significant of one important fact: he was not only the young man in love. He was, and increasingly would have to be, the priest, also.

Before he left for the Coles' he ran over to his study, glanced at the mail, told Hastings the news of the tragedy and his whereabouts for the day. On the way out, he all but knocked over a young woman waiting at the door. She was slight and he lifted her to her feet as he made his apologies.

"That's quite all right," she said, laughing a little. "I must have seemed like an eavesdropper listening at the keyhole. As a matter of fact I was getting my courage up to knock. I'm Miss Mowbray, Dr. Partridge's secretary, and I wondered if you will want me to stay on."

He looked at her keenly. Hastings was right. She was homely. Nose a shade too long, mouth too big, no feature exactly ugly and yet all failing to correlate with each other into beauty or even prettiness. She looked intelligent, though, and her voice was one of the nicest he had ever heard.

"Of course I'll need you," he answered heartily. "I was going to get in touch with you. Could you start, say, next Monday, after I've had a chance to get settled a little?"

She nodded. "If you need me sooner Hastings can give you my phone number."

"You're sure you're not hurt? I wouldn't have come charging out like that except that I'm in a desperate hurry."

"Good-bye," she said simply, smiling. "I'll come in next week."

Hilary thought of her briefly as he drove to the Coles'. Plain, intelligent, capable. Knew the work, knew the parish. She would be a godsend. Between her and Hastings he ought to learn the ropes fairly soon.

He found Mrs. Cole a slender woman just past her first great beauty. Hilary respected her at once. She was ghostly white and drawn and her hands trembled each time she tried to raise them, but she was controlled. Hilary's own eyes filled as he looked into hers. Once again the whole weight of pain seemed to lie upon his own heart.

"You are very kind to come," she said. "My husband told me how you helped him last night. I'm so confused, but there are things we must settle and the doctor feels my husband should sleep now that he's relaxed."

"I want to help you in every way possible, Mrs. Cole."

"About the—funeral." She paused, her lips quivering. "I know it cannot be held in the church. But even here at the house there will be a great many people. Our close friends and Steve's. The thing I wanted most to ask you was whether you could still use some sort of service which would seem as normal as possible. Even a little beautiful—for Steve's sake?"

He caught her shaking hands in his and held them fast.

"Mrs. Cole, the rubric of the church is not our highest authority. The service will be as beautiful and as comforting as I can make it."

She thanked him with her eyes.

"Steve loved music so," she went on. "He was always playing his symphony records. I wondered if it would be out of place to have music at that time? I'm sure there will be many young people here. Steve had so many friends. I would like to keep the note of—of tragedy as far away as we can, for their sakes."

She could not go on.

"The music would be right and possible," Hilary said quickly. "Could I help to arrange it?"

"If you would speak to Mr. Forrest, the organist. It's so hard for me. I had thought of instruments—violin and cello, perhaps. But he will know just what to have."

Hilary promised. As he did so, it came over him with a shock that he had not even met the organist yet. He must look him up that very day in any case, for there would be much to talk over together.

It was nearly one when he finally left the house. He had talked to Mrs. Cole, when the simple plans were completed, drawing upon all his powers, physical and spiritual, to give her strength. He had stopped in young Steve's room—a hard thing—had found the listing of the records

36

with his favorites marked upon it, as his mother had said they would be. After Hilary had written these carefully on a card for later reference, he had looked hesitantly around the room. It seemed incredible that only last night he had come in here at the risk of his life, and had prayed beside the dead boy upon the bed.

The room was fresh now and empty. In spite of the luxurious furnishings, the simplicity of Steve's spirit seemed to dominate it. There was a collection of china dogs in a case, and an intricate ship's model, half completed, on a table. The books, the pictures on the wall, the tray of pipes, the snapshot of a girl in skirt and sweater, tucked in the mirror frame— these details looked so normal, so far removed from stark despair, Hilary wondered intensely for the first time what had been the cause of it. Up till this moment his attention had been focused upon the results. Now he was deeply curious as to the strange reasons leading up to the final act. Perhaps no one will ever know, he thought, as he went out and gently closed the door behind him.

He drove straight to the McCollys'. Jarvis, the butler, opened the door.

"Is Mrs. McColly in?" Hilary asked.

"Yes, Mr. Laurens, I'll tell her. And Miss Alexa?" Jarvis smiled as far as he could achieve that effect.

"Of course." Hilary tried to return the smile but he was uneasy.

He waited in the familiar room, watching the sunlight stream through the casements upon the bowl of daffodils on the window sill and his own roses still upon the table.

He turned swiftly as he heard a step. It was Mrs. McColly. During the time he had been coming to the house he had never grown to feel any closer to this woman whom he hoped some day he could name as mother. She was pretty to look upon even now, though with no trace of Lex's vibrant beauty. She was a slender woman with cool patrician features, blond hair and gray eyes; always charming, always correct. The results of her inheritance and upbringing had remained unchanged through the years of her marriage with Alex McColly. There was an even propriety about her actions. Once and once only she had done the unconventional thing. Perhaps because of that she had retreated farther into her natural citadel of conservatism than her friends who had made "suitable" marriages in their youth. Perhaps she only seemed more conservative than most women because old Alex and young Alex were both openly radical upon all minor points of conduct.

Hilary went up to her. "I'm so glad I found you in."

"We're very proud of you, Hilary. How are the first days going?"

"Rather mixed, but I'll feel more at home soon. I wonder if Lex told you about last night?"

"Sit down. Lex isn't quite ready and I really want to talk to you about that. What happened to the Cole boy?"

Hilary told her as briefly as he could.

"It hit me so hard, for I'd just come from my evening with Lex. I was pretty happy. I wonder if she told you?"

"Yes, she did," Mrs. McColly said.

"It was such desperate news to get at the very moment I opened the Rectory door. You do see why I didn't even wait to phone her, don't you? I should have. It would not have taken long. The thing of it was . . ."

"You never thought of it."

Hilary's clear, honest eyes were raised to her face.

"That's right. I can't explain it to myself, let alone to Lex."

"There will be many such times, you know," she said. "That's what I fear a little if Lex marries you. Perhaps unscrupulous men make the best husbands."

Hilary's startled face made her go on hastily.

"I'm joking, of course. But I do know that if it were a choice between me and his duty my husband would unhesitatingly choose me. You, Hilary, will always, consciously or unconsciously, put what you conceive to be your duty first. Even before Lex. My fear is that she may never adjust herself to that."

"But, Mrs. McColly, I could never put anything before my *love* for Lex. It's only that as a priest . . ."

"I know, dear boy. You will do what your profession demands of you. It is right that you should. Only"—she broke off, looking down at the circlet of stones she turned on her finger—"we women want everything. We want our husbands to run the affairs of the world and still keep us in the background of their thoughts every waking minute. We want them to be men of honor whom we can respect and yet we want them to give in to our wishes, right or wrong. We want to eat our cake and have it. As I say, we unreasonably want everything, and . . ."

She raised her eyes, and Hilary felt in that second he knew her better than ever before.

"Some of us give everything," she finished.

Hilary fumbled for words. They seemed trite when they came.

"I'm sure I could make Lex happy. When we love each other, every obstacle will smooth out."

"Don't hurry her," Mrs. McColly said softly, for they could hear Lex on the stairs. "Just be sure, both of you!"

Lex came into the room slowly and did not speak as she came. Mrs. McColly covered the awkward moment.

"You must come to dinner soon, Hilary. Alex will want to see you.

38

Now I must be off to do some shopping. Such a nuisance this nice spring day!"

She was gone. Hilary and Lex stood looking into each other's eyes. Then he caught her to him. When he released her she looked up with the same startled expression she had worn the night before.

"All right, you needn't ask. I suppose I'll have to forgive you. This time. But I didn't like it and I was very angry, so that's that. What happened to the Cole boy?"

He repeated the details again. "But now," he went on, "I've done all I can for them at the moment. This afternoon is our own. Do you realize this is the first time I've ever taken you out knowing that you love me? Every other time I was so tortured with uncertainty I couldn't half enjoy it. But today! Oh, Lex, you're beautiful!"

She colored under his gaze.

"No more blandishments! I'm not in the best mood yet. But come on, let's go. Maybe it will improve."

They went first to the florist's, where Hilary spent an absurdly long time examining violets. When he had at last found the perfect bunch, he fastened them himself to Lexa's fur. She watched his long, strong fingers not quite steady, and the hard light melted in her eyes.

"Oh, Hil, you *are* sweet," she whispered. "Come on before I make a fool of myself. It's going to be dreadful if I can't stay mad at you even for one morning! You'll get out of hand entirely. You and your precious parish!"

They walked slowly up to Moxam's, leaving the car by the florist's. The spring sun was warm and bright. The stir of the crowds about them only shut them in more closely, more securely to themselves. By the time they had reached the old, high-ceilinged restaurant with its shining tables and urbane atmosphere they were once more two young people, happy in a love newly confessed.

The head waiter recognized Lex at once, bowed deferentially to Hilary and escorted them to a choice table at one of the tall windows overlooking the park. They sat for a long time without speaking, forgetting even to order.

"You do forgive me?" Hilary asked at last.

"I guess so, only don't do it again."

"I'll try not to. Can't you see, though, that no matter what I may have to do, there will always be you and only you in my heart? Isn't that enough?"

"Would it be for you?"

"What do you mean?"

"Perhaps I'll show you some time."

Hilary looked sober and then smiled again.

"Don't threaten me. I'm still too happy. Tell me again. Was it really from the first, Lex? That night by the river?"

She nodded slowly, the color rising again in her cheeks.

"I thought I was crazy. That's why I went off to Canada. You've caused me an awful lot of trouble, Hil."

"And what about me? But it's over now."

"I'm not so sure!" Then after they had ordered, she looked up with a glorious light on her face. Hilary felt blinded by it. "Oh, let's not argue. I want to be happy today, myself. Let's forget last night and all the *if*'s to come! Let's forget St. Matthews!"

"That's not hard, when I'm with you!"

The sun of the new spring streamed in upon them. There was in it a fresh young quality of delight. They basked in it and drew from it a vast confidence.

"It was so silly of me to be angry last night," Lex said.

"It was not," Hilary maintained stoutly. "I should have stopped to phone you. But we'll both be right as right from now on."

Near the end of the meal Lex, glancing over her shoulder, frowned suddenly.

"How the affairs of the parish do intrude! That's old J. V. Dunn who just came in. I don't know the man with him."

"Who is Dunn?" Hilary asked innocently.

"Oh, Hil, you have got such a lot to learn! He's one of the richest men in St. Matthews, and a regular old devil if you ask me. He won't be a vestryman, they say, but he likes to pull strings from behind. Politics. You know. He doesn't approve of me."

"Why on earth not?"

"Oh, he thinks our crowd is *fast*. He's got one daughter. Poor Maudie! She doesn't know her nose is her own. I'll venture to say he has you all picked out for her. So, watch yourself!"

Hilary was amused. "What's she like? So I'll be on guard at once."

Lex did not answer for a moment. Instead she sat watching him intently.

"You're so awfully good-looking, Hil. I never thought about it before, but you're bound to have women falling in love with you. They always do with preachers. Maybe I'll have trouble on that score."

Hilary threw back his head and laughed heartily.

"When you are jealous of me, that will be something," he replied inelegantly. "But don't let's talk nonsense!"

"All the same," Lex went on, "if I ever really do marry you I'll want you to tell me everything. Every single thing. Promise?"

40

He looked grave. "All my own life will be an open book to you, darling. That goes without saying. But a clergyman gets entangled in a lot of confidences. The 'secrets of the confessional,' so to speak, I couldn't repeat even to you."

"I see. I'm not sure I like that idea."

"Listen, sweet. We're being foolish again. Can't we just trust each other and the future too?"

"I guess so."

As they were leaving the dining room, Hilary whispered, "Which one is Dunn?"

"Over there, next the wall. The one with the beak like a vulture."

To Hilary's amusement, he spotted him instantly from the description. Tough old customer, he thought to himself. He hoped he could get on the good side of him.

It was four when he got back to his study. He found Hastings waiting for him with a sheaf of messages. There were several cards also. Two of the vestrymen had already dropped in at the study to call; one was Henry Alvord, Senior Warden. Hilary was especially sorry to have missed him, for he had suspected a lack of confidence in Alvord's attitude.

Feeling a faint reproach in Hastings' tone, Hilary hastened to reassure him.

"During the rest of the week I expect to be right here. Today I've had to be out. Now, first of all, how can I get in touch with Mr. Forrest, the organist?"

"Maybe he's at the organ now. Usually is round this time. Always likes to practice in the late afternoon." He opened the window nearest the choir. A faint sound of music could be heard.

"That's him. You'd better go right down."

"Come along then and introduce me," Hilary said, knowing it would please the old man.

As they entered the church, Hilary gave a sound of surprise.

"He doesn't have the lights on!"

Hastings stopped. "He don't need them. Hasn't anyone told you? He's blind."

Hilary stood still. The vestrymen had stated proudly that they thought they had the best organist in the country. "Forrest, you know." As though the mere mention of the name was all that was necessary. And he had replied, "Oh, yes, Forrest. Of course. I'm sure we've used his music."

But beyond that they had not described him. It came over Hilary now with a frightening realization how very little of importance concerning a church was likely to be discussed before the actual union of parish and priest had taken place.

They had a fine *plant,* the vestrymen had told him. Buildings worth so much, endowment so much, pew rental so much, parish house so big. These were the corporealities of which the vestry had spoken to him. But all the imperishable elements, all those intangibles which made up the church's soul, he would have to learn for himself, gropingly, blunderingly, perhaps.

He felt strange and shy as he approached the organ. He had never had any acquaintance with a blind man before. He asked Hastings to turn on one of the chancel lights, so he saw clearly the man seated on the bench. His head was raised a little, his eyes closed, his whole countenance sensitive and spiritual.

"Mr. Forrest," Hastings said, "here's somebody wants to talk to you."

The man at the organ played on for a moment as though intent upon memorizing a strain, then he turned. "Yes, what is it?"

In full view his face was more striking than the profile had been. The features were cut thin and clean and the whole expression one of singular beauty. Hilary found himself involuntarily thinking, "Blessed are the pure in heart," for here before him he knew at once was a man in whom there was no guile.

"It's the new rector wants to meet you," Hastings stated with importance.

"Don't get up," Hilary said quickly. He slid to the bench beside Forrest and they shook hands.

"I've heard many fine things of you, Mr. Laurens."

"And I of you."

"Do you mind if I 'look' at you in my own way?"

"Please do."

The blind man touched Hilary's face lightly. He smiled. "I think we'll get on together," he said.

"I'm sure of it. There will be so much I'll want you to tell me a little later, but right now there is a sad duty to do on Thursday afternoon."

He told him then of young Cole's death and his mother's wishes for the service.

"It will be at their home of course and as simple as possible, but there will be people there, many of them young. What do you think about her suggestion?"

"I understand it," Mr. Forrest said slowly. "I'll attend to the music. There must be running through it all a note of youth and hope. I'll plan it very carefully. I know just the people for the instruments if I can get them. I'll call them up tonight. This is a tragic business. We'll do what we can."

Hilary drew the card from his pocket. "Here are some of the boy's favorite symphonies. I jotted them down." He read them over slowly. "Thank you for understanding. I must go now and not interrupt you any longer. I'm very much at sea about everything. Won't you give me your advice whenever you can?"

Mr. Forrest felt for Hilary's hand. "I'm always here in the late afternoons. Don't ever hesitate to come in if you care to. I've been at St. Matthews a good many years—like Hastings—so if I can be of any help, I'll be glad. I'm a good listener," he added smiling.

Hilary went back to his study with warmth in his heart. He would have a friend in Forrest, he knew. There would be one sensitive and sympathetic soul, at least, to whom he could go for advice and comfort.

He called Lex at dinnertime and again at ten.

"I'm in my study, darling. I'm working late tonight."

"Whatever are you doing?"

"Well, there is such a thing as a Sunday sermon, you know."

"Of course. I always keep forgetting. What are you going to preach about? I'm coming to hear you."

"Don't, please! Not my first Sunday. You might throw me off the track altogether. I mean it."

"Silly! When will I see you tomorrow?"

"Dinner if it suits. I'll work like mad all day."

When they said goodbye at last, Hilary wrote to Dick. Even as he put pen to paper he was conscious of the great void in his life. Ordinarily he would be pouring out everything to the Bishop first of all.

DEAR DICK:

Here I am in my new study feeling, as Grandy would have said, "like a cat in a strange garret!" The job scares me stiff but I may get over it. Hastings, the old sexton, after suspicious scrutiny, has taken me under his wing, the general idea being that if I give him a little lift here and there in such small matters as sermons and sacraments, he will be able to run the parish as usual. Funny old bird but I like him.

I ran into tragedy the first thing. A young fellow shot himself last night, the son of one of my vestrymen. Funeral Thursday. It's pretty tough. Kind of thing makes me wish I were a truck driver instead of a parson. What can I say or do in such an extremity?

Look, old man, here's something I want you to take seriously. When you write, tell me what sort of sermon you'd like to hear if you ever went to church—which I know you

43

don't. What do you think the Average Man would like to have discussed by the clergy if he could have a vote? I may muff this whole job but at least I'm going to try my hardest to meet it honestly and with the best intelligence and conscience I've got. Please don't forget to give this question some thought and reply to it. I'm desperately in earnest.

And now, my cherished brother, for the real news. Lex and I are not formally engaged but we have what I believe the Victorians called "an understanding." She's still afraid of my profession but I'm confident now I can win her over. The main thing is, she really cares, though heaven knows why she should! I'm so slap happy now in my private life it's pretty hard to get on with my work. In one way, though, it's easier. The hell of uncertainty about her feeling is over. Well, I know you'll rejoice with me that I've got this far. Maybe you could drop Lex a line soon and intimate that I'm not such a bad egg and would make a marvellous husband. Write me soon and don't forget my question.

HIL

P.S. The wedding, when it does come off (I refuse to say *if*) will not be before next fall, so you'll have plenty of time to shine your shoes for your job. I'll have Lex pick you out a good maid of honor! I fancy the whole thing will turn out to be quite a show. Lex wants all the trimmings and we both think it would be nice to have it here in St. Matthews with her own rector from Christ Church officiating. The thought just crossed my mind that, when the time comes, it might be decent to ask Bronson to be here. Since no one knows how we really feel about him it would look like a gesture of respect for Grandy. I'll talk it over later with Lex. What do you think?

H.

The next morning before Hilary had finished his breakfast Hastings called up to say the cases of books and pictures and some other crates had arrived. Hilary was boyishly pleased. If his own things were once in place in the study his whole attitude would improve. He would feel more master of the situation. The very sermon he was working on would go better. He relayed his enthusiasm to Hastings. He would be over at once and they would work in the study all day.

He changed to a pair of slacks and his oldest sweater and hurried across the court. The sight of the boxes and crates exhilarated him. He liked to work with his hands and there was never much opportunity for it. In a short time now he was happy with a hammer, prying off boards and scattering nails.

When he uncrated the Bishop's own desk chair he stood for a long moment before it. This in itself would always bring Grandy's presence into the room. He placed it carefully and then turned to the books. He had no idea until they were finally stacked upon the floor, what a library he had brought. There were all his own volumes and the choicest of the Bishop's. He and Hastings eyed the shelves and conjectured.

"We can't attempt the pictures until we get these out of the way," Hilary said, "and this will be a job."

It was. All the long morning Hilary sorted and placed while Hastings fetched and carried as he was told. They took a few minutes off for lunch, with another hour which Hilary devoted to necessary phone calls; then they went at it again.

By four o'clock the bookcases, surprisingly commodious, were all filled, the debris cleared away, the floor swept, the rugs spread, the desk appointments in place. There remained then the pictures. Hilary was tired. The walls were high and he had already made a thousand trips up and down the ladder. Every muscle of him ached. He was dirty. His face was smudged and his sweater soiled. Moreover he was fast losing his temper with Hastings, who had a definite opinion about where each picture should be hung. Hilary paused to light his pipe, and then grasped the stepladder firmly before Hastings could capture it.

"I'll tell you what," he said. "We need a good strong cup of tea! Both of us. You go down to the basement and brew us a potful, and I'll get a picture or two hung while you're gone."

Hastings hesitated but his British blood prevailed. He was in the habit of making himself tea at intervals on a little stove in the basement, which he had pointed out to Hilary yesterday. This was a proper hour and he was properly thirsty, so with a few last pieces of advice he departed.

Hilary mounted the ladder with his hammer and a heavy nail. He particularly wanted a large picture of Magdalen Tower to hang on that wall. He leaned out, tapping gingerly for a studding. He found one. It was off the center of the space but it would do. He knew he should get down and move the ladder but he didn't want to bother, so he leaned still farther, set the nail, and was about to strike it in when he lost his balance and only saved himself from a nasty spill by a quick jump. Even so he was shaken up and uttered an unclerical expletive as he righted himself and the ladder. Suddenly behind him he heard a voice.

"Young man, are you the new rector or a new janitor?"

Hilary turned. He was uncomfortably aware of his dusty and dishevelled appearance. If he had not been, he would have read it in the stern eyes of the amazing-looking old woman who glared at him from the doorway. She leaned upon a cane and continued to study him from under a black velvet bonnet. Something in her complete assurance and disapproving stare nettled Hilary.

"I'm the rector," he said a little crisply, "but at the moment I'm not sure I shouldn't have chosen the janitorship instead."

The old lady took a few steps forward. "I am one of the trustees of the Wilson Orphanage for Boys," she stated with great positiveness, "and I came to size you up and see whether you're a person to influence them properly if they are still brought here to church."

"And what do you think?" said Hilary, feeling more annoyed by the second. "Will you sit down?"

"Not just now. I see you smoke."

"You are quite right. I also drink coffee. Very strong."

"You swear. I heard you."

Hilary bowed. "In common with most of the race of men, I do, mildly, upon strong occasion."

"You're not ashamed to be caught like this, looking like a freight-car tramp?"

"Not in the slightest."

She pointed her cane at him.

"What about your theology? Is it sound?"

"Why, not particularly," said Hilary. "Is yours?"

Suddenly the old lady's face broke up in a thousand crinkles. A low and incredibly delightful chuckle came from her throat. She tapped Hilary's chest with her cane.

"Young man, I think you'll do. Sit down here. I met Hastings and sent him back for more tea. I want to talk with you. I'm Mrs. Warner Reed."

She said it as though the name meant something. Hilary held out his hand, with his own disarming smile.

"I'm not ashamed of my clothes, Mrs. Reed, but I am of my manners. I've had a day of it getting things in shape here, and I must be a bit edgy. Please forgive me."

She held his hand firmly while she smiled back at him.

"I'm the bad-mannered one, but I never apologize. At my age, you don't have to. The truth is, I tried to catch you off guard. I always do that when I want to judge a person. Now, I'll warrant I'll know you better when I leave today than if I'd listened to your sermons and met you at dinner parties for ten years to come. You've got good eyes."

"Thank you."

46

"Where's Hastings, the old fool? He's had time to brew six pots of tea since I sent him back. He's taken a fancy to you. That's fortunate. If he hadn't you might as well pack up and leave. He knows enough about St. Matthews people to put us all in jail. You can get information from him, but don't let him browbeat you." She turned. "Oh, Hastings? That you? About time you got here. I was just telling Mr. Laurens you know all the skeleton closets in the parish. It's a wonder somebody hasn't shot you for it before this. Now you go down to my car and tell Winter to give you that box of cakes. We might as well eat them now with our tea. They're the kind you like."

Hastings departed, grinning broadly. It was not only his air of extreme deference which made Hilary realize that Mrs. Warner Reed was a person of consequence. He was forming his own opinion. Under the ancient velvet bonnet was a face of perhaps seventy-five years—strong and proud as an eagle's. Her bearing was regal, her manner the complete unself-consciousness of the born aristocrat.

"Now," she was saying, "I want to talk about my boys." Hilary saw the fierce gray eyes soften. "I've contributed to this Orphanage for fifty years but I never took the trouble to go to visit it till about five years ago. More shame to me. I didn't like conditions when I went. I got myself made a trustee. Now I'm trying to get some things done and I'll want your help. Do you like boys?"

"Very much. I was one once. And I have a brother. Between us we know about all there is to know on the subject. You would like Dick," he startled himself by saying. "When he comes to visit me, may I bring him to call?"

"I'll expect you to. Is he like you?"

"Not a bit, except in height. He has blond hair and black eyes. He's a wit and a bit of a pagan—I somehow think you and he would take to each other."

"Thank you. I know that's a compliment. Here's Hastings, so we'll get on first with our tea. Don't you think you'd better wash your hands?"

Hilary chuckled as he hastened to obey. Already he felt he had known the old lady for years. There was something so forthright, so unequivocal in her acceptance of him that he felt warmed and cheered as he had after his conversation with Forrest, though two more unlike people than the organist and Mrs. Reed would have been hard to find. Because of Hastings' presence in the background the talk over tea took on a vein of delicately veiled humor, and Hilary found his eyes meeting those of his guest with quick appreciation as they both thrust and parried. Great old person, he kept thinking over and over, and wise as she's witty. I'll need her!

47

When tea was over Mrs. Reed continued to take charge.

"Now, Hastings, take these things away. Mr. Laurens and I want to talk. How's your wife's rheumatism?"

"A little better, ma'am, thank you."

"That's good. See you take care of her. There's a box for her in the back of my car. I forgot to tell you when you went down before. Winter knows."

"Thank you, ma'am. She'll appreciate it, I'm sure."

Hastings left, more docile than Hilary had seen him before.

"Now he's out of the way," Mrs. Reed said, "let's talk about the Orphanage. It's my big interest, but somehow my plans are always getting blocked."

"Is there any special reason?"

Mrs. Reed leaned forward.

"There is. And her name's Hettie Breckenridge. You'll meet her soon enough. She thinks she owns this church, and she's been a trustee of the Orphanage for twenty years. I don't like her and she doesn't like me. Know too much about each other, I guess. When we were young we ate from the same dish practically."

Hilary's face had a strange expression but he made no comment.

"Well, that's beside the mark. The real point I'm getting at is that I want you as soon as you can to go and see the boys. Talk to them in their own language. Dr. Partridge was the pat-them-on-the-head kind. They called him 'Old Slobber-Puss.' But they'll like you."

"I hope so. I'll try to get over as early as possible."

"Good. Now I must go. You're a bachelor, I hear?"

"So far."

"Well, stick to it. It's an asset to a parson. Every woman in the church from seventy down will moon over you and forgive you anything. By the way, don't let Hettie Breckenridge ever catch you in that rig. Put on all your ecclesiastical petticoats for her. She's a stickler for form and ceremony."

"Thanks for the tip."

"And when you want to blow off steam, come over and see me."

"It may be often."

"The oftener, the better. Terrible business about the Cole boy."

Hilary nodded.

The old woman's face was suddenly rigid with a pride that asked no sympathy.

"I've had two sons and a grandson, and I've lost them all. Goodbye, Mr. Laurens. Let me know your opinion of the Orphanage. And don't break your neck on that stepladder! We don't want the bother of getting another new rector yet awhile. You needn't come down with me," she added. "I'm not decrepit yet."

When she was gone, Hilary finished the big pictures quickly, and stacked the smaller ones for a later day. He smiled often. He liked Mrs. Reed enormously and knew he would always be at home with her; and he was interested about the Orphanage. He sobered, though, as he thought of Miss Hettie Breckenridge. She must be Lexa's great-aunt. It was rather disquieting that Lex had never mentioned her. Of course, there was the old family feud of which he already knew, but since he was to be rector of this parish in which the remaining Breckenridges were prominent it was strange that Lex had never talked more freely to him about them. Suddenly he stopped with an unhappy look on his face. He recalled the expression on Lexa's own when he had asked what her parents' feeling would be about her being married in St. Matthews. "I think they'd rather like it," she had said, with that faint, enigmatic smile.

For the first time he felt displeasure toward Lex; but he thrust the thought from him violently. He would talk it all over with her. She doubtless had her own reasons and good ones for not discussing her mother's family with him before this.

The study in the late afternoon looked back at him now with a warm beauty which filled him with satisfaction. The long wall of friendly books; the familiar rugs from the old house; the pictures he most loved; the desk with the Bishop's photograph upon it, and his chair behind it; these all made the room now, Hilary felt, his own. The spirit of Dr. Partridge, however inspirational in theory, was completely banished, and he was glad. He had put down his first roots and felt a new freedom and stability because of it.

He sat down in the kindly western light, staring into Grandy's strong, spare face in the frame. If the dead lived again and held remembrance of things past, he knew Grandy was with him now. If only it were possible to consult with him as in the old days, Hilary thought.

It was now for the first time that the full responsibility of his own rectorship fell upon him. He was the priest of a great parish; he was the recognized intermediary between God and man. In the sacred robes of his office he would stand before his congregation next Sunday and preach. What had he to say that would touch their lives and melt their souls? What words of his could meet that deep unspoken sorrow, or penetrate the secret places of the heart in the men and women who would raise their eyes perfunctorily to his, or kneel—perhaps also perfunctorily— while he led them in prayer?

More than this, it being the first Sunday of the month, he would officiate before that high white altar in the church's greatest sacrament.

49

Would those kneeling before him at the altar-rail guess that behind his sacerdotal vestments his own heart was full of the same passions as their own? Or would he seem to them a man apart?

His face was suddenly very grave indeed. He must try, especially for that holy office, to put out of his mind every secular thought, which meant that he must thrust Lex forcibly from his consciousness. For it was impossible for him even to think of her tumultuous beauty without having his imagination swept away by it. So it had been at their first meeting. So it was still.

Aside from the responsibility of his first sermon, upon which he wanted to do some more polishing, there lay upon him now heavily the matter of the funeral tomorrow for young Cole. In the circumstances he was not permitted by the rubric to read the regular burial service. He must devise one of his own, and it had better be done at once.

He opened his books before him and leafed through, jotting down a line here, a passage there. Suddenly, unsatisfied with what he had done, he rose and went to the nearest bookcase. In it only a few hours ago he had carefully placed the large brown scrapbook which Grandy had bequeathed him. His experience with it these last months had been a peculiar one. At first the very feel of the book in his hands had brought him comfort. But later when he had opened it, the sight of the Bishop's small, firm, familiar handwriting, the glimpse he had caught of the carefully kept index in which the sacred and the secular—true to Grandy's nature—mingled freely, had all brought too much pain. He had closed the book without perusing it. He was too close yet, he had told himself, to his grief. Later he would look carefully into it.

Now, this hour, he felt, was the time. Even though it brought back the poignancy of his sorrow, it was the nearest possible thing to Grandy's own spoken words. And he had need of them.

He drew out the book and took it back to the desk. It was large and the paper was faded in places. Evidently it had been kept by the Bishop over a long period of time. On the front page, recently written, were the words: "To Hilary Laurens, with the love of his grandfather." And below: "This book contains the advice I have given to young ministers over a period of thirty years, together with some opinions and observations of my own which I have kept to myself. I hope it may be of some use."

Hilary looked at the index, under S. He saw at once what he sought and turned quickly to the page. There were only a few lines upon it.

"Under these tragic circumstances make up your own prayers as best you can, and for Scripture stick to the Psalms. You can never go wrong with them. God bless old David. He knew everything."

Hilary smiled. It was as though Grandy had spoken it. He quickly tore

50

up the tentative sentences he had written. The Twenty-third Psalm would be best of all, with perhaps the Twenty-seventh added to it. Then, having settled this, he began with deeper concentration to formulate the prayers he would use. As he wrote once again he felt in his own heart the parents' agony of grief. He felt the shock of the young life's ending. He wrote slowly, pausing, pondering, feeling some virtue go out of himself to be spent upon the lines.

There was the sound of feet on the stairs and a tap on the door, followed by Hastings' entrance.

"Hello," Hilary said, "I thought you'd gone."

There was a pleased air of importance about Hastings.

"There's a young couple downstairs, Mr. Laurens, wantin' to get married."

"What! At this hour?" The clock stood at six.

"Yes, sir. It's like this. They was tellin' me. They're a simple young pair. He got his thumb hurt in the shop today and got a few days off and they want to get married and catch the eight o'clock train for upstate a little ways, where the girl's got an aunt in the country. I think you'd better marry them. I brought up your cassock."

"Thanks, Hastings. Give me a minute and then show them up. Have they witnesses?"

"Yes, a man and a girl."

Hilary stripped off his sweater and shoved it into a desk drawer. He got into his cassock, tied the cincture, smoothed his hair, and wiped his face carefully with his handkerchief. At that moment Hastings ushered in the pair. Hilary warmed to them at once. The young fellow had a fresh, ruddy face, honest eyes, and a great pair of shoulders. He was embarrassed and awkward and his first word revealed him as not long from the old country. Ireland, Hilary guessed. The girl was little and dark and pretty, and, while also shy, took the situation in hand when the first introductory words were over with.

"You see," she said, "it was my idea coming here, and we never half thought to find you in and all. But I had such a wish to be married in St. Matthews not knowing if it ever could be with us just simple folk, but when Miss Nancy was married—she's the daughter of the lady I worked for for years, but my madam's dead now—well, when Miss Nancy was married, Mrs. Borden, that was her mother, the lady I worked for, well, she invited all of us help to come and sit in the gallery and see it and it was so beautiful and I thought then if I could just be married before that altar to keep thinking of all the rest of my life and Joe was agreed, for he's Protestant, North of Ireland, and I'm English, so we just come to ask if such a thing could be, sir."

51

Hilary smiled into her anxious eyes.

"Of course it can. And very proud I'll be of the wedding, for it's the first since I became rector here. You have your license?"

Joe produced it clumsily. "We've had it this while back just waitin' for a good time. Then today when I knocked up my thumb—it's nothing, but it gives me a bit of time off—we thought we'd get on with it as fast as possible. Here it is, sir."

"This is all in good order," Hilary said, scanning it, "and your witnesses?"

"My girl friend and her boy friend. They're downstairs in the Parish House waiting to see. Oh, you can't know what this will mean to me, sir."

Hilary looked again into her eager face. She was dressed plainly in a dark hat and coat with a blue dress showing bravely underneath. A good girl, and a nice boy, they were, clean and honest and upright by every token, with the beauty of this great moment before them, and then the few days' honeymoon at the aunt's in the country! Beyond this would be Joe back in the machine shop and the girl and her eventual babies, pinching out their drab existence through the years. He spoke quickly to her.

"Now, Mary, will you go down to your friends and tell them we'll be ready in a few minutes? Just wait with them till we come. Hastings, you'll attend to the church lights, and light the candles at the altar. All of them. Then bring me the proper vestments. Joe will wait here for me and we'll soon join you."

Mary and Joe looked at each other as though fearful even of this brief separation. Hastings looked inquiringly at Hilary, who blandly glanced the other way. When the two were gone, Hilary spoke soberly to Joe.

"There's one little matter. When a girl is married in a church it's the custom for her to have some flowers to carry or to wear."

"Ah, that's right. I might ha' known. I was so excited like, I never thought of a bouquet. It's a pity, an' her so set on bein' married here an' all."

"Well now, there's a little florist shop right at the corner. Why don't you run up there and get a pretty corsage—you know, the kind she can pin on her shoulder. They're not very expensive. And you'll be back here by the time I'm ready. Go down these stairs and out through the court."

Joe grinned broadly.

"I'll be back in a jiffy with it, sir, an' I'm obliged to you for puttin' me right about it."

"Don't tell her I did," Hilary warned.

"No fears. I'll take the credit to meself."

It was twenty minutes later that Hilary in his white surplice and stole stood watching as the young couple walked slowly up the center aisle.

This, too, was Mary's wish. He could see as they approached that the girl's eyes were still moist. Her delight over the flowers had been touching in the extreme.

He had officiated at many weddings during his priesthood, but never one, he was thinking, which so pleased him as this one now. Joe's responses were firm in his rich old-country voice; Mary's were clear and sweet. He had been wrong about the years of drab living. There might never be luxury or even much comfort. There might always be the pinchpenny hardships. But there would also always be love's renewal. He felt this as they knelt before him; his own voice was low and vibrant upon the final words.

"That you may so live together in this life that in the world to come ye may have life everlasting. Amen."

When they rose to their feet, they stood a moment awed and uncertain.

"You may kiss her now," Hilary whispered, smiling.

He saw them off at the church door, hearing their thanks again and wishing them well. The five-dollar bill which Joe had proudly given him he quietly returned to the bride.

"It's the custom," he said with perfect gravity. "The fee for the first wedding a new rector has, always goes back to the bride."

"It does?" she replied, beaming. "Joe, just fancy that now!"

When they were gone, Hilary walked slowly up the aisle, watching as Hastings extinguished the altar candles.

"Well," the old man observed with his Olympian air, "you're gettin' your hand in this week. Marry 'em today, bury 'em tomorrow. That's the way it is round here."

"I guess that's our job, Hastings," Hilary answered. "You go along now. I'll put out the other lights. I want to stay here a minute to rest myself."

When he was alone Hilary sat down in one of the front pews. His mind followed the newly wedded pair. They would sit close as the train tore through the night, the perfume of the roses on the girl's coat enfolding them. (He was glad he had thought of the flowers.) There would be the stop at some country station where they would alight in the darkness with their cheap suitcase. There would be the ride under the stars to a farmhouse. Then at last in some plain little spare chamber, the warm clasp of heart to heart. He felt shaken with the thought. If only some time before too long it could be even so with him and his beloved!

He rose to go, then stopped suddenly, facing the dim whiteness of the altar. He had only realized at that moment that his first act as rector of this church had been to marry a young couple by the names of Mary and Joseph! He put out the lights and hurried up to the study to call Lex.

He must tell her! He must have her know of this strange and tender coincidence.

Then, with his hand on the telephone, he hesitated. Would she understand? Perhaps his own emotion was too tenuous, too delicate to risk sharing with another. It was safest to keep it to himself.

CHAPTER IV

ON THAT FIRST Sunday morning Hilary wakened early. He had set his alarm for seven but it was an unnecessary precaution. The first birds twittering under the church eaves aroused him and while he lay thinking of what the day might have in store, he could hear Morris shuffling softly through the hall. Punctually upon the minute the old man was at the door.

"I sure do wish you well today, Mist' Hilary," he began.

"Thanks, Morris. I'm glad you're here to back me up. I won't want breakfast until after the early service. Then I can take my time."

"Yes, Mist' Hilary. That's the way the Bishop always liked. I dreamed about him last night. He be mighty proud today if he was here."

Hilary stopped to pat the bony shoulders under the black alpaca coat.

"I know. I wish he were. Run along, Morris, and fuss with the breakfast. I'll be ready for a good one. I want to get over to Church early now."

He did not know whether there would be five people or fifty at the eight o'clock communion, but it was his first service and a tremendous nervous excitement possessed him. He bathed, shaved and dressed with scrupulous, almost holy care, trying all the time to control the undue beating of his heart. At last he was ready. He went downstairs, crossed the court, entered the side door of the church and went on into the robing room. He had never felt so alone in his life. He put on his vestments and stood nervously watching the hands of the clock on the wall. When they reached eight, he opened the door, crossed slowly to the altar and knelt down before it.

The flowers were white stocks and their faint perfume filled the chancel. Through the high, rich windows the morning light came softly. There was everywhere, Hilary felt, a breath of expectancy. Priest and altar awaited; the Chalice and Paten stood ready with their mysterious symbolism of the ages; for the first time from his hands the waiting men and women would soon receive the bread and the wine. For the first time from his lips they would hear the words that would, for a moment, make them one with divinity. His flock. He, their new shepherd. With a sudden inner intensity that racked him, he prayed that with his own very body and blood he might serve this people.

Footsteps could be heard upon the stone flagging of the aisles. This was a quiet service with only the echo of past prayers and the faint fall of the footsteps until his voice should break the silence. He raised his eyes. The reredos towered in sculptured white behind the altar, with the heroic figure of the Christ uplifted against it. Beneath, on the altar itself, the rich violet of the season hung below the "fair white cloth," the tapers burned, the stocks gave out their fragrance. A great quiet rested upon the kneeling worshippers and suddenly touched his own quick beating heart. He waited for the sound of new footsteps to die away, and then bowed his head and in low tones began to repeat the Lord's Prayer.

As he passed back and forth before the kneeling communicants during the service, the slow rise and fall of his voice formed the weaving pattern of the ancient ritual. *Preserve thy body and soul unto everlasting life . . . preserve thy body and soul . . .*

A few faces at the altar, uplifted to receive the cup, became clear to him. One was that of old Mrs. Reed. Her hands were trembling, he noticed, as she touched the Chalice. His own voice broke upon the words as he recognized the Coles, kneeling there, their faces ashen and set. He found himself pausing a second before them, and then raising his hand in special benediction above their bowed heads. *"And feed on him in thy heart by faith with thanksgiving."*

The other face that suddenly and intensely imprinted itself upon his mind was that of a woman. It was a face of such graven beauty of features that it startled him. She was not young, for the hair under her hat was well mixed with gray, but there was a quality of grace in every line of her kneeling body, in her hands as she cupped them to receive the bread. There was another quality, too, which Hilary, sensitive as he was to spiritual reactions, felt at once. This was the woman's complete absorption in her own devotions. He found himself wondering who she was as he returned again to press the Chalice to her lips. *"Drink this, in remembrance that Christ's blood was shed for thee, and be thankful."*

When the service was ended and he went back to the Rectory, he had a feeling of release, of relief from some hard suppression. He permitted himself to think of Lex, almost wishing he had allowed her to come to hear him preach as she had wanted to do. But no, it was better so. He was to go to the McCollys' to dinner later and he could then talk it all over with her. After these sweet stolen thoughts now, he must again put her out of his mind and concentrate upon the grave duties yet to come.

Even though he had been accustomed from boyhood to the contrast between the early Communion and the regular eleven o'clock service, Hilary was unprepared for the startling difference in his own reactions to them today. As he returned to the church at ten-thirty he was conscious at once of a pleasant stir and the exhilaration of voices and of sounds. When he reached the study he found two of the vestrymen, Avison and Thornton, waiting to greet him. They were enthusiastic over the appearance of the room as he had arranged it and over him, himself, apparently.

"It looks as though we're going to have a big congregation. People are coming in fast, already. We had good publicity in last night's papers," Thornton said. "Well, we just wanted to give you our good wishes now before the service. You'll be at the back of the church when it's over?"

Hilary hesitated. He had an intense dislike of making a rush for the outer door, especially after Communion, and then of attempting to play the part of genial handshaker to all who passed out.

"I would rather not," he said. "Do you mind?"

The two men looked at each other.

"It has always been the custom," Avison said.

"I had planned to wait in the Chapel to speak to anyone who cared to see me there. Suppose I do that today until we can talk the whole matter over later."

"Fair enough," said Thornton. They left with expressions of confidence.

Hastings, supremely in his element and robed in his black gown, came up to confirm evidences of a large congregation. As he left, Hilary looked hurriedly again over his sermon notes and then put them in the back of his Prayer-book. He was sure he had the whole argument well fixed in his mind. He gazed intently upon the Bishop's face for a moment, then went down the stairs and on to the robing room where once again he put on his vestments and stood, watching the clock. Strangely enough he did not feel nervous now as he had done before the early service. Instead he felt an excited eagerness, a sort of sublime confidence. So, with a firm finger he pressed the button at three minutes to eleven which gave the signal to the choir in their own robing room below, and then went on into the Chapel where the procession would form.

It arranged itself quickly and quietly, giving evidence of excellent training. Hilary was thankful and approving as he watched. First came the small boys headed by a tall blond lad as Crucifer, then the older men and women, perhaps thirty of them. At the very end Hilary took his place. There was a sudden loud burst of melody as the opening bars of the hymn came from the organ. The Crucifer at the front adjusted the great gold cross, his white gloved hands grasping it more firmly. The wide doors were opened and the procession began to move slowly forward.

Hilary had been completely unprepared for the magnificence of Forrest's choir. The voices rose now in such richness and volume that he felt himself lifted with them as upon a tidal wave. He, himself, had chosen the hymn because it was the Bishop's favorite processional. So it rang out now, majestic, triumphant, to the highest vaulted stone:

> "Ten thousand times ten thousand,
> In sparkling raiment bright,
> The armies of the ransomed saints
> Throng up the steeps of light."

As they moved along the front of the church, Hilary's eyes swept the congregation. Hastings had been right. It looked as though every seat was filled. The throbbing eagerness in his breast increased. It was as though Something, Someone, not himself, was giving him strength.

They were moving up the steps into the chancel now; then the choir filed slowly into their stalls. As Hilary knelt in his place, the last great burst of song rose heavenward. The heart of the organ seemed to strain with the joy of it; the hymn reached its final exultant crescendo and then died softly away in the Amen. Into the hush which followed there came a voice which Hilary scarcely recognized as his own, so strong, so measured, so resonant it was:

" 'The Lord is in his holy temple; Let all the earth keep silence before him!' "

The service as it progressed, Hilary felt, was the most beautiful he had ever known. The vast traditional dignity of the ritual and the moving power of the prayers seemed to come to their very flower as he read. Then, when he was at last in the pulpit, looking over the congregation with their upturned faces, he knew by that delicately unerring instinct which every public speaker possesses, that he held them in the hollow of his hand. Something of personal magnetism, of quality of voice, of mental power, of strength of spirit—something of all these combined, now held these thousand diverse human beings to himself. He knew this, without pride, and because he knew it, he began to speak with complete simplicity and ease.

He had searched for the text for this day's sermon with long and anxious thought. Finally he had chosen one upon which he had always wanted to preach; the one he considered the most arresting in the Bible. He announced it now with slow and full emphasis: " 'Be ye therefore perfect.' " Then with steady, resistless logic he began to reveal its implications. Since the Great Teacher never spoke lightly he must have believed mankind capable of some sort of perfection or he would never have given this amazing command with such complete assurance. Did this not then constitute the greatest tribute ever paid to the human race?

Still quietly, but with the same remorseless logic he continued. Since from the context Jesus was apparently laying especial emphasis upon perfection in love, there must lie upon ordinary men and women, who had always considered perfection the one thing unattainable in this world, a peculiar compulsion to strive for it; to be satisfied with nothing less; to find strength for the full achieving in the knowledge that it was possible —a perfection of love, in the closest of human relations, in the wider circle of friends and acquaintances, and finally in respect to the whole needy world.

As he neared the close, there was not a breath to break the hush of the listening congregation.

"I stand before you," he concluded, "on this first Sunday of our union as people and priest. I bring you these amazing words of Jesus as the keynote of our service together; as the constant ringing challenge to guide us in all our work; as a measure of deep comfort in the knowledge of God's faith in us as human beings and in our own renewed faith in ourselves and in each other."

He was back before the altar taking up the Alms Basins, thinking, Did I get it across? Did they feel it? Then he was advancing to the front of the chancel. He watched the eight vestrymen who were ushering that day come toward him, with the atmosphere of the world enveloping them, impeccably suited and boutonniered, to receive the Basins from his hands and then proceed down the aisles as the choir began gloriously upon the anthem.

The Communion service which followed was long. Hilary realized in the back of his mind, as he passed and repassed before the kneeling men and women, that he would be compelled to find an assistant soon, as the vestrymen had suggested. Today, however, the people stood patiently upon the chancel tiles awaiting their turn at the altar, while once again the low, mystic words, like an oft repeated celestial refrain, hung upon the air.

The last communicant had received the wine, the last footfalls of retreating steps had died away, as Hilary faced the altar and knelt for the final prayers. Then again came a burst of melody as Forrest started upon the Recessional.

Once more the great gold cross advanced and the procession moved down the chancel steps to the accompaniment of the rich diapason of organ and voices. Hilary followed with uplifted heart. It was over and it had gone well. If only Grandy could have lived to see this day! He found himself joining in the familiar words with the choir.

They were back in the chapel; the last softened echoes of the hymn ceased, and Hilary's voice, in cloistered tones, rose in the final words of the service. Then in an incredibly short time, the room seemed filled with people. Hastings, jubilantly important, kept ushering in more and more. The apparent pleasure and satisfaction upon all the faces sent Hilary's spirits up still higher. A personal note was evident in the voices of the vestrymen.

"My wife, Mr. Laurens. That was a wonderful sermon!"

"I can't tell you how delighted we are! Such a very fine sermon! We hope to have you to dinner soon."

"Well, you've made a great start this morning, my boy! Helen, this is Mr. Laurens."

Hilary started as he recognized J. V. Dunn, of the vulture beak, approaching. He had with him an elderly feminine duplicate of himself and a young woman obviously ill at ease.

"Mr. Laurens, my name is Dunn. Pewholder here for thirty years. Thought your sermon very good. Want to introduce my sister and daughter."

With this he caught the young woman's arm and brought her close to Hilary.

"My daughter, Maudie," he repeated.

The girl's rather anaemic face broke up in small twitchings just as her voice began to emit indefinite sounds which never quite became words.

"Maudie's very much interested in church work," (more faint sounds from Maudie), "so you'll be seeing her around here."

"We hope you'll honor us by coming to dinner soon," the older Miss Dunn said as they gave place to the next comers. "I shall write you."

Hilary would have been less than human if he had not felt his heart swell with the warmth of the greetings and the very evident enthusiasm of those who spoke to him. He tried with intensity to fix names and faces in his mind while the word *wonderful* seemed to hover in the air.

"My name is Haverstraw. I just wanted to welcome you and thank you for that wonderful sermon."

"I'm Mrs. Lester White. I want you to know how happy we are to have you as our rector. Your sermon was wonderful."

As the crowd thinned, Hilary saw old Mrs. Reed rise stiffly from a chair at the back of the room and come slowly toward him. There was a look upon her face resembling the one with which she had first greeted him. She did not smile. Indeed her eyes were anxious.

"Now listen," she said as she reached him, "you're all right. You're good. But don't go and get a swelled head."

Hilary looked soberly back at her. He had a swift sense of contrast between the hushed service at the altar and the near joviality of the informal reception.

"I won't," he said gravely. "But I'm glad to be reminded."

They eyed each other, still unsmiling, until she turned away.

At last there was no one left in the chapel except Hastings and himself. Hastings drew confidentially close and produced two white missives.

"Well, here's the first ones. I suppose you're used to this sort of thing. Only bein' young you'd better keep your eyes open. These were both some dames though that give me these. One of them belongs here but the other's a new one. I guess you can handle 'em. Well, I don't think you did too bad today."

"Thank you, Hastings." Hilary felt this and Mrs. Reed's pronouncement were his sincerest compliments.

He took the notes from Hastings and went on up to the study to relax for a few minutes before he went to the McCollys. He faced the Bishop's portrait with a smile. His head was not swelled, but he knew the morning had gone extremely well and he was grateful and happy. If he only knew where Dick was at the moment he would put in a long distance call and talk to him. He fairly craved this. But he knew how difficult it was to locate Dick. This last mining job he was on was more erratic than usual. In any case he would soon see Lex and talk it all over with her. He wished now with all his heart that he had let her come to the service.

He remembered the two notes in his hand. The first was a visiting card, bearing the name: Mrs. Frederick Waltham Downes. The message and address were written below in pencil, apparently during the service:

> Your sermon has touched me deeply. I am greatly in need
> of counsel. Could you call at your earliest convenience?

Hilary drew his brows, recalling Hastings' comment. This was the sort of thing one had to look out for, from a woman. But he would have to go to see her, of course. It was doubtless genuine.

The second missive was a letter, sealed and addressed to him. It was written carefully in ink. He read:

> I am the only person who knows the truth about Steve
> Cole's death. I was at the funeral and heard you there. I feel
> as if I could talk to you. I've got to talk to someone or I'll
> go crazy. Could I come to your study? Any afternoon
> around five. If you'll let me come, please call Woodside 327
> and leave the message for Mary Smith. I'll get it. Please
> make it soon if you can.

Hilary sat staring at the paper. So it had been a girl. He found himself dreading the encounter with sharp distaste. He could imagine what the main details of the story would be. Yet he must accede to this request also. He made quick notes upon his desk pad and then tore both missives to bits and dropped them in the waste basket. The week just coming would be full enough!

When he reached the McCollys upon the hour, he found them all in the living room. There was a new warmth in Mrs. McColly's greeting and old Alex grasped his hand.

"Well, well, I'm glad to see you, Hilary. Glad to see you! We've just been hearing about the service. I knew you'd never keep Lex away this first Sunday. No, sir!"

"You were there, then, after all?" Hilary said, turning to Lex, his voice showing more pleasure than he knew.

"I'm glad you're not mad at me. It was all beautiful, Hil. I didn't know I could be so proud of you!"

The red crept up in Hilary's cheeks. "But to think you were there and I never saw you! You didn't take Communion."

"No. Muff wouldn't let me. She was more jittery than you were. I sat up in the gallery. Just melted into the landscape. One more sinner."

In spite of their laughter, Hilary felt a sudden qualm of uneasiness. There was a gravity in Lex's eyes. During dinner as they talked together of the day and of his work in general, he became more unhappily convinced that all was not well. He kept trying to meet Lex's glance and failed each time. When dessert was finished, she appealed to her mother.

"Do you mind if Hilary and I have our coffee in the living room?"

"Of course not," Mrs. McColly agreed instantly. "Your father and I are going right up to the library to wrestle with this Benefit business we've gotten ourselves into, and we'll have ours there while we work. Come on, Alex."

Hilary smiled frankly into her eyes. No longer was it necessary to conceal his eagerness to be alone with Lex.

"Thanks," he said. "I haven't too much time. Vespers at four, you know."

" 'Pon my soul," Old Alex exclaimed, "I never thought parsons worked much for a living, but it looks as if you put in a full day on Sundays, anyway."

"I'd forgotten about vespers," Lex said in a startled voice. "Let's go, Hil."

Back in the living room he took her in his arms.

"What is it?" he soon asked anxiously. "Were you somehow disappointed in the service? Tell me the truth. I'll always count on you to do that."

To his amazement her eyes filled with tears.

"Disappointed?" she said. "I don't know how to say it, Hil, but I've never been so moved, so completely shaken in my life. That's the trouble. That's what I have to explain to you."

She drew away from him. He saw that her hands, the little, slim hands he so loved, were trembling.

"If I've been uncertain before about—us—I'm terrified now. Do you realize, Hilary, that I've known you for two years, but always in what we might call your 'off' moments? Never till today have I seen you in your vestments or heard you pray or preach or give Communion. As I sat there and looked at you and listened to you I felt you were an utter stranger."

"Lex! How can you say such a thing?"

"It's true. That's the way you seemed to me. A stranger. So far away I couldn't even reach you."

"That is absolute foolishness!"

"And then your sermon. Honestly, Hil, I never knew you were like that. Such a mind. Such power over an audience. It wasn't just me. I could feel how all the people around me were fairly holding their breath. And then this thing you preached about, this 'perfection of love.' "

He tried to draw her close again, but she resisted, turned away and walked to the window.

"I'd rather never marry you than fail you, Hilary. And I just don't think I can live on your heights."

He strode over to her then and turned her toward him. His face was set.

"I don't want you on the heights. I want you . . ."

"I know." Her face suddenly became suffused with color. "That's part of our trouble, I think. But if we marry we get let in for the whole of each other, don't we? I came to a decision in church. I hate to tell you but you can't move me from it."

He could not speak. His face had gone white.

"I ran away after that first night. I'm going to do it again. I'm going abroad. Muff will come. She loves to travel. I'll stay all summer and come back to Maine early in September. You can come up then. If we simply can't help it, we'll go ahead and get married and take the chances. But I think by that time we'll know."

"*We* will know!" Hilary's tone was almost bitter.

"Well, I will, then. You see, Hil, if we don't see each other at all for six months, it will give us both a better chance. You'll be able to concentrate on your work and get it started. I'll be able to decide whether I can do without you or not. This will be the final test."

As he still looked at her, speechless, she went on.

63

"Before this, I've really been thinking only of myself. I know that now. Whether *I* would be happy as your wife. But now you've got to believe me, I'm thinking of you, too. That's what your sermon did to me."

He knew from the gravity of her eyes and the whole fixed expression on her face that argument was useless. It was Young Alex who had spoken, with the force and determination of her sire. There was behind the words, too, Hilary realized, an intuitive wisdom. In spite of his coming loneliness, his work during these first difficult months would be easier with Lex far away. More deeply and with a pain akin to shame, he knew that Lex had also sensed, as he himself had at times, that the strongest bond that held them was a physical one.

He stood silent so long that Lex seemed frightened.

"Say something, Hil. Anything. Only don't look like that."

"When will you go?"

"Right away. We'll get sailings for this week. Dad can always fix things. Oh, Hil, I am as I am. I can't help it."

"Is it to be good-bye now?"

"I think it would be best. No use torturing ourselves. And I might as well admit," she burst out, "that it *is* torture to me to leave you. But I've got to. Let's cut clean now, Hil. I'll phone you my plans and of course we'll write."

He held her as though he would never let her go; then when the embrace was over, he left quickly.

As he drove back, a wave of physical sickness and weakness swept over him. He realized that every nerve in him had been keyed to the highest point for the morning's services. The elation afterwards had buoyed him up until Lex had told him of her decision. Now physically and spiritually the reaction overcame him. For six months he would not see Lex. For that period the old uncertainty would once more fasten itself upon him. Indeed, for the first time since he had fallen in love, he now felt utterly hopeless. Was there actually too great a gulf fixed between his life and Lexa's? Even though she loved him, would she ultimately refuse to marry him? And if so, how could he ever countenance the oncoming years?

With a sudden wave of anger he thought of his sermon on the perfection of love. This sermon, over which he had prayed and labored for weeks, and delivered that morning with a kind of holy joy, had evidently been the concrete cause of Lexa's new decision. He hated it.

He went through vespers in a sort of trance. Fortunately there was only a brief address. It was really Forrest's service and if Hilary's misery had not been so deep-seated he knew he would have been stirred by the tender beauty of the music. He forced himself to complete concentration

64

upon the lessons and the prayers; then after the benediction he left immediately, not even waiting to speak to Forrest as he had intended. He would see him the next day in any case as they had arranged that the organist would come to his study each Monday morning, at which time they would consult together about the week's plans.

Now Hilary, pleading weariness to Hastings, slipped out quickly to the court and made his way in a black misery to the side of the rectory. As usual, no matter at what door he entered, Morris, apprized of his approach by some sixth sense apparently, was there waiting for him.

"You all done for the day now, Mist' Hilary?"

The eager kindness in the wrinkled face brought a sting to Hilary's eyes. As long as the old man lived, the house would have some atmosphere of home.

"Done and done in, both, Morris."

"Did things—did they go all right?"

"Yes, I think they did," Hilary replied slowly. "I believe, Morris, that the Bishop would have been pleased with every service. I'm just tired now, that's all."

"I got the fire made up in the library an' I'm bringin' your supper right in there. That's good, Mist' Hilary, 'bout the services. I knowed they'd be fine. You just go in there now an' rest yourself."

The room looked welcoming with the great fireplace alight. After his supper, during which he told Morris all the details of the day which might interest him, Hilary allowed himself to relax completely. Tomorrow a flood of duties would engulf him, enough perhaps to drown out part of his pain. Tonight he felt weary and bruised and lonely.

His mind moved slowly over the events of the day. He remembered the faces of the Coles at the early service. To be there at all must have taken a high courage on their part. Fine people. He would prize their friendship and would try to do all he could to help them in their grief. What of the girl whom he must see soon? Would her story be one he could ever tell to Steve's mother and father? He doubted it. He had a swift intuition that one of his coming burdens would be the weight upon his heart of secrets which he might never share.

He thought of the woman with the beautiful face and form who had knelt at the altar, lost in the sacrament. He had felt a spiritual kinship with her though they had spoken no word to each other. He thought of the later service and the glory and exhilaration of it. At least there would never be any difficulties for him in connection with the music! Forrest was a master.

Before long he must call a vestry meeting. He knew he had the support and confidence of the majority of them, or he would not be here.

But there were one or two who had held aloof. He must win them if possible. He sighed heavily. There would probably be conflict enough in his work without the inner fears and problems of his heart. *Lexa!* No matter where his thoughts started, they ended with her.

Morris suddenly appeared.

"Lady on the phone, Mist' Hilary."

He almost fell in his haste.

"Hello," he said, his heart thudding.

The voice which came was that of old Mrs. Reed.

"This is once I am going to apologize. I shouldn't have said what I did this morning. I'm a bad-tempered, critical, bossy old—"

"Please. Don't retract. That's unworthy of you. You were exactly right and I'm going to need all your advice and warning to keep me straight."

Mrs. Reed lowered her voice.

"Listen. What I really waited for this morning was to tell you that your sermon was the finest I ever heard. Somehow after I listened to all the other cackling I couldn't say it. But now you know."

"Thank you," Hilary said gently. "I need that tonight much more than I did this morning."

When he had said good-bye he sat, nervous, his hand still on the telephone. He wanted desperately, feverishly to call Lexa; but something held him back. At last he rose, told Morris that he would go on up to bed early, and slowly and heavily climbed the stairs.

When he was finally propped against the pillows he picked up *The Imitation* from the table beside him to read a little from it as his custom was each night. This time he leafed through the book until the words he sought leaped to his eyes.

> Though weary, love is not tired; though pressed, it is not straitened; though alarmed, it is not confounded; but as a lively flame and burning torch it forces its way upwards and securely passes through all. If any man love, he knoweth what is the cry of this voice.

Slowly, Hilary closed the book and put out the light.

CHAPTER V

ON MONDAY MORNING Hilary found Miss Mowbray in her little office outside his study already at work on the files when he got there. He was immediately at ease with her. The homeliness of her irregular features was alleviated by the brightness of her gray eyes and the pleasing quality of her voice. Good girl, Hilary thought to himself. Good, sensible girl!

Before many days had passed he reverently thanked God for her. She knew everyone and everything. She had a way of listening intently to a question, weighing it for a second and then giving the right answer modestly. She showed no embarrassing tendency to load him with information before he asked for it.

Together they went over the Parish records and planned a new system of filing.

"Don't tell me about any of these people," Hilary said at the start. "I know you could, but I've got to have a clean slate and form my own opinions. If you'll just indicate the ones who are sick or in trouble I'll go to see them first."

They went to work on this list, a long one. Then on two sets of new cards Miss Mowbray typed all Parish names and addresses, one set to be filed alphabetically, the other—Hilary's idea—geographically, so that calling might be zoned, as it were, to save time.

"Have you any ideas about an assistant?" Miss Mowbray inquired once, as she saw Hilary's growing realization of the magnitude of his job.

"Not a thought. I'll have to come to it soon, though, I can see that. My feeling was that I wanted to get acquainted with the work a little myself before I tried to train anybody else."

"There were two curates here for a long time, and they were both busy enough. In the last years there was only one. Dr. Partridge did not delegate power too easily," she said, smiling.

In addition to the reorganization of the files the mail demanded increasing attention, for it grew heavier by the day. The invitations to dinner gave Hilary the greatest immediate concern. They ranged from engraved cards to informal notes. One thing was certain. It would be a physical impossibility to accept them all. He had Miss Mowbray sort out those of the vestrymen's wives first, and then guided by a curious intuition born of Lexa's warning he put with these the chastely correct missive from Miss Dunn. Before the week was out he had added another, not without foreboding. It was the crested card of Miss Hettie Breckenridge.

The other letters were a strange mixture. Most of them were welcoming him to the parish and the city, many of them were begging, some were evidently sincere appeals for help, some were the work of cranks. Out of them all two hit Hilary very hard. The one was a bitterly critical attack upon his first Sunday's sermon.

> DEAR MR. LAURENS:
>
> Although not a member of St. Matthews I went to service on Sunday hoping, from the statements of the press, to find in you the preacher I long have sought. I was grievously disappointed. If any parish in this city needs a thorough arousing from its velvet cushions of comfortable sloth, it is St. Matthews. And to these complacent capitalists you suggest gently that perfection is almost within their grasp. What they need is a John the Baptist. What they have apparently got—if you'll excuse the brutal frankness—is a handsome lounge lizard in a cassock.
>
> A STRANGER

The very next letter he read ran as follows:

> DEAR RECTOR:
>
> Your sermon on the possibility of perfection in love moved me as nothing has done in many years. In all humility I am going to try to put it into practice. Will you use the enclosed according to your discretion for some corner of "the needy world"?
>
> AN OLD PARISHIONER

It was a hundred-dollar bill.

The curious juxtaposition of the two types of letter was to become familiar to Hilary as time passed. During these first days, however, he brooded over it. He laid them both carefully in a drawer where he could re-read them, reminding himslf of the diverse characters among his audience each Sunday, and of the heavy compulsion resting upon him to be "all things to all men."

While the letter from "A Stranger" was probably the work of a religious eccentric, yet there was a note in it which he could not afford to disregard. The main membership of St. Matthews was indeed made up of people of wealth or at least of a comfortable competence of this world's goods. While they would of course be vulnerable along with the rest of mankind to the inevitable blows of sickness and death, they would still be untouched by the peculiar sorrows of the poor. Each day as he walked the surrounding streets he was more conscious of the contrast between the beauty and comfort of the church itself and the drab poverty represented in the string of tenements and cheap apartments just behind it.

He sat late at his desk one night, considering, and finally made his first great decision relative to his ministry. In so far as he was capable he resolved to divide his time and attention between the present pew holders of St. Matthews and another yet invisible congregation which he had in mind to serve. Past the great church each day walked a motley multitude. Unknown men and women worked in the lofts and factories all about. Within easy access were endless dwellings where poverty ruled, where even hunger and cold might exist. What was he going to do about this? He already had several ideas. With the hundred-dollar bill as a nucleus he would try to build up a so-called discretionary fund, the many uses of which he could already imagine. This could be only the proverbial drop in the bucket but it would be at least concrete.

But more than this. Above the long blocks of rented pews in St. Matthews ran the gallery. This was free, and as Hastings had reported, usually empty except for a few transients and the Orphanage boys. Hilary had an immediate picture of a strong, integrated gallery congregation, drawn from the ranks of the humble.

Then there was the Parish House. Its uses had deteriorated somewhat during Dr. Partridge's declining years, he gathered from bits of evidence here and there, but the building was amply furnished, ready and available for whatever uses he wished to put it.

Night after night, Hilary sat at his desk, weighing one course of action against another, always measuring his judgment by meeting the Bishop's eyes in the frame. He was preparing for the special meeting with his vestry at which time he would outline his plans.

Meanwhile his personal problems had resolved themselves temporarily. Lex was gone. In accordance with her usual promptness of action she had sailed with Muff for France ten days after their talk. In spite of their first decision Hilary had gone to see her off, his heart like lead in his breast. She had never seemed so utterly dear to him as in that last moment when she had broken down, raising misty eyes to his.

"I don't know whether I'm more afraid to go or to stay," she had whispered.

Then the bell rang, the crowd jostled, and he had found himself ashore with her father and mother, watching, waving, until her small figure in the shadow of Muff's tall, protecting one was lost to the sight. He had come back with something in his heart poorer than hope and a little better than despair. One thing he had to admit as the days passed, and that was the fact that her complete absence gave him a feeling of mental release. The fact, though, that she had been wise enough to foresee this, frightened him. Did this mean then that there was wisdom in her other conclusions also? In so far as it was possible he drove this idea from his mind and his hunger for her from his heart and concentrated fiercely upon his work.

On a dull, rainy afternoon, Hilary sat at his desk with a nervousness he could not control. He had left the message for "Mary Smith" suggesting five o'clock that day. Would she come? What would she be like? What story would she tell about Steve Cole? He somehow hated this encounter. He had dined quietly with the Coles a few nights before and their dignity, self-control and essential courage had again moved him deeply. Two rare souls, they were, who claimed him now as a friend. To him at least they talked of Steve as though it eased their unendurable grief. Through their unconscious illumination, the young man himself had emerged full grown before him, fine, sensitive, gifted, full of promise. He was to have been a doctor. His own dread now was that the coming interview would do violence to this character.

There was a tap on the study door and Miss Mowbray's voice.

"Miss Smith is here."

Hilary stood up and looked at his caller. He saw a tall, slender girl in a small hat and a raincoat. Her thin face was shockingly white and taut, as though the bones might at any moment pierce the delicate skin. Her eyes were the saddest he had ever seen.

He went forward to meet her and drew a chair.

"Sit down," he said warmly. "It's a nasty day out. I didn't know when I called up that the weather was going to be like this."

She made a small gesture as though dismissing the weather.

"My real name is Francine Avery," she began in a voice with a faint, alluring accent. "Since a sad story should not be long I will try to tell you quickly. It is very hard but it is harder still to keep silent. I have to talk to someone. I felt it must be you."

Hilary met her gravity instantly. His voice was very gentle.

"Please tell me all that lies upon your heart, Miss Avery. I think I understand your feeling. It helps to 'give sorrow words'."

70

She sat tensely forward in her chair, the raincoat which she had not taken the trouble to remove giving her the appearance of a child. She fixed her dark eyes firmly on the window behind Hilary and began.

"I grew up in France. My mother was French, my father English. He died when I was very small. My mother was a dancer. I am also. We lived very strangely abroad, very unconventionally. I do not mean to excuse myself, only to tell the truth. I was not brought up as the usual French jeune fille. When my mother died I came to this country with a man I—knew. I have had some success here. There have been several men who—helped me. It was of small meaning to me, what happened between me and them. I cared for none of these men."

She gave a tragic little gesture. "This is what is so necessary for you to believe. My heart felt nothing—nothing. I wanted to get on in my profession. I did only what seemed to me practical and, as I had been brought up, natural."

She stopped, her eyes on his face with an alarming fixity. "I cannot go on unless you believe this."

"I do believe you," Hilary said.

Something of the tension in her slight figure relaxed.

"Yes," she said, "I see that you do. I met Steve at the night club where I was dancing. From that moment we loved each other. At first I did not question anything. I had always taken whatever came without question, as my mother had taught me. Then, when Steve wished to take me home to meet his mother and father, I was suddenly afraid."

Her hands were clasped so tightly now that Hilary felt in himself the hurt of the clenched fingers.

"I considered saying nothing of my life before. But he was too good. I loved him too much. That last afternoon I told him everything. The reason I can't sleep now is seeing the look on his face. He was so very white. He kept saying, 'There will be some way; don't worry.' Then he went home. The next day I read in the paper what happened."

She stopped. The story was told. Hilary sat, looking at her, shaken. The violence of the contrast between the truth and his own imaginings left him speechless.

"The thing which makes me so confused," the girl went on slowly, "is that I did what I felt to be right in telling him. And if I had not done so, he would now be alive and we could have been happy always. Now since I killed him I do not care to live. I would rather do as he did."

Her eyes met his, seeking, distraught.

The old feeling of inadequacy for a moment engulfed Hilary. How could he guide her, comfort her? What words would be given him to speak? Looking at the girl, though worn now and careless of her beauty,

71

he could see why Steve had loved her. Her strange charm, the compelling quality of her personality, her essential sincerity of heart and the dancer's grace of her body, would attract any man. But by the extremity of the moment, and the deep prayer of his own heart, he felt himself entirely removed from all of this. He was not a man, he was completely the priest of God.

"Francine," he said, using her name simply, "my dear child, you must consider first of all that with honesty and courage you did what you thought was your duty. The consequences are not your responsibility. Leave them in the hands of God. In the next place you must put from you all thought of ending your own life. I believe in another world after this. I believe Steve is there now."

"You do?" Her tone was full of amazement.

"Of course. God is surely not less understanding than we poor humans. But Steve's immortality in this world depends upon those who loved him. A part of him will always live on in your heart. You must treasure that and see that no violence comes to it through you. This, too, is a duty. Do you understand?"

She was very still for a moment, then slowly nodded her head.

"I had not thought of it in that way."

"Are you a Catholic?" he asked.

"No. I'm not anything, really. I think I was christened as an infant."

"I want you to come to church, to Steve's church, and eventually to be confirmed. But right now, next Sunday, if you don't mind getting up early, I want you to come to the eight o'clock Communion. No one else will know whether you are a member or not. Come and say a little prayer for Steve's soul and for your own. It will do you good. Will you?"

Once again she thought his words over.

"Would I know what to do?"

"Just follow the others. It's very easy. And now, most of all, you must drop this burden you've been carrying. I do not of course mean your grief. But put all that you should forget out of your mind, out of your life. Start all over. Keep your love for Steve and begin now to be all he thought you were. Forget the rest." His voice was firm. "Work and rest, pray often, *and go on living.*"

He held her eyes to his until he saw them suddenly overflow with tears.

"I haven't been able to weep before."

Hilary rose. "It will relax you. I want to speak to my secretary. Excuse me for a moment."

Once outside he said to Miss Mowbray. "What about a good strong cup of tea?"

She smiled. "It's ready. I thought from the look of her we might need it."

She brought a small tray with two cups. "I'll set it in. I think you can do with one yourself."

The girl was still weeping when he returned, slumped in complete exhaustion in the chair. He wondered anxiously if there would be strength enough in her body to enable her to rise eventually.

Miss Mowbray set down the tray and left as quietly as she came. The cup shook in Francine's hand, but she drank the tea gratefully and then with a great effort pulled herself together, and rose.

"I must go," she said. "I can never thank you enough. Please know . . ."

"Of course," Hilary said. "I only want you to promise to come back whenever I can help. Will you?"

"And Sunday morning?"

"I shall count on your being there."

She stood a moment, hesitant.

"And you really think—you feel even in spite of all I've told you—I can . . ."

She faltered and stopped.

The words came instinctively to Hilary's lips.

"May the Lord bless you and keep you, Francine. May he lift up the light of his countenance upon you and give you peace."

As she left, she turned and for the first time smiled. Even through the tears the smile transformed her face.

Hilary realized again how young Steve must have loved her. Oh, the torturing, agonizing sorrows of love! How mysteriously for his own vast purposes the Creator had wrought the miracle of sex! Sex and religion, he brooded, as he sat down again at his desk. The two most powerful forces in life!

He wondered anxiously, as always, if he had said the right thing. Had he said enough? Reflecting now, he felt his words had been perhaps too few. Should he have given a different sort of counsel, dwelling more upon that period of her life, the irregularities of which had brought about the tragedy? Should he have spoken of penance and sackcloth and ashes?

No, he decided with vehemence. Not that. Her anguished eyes gave their own proof. It seemed to him clearly a case of "Neither do I condemn thee."

As to his urging her who belonged to no church whatsoever to come to Communion, that was perhaps open to criticism. And yet the whole meaning of the sacrament, as he saw it, was the union of the weak, needy soul of man with the great, suffering, compassionate soul of God. Well, then. Surely in this case the conditions were met. A purely technical exception could be made. Wouldn't Bronson be scandalized though if he knew? Hilary smiled a little wryly. No matter, he thought, I must serve humanity in my own way.

It was some days later that he answered in person the other missive of that first Sunday. He found Mrs. Frederick Waltham Downes a young woman in a luxuriously modernistic apartment. She was tall, with dark hair brushed high above small ears, her skin creamy against the red violence of her lips. She wore a black dress which enhanced every line of her beautiful figure, and her voice was low, soft and sad.

"This is so good of you, Mr. Laurens. I had scarcely hoped you would come so soon, but I need help terribly."

"I am anxious to serve you if I can," Hilary said sympathetically. "A new rector is always at a disadvantage at first. He must try to know so many people so quickly. And fails, of course. You must tell me, if you will, what I can do for you."

She looked down at her hands, white and ringless in her lap.

"My husband died eight months ago. I have no child, almost no relatives. I am inexpressibly lonely to the point of melancholy. My life is completely empty. I feel I must cultivate some new power within myself and I can't do it alone. If I had a new interest, too, it would help."

She hesitated and raised her eyes, very large, dark and luminous, to his face.

"Would there be any way you could use me in church work?"

Hilary was touched. He chose his words carefully, as he first recommended certain daily spiritual exercises.

"I'll send you some books which I think will be of great help to you. Keep them as long as you need them. And as to church work, of course we can use you. It's rather wonderful for anyone to ask for it as you have. Shall I let you know as soon as our organizations get started?"

"Oh, please do! I feel already that I have something to live for. The friends I have"—she smiled with a gentle tolerance—"are not the type to help me in matters of the spirit."

She rang for tea; then, as she served it, began to speak lightly of other things—books, plays, travel. Without losing the veil of sadness which enveloped her, she seemed unselfishly eager to keep from intruding her sorrow further upon her guest. Her pitiful courage appealed to Hilary and he exerted himself to his utmost to be entertaining.

"You have done so much for me," she said as he left. "I promise not to make a nuisance of myself, but if I get down too deeply in the depths again, may I . . ."

"Please call me," Hilary said earnestly, "and read the devotional books I'm sending you very carefully. They have helped me. And now, be brave."

The impression of the farewell handshake gave him a slight uneasiness as the elevator bore him down to the lobby. It had been a prolonged one for the simple reason that Mrs. Downes had not let go. She was merely grateful, Hilary thought. And don't be a vain ass, he adjured himself severely.

The most disquieting experience of his first weeks was a call from Henry Alvord, Senior Warden, the one man on the vestry for whom Hilary had held a mental reservation. He dropped in one day, pleasantly enough. He was a tall, spare man with a waxed gray mustache and cool, calculating eyes. His contribution to the church represented the largest single item of its support. He talked on in friendly fashion of generalities while Hilary felt his heart sinking into his shoes. He had a premonition that there was more to this call than met the eye.

Alvord finally leaned back in his chair with easy grace and slowly put out his cigarette.

"I'm sure you'll not resent a word or two of advice from an old member of St. Matthews?"

"I should welcome it," Hilary replied.

"Churches are like families," Alvord began deliberately. "Some either have no roots or they are negligible. Others have very deep roots and very distinct traditions. St. Matthews is one of these. For a hundred years this church has served the type of people who appreciate the beauty and dignity of its edifice and its service. They have built through the years certain traditions which I hope may never be broken or infringed upon in any way."

He paused, watching Hilary.

"I understand perfectly what you mean," Hilary said quietly, meeting his eyes.

Alvord looked gratified.

"Another thing—forgive me for speaking so plainly, but it is as an old man to a young one. Many young men in their twenties and thirties are moved by a great desire to change the existing social and economic order. It is perhaps a more or less normal youthful reaction. They would, if they could, overthrow certain—ah—systems which have been long in operation. Now, I've lived for nearly seventy years. I've watched many young men foolishly break their heads against a wall which is essentially a *good* wall. The tried and proven order is the best. I am quite sure the great majority of St. Matthews' membership believe this as firmly as I do. I wonder if you—ah—follow me?"

Hilary nodded. "Once again I understand you perfectly."

Alvord rose, smiling.

"I've enjoyed this call. I hear nothing but the highest praise of you in every quarter. You have here in St. Matthews the greatest opportunity that any young clergyman could ask for. I'm sure you will fulfill our expectations."

Hilary stood silent for a moment.

"I'm glad you came in, Mr. Alvord. And I'm very glad also that you have told me so frankly what you would like my policies at St. Matthews to be."

The older man looked somewhat startled and his dark, straight brows contracted a little.

"I have told you that I understand," Hilary went on. "This does not mean, however, that I agree. But understanding is the real basis of friendship and I want very much to be your friend. May we leave things so while I think over carefully all that you have said?"

Hilary smiled with his unconscious, disarming sincerity and held out his hand. Alvord grasped it.

"I'm sure you'll agree," he said. "For your success here, as I see it, depends largely upon that."

As Hilary walked to the door with him he said earnestly, "Will you drop in again and give me your advice and help? I need plenty."

The older man looked touched and gratified as he promised. But after he was gone Hilary went back to his desk and slumped into the Bishop's chair.

"No change in the type of membership and no socialistic tendencies on the part of the rector—or else!" he muttered dispiritedly.

He felt defeated before he had rightly begun. The queer presentiment he had had from his first meeting with Alvord had not been without foundation. He had noticed that the other vestrymen deferred to the Senior Warden's opinion; and now he had read in the older man's eyes during the interview Alvord's complete confidence in being able to manipulate the new young rector's policies to his will.

Hilary's strong chin stiffened. This, then, was probably to be his first major conflict. He must win over Alvord or lose him. With a deadly clarity he saw the full possibilities of his position. Even as Alvord had said, no young man could ask for a greater opportunity. With the least compliance, the least compromise of which no one but himself would ever be aware, he knew he would have steadily mounting success. He realized with a sudden complete perception the extent of his own powers. He knew, too, half ashamed, that a great ambition lay buried in his heart. A bishopric some day, even as Grandy.

Yet Grandy had never compromised. The very thought of such a thing in relation to his nature was absurd. Hilary remembered his grandfather's face once a few years ago, lean and finely tempered and whimsical in the firelight, as he had sat talking of diocesan affairs.

"When a stubborn and worldly man insists upon pulling you round by the nose, Hilary, there's just one way to deal with him. Tell him to go to hell. Not in those'words, of course, but make the general idea clear."

No, Grandy had bowed his righteous head to none in a matter of principle, but his career had been the exact opposite to Hilary's. He had come up from the bottom, as it were. Slowly, steadily mounting through small parishes to greater ones, his influence and personality had gradually made themselves felt throughout the diocese.

In Hilary's case, he was beginning at the top. There would surround him from now on the glare of publicity which would throw his every act into sharp relief, often accentuating the outlines out of proportion to their true relations. If only it were possible . . .

He did not hear the door open. So when the voice came he jumped with such violence that he overturned the chair.

"Well, how's the Man of God?"

It was Dick, sauntering casually toward him, as though he had been there only the day before, his black eyes twinkling, his long, blond face set in its customary quizzical grin. Hilary grabbed him by the shoulders and found he could not speak. Never in all his life had he been so glad to see any one. There was a queer but unmistakable mist in his eyes. Dick looked straight through him as usual, and then slapped him heartily on the back.

"Steady, you big lug. I thought for a minute you were going to kiss me. Quite a set-up you've got here, Hil."

"The Lord certainly sent you!"

"Well, I doubt if he bothers much about my movements but I'm here anyway. Hadn't time to write so I came instead. How are things going?"

"Come on, let's go over to the house and let Morris know right away. After we eat, we can talk all night. How long can you stay?"

Dick shrugged. "Oh, a few days. Have a little business here I want to attend to. How's Lex?"

"She's gone abroad. I'll tell you all about it later. How do you like my study?"

Dick roamed around, commenting upon familiar books and objects, then came to a standstill in front of the Bishop's picture.

"Still cuts pretty deep, doesn't it? I'm always expecting a letter—forgetting, you know. Well, let's get going. I want to see your ecclesiastical habitation."

When Morris opened the door, he all but tottered in his surprise. His delight was pitiful. He couldn't let Dick out of his sight. When the brothers were finally seated at dinner his ministrations were almost annoyingly persistent.

"I feel like an infant robin," Dick said once when the old man was in the kitchen. "Any moment I expect him to drop a worm in my mouth. By the way, why don't we just have him sit down and eat with us? He's the nearest thing to a parent we've got now."

Hilary considered. "For one thing he wouldn't like it. It would disturb and confuse him. He's completely happy doing what he likes best to do, taking care of us. I guess just letting him overdo it to his heart's content is the kindest thing on our part."

"He's aged shockingly these last months. He's not young any more, Hil."

"I know. I worry about him. He's lonesome and there's not much I can do about it, until—unless . . ."

"Of course," Dick filled in quickly. Then as they went back to the library, he added. "Tell me as much as you want, old man. You seem bottled up. I thought from your letter all was rosy. What went wrong?"

"It's the same thing, only worse. The parson stuff. She came to my first service and got completely scared out. The devil of it is I understand how she must feel. I almost wish I didn't. I could fight harder then. Anyway, she's gone abroad with Muff to be gone all summer. In September we're to meet up in Maine, and then it will either be all on or all off. The last throw."

"Meanwhile, as St. Paul delicately puts it, you burn."

"Right."

They smoked in silence for a while and then Dick said suddenly, "It's a funny thing about us. Hailing from the same loins and yet as different as day from night. I have no desire whatever to get married. Women, yes. I'm normal enough, God wotteth, but to look at the same one for the rest of my life—no. The thing I couldn't stand if I had a wife would be to watch the slow deterioration of the years upon her. Time is so damned cruel to women. That's their primeval curse, I guess. Well, I wouldn't want to watch the thing operating behind my own breakfast coffeepot, that's all."

Hilary laughed. "You forget, my lad, that time would also be operating behind the bacon-and-egg platter!"

"I know, but it's not quite the same. Nature gave men the best break by a jugful."

"It's odd you should bring up just this," Hilary said soberly, "for I was thinking only a few days ago that if I were lucky enough to marry Lex I would like watching her grow older. I'm sure I would never mind time's changes in her face. The thing that set me off on this was seeing a woman who comes to early communion every Sunday."

He paused to fill his pipe. "I don't know yet who she is but her face

78

haunts me and she's far from young. Fifties, maybe. There's something about her that makes a girl look a bit empty, if you see what I mean. No, if all I have to worry about is women's primeval curse, as you call it, I'll take it and jump at the chance. By the way, about my letter. I asked for some advice, and I was dead in earnest. I hope you've thought it over."

"Oh, your sermons. Now, there was an unexpected compliment!"

To Hilary's surprise, however, Dick did not proceed with his usual raillery. He was serious.

"I honestly don't know what to tell you. I can't think of anything in particular I'd like to have preached at me. But there's one thing I've always felt very strongly about. I don't think any parson has a right to harangue a congregation as though they were a bunch of sinners."

"Why, aren't we all?" Hilary asked in mild surprise.

"So we're always being told. But somehow I can't see it. People have such a darned lot to bear from life. And remember, they never asked to be born in the first place. They have to take the blows as they come and do the best they can. Take old Sickle-Back at college."

"Yes."

"About the only thing I remember from that course is the way he used to look up suddenly and say:

"O Thou who Man of baser earth didst make
And even with Paradise devise the Snake;
For all the sin wherewith the face of man
Is blackened, Man's forgiveness give—*and take!*"

"I remember that, too. Poor old Sickle-Back! They said he always quoted it when the pain got past bearing, which was pretty often. Great eyes, he had. Really a handsome man, if he hadn't been deformed. I got a lot out of that course of his. And look, I do see what you're driving at. But it's a new idea in a way, one I've got to think over. 'Man's forgiveness, give *and take.*' That line never fully hit me before. You see the whole problem of sin is involved . . ."

"Not tonight, it isn't!" Dick interrupted with a laugh. "I've been serious long enough for once. Tell me the lighter news of the parish. What have you been doing socially? Have you met some nice people? Have you run into your first lonely widow yet?"

Hilary turned and stared at his brother. "Now what in the world made you ask that last question?"

Dick grinned. "Touché, eh? Oh, I guess that old parody Grandy used to chuckle over made me think of it. Some other Bishop told it to him. Don't you remember? 'Pure religion and undefiled for the parson is this: To visit the widow in her affliction and keep himself unspotted . . .'"

Hilary laughed heartily and then looked troubled.

"There *is* a widow and a mighty good-looking one. But she's perfectly sincere. Yes, I'm sure she is."

"Well, watch your step. You're a personable youth!"

"Mist' Hilary." It was Morris at the door. "Telephone for you."

When Hilary answered, a woman's breathless voice spoke.

"Mr. Laurens, this is Mary McComb. You mind you married Joe and me? Well, Joe's sick and I'm so frightened. The doctor's been and he says it's his appendix and he's to get to the hospital at once and he's called the ambulance and he told me it might be too late, for Joe wouldn't have a doctor sooner and I'm afraid they'll just let any one operate when we get there and he's bad, you know. I don't know what to do."

"Where do you live?"

"Right back of the church at 600 Sinclair Street. We're on the second floor."

"I'll be right over."

Somehow he sensed it was a matter of life and death. He grabbed his hat and called to Dick.

"Sick call and it looks serious. I've got to hurry."

Dick was at the door in a flash. "Good luck, old man. Take it easy. I'll wait up."

It was quicker to walk than get the car. As a matter of fact Hilary ran most of the way, hoping no policeman would stop him. He found Mary white and terrified and one glance at Joe on the bed confirmed his fears.

"Where's the doctor?"

"He had to leave after he called the ambulance. He said he couldn't do anything more just now."

"Which hospital is Joe to go to?"

"St. Luke's."

Hilary thought fast. At a dinner the week before he had met a Dr. Shane, a bachelor, a dark, quiet man who, his host had told him on the side, was considered the finest surgeon in the city. To call him now was utterly preposterous. But Hilary did not hesitate. He found the number in the telephone book and dialled quickly. It was a chance in a thousand he would even be at home, for he was socially prominent.

He was at home, and still at dinner. The butler made it clear, however, that he should not be disturbed.

"Please tell him this is the rector of St. Matthews calling and that it is very urgent."

In a moment he heard Dr. Shane's voice.

"This is Hilary Laurens, Doctor; I'm ashamed to trouble you, but I'm with a young man who's in a bad way. Appendix. The doctor they finally called in said he feared it was too late to operate but ordered an ambulance from St. Luke's. Could you possibly help us?"

"Glad it's St. Luke's. Tell the men when they get there that I'm operating and they're to handle the patient carefully. What's the man's name?"

"Joseph McComb."

"I'll be at the hospital. Good-bye."

Hilary was stunned at the brevity and the compliance. He turned to Mary.

"I'll go down to the sidewalk and wait for the ambulance. Be brave now. We've got the best man in town."

The ambulance came in a few minutes. The young internes showed a slight change of expression at mention of Dr. Shane. They worked skillfully, and in the shortest possible time they were all on their way.

It was the first time Hilary had ridden in an ambulance. So often he had watched them passing swiftly along the street with their still burdens, part of the world of sickness and suffering and death to be noted and then forgotten as quickly as possible by those who in happiness and health pursued their normal way. Now as an integral part of that darker world, he rode along, conscious of Joe's big body inert on the narrow cot, of the interne with the keen eyes bending above him; of the bride, Mary, stricken, her heart hanging in the balance with Joe; of the driver's steady, casual expertness.

It was a long wait in one of the hospital's sunrooms. Hilary and Mary were alone in the impersonal, institutional atmosphere. They could see nurses passing unconcerned through the halls, each living her own removed emotional life below the professional surface. They could hear the dull metallic movements of the elevator as it made its steady trips up and down. Night and what peace it could bring had descended upon the great building. But somewhere, they knew, Dr. Shane, instead of having coffee at home after dinner, was standing white-robed in a hot glare, his dark face intent, his trained fingers at work upon Joe's flesh.

Hilary sat beside Mary on the reed settee and held her hand in his own strong one. Once in a while he spoke but most of the time they both prayed. He could see Mary's blue lips moving; and as to himself, with agonizing intensity he offered his own supplications that Dr. Shane might have skill, speed, accuracy, wisdom, and that Joe might live.

Once as he wrestled through the powers of darkness up, as he hoped, to the throne, a line he had once read came to his mind: "Great sin is there in taking Heaven by storm."

Was it indeed wrong or unethical, he wondered suddenly, to try to tear through the veils of flesh to reach the spirit of God, and demand his favor and intervention? Sometime he must think of this more carefully, but not now. He went on praying, and the first slow hour became two. As the third passed he found his petitions concentrating upon Dr. Shane.

Once Mary gave a sob. "Maybe we loved each other too much! We've been *so* happy."

"You can never love too much," Hilary said quietly, "and God grant you may still be happy."

When Dr. Shane appeared at last, they did not speak as he came toward them. His face showed nothing.

"Are you the young man's wife?" he asked Mary.

"Yes." It was a whisper.

"Well, he certainly gave me the toughest job I've ever tackled. What is he, Irish?"

"Yes." Again a whisper with her eyes beseeching.

"I thought so. That old-country constitution is going to help him now. I think he'll pull through. Did you two come in the ambulance?"

"Yes, we did," Hilary answered.

"I've got my car. I'll drop you both off."

"You think he'll live?" Mary begged unsteadily.

"I think so. He'll be pretty sick for a few days, but if I'm not badly mistaken he'll make a good come-back. There's no point in your seeing him now. I've arranged everything. He'll have good care. You come on home and get to bed. Tomorrow you can come up and have a look at him."

His steady casualness was what was needed to bring both Mary and Hilary down to the calmness of familiar things. They went out to the car. Dr. Shane drove himself, speaking little except to ask directions. When they got to the cheap apartment house, Hilary went inside a moment with Mary.

"You're sure you're all right now?" he asked.

She nodded, the tears of her gratitude brimming over. She held his hand tightly in both her own, but could not speak.

"Get a good sleep now," Hilary said. "I'll try to get over to the hospital soon to see Joe. And please call me at any time if I can help you."

"Mr. Laurens, thank you—thank you!"

"That's all right, Mary. I'm almost as glad as you are that everything went well. Good night!"

He hurried out to the car and got in the front seat.

"Of course," he began, "I realize that it was unforgivable presumption of me to call you tonight."

"Glad you did," Shane said. "It was a bad mess. I used all the tricks I knew and then some. But I'm sure I've got him in decent shape. He has the constitution of an ox, and that ought to do the rest. Who are they? Friends of yours?"

"This is only the second time I've laid eyes on them. I married them a few weeks ago—my first wedding here. I liked them. Nice boy and girl. He works in a machine shop. She was somebody or other's maid. She called me tonight in desperation. That's the story."

"I see," Shane replied. "And you consider all you've done tonight in line with your professional duties?"

"Of course," Hilary said, surprised. "A clergyman responds to a sick call just the same as a doctor, you know. It's part of the job."

"I don't believe they all see a thing through as you've done tonight. I'm not a churchman and I haven't had much dealings with parsons, but you seem to me a different type from the ordinary run. Theoretically you should just come in when the doctor gives up; but you were on the job first tonight."

Hilary laughed as Shane drew the car to a stop at the rectory. "Pure accident. Seriously though, I can't even attempt to thank you for what you did tonight. It was tremendously fine of you to come to our help without a question. Leaving your dinner too! I shall never forget it. And by the way, will you please send the bill to me? I'll arrange for it."

Shane was silent for a moment.

"It's rather a curious thing that the two professions that are supposed to minister to humanity's needs have so little dealing with each other, isn't it? Doctors and preachers never seem to hobnob much together. I suppose because most doctors don't go to church and that gives them a black eye with the clergy. I'm a heretic out and out, but still I hope we'll meet again."

"If you should have a free night some time to join me here at the rectory at a bachelor dinner, I should be delighted," Hilary said.

"Fine," said Shane. "I'd really like that."

"I'll call then when I'm a bit more settled, and see about a date. A thousand thanks again meanwhile for tonight."

"That's all right," Shane said, adding gruffly over his shoulder as he started the car, "and there will be no bill."

Hilary ran up the steps and into the house. He was physically tired but his heart was light. It was good to think Dick was here waiting for him. Good to have some one to whom he could pour it all out.

Dick was already in the upper hall. "Well," he remarked, "you look chipper enough. Mother and child doing well, I take it."

Hilary laughed and told his story while they smoked in Dick's room.

"Did you ever hear of such consummate cheek on my part?" Hilary kept asking elatedly. "But the young chap would have died otherwise. Shane as much as intimated that. He's a great chap, Shane. Says he's an arch heretic, but I think we're going to hit it off. Why do I always warm up so to the sinners?"

"My influence," Dick replied cheerfully. "Say, some old dame called up. I answered the phone and she apparently knows all about me. How come? She insists upon pouring some tea down my northwest passage tomorrow afternoon at four. You're also invited. Name is Sneed or Weed or some such."

"That's old Mrs. Reed. She's a real person. I've told her about you. Of course we'll go. She'll eat from your hand. Now, I guess we ought to get to bed. I've got plenty of work tomorrow. By the way, you haven't said a thing about your own business. I've been a swine to talk nothing but my own shop. How's the mine working out?"

Dick's black eyes lighted up but he shook his head.

"I'll tell you all tomorrow," he said. "Just now, Brother Laurens, you should seek your cell."

He stood up, crossed the cords of his bath robe ceremoniously over his abdomen, assumed an air of bland innocence and winked.

"Pax vobiscum," he said, "and don't snore."

CHAPTER VI

DURING DICK'S VISIT Hilary saw little of him except in the evenings. They went together to Mrs. Reed's to tea, however. She received them in her little Victorian upstairs sitting room, and, as Hilary had predicted, it was love at first sight between her and Dick. Before the afternoon was over he was telling her one of his best stories and the old lady was insisting through her laughter that he was a devil but that she couldn't resist him.

There was one tender moment, also, when she brought out the pictures of her sons and grandson.

"Gone," she said. "All gone, and my life empty. Why should it be so? But I still say my prayers," she added, looking at Hilary.

"Do you know," she went on to Dick, "this brother of yours has taken the town by storm? A parson's supposed to have morals and bowels of compassion and all that, but this fellow's got brains too. It's hard on me. He keeps me awake Sundays during the sermon and I'm not used to it."

When they were leaving she patted them both on the back.

"Nice boys," she said. "Come to see me, Dick, whenever you're in town. And you, Hilary"—using his Christian name for the first time—"drop in when you want to, and blow off steam. Nothing said in this room ever goes any further."

It was the night before Dick left that he made his confession. Hilary had noticed that his eyes looked very bright and there was an excitement in his movements and speech more than his natural restless energy. He had turned off all questions about his business in the city, chiefly, Hilary had supposed, because there was nothing to tell. He had decided Dick had come on now solely to see him in his new environment, as he would certainly have done sooner or later.

But on their last evening Dick suddenly stopped roaming about the library and faced his brother.

"I think I've hit it at last, Hil. We've got a mine out there that's going to pay off. I'm putting my last shirt into it, and, by the black mare's tail, I'm going to be rich this time."

Hilary felt his heart sink. It was not the first time Dick had invested in a mine. His get-rich-quick efforts had constituted one of the Bishop's major anxieties. But he tried now to answer casually.

"You think it's a good risk?"

"It's the real thing! I believe it's the chance of a lifetime. I've talked to a couple of fellows here in the city who know copper mines, and they're keen too. Do you want to come in on it?"

Hilary shook his head. "I don't believe so. You're not putting what you got from Grandy in it, are you?"

"I'd planned to. It's a dead sure thing, Hil."

"Nothing's sure in this vain and transitory world. You ought to know that. But you're of age. You can do as you please, only if I were you I'd keep some of Grandy's safe. Sentiment maybe. He planned his investments pretty carefully, thinking of us."

Dick's brows darkened. "I know what you're driving at. I know I've backed some wrong horses in my time, but this is different. I'm pretty excited over it. I didn't mention it before because I knew you'd preach. But nothing you can say will change me. I know it will pay off. But even if I weren't so sure—" He laughed, his eyes very black and intense. "I'd still like the gamble," he added. "I need a touch of excitement to keep me cheerful. Let me go my own gait, Hil. I will in any case, you know."

"All right," Hilary said slowly, "but take it as easy as you can. There's plenty of excitement to be had in this world without risking your last dollar on it."

When they had gone to their rooms, Hilary lay, wakeful. He was deeply disturbed over Dick's news. It was, however, entirely to be expected. Dick was always impetuous, overenthusiastic, a born gambler. Already on other unlucky ventures he had lost all of his share of the inheritance which had come to the boys from their mother. Now, with Grandy's fairly considerable estate settled, Dick was once again in possession of funds to invest. Of course, Hilary tried to reason, Dick was thirty, unattached and a free agent. If this sort of thing gave him pleasure, why worry about it? There was still, however, fresh in his mind, Grandy's parting request that he should keep an eye on his brother.

Suddenly, as a thought struck him, he sprang out of bed. Dick's light was still on, for he was always a night owl, so Hilary went into his room and sat down on the side of the bed.

"How now, O righteous one?" Dick inquired, grinning, as he put down his book and reared up from the pillows. "More sound advice?"

Hilary shook his head. "No, an idea just hit me. You know Grandy's folks out in Maryville? Well, I keep thinking about them. In that last letter Grandy wrote to me he said he was planning to go out there this summer. Wanted me to go along. There's an old cousin of his in the village

86

and a great-nephew on the old farm. I wondered. I can't possibly leave here this summer. But we oughtn't to lose touch with them. I'll write of course now and then, but I thought just possibly sometime you were coming through Pittsburgh—you get a jerkwater train there or a bus or something . . ."

He stopped. Dick's face had gone serious.

"Look," he said, "I'll come and preach for you sometime if you want me to, but I'll be damned if I'll go out to some forty-second cousin's farm and visit cows. I hate cows. I wouldn't know the north side of one from the south. You couldn't do this to me, Hil."

"It's only because Grandy had planned the visit, I thought . . ."

"Well, good heavens, I'd do anything he would have wanted except go and twaddle over pigs and chickens. I can't stand yokels. I wouldn't get on with them. I'd bust wide open and shock the livers out of them."

His real distress made Hilary laugh. "Don't worry," he said. "I guess you're right. We'll let it all ride until sometime I can go myself. I'd really like to. I was there once with Grandy, you remember, years ago."

"Yes, I didn't want to go even then, so Grandy sent me to camp and took you along. Well, you think then we can leave it at that? I don't want to let either you or Grandy down."

"It's much better this way. I hadn't thought the thing through when I spoke. Now, get back to your book. I'm going to sleep."

"Hil."

"Yes."

"Don't give up about Lex. I've got a hunch she'll come to hand. She's worth waiting for. And so are you, for that matter."

"Thanks, Bib." It was his childhood nickname for his brother, and Hilary was startled to find it suddenly upon his lips after so many years. Perhaps it was loneliness that had brought it forth. It hurt to see Dick go.

The following days were so full, however, that he had no time to think of anything except his work. Always, always there was the next sermon to be prepared, and because he was intellectually active, even brilliant, and also because he felt—perhaps through a strain of Scotch Presbyterianism in his blood—that the sermon was the most important part of the service next to the Sacrament, he poured out upon it the best effort of which he was capable. He was surprised now, since he had done little preaching during his Chicago curateship, to discover that instead of having to search for a subject, it was a matter of selection. Dozens of ideas, of themes, of texts, jostled each other in his mind, eager for consideration. He was glad of this. He liked this warm rich feeling of mental fertility. But once the idea was chosen, there was hard, gruelling work to be done. For the weight of a perfectionistic compulsion lay upon him. The most difficult thing was to compress all that he wanted to say into twenty minutes. It would be infinitely easier to speak for an hour. The narrow space of time meant ruthless pruning of sentences, continual readjustment of material, painstaking care in highlighting and emphasis.

Then there was all the unexpected work of the priest. Already he had baptized babies at odd hours, married a half dozen strange couples who had drifted in and also a number of parish young people, in addition to officiating at several funerals. In between were the sick calls—and the evening dinner parties!

Steadily, though, he was working out his main program of parish work as he expected to lay it before the vestry when they met. He had postponed calling them together for this special meeting until he had grown better acquainted with the parish and also the community in which St. Matthews was located. Daily his mind revolved around this latter problem. Here stood the great edifice itself, with the rectory and the parish house adjacent. And here also pressing close upon three sides was the poverty of the city. Each noon he walked the streets slowly, sizing up the people and the cheap dwellings which housed them. Through his calls upon Joe and Mary McComb he had met some of their neighbors, decent self-respecting people, making the most of their very little. One young woman, a friend of Mary's, he had invited to come to church. She had looked at him in amazement.

"Me?" she said. "Go to St. Matthews? Why it's the big bugs' church."

"It is God's church," Hilary had replied. "And you're welcome there. Mary and Joe are coming. Get your husband and come along."

But her words stuck in his mind.

One day before Miss Mowbray was back from lunch Hilary suddenly started out. He had called the vestry meeting at last for the following week. He wanted very much to present to them some concrete facts on the subject of the surrounding neighborhood. He decided to take a few hours and make a personal canvass of some of the apartments and tenements nearby. His best talking point was the fact that the church itself could be plainly seen from all their windows; and his clerical vest served as its own introduction. At least, he thought, they won't take me for a brush salesman.

He had been prepared for strange encounters, and he had them; but in the main people were courteous, even when apathetic. By four-thirty he was thoroughly tired, but he had now in his possession some information he had very much wanted. Out of three tenements he had visited not a single Protestant family attended church!

He walked back, hot, weary, and perspiring, for it was one of those bright, unseasonably warm days in early May. As he turned the corner in sight of the church he was surprised to see Miss Mowbray on the sidewalk looking up and down the street, her whole bearing one of tenseness and extreme anxiety. As she caught sight of him, she signed frantically for him to hurry, starting herself to meet him. At the same moment Hastings came running down the steps like a wild man, and Morris emerged from the rectory. Hilary's heart stood still. Was it Lex? Was it Dick? What had happened?

"What is it?" he said when he and Miss Mowbray got close enough to speak.

"The wedding!" she panted. "The Pettigrew wedding at four!"

A cold streak ran up Hilary's spine.

He looked at her aghast, unable to speak.

"Hurry. We've got a car waiting and a man from the garage to drive it. I've got your vestments and Prayer-book in the bag in the car. *Hurry*. They've been calling every ten minutes. They're waiting till five. You can just make it—I've given the man the directions . . ."

She had grabbed his arm though he needed no urging. They ran the rest of the way and he threw himself into the car.

"Step on it," he said to the driver through his teeth. "This is awful."

He spoke only once again on the way, his eyes glued to the clock. "Can we make it by five?"

"Do my best, Reverend. All depends on the traffic."

The feeling of abject shame which engulfed Hilary seemed to paralyze his very members. The incredible, the unforgivable fact that he had forgotten the wedding stunned him. He had been at the rehearsal the night before; he had thought of the event as he woke up that morning; the notation regarding it was plainly written on his desk calendar. Heavy beads of perspiration stood on his brow. Why, he must be suffering from a nightmare! He *couldn't* have forgotten it! But he had. In the sudden intensity of his new plan to make a personal survey of the tenements, everything outside the actual experience itself had been wiped from his mind. And now, what should he say, what should he do when he got there?

The cab swung at last into the drive on two wheels at five o'clock flat. The wide beautiful grounds looked festive. A bright marquee for dancing had been erected at the side. Small tables were set under the trees. Men and women in afternoon dress covered the lawns, and stood about on the tall pillared porch. It seemed to Hilary as though every eye centered and froze upon him as he got out of the cab, and clutching his bag, hurried up the steps. Mr. Pettigrew met him, his eyes dark, his face worried, his lips in a forced smile.

"Come this way, Mr. Laurens. We're certainly relieved to see you at last."

He nodded to the guests who happened to be near.

"Just pass the word around. We'll be ready in a few minutes." He turned to Hilary. "Everyone was in the house of course at four, but they finally scattered and have been drifting around. *What delayed you?*"

"I can't explain now," Hilary said. "I'm desperately sorry. Just show me where I can put on my vestments and I'll be ready in five minutes."

He could feel the air of anxious, curious tension that still pervaded the house and overcame the normal pleasant suspense of the moments before a wedding. From the small bedroom where he changed he could hear Mr. Pettigrew's flurried orders to the servants and the voice of the professional director just outside in the hall.

Tell Miss Pettigrew that Mr. Laurens has come. Tell Mr. Mallory. Tell Mrs. Pettigrew. Tell the bridesmaids. Tell Mrs. Armstrong. (Hilary knew the latter was the invalid grandmother for whose sake the wedding was a home one.) Tell the guests to come into the drawing room and be seated. Tell the musicians to get ready to start the wedding music. Tell the caterer in the kitchen . . .

There was confusion. Controlled, but still confusion. He felt his cheeks grow scarlet as he donned his cassock and surplice and adjusted the heavy white silk stole. He snatched a comb from the dresser, ran it through his hair, wiped his dusty shoes at the last moment on his handkerchief which he tossed back into the bag, picked up his Prayer-book and stepped outside in the wide upper hall to announce his readiness.

The director was a pleasant, youngish woman with efficiency written all over her. She spoke to him with eyebrows raised.

"What in the world happened? Everybody's been frantic! To hold a wedding for over an hour is some job."

"I know. I'm so desperately sorry. But I'm ready now."

"Here are Mr. Mallory and the best man. You know the stairway you are to take. I'll get the rest lined up as soon as you are gone."

The bridegroom was a pleasant chap, but he, too, looked worried and angry.

"What happened?" he said.

"It's a long story," Hilary replied nervously. "I feel as though I could shoot myself if it would do any good. Will the delay upset your plans too much?"

"Well, you see we're sailing tonight and we had arranged the time element pretty carefully. It will cut the party short for us, that's sure. I don't mind so much but I know Helen will. All right, let's go."

Hilary felt utterly miserable. He must tell some one the straight truth before he left but he had decided to wait and make his confession to Mr. Pettigrew himself. He could hear the music below and the sound of the guests taking their places in the great drawing room at the end of which an altar had been improvised. The Pettigrews, aside from their wealth, were of the city's blood royal. The wedding was a social event of the first water, and Hilary knew that all the beautifully correct arrangements had been made months in advance.

He and the groom and the best man were now in the library awaiting their signal. Hilary opened his Prayer-book at the service and the best man checked again on the ring. The groom was nervous and not inclined to talk. Hilary guessed that he might suspect the real fact and could not forgive it. And I certainly don't blame him, he thought to himself. I never felt like such a heel in my life.

At last the signal came and they walked into the drawing room and took their places. As Hilary faced about he was amazed at the size of the company, and at the complete transformation of the room. It looked, indeed, like an exquisite chapel. As he noted each detail, his heart smote him anew that he should have been the one to mar the perfection of the plans.

The wedding march began, the bridal procession advanced slowly through the wide doorway from the hall and up the flower-decked aisle. At last came Helen, white and beautiful, on her father's arm.

It was at the moment that the bridegroom had taken her hand and they had moved to their places before him that a thought of horror swept through Hilary's brain. What was the bridegroom's real name? They all called him Ted. Was it Theodore or Edward? He had thought of this last night in bed after the rehearsal and had meant to clear it up just before the wedding. He tried desperately to recall the name upon the license but he could not. As he had looked at it the night before the groom had been talking to him animatedly about their plans for the trip abroad.

There was no help for it. With the room in a breathless hush Hilary took a step forward.

"What's your name?" he whispered as low as he could.

The groom glared at him as if this was indeed the last straw. "What?" he asked huskily.

"Your first name?" Hilary repeated a little louder, horribly conscious that the strange conversation was now audible to all the first rows and that a faint breath of question and surprise was sweeping the room.

"Edward," the young man answered in a throaty whisper.

Within the second, in a voice as rich and sonorous as he could make it, Hilary began the service.

"Dearly beloved, we are gathered together here in the sight of God and in the face of this company . . ."

Never had he so exerted every effort in his power to make a wedding service memorably beautiful in the reading. Underneath he prayed wordlessly that his mistakes might somehow be forgiven, and the wedding not completely spoiled.

When he came to the last words he knew that the ceremony at least, had been perfect, except for the blundering question and the answer at the beginning. There was now the usual joyful recessional, then the normal confusion of talk and laughter and the gay crowding of the receiving line. When the champagne was being passed, Hilary saw Mr. Pettigrew coming toward him.

"Let's go into my study for a moment," he said.

Once there he faced Hilary squarely.

"Now, I'd like an explanation," he said. "I believe it is due me." He was still very angry.

"It is," Hilary answered gravely. "I wish I could tell you I was delayed by an accident—by anything legitimate. Even then it would be bad enough. But the truth is I forgot it. I was checking up on that section just back of the church, going through those tenements, and—"

"You forgot it! And you admit it?"

"Yes. I feel utterly wretched."

Pettigrew faced him coldly.

"Well, if I had been in your place I would have made up some sort of plausible story and stuck to it. Now, I've got to do it myself. I'm not going to have every gossip in the city buzzing that Helen Pettigrew's wedding was an hour and a half late because the preacher forgot to come. That, I couldn't stand. I'm going to tell my own story and I'll thank you to confirm it when you need to. I want you to leave at once. Then I'll let it be known that you're not well. That was the reason you were late. Out making calls, overtired, overworked, seized with sudden faintness—God knows what—but anyway you came as soon as you could and then left immediately after the ceremony. That will at least sound dignified. And," he added, his blue eyes scathing, "I'm not doing this to save *your* skin, mind you. I damned well don't care at this moment what happens to you. But I'm not going to have my daughter's wedding made a laughing stock."

Hilary bowed his head. "You're probably right," he said.

"She's our only child. This wedding is not only the biggest thing in her life but in her mother's and mine as well. We've planned this for months, spared no expense. Her friends have come from all over the country. She and Ted counted on two hours of party after refreshments before they left. Helen particularly looked forward to that. What girl wouldn't? Now, they'll be lucky if they get one dance. Well, Mr. Laurens, I believe that's all. Except that I'll be grateful if you leave at once."

"I'll wait only to speak to your daughter for a moment. I've had no chance yet. I won't ask any of you to forgive me. I don't think you ever could. But, believe me, I couldn't feel sorrier."

"I'll have a car at the west porch for you in five minutes," was Mr. Pettigrew's only answer. Then, as though the thought had just struck him, he added, "And you even bungled up the service! It was your business to know Ted's name beforehand."

Hilary went out into the gay, moving crowd. The bride's table was in the main dining room. He slipped in unobtrusively and finally went over to where she sat.

"Mrs. Mallory, may I interrupt you just long enough to say good-bye and to wish you both the happiest honeymoon any two people ever had?"

She looked up, her eyes overcast for the second.

"I've explained my lateness to your father. I've never felt so miserable over anything in my life."

She smiled slowly. "You mustn't feel so on my wedding day. And you— you read the service beautifully."

"Those are the kindest words any one has ever spoken to me. Now, God bless you both!"

He shook hands quickly and made his way to the west door, keeping out of sight of people he knew in so far as it was possible. He got into the car, realized he was still in his vestments, hurried back to the room, changed and finally left feeling as though all the strength and breath had been knocked out of him.

Once back in the rectory he phoned Miss Mowbray to thank her for her part and give her the brief details, then he sat in the library with his head in his hands. All Morris' efforts were in vain. He could eat nothing. The thought of food choked him. He began to feel that he must talk to someone, but to whom? Old Mrs. Reed? No, not this. He knew he would accept the offer of her little sitting room as a confession chamber many times as the years went on, but this . . .

Suddenly he knew to whom he could confide. Forrest. He of the sensitive face, the wise and gentle voice. "I'm a good listener," he had told him that first afternoon.

He dialled quickly. Forrest was at home, alone, and would be glad to see him. He left at once.

When he entered the blind man's bachelor quarters he had a distinct feeling of surprise and pleasure. The rooms were in an old apartment house in a section of the city which seemed to have been forgotten by the onsurge of progress. It was a fourth floor walk-up, but the living room was large and airy with a small iron balcony opening from it, which overlooked a bit of garden. The furniture was good and comfortably shabby by long use. The great piano, a few fine etchings, and a number of unusually good pieces of sculpture gave the room distinction and charm.

"This is a great pleasure," Forrest said, coming to meet him. "I'll confess I've been looking forward to this, but I've never had the courage to ask you. I know what these first months are. Sit over here near the balcony. It's cooler."

Hilary sank down gratefully. There was something about the room which reminded him of the old library at home.

"I'm in trouble," he said. "I've made an awful mess of something and I felt I'd like to talk it over with you."

"You honor me," Forrest said. "I'm glad you came. Do you want to go ahead and get it off your chest at once?"

Hilary plunged into the story, telling it in full. When he had finished Forrest did not speak for a long moment.

"It is bad," he said slowly at last. "There's no use denying it. But I think you must accept it as part of the whole pattern of your ministry. There's no doctrine, you know, of the infallibility of *priests!* You are, after all, a man like unto other men. You will of necessity make mistakes. And I'm not so sure—"

He stopped, half smiling, one thin hand supporting the sensitively thoughtful face.

"Will you forgive me if I make a strange statement? I was about to say that as far as you yourself are concerned I'm almost glad this has happened."

"Why?" The word fairly burst from Hilary.

"Well, there is one Biblical *woe* which most people don't have to worry about. 'Woe unto you when all men shall speak well of you.' But as far as I have been able to gather you've been in just that position. You've made a phenomenally good impression. Your praises are sung everywhere."

"And you think this is dangerous?"

"I think you have been singularly untouched by it, but perhaps a big mistake such as this may preserve a certain needed balance. Please don't hate me for saying this."

"On the contrary," Hilary said slowly, "I think you may be right in principle. But you see, if Pettigrew tells everyone I was sick, I still won't be blamed as far as the congregation in general is concerned."

"But you'll have to forgive yourself. That's often harder than forgiving other people. You'll have to live with this mistake and accept your own limitations along with your own great powers. And you can be sure there

94

will be one family at least who won't be 'speaking well' of you for some time to come."

"I'm sure of that."

"I hope you won't think I'm brutal in saying what I have."

"No," Hilary said slowly. "You sound very like my grandfather. I believe that's exactly what he might have said. I hope you'll believe me though when I tell you that the reason this thing has hit me so hard is not because I'm afraid of the effect on myself, but because I realize I have made a number of people very unhappy. To have spoiled a wedding for all involved—that makes me wretched beyond words. And there is something else, too."

"Tell me," said Forrest.

"Well, it's hard to explain because I'm a bit confused myself. You see, in Chicago I was merely a curate. I was learning my trade, as it were, doing what I was told. My responsibility to the—outside world, shall we call it?—didn't strike me there. When I came to St. Matthews it hit me full in the face. All those tenements just back of the church. All the people working in the factories and lofts around it. The city! The city! It beats upon me. I feel the whole weight of it. I've got to do something about it. I've got to reach out to it, serve it, somehow—"

He broke off. Forrest still sat with his hand against his cheek, his eyes closed, but his whole face seemed to change, to become animated.

"The city!" he repeated. "The ultimate unit of society. The concentrated essence of civilization. It's the city that lives after the nation has fallen. I can't see it with my eyes, but I feel it with all my other senses. I couldn't be happy out of it. It intoxicates me, stimulates me—all of it."

Hilary watched him, surprised. He had thought of Forrest as the deeply contemplative type who would doubtless have preferred the quiet of the country if he could have had it.

"I know what you mean, though," the older man went on, "about the tragic cry of the city. I get my secretary to take me for long walks in the slums, down along Water Street. Once we went to the Redeemer Mission. You ought to go some time. It's an experience. I go in order to get deeper tones into my music, something of the poor, wretched, suffering souls of men."

"That's it," Hilary broke in eagerly. "I was so full of zeal to help them that today I forgot my first duty, which is to St. Matthews. I've got to be very careful to serve my own people first. I've got to realize that rich people can be as unhappy as poor people. In other words I've got to restrain a lot of my first impulses because of this afternoon's experience."

"I think I see what you mean," Forrest said, "but don't be discouraged over that." He smiled. "You may have to revise your plans still more after your vestry meetings. Ease into things gradually. That's not cowardice. It's merely good sense and efficiency in the long run. How about an assistant?"

"I must find one soon. So far I've been trying to get my own bearings. But I'm ready now to start the search. Any suggestions?"

Forrest hesitated. "I have one but I am biased at the outset. The man is an old friend."

"Really?" said Hilary. "That's a recommendation in itself. Tell me about him."

"Well," said Forrest, "it's a long story. He's from a little town in the middle west and his wife still is, if you get what I mean. That's been his trouble. A boy and girl romance to which he held, by conscience or a sense of chivalry, I fancy, after he'd come east here to the Seminary. He's grown, she hasn't. He's got a little church now somewhere in upper New York state where all his talents are wasted. He would fit into this place perfectly, I feel sure. But while she can run a mother's meeting or a cake sale with one hand she wouldn't be socially acceptable to St. Matthews. Do you see the picture?"

"Yes and it interests me," Hilary said slowly. "How old is he?"

"He's all of sixty; so is she but neither of them look it."

"Would he care to be an assistant to a younger man?"

Forrest's expression told more than his words. "He has not had much chance to develop pride during the years. I don't believe that thought would even cross his mind. He loves beauty. To serve before the altar of St. Matthews in any capacity would be to him, I imagine, the great fulfillment."

"Tell me more about the woman."

"Well, let me think. First of all, practical and utterly devoid of imagination. Voice too loud with a good many little provincialisms of speech. No social graces but a heart of gold. There's one thing more I must tell you about him, though. Two or three times during the years, he's gotten drunk. And he doesn't drink, mind you."

In spite of himself Hilary laughed. "He doesn't drink, he just gets drunk!"

"That's it in a nutshell. He definitely does not drink, in the usual sense. Never did even before he took orders. What has happened is this: his whole life has been one long frustration; several times when he felt completely hopeless he shut himself in his study with a bottle of Scotch and finished it. Twice by devilish ill luck he was discovered. Of course people thought the worst, though I will say they tried to keep it quiet. Both times, though, he left and moved on. In a little town a thing like that could never be condoned."

"You think it could be here, for example?"

"I don't think it would ever happen here. If, conceivably, he were to come here as your assistant, he would have constantly the kind of contacts, the kind of outlet for his resources, which he has always craved. Don't you see? I could almost guarantee there would be no problem there, though of course I had to give you all the facts. And, I'm sure he and you would take to each other. I've thought of it often since you came but hesitated— Tonight seemed the perfect opportunity to tell you about him."

Hilary sat thoughtful for some minutes. "In many ways I would like an older man. I hate the thought of breaking in a young one. This set-up, if it should work out, would give our ministry a sort of balance. And as to the woman—I'm not so sure but that I could use her. Would she expect to do any church work?"

"Good heavens, yes! That would be just the trouble. She's the hearty, efficient kind, born to run country-church suppers and pack missionary barrels. But as you know, St. Matthews doesn't need just those qualifications."

Hilary drew slowly upon his pipe. "I'm not so sure about that," he repeated. "I have some plans in mind where she might possibly fit in. How can I see these people?"

"I'll ask them down for a night. I often do as a matter of fact. It seems to give him a lift. I'll not drop even a hint of what we've talked about. I'll just take him over to the study because I want him to meet you. Then you can size him up. If you want to see her, we can manage that too. I don't want to press this, remember, or lay any sort of obligation upon you. It's merely a suggestion and no more."

"I understand. It's something to think about though. I'm grateful for even the possibility. Now I mustn't keep you up any longer. You've helped me tonight as I'm sure no one else could. I can't ever thank you."

Forrest only smiled. "It was wonderfully nice of you to come. How about something to eat before you go? Katy always leaves a pretty full icebox. Let's go forage."

"By George," said Hilary, "I've just remembered I had no dinner! I couldn't eat when I got back from the wedding. It's not fair to raid your icebox under those conditions."

Forrest laughed and led the way. Hilary marvelled at his ease. With perfect assurance he moved about the kitchen, reaching one article and another as though by sight. They sat down at last with a tray of sandwiches between them.

"By the way, what is the name of this man, your friend?" Hilary asked suddenly.

"Adams. Stupid of me not to mention it. Samuel Adams. And she"—he paused, smiling—"she is Samantha!"

Hilary rolled the name upon his tongue. "If they should ever come I know I'd call her Aunt Samantha."

"She would love it," Forrest said. "But she would try to boss you, make you wear rubbers, and smell camphor for a cold. I warn you."

"But she's kind."

Forrest's expression was strange. "She's the kindest person I know," he said.

When Hilary got back at last to the rectory, Morris was waiting up.

"Mist' Hilary, you all right?"

"Fine, Morris. I was tired and worried, but I've got my second wind now."

"Lots of people callin' up tonight askin' how you is."

Hilary stopped dead with his foot on the stair. He had not foreseen this contingency.

"What did you tell them?"

"I just say you feelin' poorly."

"Did you say I was out?"

"No, Mist' Hilary, I just say you feelin' poorly. I mind once the Bishop tell me that was the safest if I wasn't sure, 'cause folks could always get well quick if they needed to."

Hilary laughed. "Good! That will be the way with me. Tomorrow if any one calls just say I'm feeling a little better and am at the study. By the way, do you think you could manage a dinner party for me some night?"

The change in the old colored man was electrical. His shrunken shoulders straightened; life came back into his eyes; his lips trembled with eagerness.

"Dinner party? Now, Mist' Hilary there's nothin' do me as much good as cookin' a dinner for comp'ny. How many folks?"

"Oh, eight or ten, perhaps. I'll tell you in a few days when it will be. Good night, Morris, you're a good fellow!"

At the top of the stairs he heard Morris speaking excitedly.

"Mist' Hilary, you forgot something. That's why I know this afternoon you feelin' mighty low." He was coming up the stairs as fast as his stiff knees could bring him. Hilary saw then the silver tray in his hand with a letter upon it. A letter from Lex! He grasped it, grinning his thanks, and took the rest of the stairs two at a time. How could he have missed it? Morris, having been told nothing, yet with the instinct of his race for knowing everything, always propped her letters ostentatiously, as they came, upon the hall table. Hilary's eyes sought the spot each day as he came through the door, hopefully, fearfully. Tonight in his deep distress of mind he had not even noticed.

He opened it now and read it through swiftly, then sitting down, read it slowly again.

HIL DEAR:

We're in Paris, as you'll note. Muff is sick in bed with tonsillitis and I might as well be, for she gets in a state every time I go out alone. We're at a very elegant but very quiet little hotel just near the Crillon. Too near, for I can get tantalizing glimpses of the gaiety there and feel horribly shut out of it. Scores of handsome and distinguished-looking males pass in and out the portals. Any day now I shall drop my hanky at the feet of one of them and allow myself to be persuaded to have lunch or tea with him. Beyond that —"Oh, my *dear* Monsieur, how could you so misjudge me!"

I've done all the things I can decently do by myself. Shopping, the flower market, some churches. Do you know the church I love most here? The Madeleine. The first time I saw it I thought it was a bit gaudy and ornate, but now I don't. That white and gold seems to suit the character of the Magdalene. The whole thing *means* something. It may surprise you, but I knelt there today and said a little prayer for us. Hil, if you were a lawyer or a doctor I'd take the next ship home. I do miss you. Terribly. I hope everything is going all right at the church. Tell me what you're preaching about. Are all the women swooning over you? You asked in your letter about Aunt Hettie Breckenridge. She's Mother's aunt and an old harpy. She hates Dad and thinks I'm a spoiled brat. If she thought you were considering me for the Rector-ess of St. Matthews she'd die of apoplexy. So don't tell her—yet. As to your other question, I can only say this. I've never thought so hard about anything in my life as I am now every day about us.

Love—
LEX

Hilary read it over once more and then on a sudden impulse slipped down the stairs again, out across the court and let himself in to the rear of the church. He turned on one light only so the chancel was dim. He walked into it slowly as he had done on his first day, and knelt before the altar. For a few minutes the happenings of the afternoon and evening passed fluidly through his mind. The tenements he had visited, with their poor, drab inhabitants; the luxurious beauty of the Pettigrew wedding which his own forgetfulness had so grievously marred; his call upon Forrest and the strange problem of Samuel and Samantha Adams; now the letter from Lex and his own aching, longing heart.

His head fell upon his hands and he prayed.

CHAPTER VII

THE NEXT MORNING at seven, before he was dressed, Hilary heard Hastings' voice in the hall below. This boded no good. He got into his clothes quickly and went down. The old verger waited in the dining room, his lean face melancholy as usual, a bunch of newpsapers in his hand.

"What's up, Hastings?" Hilary asked anxiously.

"I just thought you'd better see these," he said, "before you leave the house."

Hilary grabbed the papers, all opened and folded at the account of the Pettigrew wedding. The conservative ones ran the familiar headings, but did not fail to mention the unusual fact of the ceremony's delay due to the sudden illness of the rector of St. Matthews just prior to the hour. The tabloids, however, ran riot:

"Sudden Illness of Rector Delays Fashionable Wedding! . . . St. Matthews' Rector Suffers Heart Attack. . . . Pettigrew-Mallory Nuptials an Hour Late Due to Clergyman's Seizure."

He read them all and groaned.

" 'Bout the best you could do, I s'pose," Hastings was remarking judicially. "My father used to say, 'Tell a whopper when you have to an' then stick to it.' "

"But, Hastings," Hilary burst out, "don't think *I* made up this excuse. I told Mr. Pettigrew the absolute truth, of course. He felt it sounded too undignified to give out, so he invented this tale and asked me as a favor to confirm it if I needed to. Now I *am* in a jam. I never thought of the papers taking it up."

"So that's the way it was," Hastings said, his bleak gray eyes softening. "Me an' Miss Mowbray just wondered. Now you listen. You get right back up to your room an' stay there. It won't hurt you to rest up a day or so after tearin' round like mad the way you've been doin'. Miss Mowbray can bring the mail over an' do it here. I'll take care of the phone over at the study, an' this here gentleman," indicating Morris, "can do the same here. We're in this thing now, an' we've got to see it through."

"I'll have to lie doggo today, at least, I suppose," Hilary agreed slowly, "but I hate all this like poison."

Hastings was scratching his bald head. "Just one thing bothers me. This heart attack business. That ain't good for a new preacher. Every Sunday now, the old ladies 'll all be lookin' for you to keel over in the pulpit. We got to think you up some other disease. I s'pose," he said apologetically, "you wouldn't want me to say something had *disagreed* with you."

Hilary laughed, but without much mirth. "I feel so low that a little more embarrassment wouldn't matter much. Wait a minute."

He jumped up quickly and went to the telephone. It was only seven-thirty. He might be able to catch Shane before he left the house. Luck had been with him once before. It was again. In a few seconds he heard Shane's voice.

"This is Hilary Laurens, doctor. I'm always asking favors, I fear."

"What's this I see in the morning papers about you? How are you?"

"Too well, considering the write-ups. Would it be possible for you to step in here at the rectory for a few minutes? It's a lot to ask you."

"Are you sure I'm the doctor you want? I can give you the name of the best heart specialist in the city."

"You're the very one I want, if I can get you."

"I'll be over in about ten minutes on my way to the hospital," he said.

Hilary told Hastings to wait, and went back up to his room. He had never felt so thoroughly uncomfortable and ashamed. Morris, always delighted at any excuse for a tray, brought him up his breakfast and insisted upon hanging up his coat and helping him into a dressing gown. The most remarkable fact of all was that, once relaxed in his chair, he felt inexpressibly weary and willing to stay there.

When Shane came, he told him the facts.

"You see I'm in for it for a decent interval at least. But as Hastings down there has just pointed out to me, it's not good to spread the word that I've had a heart attack. What reasonable disease can I have and recover from quickly?"

Shane listened to his chest.

"Much athletics in college?"

"Track."

"Sounds like it. No real trouble, though, if you use common sense. You look pretty tired to me. Give me an idea of your routine."

"Oh, up at seven or before. At the study by a quarter to eight. Mail first, then work on my sermon. Calls all afternoon. Dinner parties most nights. If it's not too late after that, some reading or study. Of course in between all this the usual number of weddings and funerals and callers."

Shane nodded.

"Pretty full schedule. Well, just to ease your conscience I'll tell you

you're a pretty tired young man, and I prescribe two days in bed for you. We'll call it grippe. Good old grippe. Heart not affected in the least but rest definitely ordered. How's that?"

"You're a brick. But I hate this whole dissembling business. I should never have gotten into it but I felt so ashamed of myself and so sorry for the Pettigrews. But it's bad. I have a sort of fanatical regard for the truth. And this thing is nauseating to me."

"Ah," said Shane, "we'll have to have a talk about *truth* some time. One of my pet topics. When does the moral worth of an ultimate good take precedence over adherence to the present fact? Where in the field of ethics does pragmatic lying fit in? Do doctors and preachers come to a line where they have to lie about a thing *in order to make it come true?* I've often said to a sick man *'You're going to get well,'* when I was certain sure he wasn't. Then, damn me, if he didn't up and recover, making me a liar if I'd told what I believed before to be the truth. Very complicated. I'll bet you preachers run into the same thing."

Shane slapped him on the shoulder.

"Now take it easy. I'll leave a prescription. You definitely need the rest. Oh, by the way, let's have a look in your throat. By George, it *is* a bit red. Wonderful! Gargle with salt water, take your tonic and keep to your room, for two days. Let me know if you run into more trouble. Well, goodbye."

He was off before Hilary could more than thank him.

The fact that now he had some justification for his rest made him relax completely. He realized under what a terrific emotional and physical strain he had been working for weeks. Now that he had let go, he felt limp. As he glanced at the bed he could think of nothing more desirable than crawling back into it and sleeping for a whole day.

He went to the door and called Hastings, who came up at once.

"Dr. Shane says you aren't in too good shape an' no foolin'. You go at things hammer an' tongs. I've told you well of it, mind. You've got to slow up. Now you stay here an' behave yourself an' me an' Miss Mowbray, we'll run things. What about the mail?"

The old man's solicitude made his voice harsh.

"Now listen, Hastings. Don't get excited. I am pretty tired and the doctor says I have a red throat. I'm going to turn in again and sleep all day. Tomorrow morning I'll be down in the library, and Miss Mowbray can bring all the mail over and we'll handle it here. And on the phone just say the doctor calls it grippe and the heart-attack story was a mistake. I know you'll be diplomatic. O.K.?"

"O.K.," Hastings said suspiciously. "But you're sure you're not sicker than you let on?"

"Absolutely. Now run along and do just what I've told you. Oh, and ask Miss Mowbray to check my calendar and be sure I'm not forgetting anything else."

When Hastings was gone, there was still Morris to reassure; then Hilary went back to bed.

"An' I'll catch the phone, Mist' Hilary, 'fore it's got time to peep up here."

He did not wake until four o'clock in the afternoon, then lay for a moment looking across at the gray stone cornices of the church roof where pigeons were ruffling their lavender and gold feathers in the sun. Below, the stained glass of one of the side windows dimly caught the afternoon light.

There was in this room, as he had felt from the first, a certain atmosphere of withdrawal from the world—a sort of monastic seclusion. All the city was shut away; there was no view from his bed except the stained glass, the weathered gray stone and the cooing pigeons; if he rose and went closer to the window there would be only the small cloistered court and the fountain. It was as though, like the young Samuel of old, he was dwelling in the very temple itself. I'll always keep this room, he thought to himself, very simple and plain. It will rest me when I get too tired.

For he felt rested now already. He got up and dressed and went downstairs. Even on the landing his nose detected a heavy, unnatural fragrance. When he got to the foot of the stairs he stopped aghast.

"Good heavens!" he exclaimed to himself. "Am I dead and don't know it?"

For the library seemed filled with flowers. Even at the moment Morris came from the pantry regions bearing two more vases.

"Mist' Hilary, I ain't done nothin' all day but answer the phone an' take in flowers. It's been like when the Bishop—I mean there's more here than you really need 'ceptin' at a funeral."

"To put it conservatively, yes," Hilary said, moving about to look at the cards which Morris had carefully placed under each bouquet.

"These here, Mist' Hilary," he said now, pointing to a huge bunch of red roses, "these here is something mighty special. Lady bring 'em herself an' leave this note. She ask me all kinds of questions how you is."

Hilary took the heavy square envelope and opened it. It read:

DEAR MR. LAURENS:
    I am deeply concerned over your sudden illness. Is there anything I could possibly send you or do for you? You have no idea how much you have helped me already and I am

most eager to show my gratitude. As soon as you are able will you come in again to tea and perhaps let me tell you more of my problems? Loneliness is, of course, still the greatest, but that I suppose I must endure. Your sympathy and guidance have helped *so* much. I shall call up tomorrow and hope for the good news that you are better.

With deepest gratitude,

DIANA DOWNES

"H'm," said Hilary, as Dick's wicked quotation about widows came to his mind. He thrust it aside, though, as unworthy.

"Lots of folks call up this mornin', then the flowers come this afternoon," Morris kept explaining. "I got all the names here on a paper."

"Good fellow! Let me have it, will you? Then take some of these out, Morris. Put them anywhere. I can't stand so many round me."

The list surprised him. There were the names of those whom he already regarded as friends: old Mrs. Reed, the Coles, others of the vestry. But there were many he did not even recognize. Morris wrote fairly plainly if shakily, but there was one name he puzzled over. At last he made it out. It was Francine Avery.

He had not spoken to her in ordinary conversation since the talk in his study on that bleak, rainy afternoon. But every Sunday morning since, she had been at eight o'clock Communion. He was intending to give her a little more time and then urge her to become confirmed. Now, she too had called up. It strangely warmed his heart.

He ate dinner with relish and then settled down in the library to write to Lex. Phone calls still came at intervals but Morris answered, as Hilary noted, with firmness and great discretion.

LEX DARLING:

Each time I start to write you all the details of my doings I find myself wanting to say only one thing. I love you. I want you. I don't know how to live without you. So consider that as the substance of this letter and the rest unimportant. Relatively, I mean. Here's what happened yesterday, though. The Pettigrew-Mallory wedding was set for four. I clean, absolutely, abysmally forgot it! I got there, only by grace of Miss Mowbray and Hastings and a dare-devil taxi driver, at five, hot, dishevelled and wishing I could jump in the lake. It was all awful. Mr. P., furious, made up a tale I was sick and the papers got hold of it. I've stayed in today for looks' sake and the whole parish has sent flowers and I feel like a heel. Now if you had been my wife, dearest, it couldn't have happened. You'd have been talking all through lunch about the wedding and what you were going to wear! Everything only leads to this: I love you with my very soul. When you love me too, how can you be afraid? How can you hesitate? There can be no . . .

Morris appeared in the doorway.

"It's that Mrs. Downes, Mist' Hilary, on the phone. The one that brought the big red roses. She say can she please speak to you. She plead mighty hard."

"I suppose so," Hilary said slowly, as he rose.

Diana Downes' voice was husky and tender with anxiety.

"Mr. Laurens? This is good of you to speak to me. I've been so concerned about you, for I've thought for the last two Sundays you looked very tired. Are you really better?"

"Oh, much, thank you. The doctor says a few days' rest will be all I need. Thank you for the gorgeous roses. It was most kind of you."

"I've called you several times before but never found you in. I'm loath to speak of myself now but I am really—frightened. You helped me before. Could you possibly stop in again—next week perhaps—if you are able? Could you? Any afternoon would suit me."

Hilary knit his dark brows.

"Next week is very full for me, Mrs. Downes." He hesitated, and she said nothing at all, which made it harder to refuse.

"Perhaps on Thursday I could run in for a few minutes around five."

"Oh, that's so good of you! And do be careful now. You have become important to a great many people. Certainly . . ." Her voice broke off gently. "I shall expect you next Thursday then, at five, and thank you so very much."

Hilary returned to his letter in a baffled mood. He hated himself for doubting this woman, and yet he did.

He had barely put pen to paper when Morris appeared again.

"It's Mr. Forrest, Mist' Hilary. He say he think you'd want to speak to him."

"Of course." He jumped up quickly.

"Hello, Mr. Forrest. I should have called you before. I'm ashamed to say I've been asleep all day. The queer part is I actually seemed to need it. Thanks again for last night."

"It's about the Adamses I wanted to speak to you," Forrest said. "I began to feel that since you're interested no time should be wasted in at least bringing about a meeting. The rest, of course, is entirely up to you.

I called Sam this afternoon. I think he's perhaps been through a bad time again. He jumped at my invitation to come down. I insisted he bring Samantha, too. He often comes alone but I told him I thought she needed a change. So they're both coming next Monday. What time should I bring Sam over to the study?"

"Between three and four? Then you could leave us together while you are at the organ."

"Fine. Now get to bed, and rest some more. You sounded last night as though you needed it."

"Thanks, I will. I have an optimistic hunch about the Adamses, somehow."

"Well, of course I hope something may come of it. But don't feel in any way bound. Goodbye."

Hilary finished his letter and sat thinking of the coming week. He could not reassure himself that its manifold duties were unusual. Such weeks in general would be his constant and familiar fare, though the details would vary. Approaching now were the decision he must soon make concerning the Adamses; the problem of Diana Downes; the specially called meeting of the vestry for Friday night which he had decided to turn into a dinner; two other important dinner engagements which he dreaded and yet had felt constrained to accept; in addition to all of which was the constant overhanging weight of the weekly sermon, the urgent sick calls upon those near to death's door, probably an unexpected funeral or two . . . So it went. So it would continue to go.

If he and Lex were actually married, could he shake off all this weight of responsibility, this bearing of the burdens of others, and be a normal companion to her? It would not be fair to load upon her also the troubles of a parish. And yet he knew he would crave desperately the relief of sharing them with her—all but the secrets, such as Francine Avery's. Ah, well, the first great anxiety was still whether she would marry him at all. They could work out their life together, if they got the chance, he felt sure. With his thoughts full of her and with a sudden optimism born of rested nerves he finally went up to his room.

The next day he slept late and woke feeling better than he had for weeks. At the big desk in the library he and Miss Mowbray wrestled throughout the morning with the accumulated mail. Invitations to speak at all sorts of affairs were pouring in. These Hilary considered seriously. It was essential that he assume his position in the city and accept his responsibility toward its varied life. But he knew also how easily his time and energy could be frittered away upon trifling occasions. He armed himself against the insidious flattery inherent in each request and finally declined all except the invitation to address a group of theological graduates in June. Next fall and winter, he reasoned, when he was securely established he could perhaps do more speaking, for he knew he had the gift for it.

As they worked in the unwonted intimacy of the library, he became conscious of Miss Mowbray's peculiar charm. Her homeliness of feature became subordinated to her warm, friendly personality. Her voice, as he had noted on their first meeting, was at one with Cordelia's own. Her laughter was pleasant. She had both wit and wisdom; and all about her clung a sweet-scented freshness of person and clothing. She's made the most of herself, Hilary thought as he eyed her once. It became easy, when you were with her for a time, to forget entirely her lack of beauty. He especially liked her smoothly brushed ash-blond hair and her strong, white hands.

"I had a special phone call for you today," she said suddenly. "It was from Miss Celeste Barton of the Varny Street Settlement."

"Oh, yes?"

"She's a remarkable person. You'll enjoy knowing her. I think I've never admired a woman as much as I do her. She would like to meet you some day soon either at your study or at the settlement to discuss Fresh Air problems. She felt your plans might overlap."

"I see."

"She's doing a wonderful work there. She's given her life to it. She comes of an old family, and she's so beautiful she could have had anything." There was a certain wistfulness in Miss Mowbray's voice. "But she chose to do this. They call her the Angel of Varny Street."

"Does she belong to St. Matthews?"

"Yes, but she never comes except to eight o'clock Communion. She's always so busy—"

Hilary sat up suddenly.

"How old is she?"

"Oh, in the fifties, I should say. But she's slender and looks younger."

"Then that's the one!"

At Miss Mowbray's look of surprise he explained. "I've watched her Sunday after Sunday at the altar and wondered who she was. Let's make an appointment for week after next. This coming one is too full, but I'd like to talk with her as soon as possible."

The last letter Hilary dictated was to Francine Avery.

> DEAR MISS AVERY:
>
> I have watched you with deep thankfulness at the early service each Sunday. It has seemed to me that you have found peace. I do not wish to hurry you in any way, but as

soon as you feel like it I should be glad to talk over with you the steps leading to confirmation. There are many reasons why you should consider this seriously. Meanwhile, please accept my admiration for your honesty and courage and my sincere wish to be of service to you in any way possible.

Faithfully yours,

"Now, I think that's all," he said. "I'm afraid I've worked you very hard this morning."

She gathered up her papers. "I enjoy it," she said, smiling. "For sheer variety I'm sure a clergyman's mail must rival a movie star's. You're certain you're all right again?"

"Oh, yes. Perfectly. This has all been a queer mess, but out of it I have picked up a little rest. I've never really thanked you enough for getting me off in the cab that day—packing my vestments and all that. You certainly saved what small shred of reputation was left me. It was all pretty bad, wasn't it?"

She looked into his eyes. Her own were soft. "Don't worry. In a very little while everyone will forget about it."

"Even the bride and groom?"

"Most of all the bride and groom, I should think," she laughed. "Well, I'll be at the office as usual then, tomorrow. And do rest up today."

When she had gone Hilary reflected upon his good fortune in having her services. Her efficiency and quiet kindliness constantly encouraged him. Yes, fate had been gracious in giving him Margaret Mowbray.

Early the next morning Mrs. McColly called up, perturbed and anxious. She had been out of town and only belatedly heard the story of the delayed wedding and the supposed heart attack. Hilary allayed her fears and promised willingly to take dinner there on Sunday. The thought buoyed him up during the intervening time, but when he finally entered the house, the emptiness of it struck him like a dart. He told all his story and then the conversation turned at once to Lex.

"I don't like her prowling around Europe this summer," Old Alex said. "You know what I think? There's going to be war over there by fall."

"Don't pay any attention to him, Hilary. He's a male Cassandra if there ever was one. War is unthinkable."

"Tell that to that German jackass. I've had reports. I've got agents over there. And I was talking to a newspaper man who's been over. Those fellows know. They don't bet whether there'll be a war or not. They bet on the month it's goin' to break. I want Lex home before August. Can't you put some pressure on her, Hilary?"

Hilary's expression was pure amazement. "War," he said. "Why, I've never even taken the thought seriously. What grounds have you for being so alarmed?"

"Grounds? Good God, man, don't you read the papers? These last two months have pretty nearly told the story. Middle of March Hitler takes over all that's left of Czechoslovakia. Does he stop there? Like hell he does. He's in Lithuania in a week. The Italians are bombing Albania without warning in another week. Chamberlain announces conscription in England. This all mean anything to you? I want Lex home."

Her mother sighed softly.

"She'll come when she gets ready, and not before. You should know that by this time, Alex. Besides, I think you are ridiculously wrought up over this. Lex has made her plans to go to the Riviera for a month and then to Switzerland. She'll not be back before August, I'm sure."

"And I don't like that mountain climbing business, either," Old Alex growled. "Put some pressure on her, Hilary."

"I'm not quite in a position to do that, I'm afraid," Hilary said, smiling.

"Well, I hope you soon will be," Alex said bluntly.

"You don't hope it as much as I do," Hilary answered. Then they all laughed together, forgetting other talk. Lex, only Lex, was the subject and in the close circle of their common love they seemed to bring her near.

On Monday Hilary felt a nervousness overtake him as the time approached three. Fortunately Forrest was prompt. Miss Mowbray ushered the two men in on the stroke of the hour. Forrest took charge.

"Mr. Laurens, I want to introduce an old friend of mine, Samuel Adams. I thought you two good parsons should know each other. He and his wife are my guests for a few days and I brought him along to meet you."

"This is good of you," Hilary said, shaking hands. "I'm glad to meet you, Mr. Adams. Sit down."

"I feel almost acquainted with you," Adams returned, "for I was a deep admirer of the Bishop, your grandfather."

"You knew my grandfather?"

"I had the pleasure of meeting him at church conventions and of once long ago serving on a committee under him. And of course I've read all his books. He was a great man."

Hilary's face had lighted. "Nothing could make me feel as close to you as for you to say just that."

Forrest had risen. "Would you two like to talk a while? I'll go down to the organ and when you're ready, Sam, come on down."

When he was gone, Hilary faced his guest with eager interest. He saw a man, younger looking than sixty, with a finely featured and sensitive face, scholarly forehead, tired-looking blue eyes and a kindly mouth encased in lines worn there by hopelessness.

"You have a fine church here," Adams was saying, "the most beautiful one I know."

"I feel the same way. I'm still new and completely swamped with work. Maybe from your longer experience you can give me some advice. Just now it's the Parish House work that I must plan. I have some rather definite and perhaps not too popular ideas on the subject."

"As it happens, so have I," Adams responded, smiling, "though I've never had a chance to use them."

"Come on, then. Let's air them together."

As they talked, Hilary knew that he wanted this man if he could get him. Adams was intelligent, even scholarly. While hesitant at first, a growing confidence came into his voice as he forgot himself and discussed the problems of St. Matthew. Hilary was quick to note that, while he had had no city experience, he had apparently studied human nature to good purpose where he had been. He had a sympathetic heart, Hilary was sure, and—perhaps a small thing by comparison and yet important in its own way—a naturally deep, fine, resonant voice. In addition to all other considerations, and in a way topping them, was Adams' acquaintance with and admiration for Grandy. That would be a sound bond between them.

At the end of an hour Hilary made a quick decision. I'm going to take a chance on Aunt Samantha, he thought. This man's qualities will surely outweigh any difficulties with her, and I'm going to speak out right now.

"Mr. Adams," he said, "I'm desperately in need of an assistant. I believe you and I would be congenial and could work together. Would you consider coming to St. Matthews in that capacity?"

He was completely unprepared for the effect on the man before him. Adams stared at him, his face slowly turning white and rigid. He said nothing. At last he rose and walked to the window. He stood, his back to Hilary, looking down at the court, still without speaking.

"You may not be interested at all," Hilary went on, embarrassed. "I have rather blurted out the suggestion, and you will want time to think it over. We can go into it more in detail tomorrow if you care to—the salary, etc."

Adams turned at last. His face was still an anguished white. He looked like a drowning man disappearing for the third time.

"I can't thank you enough for the offer. There is nothing I should like so much to do as to accept. But for certain reasons I cannot."

Before the sharp tragedy of his face the words sounded blunt and almost casual. Hilary's respect for him deepened.

"If, knowing the possible reasons for your refusal, I still begged you to accept, would that change your attitude?" Hilary asked slowly, looking down at his desk.

Adams' voice was tense.

"Has Forrest talked to you?"

"Yes."

"He told you—everything?"

"Everything. I repeat, I hope you will come to St. Matthews."

Adams turned again to the window. Hilary guessed he was struggling for control. He himself had a hot sense of shame and indecency as though he were looking at a man's naked soul.

At last Adams came back and sat down. His eyes were wet.

"To serve here at St. Matthews with you would be to me the greatest possible joy. And for myself, since you evidently know my—disability, I would accept at once. But there is still the question of whether my wife would care for city life."

He spoke slowly, with meticulous respect for her, Hilary noted.

"You see, she has been accustomed to the work of small-town and rural parishes. She might not— There is a great difference, you know. Perhaps we should wait until you meet her, and then we can all talk it over."

He was leaving them all a loophole, Hilary saw, and liked him for it.

"Good. I have a dinner engagement tonight, and no doubt you are busy too; but if you could drop in tomorrow afternoon at this time I'll be delighted to meet Mrs. Adams. Wouldn't you like to have a look around the building? You should see what you're getting into before you decide, you know."

When they had completed their survey of the Parish House they returned to the church. Hilary turned on the chancel lights and together they stood looking up at the altar. Forrest's music came to them softly like the brushing of angels' wings. Hilary held his breath in sudden fear, but Adams did not fail him. He remained silent. No casual secularity, no fatuous exclamations of beauty. When the moment was passed, Hilary said goodbye quietly and left. There was no doubt about it, Adams was a man to his liking if the wife did not upset the calculations. I would put up with a good deal of Samantha, Hilary found himself muttering with a smile, for the sake of Samuel.

That night he was to dine at the Breckenridges'. It was a thrice post-poned event giving it to Hilary in advance a warmed over effect. Besides this, he was afraid of this meeting with Lex's aged relatives, spinster and bachelor, Miss Hettie and Mr. Edward. He had been at the point of asking Mrs. McColly for some advice the day before but had thought better of it. So, armed now with nothing more encouraging than old Mrs. Reed's early comment and Lex's recent one, he set out for the house, which he found ponderously elegant and dark, throwing a prophetic shadow over the evening.

Miss Hettie, spare, aquiline, patrician, rose to greet him from a tall chair by the fireside. It was not only that her skinny hands were icy, there was a sort of frozen virginity about her whole person, reminding Hilary of a stone effigy. Her brother was a small man, evidently dominated completely by her—the White Rabbit, as Lex always referred to him. Any moment, Hilary thought to himself, he will say: "Oh, my ears and whiskers! How late it's getting!" So pleased was he by this idea that he did not quite catch Miss Hettie's remark.

"I beg your pardon," he said hastily.

"I was saying that your rectorship though brief so far has been marked by very distinguished success."

"I appreciate your feeling so."

"I trust, as time goes on, this success will mount. Those of us who have been pewholders in St. Matthews for thirty years and more, naturally hold her interests very close to our hearts."

"Naturally," Hilary echoed, feeling uncomfortably that this was a lead-up to something.

Dinner progressed, in spite of all his own efforts, with an exchange of chilly banalities. Underneath, he felt Miss Hettie's penetrating eye upon him as though she were studying his very skeleton structure. Something about him, he felt sure, did not please her in spite of her praise. He tried to engage her brother's attention; but Mr. Edward deferred constantly to his sister.

At last, back in the drawing room (where the chariot wheels of conversation had still dragged heavily) shortly before Hilary took his leave, the bombshell dropped.

"I believe," Miss Hettie said with measured calm, "that you are acquainted with my great-niece, Alexa McColly."

Hilary was so completely taken back that for a moment he could not reply; then he felt himself flushing like a schoolboy.

"I am, indeed," he managed to reply. "I've known Lex for two years."

There was a dead pause. Into it he injected at random, "I think she is the most beautiful girl I have ever met."

This, at least, he felt would be a suitable and safe admission.

Miss Hettie allowed it to sink into the heavy silence for a moment and then uttered her own pronouncement.

"Alex is a spoiled, turbulent, selfish, willful girl. She's been indulged since she was born. She goes with a crowd of young people who think of nothing but cocktail parties and night clubs. I am sure you and she could have nothing in common."

Hilary felt hot with anger. If it had been a stranger speaking he would have lashed out violently in defense of his beloved. But he restrained himself. There was danger here. Somehow the old lady suspected the truth about him and Lex.

"Outward behavior is often misleading," he said crisply. "You knew Lex was abroad at the present?"

"I did. We have no intercourse with the McCollys, but I usually hear the news of the family from outsiders. I still would like to suggest to you that, by the very nature of a clergyman's office, even his friendships are subject to comment. I'm sure as time goes on yours will bear the closest scrutiny."

"I trust so," Hilary replied shortly, then very firmly changed the subject, chatted for a few minutes with outward amiability and took his leave.

He was deeply disturbed. Miss Hettie's sharp remarks had been meant as a warning, he felt sure. Why, the insufferable, meddlesome old harpy! How dared she with no real acquaintance with Lex say what she had said? He wished now he had stood up to it firmly like a man. He feared he had pussyfooted the whole attack. His instinctive reaction, however, had been the protection of their relationship by his silence. If news of any violent outbreak over her between him and Miss Hettie got around, it might even be the last straw to convince Lex their marriage would be fatal to his career. No, on second thought, he believed he had done wisely, though it had been a hard pill to swallow. He wondered, though, how many other people in the parish suspected his friendship with Lex. Not many, he was sure. During the time he had come on from Chicago to see her, he was in the city for one night only. And because they had so much to say to each other they usually spent the one precious evening in the McCollys' living room, after dinner here or there. They had never, as he recalled it, run into any St. Matthews people whom he had now come to know. And Lex, he had reason to believe, had not discussed him much with her own friends.

"I can't kid about you, Hil," she had said once. "You've been too serious from the start."

So, if their engagement was ever actually announced, it would come as a complete surprise to most of the parish. He would have to tell the vestry first, of course, out of courtesy. But in a church such as St. Matthews the main requirement in the rector's wife would be that she must be socially eligible, and Lex qualified for that. Even old Hettie, however disapproving, could not deny that on one side of the family at least, she was of the city's blood royal. Which thought brought him sharply up against the problem of Samantha Adams.

It remained uppermost in his mind all the next morning. Toward three he found himself listening for the arrival of his callers, and suddenly, before they had reached the study, he heard them. At least he heard Samantha. Her strong, positive voice found intervening space no barrier.

"There's really no reason, Sammy, why we can't get a new chancel window for our church! Let's just look round while we're here and get ideas. I'll start right in when I go back and talk to the Women's Society about it. We can use the Bazaar money for a starter."

He hasn't told her anything yet, Hilary thought with surprise. He's waiting until I meet her!

The voice continued all the way up the stairs, growing stronger all the time. Then Miss Mowbray opened the door and ushered in the guests.

Adams' face was very pale. He looked like a man who had put in a sleepless night.

"My wife, Mr. Laurens," he said.

Samantha advanced with smiling confidence. She was short and plump and dumpy. Her dress was long, her shoes utilitarian. Her face was round under the gray hair, and her bright, dark eyes looked through round shell-rimmed glasses. She was bounded entirely by curved lines and she was completely and heartily at ease.

"Well, Mr. Laurens, I'm very glad to meet you face to face, for Matt Forrest has certainly talked enough about you. He's young, isn't he, Sammy, to have a church like this? You look younger than I'd pictured you, even. Sam and I here are sort of getting on, but, as I always tell him, you're just as old as you feel."

"That's right," Hilary returned. "How do you like the city, Mrs. Adams?"

"Scares me to death! I don't see how people stand it to live here. Now I like a little town where you know everybody and where you can have a garden and neighbors running in and all. As I always say, them that like the city can have it, but give me the country!"

"Mr. Forrest tells me you take quite an active part in your church work there."

"Yes," Samantha said with a certain complacence, "I've always tried to hold up my end as well as I could. Keeps me busy, too, with the Altar Guild and the Ladies' Aid and calls on the shut-ins, and I do all my own work. Sammy, don't let me forget to send a card to old Mrs. Holmes.

I nearly missed her. She's a Methodist," she added, turning to Hilary, "but as I always say, we're all one in Christ. I try to send cards to all the town's sick when we're away. It pleases them."

Hilary leaned forward. "Mrs. Adams," he began, "one thing that weighs heavily on my mind just now is this tenement district just back of the church. I want to do something for those people. You are a woman. What would be your approach to a tired, slatternly young mother with three little children at her heels, and two dirty rooms for a home? I saw that scene with my own eyes last week. Suppose you called at a place like that, what would you say to such a woman? In the name of the Lord, I mean," he added smiling.

Samantha Adams' round face concentrated upon the problem. She pursed her lips. There was written upon her the plain common sense of long generations of small-town women.

"Well," she stated in her unmodulated voice, "I'd say to her, 'You get yourself dressed and get out and get some fresh air, and I'll take care of the children for you.' And then I'd clean the place up while she was gone, and if there was anything in the house to cook I'd cook up a little supper and have it ready when she'd come back. As a matter of fact," she said, adjusting her horn-rimmed glasses, "it might be a good idea to take a soup bone along under your arm. You know, Mr. Laurens, what a lot of people don't realize is that you can make a very good dinner out of a *soup bone*. Stew, with dumplings. You wouldn't believe it. Well, that's what I'd do if that woman was in *my* parish."

Hilary glanced at Adams. His face was not pale now, it was scarlet. He returned to Samantha.

"You like people, don't you?"

The expansive kindliness of her face seemed to fill the room.

"Oh, my, yes! As I always say, the Lord never made a person I couldn't take to my heart if I had to."

Hilary rose and stood before her.

"Mrs. Adams," he said, "I think your husband has kept something as a surprise for you. I'm going to tell you now, and I hope very much you may feel as he does about it. I asked him yesterday to come to St. Matthews as assistant rector."

Samantha's reaction was as startling as Adams' own had been. She stared disbelievingly up at Hilary, her eyes enormous behind their frames.

"No!" she said. "No, you can't mean it! I've dreamed it so often, that Sammy would get his big chance. You've asked him *here* to St. Matthews?"

"Yes. I want him very much, if you would both be satisfied to come."

"Satisfied! Oh, Sam, how often have I told you it would come! I've never given up praying. All through the years, you know, I haven't. And now it's happened!"

Suddenly her face fell, as she looked toward her husband piteously. Hilary read the signs at once and fended off the spoken word.

"I've just remembered something," he said. "I've got to go out for a short time. You two stay here as long as you want, and talk things over. Then you can let me know tomorrow. I think we can make the matter of salary satisfactory."

He shook hands warmly with them both and left precipitately.

I know I'm taking big chances, he told himself as he walked along the street, but for once I'm going to play my hunch. Then he glanced toward the tenements and smiled. She'll be showing every woman there how to make a good dinner out of a soup bone before she's been here a month, he thought.

The next day it was all settled. The salary was named and accepted. Miss Mowbray would do the preliminary apartment hunting in the suburbs for them. They would try to wind up their present work and start in at St. Matthews in September. While Adams was consulting with Miss Mowbray in her office, Hilary spoke frankly to Samantha.

"You may be lonely here. You won't have neighbors of the sort you are used to. Your work will not be with the Woman's Society or the Altar Guild. There are plenty of women who can do that. I need you and want you to help with the Parish House. I do so hope you'll be happy doing that."

She looked at him earnestly.

"I will be. But that wouldn't matter. It's only Sam that counts. He's never had a church worthy of him, and I've never understood why. Even years ago, for some reason he never seemed—I mean things would start up and just when we'd think there was going to be a call, it would all fall through. I think it's because Sam doesn't put his best foot forward. He needs someone else to speak up for him, just like Matt Forrest did now to you. My, you don't know what this will mean to Sam! And this I will say for him. Even when he's had small churches he's kept up with his books. Such a reader! He always was a born student. Well, as I've always said, 'God moves in a mysterious way his wonders to perform.' We've waited a long time, but you've given Sam and I our big opportunity at last."

Hilary could feel Adams wincing through the years at Samantha's lapses in English, but her face as she looked up at him now was bathed in a love purely selfless.

Hilary's calendar for the week was moving steadily on toward the vestry dinner meeting on Friday night, but in between were two more engagements to which he did not look forward with joy. Dinner with the J. V. Dunns on Wednesday night turned out, however, to be quite different in atmosphere from that of the Breckenridges. Indeed there was a lushness of warmth in his reception that somewhat startled him. J. V.'s nose looked less long and beaked as he talked and his frost-bitten New England countenance thawed in smiles. His sister, too, was almost embarrassingly cordial in her welcome. The daughter, Maudie, tricked out in a very bright dinner dress, put in frequent nervous little comments which usually trailed off into nothing before they were finished. As dinner progressed Hilary saw that the great light on J. V.'s face came as he looked from Maudie to him and back again to his daughter. Great Jupiter, he thought, there's something here I've got to watch out for.

J. V., without apparently having been born to social grace, still did a most masterly job as host. He talked well, not omitting to slip in here and there veiled references to business which might carry their own weight. He made it easy for Hilary to talk. He even drew Miss Dunn into the conversation. Only Maudie was allowed to sit quiet except for her little sentences which began and ended nowhere. After leisurely coffee, however, the pattern of the evening began to take form. J. V. rose with what was evidently a great attempt at casual apology.

"I wonder if you would excuse me if I go up to my study for a few minutes. I've had a most peculiar headache today. Maybe just a cold coming on—so sorry to miss any part of your visit."

Miss Dunn got up at once.

"I'll go with you and get you an aspirin. These spring colds are not to be trifled with. You'll forgive us, won't you, Mr. Laurens? We'll be down a little later."

When they were gone, to Hilary's surprise and alarm he saw Maudie's pale blue eyes suffuse with tears. He did not pretend to ignore it.

"What is the matter, Miss Dunn?" he asked kindly.

She made a little gesture of despair.

"I'm not going to put up any pretense with you. You can see for yourself how it is. This matter of getting me married has come to be a perfect obsession with Father. He wants it so desperately. He invites to dinner every eligible young man he comes across. And his standards are high, let me tell you! No fortune hunters. Then he and Auntie always have to be excused to leave us alone. Oh, I think sometimes I'd rather die than be so humiliated."

She stopped to mop her eyes but rushed on. Hilary noticed with amazement that her sentences were coming clear-cut and complete, and that the small twitchings of her face had ceased. The girl wasn't bad-looking when she was in control of herself, though rather anemic and negative.

"I have to make this all plain to you, for I want to go to church and not feel ashamed to look at you. It's all Father's doing, whatever happens, not mine."

Hilary spoke quickly now. "You can feel perfectly free with me, Miss Dunn, for I'm terribly in love with a girl whom I hope some day to marry. I'd like to be your friend, though. Maybe sometime I could be of help to you."

"You are already, for I've never come out with this before to a human soul. It helps just to confess that I'm desperate. I'm not attractive. I know it. I'm not good-looking, and I haven't any poise or self-control. I sort of go to pieces each time I'm with a man. I get tongue-tied. I twitch. I'm scared to death, for I know I'm a failure. But I'm twenty-seven and Father—"

The tears came again. "I'm so sorry for Father. I've been an awful disappointment, and if I never— Do you mind my talking on in this way?"

"Please do," Hilary said. Somehow he felt deeply moved by the girl's strange tragedy. With the intuitive sympathy which was a part of him he saw clearly the whole drama.

"I wanted to go to college. I would have loved that. But no. Father wouldn't hear of it. I had to go to Miss Hestor's classes, and then have a big coming-out party. It cost a fortune, but it was ghastly. I think every girl there had a wonderful time but me. Boys scared me stiff even then, before I got into this state I'm in now. At the dances then the boys were always getting stuck with me. They used money. You remember how that worked? Well, I was a five-dollar girl. It took that much to buy a cut-in. That's me."

Maudie leaned her head on her hands. Hilary spoke quickly.

"Couldn't you try to put this out of your mind—marriage and men? You know the old saying, 'Flee love and it will follow you.' Maybe it would work that way with you. You certainly aren't unattractive when you control yourself. You are honest and intelligent and kind. If you could only forget—"

"But how can I? When Father finds you aren't interested in me he'll bring some one else. He'll *never* give up. You don't know Father! You see it's not just that he wants to see me married. He wants an heir."

Maudie flushed, but she went on. "There has to be an heir for all the damned money. Excuse me, but that's the way I feel about it. If we were poor I'd be a happier person."

"What you need is a job!" Hilary said emphatically.

Maudie's pale eyes lighted. "Yes, I know. I'd love it. I even envy the elevator girls in department stores. But Father wouldn't hear of it. It would mean breaking completely with him. I haven't got the courage and, besides, I'm sorry for him. Church or charity work is all he'll let me do."

"We're going to get the Parish House running again by fall, and I'll see you get plenty to do there. Meanwhile, if it's any help, you can always talk to me. I'm glad you've told me what you have tonight."

Before Maudie could reply, they heard the elder Dunns coming down the stairs.

Maudie spoke very low, her nervousness returning.

"Tickets," she whispered. "Next step."

J. V. was smiling broadly as he returned. "I just remembered," he said after they had all talked for an hour, "that I've got tickets for this new show, *Farthingale,* for two weeks from tonight and I can't make it. Got an engagement. I wonder, Mr. Laurens, if you'd care to take my place? I know Maudie and her aunt would be very grateful, and so would I."

It sounded like a royal command. Hilary was uncertain what to do.

"That's very kind. May I let you know after I look at my calendar? And now, I fear I must be going. It's been a delightful evening."

He got through the farewells as quickly as possible. He had time to note the change in Maudie, however, under her father's scrutiny. Her voice broke again into nebulous little phrases; her lips twitched; her hands were nervous. Plainly, he thought as he drove back to the rectory, a most interesting case for a psychiatrist. He would make a note of this and see if he could do something for the girl.

The next afternoon at five he found himself being borne upward in the beige and chrome elevator to Diana Downes' beige and chrome penthouse. She received him in a soft rose silk affair, frothy with lace. Hilary assumed it was meant to be a hostess gown, but he recognized uncomfortably that it missed being a negligee by a very small margin. The tea table was set before the wide window overlooking the city, and he had to admit that she made a striking picture as she faced him there in the late afternoon light. Her satiny black hair was again brushed smoothly from her forehead to a cluster of curls at the back. He was struck by the beauty of her small ears, and the general delicacy of her features. She looked like a Rossetti painting.

When she leaned over to pour the tea, however, Hilary jerked his eyes away quickly and fixed his gaze across the room.

"That's a fine picture of Capri," he said in a cool and matter-of-fact voice.

He fancied a surprised annoyance in her own.

"Oh, that! Just a little thing I picked up once when I was over there."

Hilary decided to take the situation firmly in hand.

"I'm sorry to have to be rather in a rush today. I hope to have my time organized a little better later on. Won't you tell me at once about the books I sent you? Were they of any help?"

Diana set down her cup. Her slim figure seemed to slump. Her large eyes became darkly tragic.

"I've tried so hard," she said, pitifully. "For a time the books helped. I read the passages you had marked night and morning. I repeated to myself constantly the advice you gave me when you were here last. Then everything seemed futile. I lost my grip again. It's the feeling of being utterly alone in the world, of having no one close who really cares. That's what undoes me. Of late I've felt so desperate at times that I've almost— I mean I've been afraid . . ."

She left the sentence ominously in mid-air.

Hilary's natural faith in humankind rose again within him. What a cad he would be to impute motives to this woman which she might never have had! Perhaps she was actually in danger. He bent himself earnestly to the task of helping her, pouring out his warm sympathy unstintedly upon her. Slowly, as a wilting flower revives, she drew herself erect. Her dark eyes began to shine.

"You seem to give me a reason for living. You give me courage and hope again. I'll try to follow all your advice. If only—" She hesitated.

"If only what?"

"If only I may occasionally talk with you as I would to a doctor. I suppose you are indeed a physician of souls, aren't you? Will you be in the city during the summer?"

"Most of it. I have so much to do."

"I plan to be here a great deal, too. It seems less lonely than the country, though I'll open the house there for week ends. So if I can report to you from time to time I think it will help me from getting so very low again. Do you know, I don't like that secretary at the church."

"Miss Mowbray? Why not?"

"She seems so mechanical. So devoid of sympathy. I've called up several times and I went over to the study once when I was completely desperate, but she insisted each time you were out!"

"I doubtless was."

"Did you get my telephone messages?"

"No, I didn't." Hilary hated to admit it, for it seemed to incriminate Miss Mowbray.

"I knew it!" Diana was triumphant. "I felt certain you would have gotten in touch with me before this if you had received them. But you can understand now why I disapprove of your secretary."

"I'm sure there was some sort of mistake," Hilary said carefully, "but I'll mention it to her."

He took his leave, releasing his hand this time as quickly as possible, and made his way home, still puzzled and uncomfortable.

The next morning he spoke to Miss Mowbray. It was a close, muggy day and her white blouse looked as cool as snow. She was the *cleanest*-looking woman, he decided, that he had ever seen.

"Yesterday," he began, "I received my first criticism of you as a secretary."

Her wide gray eyes looked up, startled, into his.

"A certain Mrs. Diana Downes said that she had called me a number of times and suspected I never received the messages. I had to admit I had not. What have you to say?"

A faint flush rose in Miss Mowbray's cheeks, but her lips parted in a half-smile.

"Guilty," she said.

"I think you'd better tell me all you know, hadn't you?"

She hesitated. "The trouble is, my reasons would never stand in court. I don't honestly *know* anything about Mrs. Downes. But I've heard a few rumors and I used my own intuition. My guess is that she might be a somewhat unscrupulous woman. Each time she called you really were out. But I'll not take things into my own hands again, I promise." Her face looked earnest and troubled.

"It's just that now when you are new and feeling your way I wanted to spare you any unnecessary complications."

Hilary grinned. "You felt I would be inadequate to cope with this particular type?"

"Now, you are being nasty," she said. And suddenly they laughed together. But Hilary took careful note of the incident.

On the evening of the specially called meeting of the vestry, Hilary felt nervous. Eight men out of the ten had accepted for dinner. Morris was in his element, the big library and dining room were both graciously correct and welcoming, but still Hilary wished as he dressed that he had held the meeting in the study. If there should be tension it might be less embarrassing to have it there.

When the guests arrived, Hilary was struck first of all by the general urbanity of the group. They were all highly successful business and professional men, conventional in their attitudes and behavior. He had a wild wish for one blunt Alex McColly amongst them who would state his opinions with forthright and even profane conviction. These men were not so. They would be reserved, unfailingly courteous even in disapproval and strong with the power drawn from position and experience.

He welcomed them now, though, cordially: Cole, to whom he felt close already; Avison and Thornton, who were also definitely his friends; Henry Alvord, who would unquestionably oppose everything he was planning to say tonight; old Judge Ball, whom he knew slightly as yet but greatly admired; and three others who from the first had seemed to him rather negligible—Hartley, Powers, and Weston.

To his surprise the talk at dinner turned upon the same fears Alex McColly had voiced. The word "war" was tossed back and forth around the table. Would it come? Had Chamberlain failed? Would England call Hitler's bluff? Should she, or should she let Europe fight it out herself? What the United States had to do this time, however, was to keep well out of it, that was certain.

Judge Ball raised his heavy voice.

"That sort of talk seems to me foolish. Whether we like it or not, we stand or fall with England. We may love her or hate her or be indifferent to her but our destiny as the English-speaking peoples of the world lies together."

A storm of argument was at once under way. Hilary listened, amazed and alarmed. So deeply engrossed had he been with the affairs of the church that he had given scant attention to the seething problems beyond the sea. Now, suddenly, he felt as though all his own plans, looming so large in his mind, had become dwarfed before the death throes of nations. He talked little, drawing out his guests. The food was excellent, and Morris' service beyond all comparison. He could see the men relaxing and mellowing as the meal progressed.

Back in the library with the tobacco smoke making a genial haze, Hilary took his stand before the fireplace, one elbow leaning on the mantel.

"It may be the preacher complex, but I feel I can best say what I want to say on my feet," he began. "I've been here at St. Matthews now for three months. I want to say first of all that I have already grown to love the church and to feel that I belong to the parish. You have all made me welcome and I deeply appreciate it. Now, tonight, I'm eager to consult with you about some of the plans I would like to put into effect. And please feel free to break this up into a discussion at any point."

He paused and the men settled more comfortably into their chairs.

"I have three things on my mind," he went on. "First, the Sunday afternoon vesper service, second the general aim of the Parish House work, and third, what I shall call the gallery congregation. I shall try to be brief about each. As to the vesper services, I have a big ideal. The audience for these seems now to have dwindled to a handful of the faithful who have probably been at morning worship too. Now, I would like to build up a service of such beauty and distinction that it would attract that part of the cultured city group who are entirely outside the church. There would be Forrest's music, of course, and I would try to give a straightforward, honest, ten-minute talk. In short, I would definitely angle for the intellectual type. The University is within easy reach, and the Law School and the Medical College. There is a field here which I think goes undeveloped. I should like to reach it."

There was silence for a moment, then Judge Ball said in his deliberate, husky voice: "I, for one, will back you in this project to the best of my ability. No one knows better than I do what a flood of godless young intellectuals are abroad in this city. At least they think they are intellectuals, and they want to be thought godless. More than that I could name right now a score of older professional men, lawyers and doctors, brilliant men, who never darken a church door. Either they've never felt any need of the church or they believe that all parsons preach twaddle. If you can interest them and their type you will have done something exciting."

"You would not expect the regular membership then to attend these services?" Henry Alvord asked with an edge in his tone.

"Of course," Hilary replied smiling. "All who cared to come. I would like to see the church packed at vespers and I believe it is a not impossible goal."

There was a little more unimportant discussion, then Thornton said emphatically, "I think we're all with you on this plan. Let's go on to the next."

"Fine," said Hilary. "The plans for the Parish House have given me great concern. There are two ways of looking at a church plant such as we have here. We can view it as another social settlement or we can consider it a practical gateway into the church itself. I incline to this latter view."

He paused. The men were looking back at him with a puzzled expression.

"Let me make this clear. I've gone over all the records of work done here for three years back. Though the Parish House is not a large one, the number of activities is imposing. So is the number of participants. But I fail to find more than a handful of these who ever had any connection with the church itself. I've checked with Father Connelly down at St. Mary's and with Rabbi Hershman at the Synagogue on Second Street. I find that a great many of the young folks who danced or bowled at St. Matthews' Parish House Saturday night went to Mass the next morning at St. Mary's or belong to Rabbi Hershman's flock. Many of them, of course, had no connection with any church."

"I think, Mr. Laurens, you are here showing a surprising narrowness in your attitude toward the service a Parish House is meant to render." It was Alvord again.

"No," Hilary said firmly, "I don't think I am. I would actually deny no one the use of the house. But I should make it clear that we hoped each person using it would use the church also."

"How could that be?" Alvord was sharp.

"It is an ideal, I'll admit, but one I think we should strive for. I should like to see the young folks who use the house coming eventually to be confirmed. I should like to have these people, both young and old, feel that their connection with St. Matthews does not stop at the wall separating Parish House from Church. I would want to marry them, baptize their babies, bury their dead, but most of all give them communion."

Hilary had expected discussion but he had not been prepared for the violence of it. Even the three negligibles said their say emphatically, siding, Hilary was quick to note, with Alvord. The Parish House was supported by the Church but quite apart from it. Each served different types of people in different ways. This arrangement was practical and logical and should not be tampered with.

At last Mr. Cole begged a hearing.

"I think the question resolves itself to this: are we bound to regard the work of the Parish House as humanitarian but purely secular, or may we infuse it all with a spiritual purpose? As Mr. Laurens says, could we not use it as a definite gateway into the church itself? I agree with this attitude."

Before anyone else could speak Hilary began again quickly.

"My third plan is in a way related to the second. I can state it briefly. St. Matthews is a large church, employing the pew rental system. The only actual 'free' pews are in the gallery. I've gone over this section carefully with Hastings. The gallery is capable of seating two hundred people. I feel, by the very location of the church, that we have a responsibility toward the tenement section just behind us. I made a personal canvass of three cheap apartment houses there and discovered that not one Protestant family in them goes to church anywhere. I want to try to get some of them to come to St. Matthews and seat them in the gallery. Are there any objections?"

He had spoken so swiftly that for a second no one seemed ready to reply. There was a faint murmur of assent from several of the men and then Alvord cleared his throat. His eyes looked lowering and his whole face showed tension and anxiety.

"Now just a minute," he said. "You are a young man, Mr. Laurens, and quite naturally carried away by the romantic fervor of wanting to meet all the needs of the world. But one person or one institution can't do that. St. Matthews, as I once pointed out to you, has for a hundred years served a certain type of people. It is designed and organized for this particular service. The fact that its membership is comfortably well off doesn't mean that they don't need religion; that they don't marry and die and need benefit of clergy. Now how many members have we at the moment on the roll?"

"Eighteen hundred and twenty," Hilary answered.

"Good. Don't you think that's enough to keep you busy? Along with the regular work of the Parish House such as always has been done? In other words, can you adequately serve more than that number of people as a pastor? Even granting you have soon the help of at least one assistant, would it not take the full time of two men to do the work of this parish properly without trying to add an extraneous one?"

He stopped and they all sat facing Hilary with the question in their eyes.

Hilary looked back at them. "I want to be honest with you," he said. "This question which Mr. Alvord has just asked is the very one I've been asking myself. There is enough work in any large parish to keep two or three men busy all the time, and I can only assure you that I shall devote myself day and night to that task. But no church can ever be too full. And we have, as I see it, an obligation toward those less fortunate than ourselves which, busy or not, we must try to fulfill. Gentlemen, I should like your full and sympathetic support in my efforts to bring into this so-called gallery congregation those around us here who desperately need what the church has to offer."

There were a few voices of assent. Once again Cole spoke in agreement, but it was clear that Alvord was displeased and a perceptible tension hung in the air.

"I have one other matter of great importance to mention," Hilary said. "I have just this week engaged an assistant, the Reverend Samuel Adams, now rector of a church in a small town in upper New York State. He is a man older than I am, which will be, I feel, a great asset. He has a pleasing personality, a fine voice for services, and a cultured mind. He's an old friend of Mr. Forrest, which I know you will feel, as I do, is in his favor."

"Did Forrest recommend him to you?" Alvord asked.

"He mentioned him in conversation but the initiative for securing him was entirely my own. I hope you will like him and that he'll work out well. He hopes to be here by September first."

"Married?" Thornton asked.

"Yes, Mrs. Adams is much interested in social service and the plans for the Parish House work. They have no family."

Conversation suddenly switched to salary, apartment renting, and recollections of past assistants, of whom there had been a varied lot. Judging from the comments, Hilary felt he had done well. The men seemed eager now to talk in reminiscent vein. A few anecdotes of Hastings through the years paved the way for other stories, and the evening ended to outward seeming on a light and friendly note. Hilary, though, was not so sure as he shook hands with Alvord. He was more uncertain when after a half-hour the telephone rang; it was Avison.

"Mr. Laurens? I won't keep you long. I know you're tired after bucking us all this evening. Marvellous dinner and fine time all round. Just wanted to drop you a little hint of caution. Alvord—Henry Alvord—holds a pretty important place on the vestry and in the church. He's the largest single contributor, for one thing, as you probably know. Was a great friend of Dr. Partridge. Well now, if I were you I would sort of play along with him as well as you can. When you see he's opposed to something, just be diplomatic. Don't antagonize him. Do you understand? We all want to see you succeed. Thanks again for a fine evening."

Hilary stood there, the feeling of restraint and coercion strong upon him. This, however, was what he must break. Not roughly or with hard violence, but by gentle and cautious indirection. Somehow he must try to win Henry Alvord to his own point of view. To his own soul he would admit once that he didn't like the man and then try to forget it. As to the evening as a whole, he would have felt better about it if the outspoken discussion had run its full course. He realized now that something—or some one—had stopped it. Just when or how, he could not be sure, but it left him with an uncomfortable feeling of deep waters running far beneath the surface. One thing of course he must remember. He had been at St. Matthews only three months; he was young, as city clergymen went; he was just getting his bearings. He must not be too sure of himself, too obdurate. At any point he could be wrong, except one. In his great ideal for the church and its service to mankind he must never give way. Neither to Alvord nor to any other man.

He was starting slowly up the stairs when the telephone rang again. He answered it anxiously, half expecting the voice of another vestryman. Then he gripped the receiver more tightly, bent lower listening, with every nerve and muscle of his body tense. It was a cablegram.

YOU WIN. SAILING JULY FIRST ON THE QUEEN MARY.

LEX

CHAPTER VIII

THERE NEVER HAD been such June days! Even the city bloomed. The small parks were as fresh and green as though no dusty heat would ever blight them. The sky above St. Matthews was clear blue with untouchable white clouds circling the spire like celestial birds. Even the shabby newsstand at the corner was only half noisy headlines now; the other half was flowers. And old Mrs. Milligan, who kept a hole-in-the-wall coffee shop across from the church—where Hilary dropped in at odd times to snatch a cup of coffee when he didn't want to wait for Morris' meticulous service—put clean curtains in the window and a plant on the sill.

One day she leaned over the counter and studied Hilary profoundly.

"There's no use hidin' it," she said, "you're in love as plain as a pike-staff! I've been watchin' you."

"Mrs. Milligan," Hilary returned, "I wouldn't deceive you for the world. Your diagnosis is absolutely correct."

"What's she like?"

"Beautiful! I'll bring her in to meet you some day. You'll see!"

"Well, it's the first time I'm not wishin' you were a good Catholic priest. There'd be no lovin' in your life then, an' that would be a pity for I must say I think your girl's born lucky to get you. How about a piece of pie?"

"No, thanks. I've got to run. How's Mr. Milligan these days?"

"He's workin' at the present, but he'll be takin' his leisure again before I even see the color of his money. That's the way it goes. But before God I'll swear to ye he was the best-lookin' lad in the whole of County Cork an' lifted the natest pair of feet in a dance! It just shows ye never know what you're gettin' into when ye marry. When's your weddin'?"

"Not till fall. I'll let you know. You must come to it."

"*Me?* Come to your weddin'! Lord love ye, if that ain't just like ye! Well, God send her worthy of you!"

Hilary walked quickly down the street, for he was on his way at last to the settlement to meet Miss Barton. On the corner he ran into Mike Flannery, the big policeman. There had been a special bond between them, following the night the rector had found him staggering on his beat and had maneuvered him safely home. Since then Hilary had become, without any volition on his own part, the patron saint of the Flannerys.

"Hello, Mike."

"Hello, your Riverence."

"It's a great day for the Irish."

"Sure, we'll be gladly sharin' it with you!"

"Still on the wagon, Mike?"

Hilary eyed him sharply. Mike rubbed his ruddy face with a heavy fist.

"Well, you might say, your Riverence, I'm runnin' hard to ketch up with it again, anyway."

"Well, see that you do it!"

"I will that, your Riverence."

"How's Mrs. Flannery these days?"

"Well now, I'd say if her tongue was just in as good shape as the rest of her, she'd be all right. Take a tip from me, your Riverence, don't you ever get married!"

Hilary laughed and passed on. In three days Lex would sail, he was thinking. In five more she would land! There never had been such weather, such a season, such a world! There never had been a man so outrageously happy!

The settlement house sprawled for most of a block behind a row of trees and small plots planted with green. It was of faded red brick and had an old friendliness about it. Hilary stood across the street and watched the people who came and went through its several entrances: skipping children, a truck driver, an old woman on a cane, a slender young man with a portfolio, an anxious-looking young mother with a crying baby. He followed the latter through the main doorway and found himself in a large, casually comfortable room in which any one might have felt at ease. The young woman at the desk was probably efficient but she was first of all smiling and kindly in expression.

"I have an appointment to see Miss Barton at three," Hilary said, giving his card.

"Oh, yes. Just walk down that hall to the left and knock on the door at the end."

As simple as that. In another minute the door before him opened and Miss Barton welcomed him in. She was younger-looking in her blue linen than he had expected to find her. There was a light, quick slenderness about her figure too, unusual for middle age. Her graying hair was soft and abundant above the finely cut lines of her features and her expression was eager and animated.

"This is a great pleasure to me, Miss Barton. I've seen you in church, of course."

"But I've never heard you preach! It's too bad, but Sunday is such a busy day for me I can't make it. Sit here, won't you? This window always catches the breeze when there is one."

Hilary realized now that he was in a luxuriously beautiful room—the last thing he had expected here. The green carpet was lush to the foot, the chintz flowered divans were large and deep, the choice old mahogany waxed and gleaming. Above the fireplace two Dresden candelabra were reflected in what must be a priceless antique mirror. Each place his eye fell a new object of beauty met his gaze.

"I always feel it's best to explain this room at once," Miss Barton said now, her eyes twinkling at his embarrassed expression.

"I find it indescribably lovely," Hilary said.

"I like it myself. This is the way it happened. My predecessor, a remarkable woman, by the way, had this place furnished with cast-off odds and ends. Perfectly awful. She felt it was wrong for her own surroundings to be beautiful in the midst of such poverty all around. I felt differently. I was planning to spend the rest of my life here. I knew I would often be worn to tatters both physically and spiritually. I would need all the refreshment I could get. So I brought all these things from my old home and furnished my rooms just as I would have had them up town. And they've saved me from despair many a time."

"I can easily imagine it."

"But they've served much more than that purpose," she went on earnestly. "I use them as I can for my people here. Sometimes I pick out a few women who need a special kind of a lift and have them here to tea. Do it up brown, you know. Make it very swell. They love it. To them it seems like the movies. It gives them something different to think about."

Hilary was watching her bright, mobile face, fascinated.

"And now and then we have young people who I can see are definitely on their way up. I have them here, one by one, and teach them how things are done socially. We have one of our girls now studying for Grand Opera. Isn't that wonderful? Well, right here, I showed her how to use a finger bowl and how to eat an artichoke. It all helps. So, I feel happy in what seems like my unjustified luxury. Now tell me about you and your work. How's it going?"

When the little Dresden clock on the mantel struck four, Hilary jumped.

"I never knew an hour to go so fast! I apologize for staying so long. The worst of it is that I've just thought of something more I want very much to say. Could you use here a young woman with too much money and too little to do who longs for a job?"

He sketched with reticence the problem of Maudie Dunn.

"Could I use her?" Miss Barton echoed. "If she isn't afraid to work and would even add a contribution occasionally, she'd be a gift from heaven!"

"I'll tell her then to get in touch with you as soon as she's back in town this fall. You could try her out, at least. And now I must go, but may I come back soon and often?"

"Please do. I'll help you in any way I can with your Parish House plans. I confess your ideas startled me at first but I believe you may be right. In our work here we don't dare bring religion as such into it. A church parish house should be more than just another settlement, when one thinks of it. I'll be so interested in how you work it out. And meanwhile we'll take care of your Fresh Air problems this summer if you can supply the money. Is that a deal?" she laughed.

"It is, and a great relief to me right now. I'll try to have a good check for you by next week. It's been wonderful meeting you, Miss Barton."

She held his hand firmly as she looked questioningly into his eyes.

"I feel that as time goes on we will have much to say to each other."

"So do I, and thank you for everything."

He went out again into the sunshine feeling that the rich day was still richer for having Celeste Barton in it. There would be a spiritual kinship in their friendship, added to the mutuality of their problems.

He decided to hop a cab and drop in on old Mrs. Reed on his way back. He felt that he had to tell his new happiness to some one face to face or he would burst with it. He had called Dick at once on the telephone and of course Mr. and Mrs. McColly, who had just gone up to Maine. It was decided that Hilary should meet Lex at the ship and then go on up with her to join them for a week. Right now he craved desperately a conversation about nothing but Lex. He got out at the big stone house set in its wide lawn and ran up the steps. He hoped Mrs. Reed had not left town yet. She had mentioned once that she stayed away now only through July and August.

She was home, the butler assured him, and in a moment showed him up to the little Victorian sitting room which he remembered. It was comfortably untidy, reminding Hilary of a worn and much loved book which one could open at random and slip into with relaxed pleasure.

"Well, well," Mrs. Reed exclaimed, rising stiffly from her low rocker, "come in and bring the word of the Lord to me! I certainly need it after reading the editorials these days. What's brewing over in Europe anyway?"

Hilary's smile faded.

"I don't know," he said. "But I can't get too excited over it. I'm confident it won't go too far. Another war seems to me utterly impossible."

"Glad to hear you say that, for it seems the same to me. Now tell me about yourself. Are you all right again?"

"Oh, quite. I have some news though. A big—a tremendous secret. You're the only person I'm telling. Can you cross your heart on it?"

She peered at him with her wise old eyes.

"In love," she said. "It's written all over you. Who is she?"

"You really promise to keep it? I'm very serious about that, for the engagement won't be announced for some weeks probably."

"Of course I'll keep it, and I'm flattered to death that you're telling me. Is it a Chicago girl?"

"No," Hilary smiled, "from right here. It's Alexa McColly."

The old lady stared at him blankly, incredulously, then repeated the name in slow amazement.

"Not Lex McColly?"

"The very same. Do you know her?"

"Do I know her? I've known her since she was born. But I can't believe this! It's incredible!"

"Why?" Hilary asked, somewhat dashed.

"You're actually going to get married?"

"We are."

Mrs. Reed leaned her head back against the chair while a great laugh shook her whole body.

"If I could see Hettie Breckenridge when she finds out about this I'd ask nothing more in this world. Why, this is the biggest shock since Eunice eloped with Alex McColly twenty-five years ago!"

Hilary felt hurt and a little angered. At sight of his face, Mrs. Reed pulled herself together and set about atonement.

"My dear boy," she said, "you must forgive me. You don't know all the old family threads in this town the way I do and I'll admit this is a big surprise. It will be to everybody. You see, Lex is not the type you would ordinarily select for a clergyman's wife. But I'll tell you one thing. She's headstrong as a colt—always has been—but she's as honest and true as the daylight, and that's more than you can say of a lot of them."

She leaned over and patted his arm.

"And she's beautiful enough, God knows, to turn any man's head. I suppose you know she's turned plenty! Well, congratulations from my heart. And now start at the beginning and tell me all."

Somewhat cheered and mollified, Hilary complied. As he talked, Mrs. Reed's face became more and more delighted. She chuckled and looked off into space.

"The more I think about this, Hilary, the better I like it. I'm terribly fond of Lex, always have been. And maybe there are qualifications for a

132

parson's wife better than fasting and prayer. At least the rectory will never be dull with Lex in it. But the way you've both kept this thing a secret beats me! Have you told Hastings yet?"

"Why, no, hardly," said Hilary. "You're the only one I intend to tell until just before the announcement. Then, of course, I'll have to break it to the vestry."

Mrs. Reed was thoughtful. "Listen," she said at last. "If I were you I'd tell Hastings at once. Be sure to make it clear that he knows it before the vestry. You see, he can be nasty if he thinks anything connected with St. Matthews gets done without his knowledge. You really have to humor him. Whatever he may think of Lex later, this will smooth him down."

Hilary laughed. "You're probably right. Thanks for the suggestion. Now I've got to go, but it's done me good to talk to you. I don't like the feeling, though, that this is going to be too big a bombshell for Miss Hettie Breckenridge. She found out somehow that I've been seeing Lex, for she gave me a veiled warning the night I was there to dinner."

"Oh, she did!" Mrs. Reed's lips snapped close. "Well, if she tries to make any real trouble for you, I'll do what I've wanted to do for forty years."

She elucidated no further, and Hilary was afraid to question.

"Are you still at cross purposes over the Orphanage problems?"

"Oh, yes. She's president of the Trustees, and when she doesn't want action she just doesn't call a meeting. But I'm going to force one soon. Meanwhile, run in and see the boys when you can. They like you. I knew they would. And now congratulations again for you and Lex, and God bless you both!"

To his surprise she drew his head down and kissed him, and there were tears in her eyes. He held her to him tenderly, realizing how empty his life was of the love which a mother would have given him, and that this kiss had fallen like gentle rain upon a barren spot of his heart.

"Thank you," he said huskily, and because his own eyes were misty, he left without more words.

During the next week he tried desperately to cover all his necessary duties. He had a strange feeling of absolute demarcation between his life up until the moment he saw Lex at the ship and his life after. Perhaps not even marriage itself would set so fast a division in time, as this moment of meeting, to which now all his thoughts, all his senses were projected. Because of this, therefore, he instinctively strove to catch up the loose threads, to bring what might be finished to conclusion, and to leave nothing of importance undone. It was almost as a man might prepare for death itself, he kept thinking, by setting his house in order.

He called again on the most critically ill and the bereaved. He visited the Orphanage. He had three baptisms. He lunched with Henry Alvord one day, exerting every power he possessed to sell himself and his plans. He was conscious again of failure, but he would keep on trying. He talked with Francine Avery on the telephone and reassured himself that she was taking hold of life firmly. To his astonishment she told him she had decided to give up her night-club work and enter nurse's training at St. Luke's Hospital. Hilary made a note to let Shane know she was there, and also to suggest that they postpone their dinner party till fall since the weeks now had been so full.

He called on Mary and Joe McComb. Joe had lost his job and Mary was going to have a baby. He left them enough money from his discretionary fund to tide them over the next month. Joe was hopeful of a new job by then.

He had declined J. V. Dunn's invitation to the theater, but he wrote Maudie at their summer address of the opportunity for doing regular work at the Varny Street Settlement. "It would be like a job," he explained. "Regular hours and all that, but without pay. I feel sure your father will approve. Keep it in your mind during the summer."

That, he felt, would give her something to think about.

He told Hastings his secret with elaborate confidence. Hastings listened with mouth wide open, then assumed a judicial attitude.

"None of the vestry know about it yet?"

"Not one."

"Told Miss Mowbray?"

"No."

Hastings nodded. "That's right. When it comes to a matter like this, don't trust strangers with it. Alex McColly's daughter, eh?"

"That's the one."

"How'll the Breckenridges take it? They raised stink enough when this girl's mother eloped. I mind it as well as if it was yesterday. Miss Eunice never dared stick her nose back in this church the way Miss Hettie carried on. She raised Miss Eunice like she was her own child. Mother dead. The McCollys had to go over to Christ Church. A big letdown after St. Matthews, I can tell you. Now, I s'pose that's where you'll have to be married." His tone was mournful in the extreme.

"No, we thought we'd like the wedding here since it's my own church."

Hastings could never be said actually to smile, but brightness flickered over his rocky countenance and was gone.

"Well, that's good. I'll take care of everything then. Well, we'll wait an' see how this works out. By fall, if you're feeling the same way, then mebbe you'd better just go ahead with it."

Hilary returned Hastings' gaze with a perfectly straight face.

"You think so?"

"Yes. Might as well get married once you're set on a girl. No good puttin' it off too long. Pigs are apt to run through it, as the sayin' goes. You say early fall you're thinkin' of?"

"The end of September probably."

Hastings considered and then nodded his head. "I think I can be ready by then. I'll want to give this whole place the cleanin' of its life. Yes, I think mebbe end of September would suit me all right."

Like a man in a fever Hilary pushed through the last intervening days. He dropped in at Mr. Pettigrew's office a moment, the rest of the family, he had discovered, having left home for the summer. Mr. Pettigrew was frigid at first, but thawed slightly as they talked. The young people were having a perfect honeymoon abroad, though Ted wrote that he didn't like the political look of things over there. For himself, Mr. Pettigrew was sure nothing serious would come of it. Hilary mentioned the matter of the Fresh Air work, and to his surprise and delight Pettigrew gave him a check. As he was leaving, the older man's face relaxed.

"You are feeling better again?" he asked quizzically.

An enormous relief rose in Hilary's breast.

"Quite," he said, "but I was sick enough the day of the wedding!"

Pettigrew held out his hand.

"At least it's good to meet an honest man."

With the arrangement for a theological student to take the services for two Sundays, a few more calls, the transfer of the checks he had gathered for the Fresh Air work, letters to Dick and to old Cousin Mattie in Maryville, Hilary left his study one morning in June, and hurried to the rectory to pack his bag. The ship would dock at two in the afternoon and he wanted to be sure that nothing would make him late. He bade farewell to Morris affectionately. He hated leaving the old soul alone, but Morris was cheerful and full of plans for cleaning the house. Hastings and Miss Mowbray had both promised to look in on him often and see how he did.

With his bag in his hand, Hilary paused in the court, then quietly slipped into the back of the church, stayed for a moment in the dimness, watching the altar with the faint light from the rose window falling on the gold cross and the fair white cloth, bowed his head, then went out quickly into the sunshine.

Oh, the sweet, intolerably joyous pain of those minutes, trembling in time's suspension, before the face comes home at last to the waiting face; the eyes to the hungry eyes; the heart to the craving heart! Before bodies separated by unrelenting space are close again in the warm, undenied touch of reunion!

So Hilary thought as he waited at the pier. When he finally held her close her bright hair lay against his coat, her face hidden. For once she had no gay words.

"Oh, Hil," she whispered, and he knew by her voice that she was weeping, "what if something had happened to one of us before I got back?" She was holding tightly to him, and he could feel her slender body vibrating with some tremendous nervous reaction.

At last she raised her head, the tears still wet on her cheeks, and interrupted the incoherent words of his own love.

"I've learned my lesson the hard way," she said. "I've never been so wretched! Whether I'll be good for your career or not, Hil, you'll have to take me now. You'll have to take me, for I can't live without you."

On the twenty-sixth of September a bland sunshine enfolded the city. From an early-morning haze the day had emerged clear and beautiful. Even downtown amongst the hard trodden grimy streets and the darkly weathered buildings there was appreciable to the senses the contented balm of the late year's brightness. As the day reached noon the cross of St. Matthews pierced the fair blue sky with reflected gold. Far below, there was activity multiplied. A striped awning was being placed over the sidewalk, florists' vans parked, unloaded and drove off; Mike Flannery gave instructions to three extra policemen; strange men and women on various errands hurried in and out the great carved doors, and Hastings, in a fever of excitement and importance, was everywhere at once.

By two o'clock, however, the old church was ready and waiting for the great nuptial service. The gold altar vases were heavy and sweet with white stocks; the tall white candles were ready to light; ferns as delicate as lace made a green mist in the corners of the chancel, and all the long way down the center aisle ranged the fragrant white pew bouquets with broad ribbon streamers. Before the altar rail lay the white satin cushions awaiting the kneeling bride and groom.

In the rectory, Hilary and Dick sat at late lunch and tried to be calm. Hilary himself had wakened at daybreak and found it impossible to return to sleep. He and Dick had sat up very late after the rehearsal, talking about the war, so now he felt a bit lightheaded and queer.

"I'll have some coffee, Morris, after all. I guess I do need a bracer."

"What you need is a good hooker of Scotch," said Dick looking at him judicially.

"No, thanks. I never dreamed, though, that I'd be as nervous as this. Do you suppose every man is?"

"Wouldn't be surprised. It's quite an occasion after all. Look at me. I'm jumpy as a cat and I'm only the groom's brother."

"About Bronson. I can't explain exactly why I wanted him to marry us. We've never liked him and yet he seemed the closest link to Grandy that there is. Especially since he's living in the old house. And he did read the service for Grandy more beautifully than I would have thought possible. You know we commented on it at the time."

"Pleased him no end to be asked, I suppose?"

"Yes, I think it did. He seems to have mellowed a little. Not quite so spread-eagle. When I went over to the Bishop's to see him yesterday afternoon we talked most of the time of Grandy and it did me good. Strange how it often pays to follow a thoroughly illogical idea to its conclusion if you feel it strongly enough."

"I was never much on logic, myself. I do better with the Law of the First Impulse, as you may have observed."

"That's because you got all the Irish blood of the family while I got all the Scotch. Oh, say, I've something I want to read you."

He drew an envelope from his pocket and took out a letter in a fine, not too steady handwriting.

"It's from old Cousin Mattie out in Maryville," he said. "I wrote her about the wedding. I've tried to keep in touch with her for Grandy's sake. Listen to this."

> Dear Hilary—
>
> I write to congratulate you upon the occasion of your marriage, and to wish you and Alexa every happiness. Your grandfather should have lived to see this day. Although I never married I once had expectations long ago and the remembrance of that happiness has remained with me. I made quilts then as girls did in those days. I have kept them very carefully and they are as good as new. I am sending one to Alexa. The Wedding Ring pattern. Your grandfather liked it the best of all I made, that's why I'm sending it.
>
> May God bless you both.
>
> Cousin Mattie

"Damned nice of the old girl!"

"Yes, but I have a queer hunch there's more behind this. When I went through Grandy's things I found a lot of her letters. And he never kept letters as a rule. And there was a little old-fashioned picture wrapped in tissue paper of a really beautiful young girl and on the back was: 'Mattie, aged 19.' And now she's sending the quilt he liked best. Maybe they were in love once."

"Oh, in your state you'd think the very lamp posts were enamored of each other. Come on now, eat your lunch. I don't want to have to hold you up at the altar."

"The last time I called Lex, Mrs. McColly said she was too busy to come to the phone. I wonder what she was doing?"

"Why, you poor goon, she was probably taking three different baths in various perfumes and massaging her face with cold cream and putting mascara on her lashes and shaving her legs and combing her hair six times and—"

"How do *you* know all this?"

"Oh, I get around. And I read the ads. Hurry up now, we have a little refurbishing to do ourselves."

They walked up the wide stairs side by side. At the landing they stopped instinctively in the dim light. Dick gripped his brother's shoulders.

"I know what this all means to you, Hil. God, I can guess what you're feeling, and no one deserves the happiness as much as you."

Hilary was deeply moved. He and Dick had gone through all the experiences of the years together. So now would Dick stand close in this the greatest moment of his life. He held on hard, but he could only mutter, "Thanks, Bib."

At the top of the stairs in the broad light of the upper hall Dick was his usual airy self.

"Well, pax vobiscum," he grinned, "and may your troubles all be *little ones!*"

At fifteen minutes to four the two brothers stepped out into the sunshine of the court. Old Morris had left a half-hour earlier so that Hastings could seat him inconspicuously in the gallery. They went in the side way and on to the vestry room where they found Bronson already with Dr. Farley, the rector of Christ Church. Bronson looked bigger and more imposing than ever in his full ecclesiastical regalia. He spoke in friendly fashion to Dick, however, and there descended upon the four an intangible male oneness of spirit as they waited the final signal.

"Nervous?" Dr. Farley asked Hilary, smiling.

"A little."

"I remember when I was married I shook so much I thought every one could see," Bronson volunteered. Strange, Hilary thought, to hear Bronson confess to anything less than complete assurance, ever. He was speaking again.

"I am using the old English form of the marriage service. You are familiar with it, no doubt?"

"Yes. Oh, yes," Hilary said, his mind fixed upon Lex, leaving the house, driving through the streets, entering the vestibule, starting up the aisle.

"That is satisfactory to you, then?"

"Oh, quite."

There was a faint buzz from the call bell.

"O.K. Hil. Here we go," Dick whispered in his ear.

Dr. Farley pushed open the door; Bronson, broad and pontifical, passed through; last came Hilary and Dick. The church was an indistinguishable mass of faces in the soft sweet-scented light. Hilary moved mechanically to his appointed place, turned and looked down the aisle. All he could see was the blur of yellows and blues which he knew was the bridesmaids. Would their pace never quicken? Would they never cease to obscure the object his heart and his eyes sought? Then he saw her! Still far back in the church, a white vision, on her father's arm, Lex moved slowly, slowly past the flower-decked pews. Hilary could see that old Alex's gray, curly head was held high. It was as though he were flinging defiance at all those who twenty-five years before had said he was not good enough for young Eunice Breckenridge nor for St. Matthews. It was his hour of triumph. Like a cloud drifting beside his burly form Lex moved slowly on. So slowly! Yet Hilary, as he saw her face at last, knew that there was now no withholding. In a burning look that shut out all others their eyes held as he finally stepped forward to meet her and grasp her hand.

"Dearly beloved, we are gathered together here in the sight of God, and in the face of this company . . ."

He heard Dr. Farley pronounce the familiar opening words which he himself had so often uttered for others. Now, incredible wonder, it was he, himself, who was being married. He and Lex.

As they moved forward to where Bronson waited before the altar itself, Hilary felt his throat tight and choked. Would his voice be heard? Would he, who had repeated them so often before, now fumble the final vows?

"I, Hilary, take thee, Alexa . . ."

When her voice came he felt as though all the deeps within him were breaking up. After his long, torturing uncertainty he heard now clearly, unfalteringly, "I, Alexa, take thee, Hilary . . ."

He had been conscious of no great deviation from the usual service until he placed the ring upon Lex's finger; then he found himself repeating after Bronson: "With this ring I thee wed and with my body I thee worship." He had read the old form, of course, but had forgotten it. He flushed now, wondering whether Lex or the congregation at large would think the words strange. At least he could not have spoken a profounder truth.

They knelt on the white satin cushions to receive the final benediction; then in what seemed a maze of mingled light and sound they passed swiftly down the aisle and into the waiting car.

"Do you know," Lex said, after the first embrace, "the only person I actually saw, coming down the aisle, was Aunt Samantha Adams! She was at the end of a pew wearing a funny hat with a feather. Her glasses were slipped down on her nose and she was smiling and wiping her eyes at the same time."

"I hope she'll get on all right at the reception. It's her first public appearance, you know."

"Oh, she'll make out. I think she'll be good for some of these stuffed shirts. Hil, who am I now? Quick! I want to hear it first from you!"

"You are Mrs. Hilary Laurens. You are my wife, for ever and ever, Amen!"

During the weeks of the honeymoon Hilary experienced a deep and rapturous surprise. Not only was there the constant miracle of their being now one flesh but there was the wonder of Lex's bountiful love. Perhaps because he had been accustomed during their courtship to giving all and expecting nothing in return he was humbly unprepared for the passionate wholeness of Lex's giving. Sometimes his eyes were wet as he looked into her eager, adoring face. With all the strong fiery fervor of her father's blood, she now spent upon Hilary the devotion of which she was capable.

They had agreed to return for this precious period to the place they had first met. It had been easy this late in the season to secure one of the choice cabins on the lake. They were within reach of the big hotel for meals, so, as Lex pointed out, they could have both solitude and society and she could wear her new slack suits and also her trousseau evening gowns. Hilary had agreed, of course, though feeling that for his own happiness the society would be unnecessary. But after only a few days Lex's interest in dining and dancing at the hotel died completely also. From then on they had their meals sent down to the cabin, where they ate in front of the blazing wood fire, close and secure in the enchantment of their new intimacy.

Sometimes through the lightness of their laughter and the completeness of their joy a shadow fell, as though from the spire of St. Matthews.

"Don't!" Lex would say with faint petulance. "It's not fair to drag any of this into the honeymoon. You'll be back in the midst of all that soon enough. Just now you are *all mine!* Do you hear?"

And Hilary heard with amazement and delight that it should be so, though sometimes the shadow remained until her kisses had purged it away.

Upon their return to the city, Hilary faced a new surprise. This was the tremendous zest and enthusiasm with which Lex set about her housekeeping. They would keep the library practically as it was, they both agreed, also the "Prophet's Chamber," as Lex termed Hilary's small room upstairs; but the rest of the house badly needed redecorating, and of course added furniture.

"I believe," Lex said one evening as she sat at her dressing table brushing her hair, "I'll put Muff up on the third floor. Fix up a little suite for her. She'd like that."

"Muff!"

At his tone Lex looked up in surprise. "Why, of course! You surely knew Muff would go wherever I went."

"I just hadn't thought of it at all," Hilary said, "so it startled me."

"And you don't like the idea?"

"Well," he said slowly, "of course I prefer the thought of being all alone in the house with you. Regular servants don't count, but Muff is— well different."

She drew his head down and kissed him.

"You're a dear goose! But Muff won't bother you. You'll never know she's here. She'll do the mending and keep the drawers tidy and look after our clothes and tell me my duty as a wife. I really couldn't do without her, Hil. She's been with me since I was two. Please don't mind. Imagine how you'd feel giving up Morris!"

"That's true. You and Morris are certainly hitting it off together, aren't you?"

"Thick as thieves. He's a sweet old thing. He's as excited about all the decorating as I am. You know it's fun keeping house, Hil. It's fun being married to you!"

He swept her into his arms. Nothing mattered, then, nothing but her nearness.

By late November the work upon the rectory was finished. By dint of wheedling, cajoling, threatening, of unremitting shopping, surveillance, driving motive power, and, it must be admitted, a few whirlwind rages, Lex had achieved the impossible. Walls and woodwork were fresh, rugs were down, all the new furniture in order, curtains hung, the usable wedding presents in place and the rest packed in storage rooms. As in her whole personality, Lex combined in the matter of taste the infallible traditions of the Breckenridges with the impulsive daring of the McCollys. So now, while the great drawing room, for example, was elegantly conventional in its main furnishings, there was a brilliant unexpectedness about the cerise hangings and gay mantel vases against the gray walls; while the gorgeous splash of pattern on the fireside chairs startled the eye until it came to rest on the soft dove color of the divans. It was unusual, it was loud in contrasts, it was beautiful, it was Lex.

Hilary came in late one afternoon, tired and sad. He had just had the funeral of a little child. The white anguish of the young parents' faces was still graven upon his heart. Lex met him in the hall, caught his hand and danced into the drawing room. Her face was radiant and her eyes sparkled.

"It's all done at last," she said jubilantly. "I've just been waiting for you so we could gloat over it together. Isn't it really stunning, Hil?"

"It's wonderful! I don't see how you ever did it." He sank down on the couch.

"I don't like your tone. There is a 'but' in it."

"Not a single 'but.' I love the room. It's only that I've had a hard day." Suddenly it was impossible to tell her, as she pressed her glowing face close to his, about the child's funeral.

"It's been such fun doing it all, even if I have worked like a slave. But now we're all set. I'm dying to throw a big party soon. That's why I hurried so."

"I suppose we should," Hilary agreed slowly. "I've been entertained so much, and of course we've had a lot of invitations."

"Oh, them," Lex said. "I'll have to go through all that vestry-and-their-wives business later. What I mean now is a big cocktail party. All my old crowd. I'm dying to have them see the house. You know what the girls think? They think this is a sort of Jane Austen interior. Wait till they see it! And they still think you're a myth, Hil. I want them to meet you and know you're *real*. I can have thirty here without crowding. Fifty even. Mother will let me have Haskins over to fix the drinks. I don't think Morris would be up to that—"

"Lex! My darling child, you can't have a cocktail party here!" Hilary's face was stricken.

"I can't have a— Just what do you mean, Hil?" She had withdrawn from his arms and faced him now, her head up, the color drawn from her cheeks.

"Dearest, you couldn't do that here, in the rectory. It wouldn't—surely you can see for yourself—it wouldn't be proper or seemly."

"You mean to say I can't have a cocktail party here, in what I thought was my own home? After all my work and planning! Don't you think every bride wants to give a party and have her friends? And I was so happy— Hil, why? Give me one good reason why?"

He could see by the tension of her face that she was holding back her anger with difficulty. The blank astonishment in her eyes was even harder to bear.

He could not speak. He had never once thought of this situation. In all their times together the matter of drinking had been touched upon but lightly. "Cocktail, Hilary?" "No, thanks." Once he remembered she had said, "I don't really care for them myself—it's just routine."

She had moved nearer to him now. Her voice was less angry and more pleading.

"Aren't you just setting up a straw man, Hil? Everybody gives cocktail parties now. How else would they entertain a big crowd? And I know for a fact every one of your vestrymen's families have them. Why, the biggest thing of the kind I ever went to was at Judge Ball's! You know Clarissa, his granddaughter, lives with him. When they all do it, why on earth couldn't we? And besides, Hil, try to think of my side. What will I *do* with myself if I can't have my own crowd at my own house? I wanted you to meet them all. To show you off! The wedding reception didn't count. There was such a mob."

Suddenly she turned and buried her head in the cushion. Her weeping made no sound, but her shoulders shook with it. Hilary tried to gather her to him again, but she resisted.

"Darling, don't, *don't* be so disappointed. Give me a little time to think it over. It all hit me so suddenly. Please, Lex. Let me try to find a way out."

She finally returned to his arms; but they were both quiet all evening, and the glory of the new drawing room had dimmed a little. Hilary lay awake most of the night. He was wondering what more he could do for the young couple who had lost their child. The whole question concerning immortality struck him afresh each time he had a funeral. It had been so today. The little form, so unspeakably, so heartbreakingly precious to the parents had seemed so small, so almost negligible in the face of all nature, of the universe. Even the beautiful hyperbole of the fallen sparrow did not completely comfort him. He felt racked with the pain of it all.

He tossed and turned, trying not to disturb Lex who slept soundly beside him. He could feel her dear form, could see as before the light went out, the glory of her hair upon the pillow, the sweetness of her lips as he had bent over her. What could he do about the cocktail party? As usual with him, he saw her side completely. There was her natural wish to show off the new home which she had literally created during these last weeks of incessant work, and to show *him* off also! Hilary smiled wryly, but he understood. By the nature of the situation he had met few of Lex's friends and contemporaries. The young married group in their twenties, and the girls and young men a few years out of college or school, caught up again into the gay life of the city, all of these socially the *crème de la crème,* would form the crowd. And there would doubtless be fifty whom she would want to invite. From her point of view a cocktail party was the natural, the inevitable, the only form of entertainment for such a number. It was also true, as Lex had pointed out, that a very large group of St. Matthews parishioners did the same thing in their own homes as a matter of course.

As always he turned instinctively to Grandy's example for help. The Bishop on this point had been firm. Wine he would use and did use in his own home or elsewhere. Hilary remembered once, when an unusually strait-laced parson had been visiting them and had not only declined a glass of wine but lectured the Bishop upon his own laxity, Grandy had listened to the end and then in a dangerously mild and gentle voice had said: "I have never felt myself quite worthy to sit in judgment upon the actions and behavior of my Master. He used wine himself and sanctioned it during his ministry. I do the same. May I offer you the sherry again, sir?" But beyond wine, Grandy never went. All forms of liquor were dangerous and the use of them easily abused, he said; therefore the clergy should set an unfailing example of abstinence. He had loathed cocktails. "A cheap invention of the devil," he called them, adding once, "and I'm not so sure it wasn't a she-devil."

The next day Hilary had an inspiration. He telephoned, got into the car, and in a few minutes was in Mrs. Reed's sitting room. She was seated by the window, knitting, and her face looked pale and old.

"I thought there would be no more war socks to do in my lifetime, but I'm at it again. Things are in a bad way, Hilary. And we're only at the beginning."

"I know," Hilary said. "I have so many daily problems I have to face that sometimes I'm afraid I'm not enough acutely conscious of the war. It rests, though, like a dark backdrop in my mind all the time. What I came to talk to you about now seems very petty compared to that, but it has to be faced and it's important in its own way."

"Tell me about it."

He told briefly of Lex's wish. He was careful to omit nothing which might support and explain her feelings. His own need not be elaborated.

Mrs. Reed sat for several minutes looking out of the window. Then she turned, and smiled.

"If you'd mentioned this to me ten years ago I would have been shocked out of my skin. But things have changed. Now I may be giving you poor advice, Hilary, but I would say let her go ahead. Have all the people she wants. Show off her house. Get it all out of her system. The chances are she may not want to do the same thing again for a long time. And you can always gamble on time. But when she does throw this thing, don't you be there. Have a convenient sick call. I'll have a stroke, if necessary. But keep clear away. Then that will put a little different face on things, if you understand me."

Hilary considered. "Of course she particularly wanted me there," he said, "but I think your idea may have something in it. It may be the solution. You think there would not be too many repercussions from the parish?"

"I doubt it. This is a big city, not a small town. The young folks move in an orbit of their own. The ones who belong to St. Matthews will likely be from families who wouldn't think it strange anyway. Unless it would be J. V. Dunn. Would she be having Maudie?"

"Oh, Maudie!" Hilary laughed. "By the way, I have great hopes of her. She started work down at the Varny Street Settlement the first of September and she's eating it up. Miss Barton tells me the girl really has ability. No, I don't imagine she goes in Lex's crowd, but I'll check. Well, you've been the greatest help and comfort. I may do as you say. I hate so desperately to disappoint Lex." The cloak of his love fell upon him.

Mrs. Reed patted his arm.

"Tell Lex I said she never deserved you but she's a good picker. And tell her I'm coming to tea. I want to see the house. Any blasts yet from Hettie Breckenridge?"

"Not a sign. I'm delighted."

"I'm not. I think it's a very ominous silence. You don't know that old girl. Well, don't worry. If worst comes to worst I'll tackle her. Listen, about these Adamses. How did that man ever marry that woman? I saw her at the reception, or rather I *heard* her. He seems a gentleman of the first water, but I can't place her."

"You probably won't see her very often," Hilary said carefully. "She is very much interested in the Parish House work and will spend a lot of time there. But when you do see her, will you do me a favor?"

"You know I will."

"Then be nice to her. *Very* nice."

"So there is a story back of them! I surmised so. Well, don't worry, I'll be nice. And give Lex her head a little on this party business. I don't believe it will shake the foundations."

That night Hilary told Lex exactly what Mrs. Reed had said. At first she flared up violently. Have it without him? Just when she wanted them all to meet him and him to get to know them? Never. That was a mean, low-down suggestion, and she'd tell Mrs. Reed so. She wondered he had considered it, even for a minute. What would they all think if he wasn't there at all?

But little by little she grew calmer. As Hilary pointed out, a doctor's wife had to put up with her husband's sudden absences, and their friends accepted the situation. It was the same in the case of a clergyman.

"But this absence would be faked," Lex said with her usual downrightness.

"Yes, but there will be plenty in days to come that won't be. And there is a very good reason for this, darling. I think it's the only way the affair can be given at all. Could you be satisfied?"

She studied his face carefully. There was a wistfulness upon it. Then she drew a deep breath.

"Why, Hil, you're disappointed yourself! You'd really *like* to be at the party."

"Well, of course! What did you suppose? I'm not exactly in my dotage!"

She drew his face down and kissed him, and he felt her cheek against his.

"Oh, Hil, you're so good you make me ashamed. I didn't realize you were making sacrifices all the time yourself for the sake of the job. Some day I'll be a really good parson's wife. I'll try so hard—after the party."

Once the matter was settled, Lex lost no time in beginning her preparations. Morris was tremendously excited. He already adored Lex. They talked together time on end out in the big kitchen, with Lex perched on a high stool and Morris leaning against the door jamb. The favorite subject with both was the boyhood of Mist' Hilary and Mist' Dick. Tender anecdotes of the Bishop were continually cropping up also, so that Lex often surprised Hilary by repeating some remark of Grandy's which he had himself forgotten. Now with burning enthusiasm, Lex poured out her plans to Morris. All the food part was to be in his hands. It must be more delicious than anything yet savored by the human race. Morris, who was an adept at hors d'œuvres and canapés, smacked his lips and beamed. There must be *millions* of them, Lex explained expansively.

"Yes, Miss Lex, I make millions! Mebbe billions. They never gonna taste anything better in their lives."

She explained about Haskins and his function, and Morris' eyes widened. There was a tinge of both jealousy and shock in them, but he recovered himself quickly as she went on to the problems of glass and linen.

In one thing Hilary was grateful to Lex's forethought. Or perhaps the credit went to Muff—who was now installed on the third floor, quietly efficient as usual, though rarely, to Hilary's eye, in view. There were no cards sent out for the party. All the invitations were telephoned.

"I'm just saying I'll be at home around five on Saturday the fourteenth.

The obnoxious word is, therefore, never mentioned," Lex said again one night. "And your name doesn't have to be brought in at all."

"Good."

They were sitting in the library having their Sunday supper in front of the fire. Hilary was in a happy mood. The morning congregation had been large and the afternoon one showed marked signs of growth. He had noted a number of young men at the latter, students, apparently, scattered here and there. He had prepared and sent out voluminous publicity to the near-by University, the Medical College, and the Law School. He believed the results were beginning to be seen. Adams had read the service that afternoon with the greatest expression, the music had been soul moving, his own little talk—well, at least he had been conscious of the intensity with which the audience listened.

Now at this moment the firelight shone on Lexa's hair and flushed her face with color. A joy as sharp as pain seized him. The rich vitality of her beauty not only fired his physical senses but seemed to pierce through to the spirit. In these perfect weeks since his marriage he had been conscious of a quickening of all his powers. It was as though certain resources within him had lain dormant until the full consummation of his love had brought them forth.

Lex looked up at him suddenly with her eyes full of mischief.

"Do you know, Hil, what a lot of these tenement families need? The ones back of us here? They should each have a cat. A nice striped tiger cat that never shows the dirt, and a Tom. Be sure it's a Tom, for he can shift better for himself. It wouldn't cost anything much to feed it—scraps and stray mice et cetera, and there's something about a cat curled up in front of a stove that makes for contentment. Poor people need a pet more than rich people."

"Lex, what on earth are you talking about?"

"And if you sit with a cat purring on your knee you can't contemplate suicide or running off with another woman's husband or abandoning your child or anything like that. At least that's what Aunt Samantha says. She's thinking of importing a basketful of tiger kittens and distributing them around."

Hilary threw back his head and laughed. Then his expression began to change.

"She might actually have something there, at that. She's the most amazing person I've ever met. She's compounded entirely of common sense and kindness. Her voice, though, is enough to drive a man crazy. Poor Adams."

Lex was serious now, too. "I like Aunt Samantha," she said. "I'm not sure that I don't like her better than Adams. There's a faint martyr complex about him, and I hate martyrs. I've asked Aunt Samantha to tea on Tuesday. I'm going to show her all over the house, and we'll shout our heads off. You can keep out of the way till dinnertime."

Hilary got up, came impetuously over and put his arms about her. He leaned his cheek against hers in a tenderness deeper than passion.

"Lex, my sweet! It's wonderful of you to do that. I've been wanting to ask you to do something for Aunt Samantha, but I thought it might bore you. It's fine of you to do this, and you don't know how I appreciate it!"

A little later she looked across the tea table into his eyes, her own crystal-clear in their honesty.

"Hil, I must tell you something. I didn't ask Aunt Samantha out of kindness. I wanted her. I love hearing her talk. I like her. You might better know the truth. If I didn't like her I wouldn't ask her."

Hilary smiled back. "Don't worry," he said. "In this case it's much better so."

As the next week moved on toward Saturday and the party, Hilary tried during the day at least to keep his mind entirely on his work, of which there was plenty. He could not escape the various implications of the coming festivity, however, when he was at home. An excitement pervaded the whole house. That which Lex, herself, manifested was a surprise to Hilary. The party meant more to her, then, than he had even guessed.

"One thing, Hil, that is going to keep this affair on a very nice safe level is the food," she said, late Saturday morning as he came in to lunch. "We're going to have tons of it, and it's going to be simply out of this world. Muff says so too. Morris gave us samples to taste. The men will all eat like pigs, and most of the girls will too. Then nobody's likely to get tight."

At the look of horror in his eyes, she hastened to reassure him.

"You know how it is. Usually there are a few who take one too many; but we're going to watch out and prevent that. It's going to be a very grand, top-drawer occasion from first to last. I can't wait for them to see the house. It does look so sort of forbidding and churchy on the outside, but they'll get the surprise of their lives once they are in."

She was setting a bowl of red roses on the desk in the library. Then she caught his hand.

"Come on. Let's have one last look all through. I've had a lot of fun doing the flowers. Here in the drawing room—well, what do you think?

Hilary caught his breath. Against the dove-gray walls with their violent cerise accents, she had used only yellow. Tall snap-dragons in the mantel vases, great bowls of chrysanthemums on the tables.

"It's simply stunning, Lex. You're a wizard."

"But wait till you see our room! It's the very sweetest. Come on up!"

Upon this, their own bedroom, Lex had lavished her finest decorative skill. There were no contrasts here to startle or challenge the eye. It was as fresh, as tenderly inviting as a summer meadow beside a murmuring stream. The dark, quaintly carved furniture rested against pale blue walls; the curtains and dressing table frills were like summer clouds; the upholstery of chairs and chaise longue repeated the darker blue of the little French tiles around the fireplace, while against the long wall, hung like a tapestry, was the Wedding Ring quilt which Cousin Mattie had sent. The placing of it so had been Lex's idea entirely, and Hilary had marveled and admired. It seemed like the gentle benediction of a past generation upon them. Lex loved it and often went close to it, pointing out to him the soft old colors and the infinity of tiny stitches which made up the pattern.

Now she was calling his attention to the flowers. On mantel, dressing table, and stand they were all white.

"I suppose the girls will make some remarks about this, but I don't care. I still feel like a bride, and the white is so darling here, don't you think so?"

It was fully five minutes before she could escape his arms; then she kissed him again and shook back her hair.

"Listen, you, I'm a busy woman. We must hurry down for lunch. We're having a stand-up in the butler's pantry, for the dining room's all set. Oh, Hil, I hope this thing goes over big. I'm really excited about it. Did I tell you Mother and Dad are coming to dinner afterwards? I wanted them to see how things look, and hear all the news. If you were only going to be— Well, I won't bring that up again. By the way, where are you going while the party's on?"

"Oh, I forgot to tell you. I'm going to Miss Mowbray's. I sort of let her in on the problem."

Lex's eyebrows lowered. "What's the idea in that?"

"Well, you see they live away out on the edge of things, and somehow or other I've never been there to call. Her mother's an invalid—arthritis or something—so it all seemed to fit for today. They'll give me tea, and I can stay as late as I want. When will the shindig be over?"

"Oh, I think by eight at the latest. Maybe we can get them all out by seven-thirty. You couldn't come in just for the tail end?"

He shook his head. "Don't tempt me, darling. Oh, Lex, I love you so!"

She pushed him gently off. "You've got a very carnal look in your eye for a parson, Mr. Laurens. I think we'd better get out of here right away. Come on. I've a million things to see to yet."

As Hilary drove slowly out to Lynton where the Mowbrays lived he felt grateful to Margaret. It had been her suggestion that he come there for the afternoon. He had told her his problem, first because he wanted her to be forewarned in case of repercussions, and second because he was puzzled about where to go on a Saturday. He knew he could go to Mrs. Reed's, but he didn't want to. This once he didn't wish to talk of Lex. He hoped to forget the party completely while it was in progress. So he had jumped at the chance when Miss Mowbray, after her usual thoughtful consideration had said: "Why not come out to see Mother? We've been wanting to have you for tea all these months but you were so busy."

He found the house small but on a good street and generally more imposing than he had expected. Inside it was filled with worn but distinguished furniture and a general air of comfort. Mrs. Mowbray was a fine-looking, elderly woman; it was clear that Margaret had not been blessed with her likeness.

"It's very like old times to see a clerical vest at our fireside," she said. "My husband, as you probably know, was a clergyman."

"But I didn't know it! Your daughter never told me!"

"I wasn't being secretive at all," Margaret smiled. "It just never came up."

The talk fell easily then into the channels Hilary knew best. He found himself quoting old stories of the Bishop and telling, what he had told no one else, about the gift of the big brown scrapbook.

Margaret served a late tea, which they all ate with heartiness, wrangling good-naturedly over books, from childhood favorites to the season's latest. Hilary was struck by their congeniality. He felt a rich sensation of having had his mind suddenly nourished as it had not been in some time.

He stayed until seven-thirty, since they insisted they were not dining till eight, and left with a feeling of warm friendship for both mother and daughter. As he drove back he turned over what seemed to him a strange situation. There was Margaret Mowbray, homely it was true but with a wealth of goodness, a keen mentality, and undeniable womanly charm. Moreover by every possible test she was ideally fitted to be a clergyman's wife. And yet, even though he had never met Lex, he was sure that any feeling of love for Margaret would have been entirely out of the question for him. How completely illogical, then, was love! Like did not necessarily call to like, neither always did mind to mind or soul to soul. Was man entirely a slave to his senses? And was anything less than their complete captivation really love? Was this dear slavery what men remembered even when they grew old and desire failed? Was it the curve of the cheek, the flowing hair, the young swell of the bosom, the shapely leg, the delicate wrist, which always launched the ships and burnt the towers, and not the beauty of soul nor the brightness of intellect?

The thought disturbed him profoundly, for it brought him face to face with a question he tried never to recognize, let alone answer. How much in addition to physical passion did he and Lex have to build upon? He thrust it again from him. Right or wrong, he had to admit that just now he asked for nothing more. At the very thought of her his whole body became alive.

As he entered the rectory by the side door, he knew by the silence that the party was over. Then he saw Lex standing in the hall like a stricken doe. With two leaps he was beside her.

"What is it, darling? Is anything wrong? Did the party not go?"

She didn't answer at once, only clung to him as she had on the day of her landing.

"Tell me, sweet; and don't worry. No matter what. Don't feel badly. It probably went much better than you think."

Her voice sounded strange and distant.

"Oh, the party. It was perfect, Hil. It was wonderful. And I felt so happy all the time! I was so busy I hadn't a chance to think about your not being here till the very end. Till I stood here saying good-bye to them, all by myself. When the last ones went and I was here alone, I don't know—something queer came over me. As though some time you wouldn't be coming in. As though some time you would really be gone far away. It was terrible."

She raised her head, and her eyes had a fey look in them. Then as Hilary kissed her, murmuring sweet, laughing assurances, she began to brighten.

"Aren't I silly? I don't know what struck me, really. It's all gone now—that ghastly feeling. Oh, Hil, there *never* was a lovelier party! I'm as proud as Punch over it. They all raved about the house, and everybody had a marvellous time—you could tell—but there wasn't the sign of a brawl! And the way they ate! You know people usually just have little nibbles of things around. And here we had simply tons of sandwiches and all Morris' other concoctions, and they fell upon them like swine. Tim Whiteside said the hot lobster puffs were better than the cocktails. Imagine Tim! It's about the first time *he's* ever gotten tight at a party!"

They went on back to the library as Muff was quietly setting things to rights in the drawing room. Lex went on rapturously.

"And you know Jake Haverstraw? Oh, no, you don't. You must meet Jake. He always does some ridiculous trick, and sometimes they're a little rough on the furniture; but today it was perfect. He sneaked up to the linen closet and got himself rigged out in a sheet and a big Indian turban made out of a rolled bath towel, and he squatted down in front of the fireplace and worked one of these paper snakes up and down like an Indian fakir. He was simply a riot. Never said a word. Linda Marshal fed him. And the girls *loved* our room, Hil! And they think you must be wonderful! They all said they hardly knew what to expect, coming to a Rectory, but that it was absolutely the best party there's been this fall! Everybody was in the most marvellous mood! I never heard such shrieks and howls of laughter. Of course we all know each other awfully well, and it was such fun getting the whole crowd together! And there wasn't a *thing* anybody could criticize, Hil, honestly! Jen and Bill Howard didn't even get high, and you know how they are. Well, anyway they *are* like that. But not today. So, you see? Now I've got to go and tell Morris what a hit his food made."

The McCollys came, and there was excited repetition and comment throughout dinner. Lex, presiding at her own table in the dignified old dining room, now gleaming with the wedding silver and crystal, was an evident source of pride to her father and mother. The setting was not unworthy of her.

"You still look like a little girl playing tea-party," Old Alex said adoringly. "Don't she, Hilary? Say, what about Tommy Tatler? What's he going to make out of this affair of yours today? He might get Hilary some bad publicity."

"Who's Tommy Tatler?" Hilary asked quickly.

"He's a snake," Lex said calmly. "Writes the Scandal Column in the *Courier*. I've known him all my life. We went to dancing school together, and he was a devil even then. But he's always been nice to me. And right now I'm glad to say he's sick."

"Lexa!"

"Well, I am. I knew that, so I hurried up the party for this week end. The girl that does his column when he's out is mild as a mouse. Sticks to weddings and blessed events. So we're safe. I'll tell you all about Tommy later, Hil, for you're bound to run into him some time. Are you ready for coffee now? Let's have it in the drawing room."

Before the McCollys left, Hilary asked Old Alex into the library.

"I wonder," he said, "if you could do a little scouting for me. I just lately discovered some tenements back here that are so horrible I couldn't sleep the night after I first saw them. They must certainly be against the Housing Law, but somebody's looking the other way and letting them stand. I want to find out who owns them, but I'd rather not go around asking questions myself. Here's the address. Do you think you could make some inquiries for me?"

Old Alex took the paper somewhat gingerly. "I don't know why you want to get mixed up in this kind of business, Hilary. Why don't you stick to your preachin'? You may get a snake by the tail before you're through. There's plenty of dirty money made on real estate, and all tracks nicely covered. Some men don't care where the revenue comes from, just so it comes. Like J. V. Dunn."

"What's wrong with Dunn?"

"Well, he owns the *Courier*. Yellowest sheet ever printed. The one we were talkin' about at dinner. Now you take me. I'm not much on religion as you know. I'll never walk up the aisle with the collection plate and a carnation in my buttonhole, but you don't ever need to worry about my money. What I've got I've fought like hell for, but it's not what I call dirty."

Old Alex paused and looked keenly at his son-in-law.

"You still want me to find out about this property?"

"I do."

"All right, if you say so, I'll see what I can nose out. And, my boy, I want to tell you again how glad I am you have our Lex. I feel safe about her. First time I ever have, as a matter of fact. So, make her happy, Hilary. Keep her happy."

CHAPTER IX

As DECEMBER drew on toward that Christmas of 1939, Hilary had never felt so deeply and richly content. There were constant heavy responsibilities, there was unceasing work, there was anxiety over the outcome of one or two major issues, there was the growing black cloud of war beyond the sea; and yet, almost to the hurt of his conscience, he felt happy. The first and main reason, of course, was because the golden thread of his love's fulfillment brightened the whole fabric of his being, and the second was because he knew with gratification and thankfulness that the work of the parish as a whole was moving forward along the lines he had conceived.

The Adamses in their strangely diverse ways were working out extremely well. The people quite generally liked Adams and he, it was clear, was reacting brilliantly to the joy of congenial work at last. As to Aunt Samantha, she had, with complete assurance and efficiency, taken the humble for her own. Already her dumpy, dowdy figure was a familiar one in the tenement district. With a small basket on her arm, containing odds and ends for the old or the sick, she made her cheerful rounds, dispensing practical advice and wholesome admonition as though she had known the women there all her life. And they in turn confided to her their many sorrows and their few joys. Best and most surprising of all, the young people took to her. The great motherly heart of her, denied by Nature the children she craved, now spent itself upon the pert little waitresses and factory girls, and the young truck drivers, bricklayers, and machinists who lived near the church. It was much more her influence, Hilary knew, than his own that made the Parish House dance hall fill up on Saturday nights. Her methods with the young folks were an increasing source of interest to Hilary. Unlike former chaperons from the ranks of the parish, she stood with complete unself-consciousness on their own level. She praised them, scolded them, comforted, and advised them. In a word, she loved them all, and they felt it and accepted her completely. In a different way, Hilary realized with thankfulness, they accepted him also.

The other manifold activities of the Parish House were progressing under carefully selected leadership, and slowly, persistently the rumor was spreading that those who came there were considered part of the church also.

One Saturday night Hilary stopped the dance music and made an announcement.

"In a big group of young people like this," he said, "there are bound to be a few who are thinking of getting married." (Laughs and a few boos from the boys, nervous giggles from the girls.) "I want to tell you that when any of you are ready for that I would like to perform the ceremony in the church, and I want you to know it won't cost you a cent. Just now the church is lighted, and I wish all of you who care to, would come in and see how beautiful it is. I would like you to learn the way, for on Christmas Eve we're having a big party in the Parish House, you know, and at midnight, just before the supper, I want you all to come to a brief service in the church itself. Mrs. Adams will tell you more about that later. But meanwhile, don't forget about the weddings."

The next week he had four! After each he felt an especial satisfaction. The youngsters had at least made a good beginning. Instead of a cheap and tawdry affair before some justice of the peace, they had plighted their troth at the altar of God.

At the other pole were the University and professional school students: young embryonic doctors and lawyers and engineers. These were coming in increasingly greater numbers to Sunday vespers. Older men were dropping in also, strangers, not of the parish. Indeed, unlike most religious audiences, this one bade fair to be predominantly male. With a desperate intensity Hilary worked over his ten-minute talks. There should be in them, he determined, no trite mediocrity, no pleasant patter of platitudes. He would start with no postulates. He must speak with all the honesty and penetration of which he was capable to what he judged were brilliant, restless, questing minds. And he must speak of the great elemental questions with which every thoughtful person is concerned. So he wrestled and prayed over his sermonettes, sometimes fearing he was being *too* honest, confessing by implication *too* candidly the strivings of his own soul. But the men kept coming.

He and Adams had decided that they would both be in the vestibule after these services. To Hilary's surprise a number of young men thanked him each time for his sermon, and here and there one asked hesitantly if he might come to talk with him. Hilary decided that after Christmas he must keep one night a week for such conferences. It would be well worth the sacrifice of an evening.

Each Sunday morning as he looked over the congregation he was conscious of that peculiar bond, like a spiritual umbilical, which unites priest and people. The faces now had ceased to be a mass and were fast becoming individuals. He could pick out swiftly now the families with whom he had rejoiced or suffered; where he had performed wedding ceremonies, baptized babies, prayed over their sick, or buried their dead. Even in these few months he had come to know magnificent souls, and petty; sacrificial lives and narrow, selfish ones. But so went the world everywhere. Here, great or small, were his people, his flock to whom he ministered with all his powers, all his growing affection.

So, as the season approached the joyful one of peace and good will, Hilary determined to postpone certain threatening issues until later and to enjoy the unreasoning happiness that possessed him. For in the rectory these days there was nothing but brightness and laughter. Lex and Morris carrying loads of holly and pine in from the car! Morris baking the fruit cake! Muff making Scotch short-bread! Lex everywhere, glowing and radiant, wrapping packages, trimming the tree, putting up the greens, planning the Christmas dinner. For Dick was coming, and it was to be a real holiday reunion.

"I'm going to have Christmas for once just the way I want it!" she said one late afternoon as she surveyed the library. "Mother never would have many greens around. She thought they made too much dirt. But I love them everywhere, over the mirrors and the pictures and twined in the stair banisters. Don't you, Hil?"

She was wearing a red dress with a ribbon to match it in her hair. His eyes devoured her.

"Do you know," he said suddenly, "I never lived with a woman before!"

"Well, I *hope* not!"

Hilary laughed. "No, but you see my mother died when Dick was born. We must have had nurses, of course, those first years, but later at Grandy's after Father's death he and Morris between them sort of brought us up. We were scared to death of old Katy, the cook, so she didn't count. It was practically an all-male establishment from the time we were kids. Can't you see why this is such heaven to me now?"

"Any nice, kind woman as a homemaker would have been all you needed, I take it?" Lex asked teasingly.

He caught her fiercely to him.

"What do *you* think?" he whispered.

A little later they sat before the fire hand in hand and, like two happy children, talked about their gifts.

"I've got the most beautiful present for you! Wait till you see it!" Hilary said.

"Is it something for the house?" Lex asked eagerly.

"Well, yes. You asked for that."

"I know. It still seems so wonderful to me to have a home of my own. It's the very nicest feeling. I never felt so much *myself* before. Oh, Hil, I hope you like what I've got for you!"

"I'm sure to."

"It's odd buying a gift for a clergyman. Should I have got you an inlaid Prayer-book or something?"

"I'm pretty well supplied."

"Well, this is purely frivolous. An any-wife-to-any-husband gift."

"Can it be true? Are you really my wife?"

"If I'm not, there's been an awful scandal," Lex said laughing. Then she added suddenly: "You remember we spoke that night after the party about the Tommy Tatler column in the *Courier*? Well, he's got something in it today about me."

"About you?" Hilary stiffened.

"I'll show you," she said, jumping up. "One of the girls told me, and I got the paper. Everybody reads it—surreptitiously, you know."

She came back in a moment with the garish tabloid, folded to the place.

"You see," she explained, "he simply gets away with murder because he never mentions a name and he calls the column, 'Through the Keyhole.' They can't ever get him for libel though plenty of people have tried. There's just nothing to pin him down to. Oh, he's a snake all right, but this is the first time he's touched me. Look, here it is."

Hilary read:

> One of the most beautiful gold-plated young women along the Atlantic Seaboard, who recently astounded her circle of fashionable ultramoderns by wedding a gentleman of the cloth, has not been seen in any of her familiar hot-plush spots for three long months. Will she continue to remain immured? Bets handled by this column.

"Why, the dirty dog!" Hilary said. "I'll go to see him. I'll tell him he's got to—"

Lex stopped him. "Don't get excited, Hil. It's not worth it. There isn't a thing you could do. You know what he'd say if you went to see him? He'd be bland as butter and tell you he was really referring to a girl in Baltimore, or Boston maybe. Curious coincidence that you felt it fitted me. You see? He squirms out of everything. He's got a wonderful racket. And it's fine for the paper's circulation, because all the set who wouldn't ordinarily touch a tabloid just snap up the *Courier* to read the dirt about all their friends. The most dangerous thing about him is that he doesn't print a thing that isn't true. And gets away with it."

"But, Lex, I hate this."

"Don't," she said. "It's really funny. I thought you'd be amused, or I wouldn't have showed you. After all, he didn't say a thing bad about me. And, Hil, I've been thinking. I won't have any more cocktail parties here. You don't need to worry about that. I know you were upset over that last one. I suppose it was very wrong of me to go ahead with it. But it did something for me. I showed all the crowd once for all that I wasn't in jail or in a nunnery. Now, you see, I can afford to do as I please. I don't have to do it again to prove anything. Do you see what I mean, Hil?"

"Yes, I think I do. And I'm enormously relieved. Fortunately there wasn't any trouble after the party, but I—well I'm more glad than I can say that you don't want to have any more."

"I didn't say that I didn't *want* to," Lex amended. "I said I wouldn't do it. Come on, let's talk some more about Christmas presents. Won't Morris be pleased over his watch?"

"You were wonderful to think of it! Here am I, devoted to every bone in his body, yet I never realized what a shabby old turnip he carried. He'll get the thrill of his life, especially having it come from you."

"If we just have the right things for Dick. Oh, Hil, I hope he has a good time. Our very first guest. Will he like the house, do you think?"

"His eyes will pop out. Do you know, I'm awfully glad we're having Christmas dinner here. Our first one."

"So am I. I did browbeat Mother and Dad a little. But we had Thanksgiving with them. Where shall we hang up our stockings? Here, don't you think?"

"Do we hang up stockings?"

"Why, Hil, don't tell me you haven't always hung up your stocking?"

Hilary shook his head. "We had a tree, and Grandy put all our presents there. I don't believe we ever had stockings even when we were kids."

Suddenly, with a sweetness that overpowered him, she drew his head against her breast.

"I'm going to make up to you for everything you missed. And to Dick, too. It's going to be the most beautiful Christmas any one ever had."

And it was. Wood fires roaring in all the fireplaces, the rich smell of the pine, the garlanded walls, the shining tree in the drawing room, bursts of music from the library as Dick and Lex alternated old carols with the latest song hit, laughter, voices calling from room to room, all sorts of joyous exclamations and warnings along with Dick's hilarious jokes, then the bulging stockings early Christmas morning as the three of them in their dressing gowns squatted like children in front of the library fireplace, the formal opening of the big gifts around the tree; the dinner, with the McCollys and old Mrs. Reed as guests; and the afternoon with its replete contentment. In between, deeply graven upon Hilary's heart, was the midnight service Christmas Eve with the young folks from the dance hall, shepherded by Aunt Samantha Adams, sitting wide-eyed amongst the worshippers, kneeling for the ancient prayers, moved as he he could see by the words and strain of the Noël as it rose and fell:

"He knows our needs; to our weakness is no stranger."

And then on Christmas morning itself, he watched with a tremendous stirring of the heart as Lex and Dick knelt side by side at the altar rail. It was the first time he had administered communion to Dick and the moment was deeply significant.

So this day ended, as all the days miraculously did now, with him and Lex alone together in the blue and white bedroom.

He had given her two beautiful and rare old perfume bottles and her delight in them knew no bounds. She sat now in a chiffon negligee on the bench before her dressing table, with Hilary beside her.

"I never was so pleased," she said again, touching the delicate glass with her finger. "They are just what my table needed. And you were so right to choose the pale pink. More blue would have been too much. I love your taste, Hil."

He leaned close. "I think it's pretty good myself," he said, his eyes upon her.

"I'm so glad my hair's not red. Then I couldn't have had a blue room. Hasn't it been a perfect day?"

"Absolutely heavenly."

"And you really do like your cuff links?"

"They are the most beautiful Christmas gift I've ever received in my whole life. Except . . ."

"Except what?" She turned her face to him, swiftly, half in alarm.

"Except you," he whispered against her hair.

The soft color mounted in her cheeks. "Silly," she said tenderly and put out the lights.

All that week, Dick stayed with them and the excited happiness continued. There were innumerable parties, to some of which Hilary went, too. When he couldn't go, Dick escorted Lex.

"You've no idea how I honor you, Alexa, my dear, for taking the curse of bachelordom from the family. 'My brother's wife,' I say now, rolling the words sweetly upon my tongue. I seem to ride in somehow myself on the tail of the kite. 'Ah, you should meet my brother's wife!' Very impressive!"

At odd times Hilary felt that Dick was worried about something. He seemed evasive when Hilary asked him one night how the mine was panning out. Instead of continuing on that subject he changed it swiftly.

"By the way, how are you making out with the handsome widow? Is she getting too tame?"

Lex was not present, so Hilary with a sort of relief aired his problem.

"I'm worried about that," he said seriously. "I'm at my wit's end how to handle it. The woman is strikingly beautiful, and in my own heart I believe she's bad. But if she is, she's diabolically clever in concealing it. The thing she continually wants from me is spiritual advice. How can I refuse that? She is lonely, she is despondent, she can't pray, she can't find God. Will I help her? Well, what else can I do?"

"What makes you think she's no good?"

"Oh, I don't know. She's had on some pretty revealing dresses when I've been to call, for one thing. And there's just a— Oh, you know how any man senses those things. She wanted to do parish work till I offered her some. Now she's afraid her health isn't quite up to it. The annoying thing is that she's always after me and I'm not dead sure but what she really needs help! It's so easy to misjudge."

"Have you told Lex?"

"No, I feel like a fool to say I think the woman's got a yen for me."

"I think you ought to tell Lex. Maybe she knows more about her than you do. And watch your step, my boy. Don't be too rough with her if you do find her out. 'Hell hath no fury, etc.,' you know. She might make trouble."

That night before they went to sleep Hilary spoke suddenly.

"Lex, do you know a woman by the name of Diana Downes?"

"Fred Downes' widow? I know her by sight. And of course everybody knows *about* her. She's considered the best-looking woman in the city. All the artists flock to paint her. There's a portrait of her in the Dale Gallery now. Why?"

"Oh, she has asked me to call several times to help her. She's very lonely."

Lex sat straight up in bed.

"*Lonely?* Diana Downes? What sort of a line has she been giving you? She never cared a hoot about Fred anyway. Why, she's the fastest thing in town. The crowd she goes with, really *steps*. Listen, has she been trying to play Madame Potiphar to your Joseph?"

Hilary was not as much surprised at her swift perception as at her classical reference.

"So you know who Madame Potiphar was?"

"My dear boy, my only real qualification for a rector's wife is that I know the Bible backwards. That's Muff's doing. She used to make me read a chapter every day. But tell me the truth, Hil. What about Diana Downes?"

"I don't exactly know," he said honestly. "She wants spiritual help."

"She does, my foot," said Lex inelegantly.

"The thing is that a gay person is often lonely at heart and could be seeking something better than worldly pleasure."

"Now you do sound like a parson. Oh, Hil, tell me truly. Do you think she's so beautiful?"

He held her close, for he had caught the note of anxiety.

"Now listen," he said. "Of course she's beautiful as a million women are. As to any response from me—well, Venus herself would leave me cold. I love one girl with all my soul, and to me she's the most beautiful being in the world. Are you satisfied?"

"Yes," she said, "but I've got a hunch that Diana is on your trail."

"She certainly knows I'm married."

"A little thing like marriage would never stop that lady. You'll be careful, Hil?"

"You can be very sure of that. Keep your ears open and tell me anything you hear about her. Meanwhile we'll forget her. Personally I hate the thought of her."

The old year ended in a round of gaiety. Then Dick went, leaving as always a void behind him; the calendar changed; the Christmas greens came down; the happy excitement merged into a memory; and the sober new year added day unto day.

To Hilary there was no real let down, for his work was piling mountain high before him, and Lex, after a brief time of restlessness, plunged with an almost fanatical fervor into the task of entertaining all the vestry and their wives. These dinners, stretching on through February, kept her busy and interested. The fact that they were unqualifiedly successful sent Hilary's pride soaring. At each she was the charming young hostess, smoothly at ease, gracefully deferent, her manner impeccable, her language faultless. No one from her outward seeming could guess that she had sworn freely to Muff while dressing, when a zipper caught in a seam, or stormed in the kitchen because the ice cream was delayed, or, when the guests were gone, had given Hilary her own résumé in her racy, modern vernacular of the table conversations. None of all these and other private outbursts marred the excellent impression of the dinners which Hilary heard mentioned on all sides.

It was with the coming of March and the beginning of Lent that Hilary felt as though a chill wind of the spirit had suddenly begun to blow upon him. In the first place the war kept looming larger. Stray sentences from the news would often fix themselves with dark threat upon his mind, as, "Finland calls twenty-year-olds to the colors." He kept thinking with a sort of irrational concern about those Finnish boys. Just the age of many of the young fellows who came to dance or bowl at the Parish House. Jim Dolton was just twenty, for example. Six foot Jim, big and clumsy as an elephant, cheerfully profane, wise with the wisdom which poverty and the slums can teach, warm-hearted and kind to a fault. It was Jim upon whom both he and Aunt Samantha depended for help when anything went wrong amongst the young people. Would the black cloud stretch across the sea as some pessimists believed? Would Jim and the rest of the boys ever have to throw their young bodies against a foreign foe? Not likely, and yet the thought haunted him.

Moreover there was a little cloud, not as yet bigger than a man's hand, between him and his vestry in the matter of policy. It came, he knew, entirely because of Henry Alvord.

This cloud which lowered over the vestry meetings was hard to deal with because it was so fluctuating, so intangible. Judge Ball and Stephen Cole were still his constant allies and Avison and Thornton his friends, but adroitly worded criticism from the others sometimes gave Hilary anxiety. Whether he wished it or not, he had become "news" in the city. His attitude toward the Parish House, for example, had been given wide publicity. So with the vesper sermons. They were striking, they were quotable. The fact that the church was at that time filled largely with men was news in itself. Reporters kept coming and presenting his views colorfully in their columns.

"One thing I should like to bring up, though I hesitate to do so," Alvord said at the March vestry meeting, "is this matter of—how shall I say it?—your rather original views as expressed at the vesper services. The newspapers make a great deal of what you say, and that is excellent as long as you do not say anything actually controversial, anything not in line with the attitude of St. Matthews as a church. Now this from last Monday's *Herald* gave me grave concern. I was not at the service, so this was the first I heard of it."

Alvord drew a clipping from his vest pocket and read the heading aloud: " 'Young Rector of St. Matthews Lashes Out Against Traditional Theology. Says Church Is Stifled by It.' I feel this demands an explanation."

Hilary smiled. "Reporters have to live, I suppose, but I get a little annoyed sometimes at the way they overemphasize certain things for effect. In the first place I didn't 'lash out' against anything. What I said, very calmly and consideredly, grew out of the talks I've been having with young students. I believe I told you that I'm setting aside Thursday evenings now to be in my study to confer with any who come. It almost looks as though one night wouldn't be enough. As to what I said on Sunday . . ."

He paused and looked at the faces around him. A dozen men, experienced in the management of large temporal affairs, good men all of them (with the possible exception of Alvord), and yet perhaps not more than half of them what he would call spiritually minded. Would they understand what he was talking about?

"What I said was that the one great mistake of the church, as I see it, is that it confuses theology and religion. Theology is man-made and likely at any point to be mistaken. Religion is the soul's search for God and dependence upon him. I said the church has put too much emphasis upon theology—is often stifled by it, in fact—and too little upon the honest, humble individual search for God."

"Now I'll say something," Judge Ball put in. "I've been hearing reports of these vesper services from a half-dozen men who never came to church before in their lives. They're telling other men like themselves about these sermons. Now it's one thing to preach to a congregation of people who believe every word you say before you say it. That's easy, relatively. It's something else again to attract men who believe nothing and send them away thinking. Mr. Laurens is doing both—and for the love of God don't lay a straw in his way."

"The only danger which I wished to point out," Alvord said icily, "and I consider it a very grave one, is that certain of our own older and most substantial members may be alarmed and estranged by these views, which seem to me somewhat out of line with traditional doctrine. I am gratified by the large attendance at vespers, but I feel it will be just as large if Mr. Laurens preaches conservatively, in a way which would be acceptable to all."

"Rot!" Judge Ball muttered under his breath.

Hilary's face went white.

"Gentlemen," he said, "I am your spiritual servant. I am trying with all my might to serve the needs of this parish. But in my sermons I must speak the truth as I see it and feel it."

"Good!" said Stephen Cole. "Go ahead."

It was five o'clock when the men were gone, but Hilary decided he would take a chance on finding Celeste Barton at home at the settlement. He craved a talk with her, and Lex was at a matinee with her mother and would not be home till late.

The Angel of Varny Street looked her full sixty years that day. Her fine, thin face was worn to the bone by weariness.

"Hilary!" she cried with unmistakable pleasure, as she opened her door. Then she laughed. "Do forgive my familiarity. It seems so natural to *tutoyer* you, as it were. But I'm terribly glad to see you. It's one of my down days."

"Mine too. That's why I came. And please continue to *tutoyer* me. I like it."

"Then you must reciprocate. Sit here. I'll light the fire and we'll have some tea. Oh, I'm weary with the world. It's been a frightful week."

"You tell first," Hilary said as the bright flame leaped up in the fireplace.

"Well, it's selfish but I'll go ahead. All in the last seven days we've had a near murder and a real suicide; one of my young men ran off with another man's wife, and little Tessie Torletto had a baby at thirteen. I have long stretches of feeling we're accomplishing something here, and then comes a succession of events like this and I feel like one of the seven maids with the mops sweeping up the sands!"

"I know," Hilary said. "I understand the feeling so well that I won't try to offer fatuous comfort. Yet it is true that it's the long stretches that count. And the good you do here simply can't be measured. You must realize that."

Celeste leaned her head against the sofa. "The worst of it all is that I sympathized with every one of these evildoers. I know now what led up to each tragedy: practically overpowering events. I wish all the people who see morality in terms of absolute black and white could live down here for a while. They'd get their eyes opened. Now, tell me your troubles. It does help of course to talk about them. I've had to keep bottled up this week for certain reasons."

"Mine may not sound as dramatic as yours, but they've been sad enough, most of them. I had to bury a little child. That always upsets me for days. I had the funeral of a man who left a lovely wife and three young sons just at the age to need him most. I've had to try to bring some comfort to three people hopelessly ill and try to patch up two homes about to break. My policeman friend, Mike Flannery, got drunk again and pawned the pants to his dress uniform. I had to get them out of hock for him so he could stand inspection. Our best soloist has left the choir to have a baby and won't be back for Easter. Hastings has taken a sudden strange dislike for Adams, my assistant, and, last but not least, some of my vestry don't like my talks at Sunday vespers."

Celeste smiled. "I saw Monday's paper. Are you up against real trouble?"

"I don't know, but I'm worried. You see I definitely went out to get the student and professional group at these meetings. Now they're coming and they're interested. I'm speaking to them simply and honestly and trying to build up something they can accept and live by. I've prayed and

164

wrestled more over these sermons than over any other thing I've ever done. I've been happy over the way the men have taken them. Perhaps I've even been a little proud. Popularity is a dangerous thing. The devil always gets a lick in at you then."

Celeste laughed.

"Come on, have a cup of hot tea. You're tired out and discouraged. No wonder. Have you thought of switching to other topics for vespers? The seven deadly sins, for example? You could be as simple and as honest as you want with them and yet not stir up any criticism."

Hilary looked at her, his eyes brightening.

"I believe your suggestion is good. Especially for Lent. I think I'll follow it. As a matter of fact a lot of the young fellows that come to talk with me want help or advice about the general problems of morality. That may be harder to handle in a sermon, though, than theology itself!"

"You'll think of a way. You'll do your young men good and pacify the old stick-in-the-muds at the same time. Temporarily, that is."

Suddenly her face brightened and became animated.

"Oh, I have one piece of nice news, only it's the greatest secret and you mustn't breathe it even in your prayers. Maudie Dunn has a boy-friend!"

"No!"

"Yes. But the affair is still in that delicate state when even a raised eyebrow might wreck it. I'm simply watching over it like a hen with one egg."

"Who on earth is he?"

"Well—don't drop your cup—he's an artist, a socialist, was threatened with a spot on his lung and hasn't two cents to rub against each other. Can you imagine her family's reaction to that?" she asked, laughing.

But Hilary did not join in the laughter. Instead, he looked anxious.

"Listen," he said, "I was responsible for getting Maudie down here. I don't want anything adverse to befall her."

"It's not adverse. I had to give it all to you dramatically, for it *is* startling. But it's wonderful just the same. This is the story. The young chap, Jerry Seaton, came here from the Middle West about a year ago to make his fortune as an artist. He has real talent. I've checked on that. But he's the shyest creature I've ever met. When we found him he was sick in a wretched little room back here, completely down and out. Now he's almost well—the doctor says he will be completely well eventually —and he's painting again."

A tender little smile crept over Celeste's face.

"At this point he and Maudie bumped into each other out here in the reception room one day. I imagine each was surprised to find another human being so embarrassed. Well, something happened in the moment

—as it does. Now they are seeing each other regularly. They take walks in the late afternoon. It's so pitiful and so sweet! He adores her with his eyes, wondering how she can stoop to look on him. Her smile is pure worship, for she can't quite dare to believe that he actually loves her for herself."

She straightened and her lips grew firm.

"And I'm going to see to it that nothing touches that love! They need each other. They're perfect for each other. Poor Maudie's life has been all but ruined. Now she's beginning to live, and you should see her! She gets prettier every day. She wears suits and blouses instead of all those frills her aunt used to pick for her. She's developing a small, growing mind of her own. She hardly ever stammers. And Jerry's gaining by leaps and bounds. He's got a reason now to live and to work. Well," she ended, laughing, "I didn't mean to browbeat you about it. I guess I'm just preparing myself for an eventual encounter with her father."

Hilary still looked grave. "I'm glad for Maudie if it looks like happiness, but I feel horribly responsible to J. V. If the thing goes on, could you manage to let me meet the young fellow some time?"

"Of course. But not for a while. Even I don't say a single word yet. I just beam on them with all I've got whenever I see them. It's all so delicate—like a little spring flower which a cold wind might kill. I know I sound like a romantic old fool, but I feel this deeply. I want those two to get married."

On his way home, Hilary kept thinking of Maudie and of J. V. If the faintest rumor of this affair reached him he would take Maudie away from the settlement—by force if necessary. Perhaps the friendship with young Seaton would serve only to give Maudie sufficient charm and assurance at last to attract another, more suitable man. This, however, would be pretty rough on Seaton if he really cared for the girl. Hilary decided he must trust Celeste's judgment for the moment but try as soon as he dared to meet Seaton and form his own opinion. Meanwhile he would continue to have a feeling of discomfort if not actual guilt, for J. V. had thanked him again with beaming eyes only a week ago, saying that the settlement work was doing Maudie so much good!

From this his own thoughts moved now to J. V.'s ownership of the *Courier* and Tommy Tatler's paragraph about Lex. It had made a deeper mark upon his heart than he had admitted. The thing kept recurring to him constantly. He hated the daring, smart-aleck words with all their implications. They not only angered him; they raised in his mind an anxiety which all but stifled him. The more so because in these last weeks, with the ending of the series of dinner parties, Lex had seemed restless. So many of his evenings were full, and in consequence hers were empty.

She went home often when he was occupied, and once or twice had gone to the theater with Clarissa Ball and the Judge. He must try hard, he decided now, to keep evenings free and to take her out himself wherever he decently could. Naturally for him night clubs were impossible during Lent. The whole weight of interests lying upon his mind and heart were a world removed from those which would naturally engage Lex. This old fact was for the first time since their marriage rising seriously to confront them.

He found her cheerful, however, when he got home. The play had been fun. Hilary must see it. She was going to help with a Junior League Benefit. Be chairman of a committee, in fact. It would be something to do.

"It's the evenings, Hil, that bother me. We never go anywhere interesting. Never do anything that's really fun. I think you need diversion too. You're awfully thin," she ended suddenly.

"Lent is always the hardest time for a clergyman. After Easter I'll rest up a little. We'll do something exciting. Maybe go off somewhere for a few days. A second honeymoon."

"I'd love that."

He drew her down to his knee. "I know you miss the excitement you were used to. Don't ever think I don't understand. But try to be patient, darling."

"I guess you're the one that must be patient. Don't pay any attention to my moods."

She was looking into the fire and suddenly she laughed aloud.

"What is it?" Hilary asked.

"I was remembering a funny night just about a year ago. There certainly is a contrast between my life then and now!"

"What about that night?"

"Oh, it was crazy, but we had such fun! We were all at Bette Haviland's dance till about two and then the party went flat, so one of the fellows suggested that eight of us go up to the Nat and swim. He was a wizard at water polo. So we went and had a marvellous time till about four, and then we were starved. One of the boys' fathers has a penthouse downtown, and he just remembered his sister was using it for a party that night and there might be food left. So we all got dressed and went down. It was a gorgeous penthouse and we ate up all the food and then played shuffleboard on one of the terraces till the sun came up."

She paused, threading her slim fingers through Hilary's long ones.

"What a sunrise! I was with Jack Brennan that night. He's a Catholic, so he suggested we go to six-thirty Mass at St. Catherine's and then get breakfast, and that's what we did. I wore Jack's handkerchief over my head to church. Imagine, with a blue chiffon evening dress! It's a wonder they let me in. The other girls looked just as bad. It was nice though, really, going to church so early. Then after Mass the boys routed out some couple they know down there who ran a little restaurant, and they cooked us sausages and pancakes! We ate like swine. I got home about eight. Sunday morning. You should have seen Muff! She was always scandalized when I was out all night."

She giggled, her face all alight.

"Our crowd was always doing the craziest things. Did I ever tell you about the night the boys took over the orchestra at the Raven Club? They were all pretty happy by that time, and no one could do a thing with them. Besides, it was so funny the whole place went mad. I was with Bill Lowden. He played the saxophone, or tried to. What a riot! What a night!"

Hilary's face had stiffened.

"Lex, there's something I've never asked you, but you must tell me now. Were you ever in love with any one else?"

She nestled closer in his arms.

"There were a lot of fellows that I was very fond of and that I always had fun with. But there's been only one man I ever wanted to marry. Give you three guesses!"

As though Celeste's advice had been prophetic, three of the young men who came to consult Hilary Thursday evening were concerned with the subject of morals. They were looking forward to professional careers. The way was long. Marriage was still far in the distance. They were earnest in their concern over their problems. Hilary was touched by their confidences, given him evidently because he, too, was a young man. He found himself promising to preach upon the matter on the third Sunday afternoon of Lent.

The fourth caller that night was of a different type entirely. He entered the study hesitantly, covered with embarrassment. Hilary's efforts to put him at his ease were unavailing. He was a fresh faced youth with dark, serious eyes. His whole countenance looked as though it was unused to laughter. After several false starts he confessed that he was ashamed of coming, but that having read certain things in the papers about the vesper sermons he had felt emboldened to do so. He was a theological student at the Calvin Seminary. Hilary had heard of the institution, one of those small, narrow-minded organizations designed, as Grandy used to say, "for the earnest propagation of ignorance and intolerance." Hilary watched the nervous young man before him with interest and a deep sympathy. He was plainly troubled.

"All my life," he was saying now, "I've believed every word of the Bible from Genesis to Revelation. I've never known a doubt until these last weeks."

At the look on Hilary's face he half smiled. "It wasn't anything you said that did it. I never heard of you until after I began to suffer so. Then when I read about your sermons in the paper I thought maybe I could talk to you. You see I'm so worried I haven't been sleeping lately."

"Tell me," Hilary said kindly. "I only hope I can help you."

"It's the miracle of feeding the five thousand. Just suddenly one day I found I couldn't believe that. I thought then it was the devil tempting me and that I could overcome it. I prayed night and day, but it didn't help. I still can't believe it. And the thing that's driving me to despair is that if I doubt one thing I may doubt another. Then everything will be swept away. And I've always wanted to preach the Gospel. I'm—I'm desperate. I don't know what to do."

The white anguish on his face went to Hilary's heart. He began speaking slowly.

"Suppose I tell you how that incident of the feeding the five thousand seems to me. As a matter of fact I love to think of it. The whole scene must have been beautiful. It happened in the spring, you remember, and the glens and slopes there at Batiha would be covered with green grass. Below, the lake would be blue and dotted with little sailboats here and there. It was sunset. The hundreds of people who had come a long way to hear Jesus preach still didn't want to leave. The disciples were nervous and anxious about the crowd and probably hungry themselves. What was to be done?"

Hilary saw that the young man had stopped his nervous fingering of his hat and was still.

"As the disciples questioned Jesus about the problem of food, a little lad, sitting evidently in the front row of the crowd, who had brought his lunch with him, impulsively offered it. Now does it not seem reasonable to you that perhaps half the crowd, or a third at least, had also been provident enough to bring some food with them, knowing the circumstances? The rest of them, human nature being as it is, had probably rushed carelessly off without any. Jesus made no demands, no suggestions. He simply accepted the lad's gift of the three little loaves and the few fishes and raising them high in the sight of all, blessed them and gave them to the disciples to distribute. What do you think probably happened then?"

The young man was leaning forward, his eyes fixed on Hilary's face.

"I am only telling you how I have always liked to interpret this story. I think that Jesus' sublime faith in them touched the selfish hearts of the crowd so that suddenly all those who had brought food turned it over to the disciples, and when it was divided and distributed it proved to be enough for all."

The young man stared in amazement but he did not speak.

"Which interpretation of the incident seems to you to have the deepest meaning for us, the greatest motivating power? The belief that Jesus by pressing some sort of supernatural button increased three loaves to the amount needed to feed a multitude, or that by his teaching and the inspiration of his personality he caused several thousand people to win a victory over selfishness and share their food with those who had none? Which?" Hilary asked.

The young man moistened his dry lips. "The latter," he answered.

"It seems so to me," Hilary said quietly. Then he added: "I'll tell you the verse that has helped me in this connection. It's this one: 'The letter killeth but the spirit giveth life.' When you try to believe the Bible according to the *letter* you will find you have killed much of its truth. If you read it only in search of the spiritual, you will find life on every page."

There was a silence. Hilary expected argument and question, but instead with a long, shaken sigh the young student got up and reached for Hilary's hand. He wrung it hard.

"Thank you," he said huskily. "Thank you. I think I can sleep tonight."

Hilary worked every extra available minute during the next week upon his sermon on morality. It did not please him. The subject itself was difficult enough in all conscience, but all his efforts to arrange constructive thoughts about it were, he felt, completely unsuccessful. Meanwhile, the topic had been announced in the newspapers and also upon the weekly bulletins which went to the University, the Medical and Law Schools. After tearing up his fifth draft, Hilary sat in his study Saturday morning in a state approaching despair. This was something he must do well or not at all. He had not so far done it well and he could think of no better approach than the ones he had already tried.

He had gone in the beginning to the brown scrapbook for help. Under "Morality" Grandy had jotted down many important notes, some of them causing the corners of Hilary's mouth to twitch, some of them so serious, with illustrations drawn from his own pastoral experience, that Hilary shuddered as he read. There was a Scriptural reference given also. It was from Proverbs, and the Bishop had added: "To my mind one of the most dramatic pieces of prose ever written."

Hilary had read these verses from the seventh and ninth chapters carefully. He had an innate susceptibility to words. He agreed with Grandy's opinion and decided at once to use them as an introduction to his sermon. But at midnight Saturday night there still was no sermon. Lex had been tired for once and gone early to bed, so, with the world shut out, Hilary worked on in his study. One o'clock came, and two. His head was hot and his hands unsteady as he wrote.

"Il ne marche pas," he said at last almost with violence, and twisting the paper in his hand, flung it into the wastebasket.

He turned to the verses he had planned to use as a text. Suddenly, as they met his eyes now, an idea leaped to his brain. Why had he not thought of it at once? What could he or any other man say on this subject to compare with what had been said by the wise, sophisticated poet-king of the long ago! He stood up, rejoicing in the relief of a perfect solution to a vexing problem, and read the passages slowly aloud. Then, with a strong inner excitement, he went down to the church itself, turned on the light at the lectern and read them again and yet again. He was content. He had his sermon.

The next afternoon at four o'clock the church was filled. Something turned over in Hilary's heart as he saw the rows upon rows of young men sitting there, their faces watchful, expectant, waiting for some sort of guidance. With most desperate earnestness he prayed silently as he knelt in his place in the chancel, that his strange message would be blessed to their need.

The music was unusually beautiful. (He had made a last-minute request for an extra anthem.) Adams' reading of the evening prayers was moving, as always. At last it was time for him. Hilary moved toward the pulpit, ascended it, faced the altar, turned, and stood for a moment looking over the large audience. Then slowly, in measured cadence he began to read.

> My son, keep my words, and lay up my commandments with thee. That they may keep thee from the strange woman, from the stranger which flattereth with her words. For at the window of my house I looked through my case-ment, and beheld among the youths, a young man devoid of understanding, passing through the street near her corner; and he went the way to her house, in the twilight, in the evening, in the black and dark night; and behold there met him a woman with the attire of an harlot and subtil of heart. So she caught him, and kissed him, and with an impudent face said unto him, I have perfumed my bed with myrrh, aloes, and cinnamon. Come, let us take our fill of love until the morning. Let us solace ourselves with loves. For the goodman is not at home, he is gone a long journey.

As Hilary read slowly on, there was a silence in the church so profound that no breath or movement stirred it. He raised his head at last and looked into the faces raised to his. He spoke the final lines with his eyes upon them, giving majestic weight to every syllable.

She saith to him, Stolen waters are sweet and bread eaten in secret is pleasant. But he knoweth not that the dead are there; and that her guests are in the depths of hell.

The vestibule was crowded after the service. Many of the young men waiting asked hesitantly to be told again where the passages just read could be found. Hilary decided in the moment to have copies printed for mailing.

When he reached the rectory at last he was so weary he could hardly hold his head up. The late night, the usual strain of the morning services along with the tension connected with vespers, had left him exhausted. He was disappointed to find the McCollys there for tea, for he would have preferred a quiet evening with Lex. He pulled himself together, however, and tried to act his part as host. Lex, in palest green, looked like the first spring flower. His eyes rested continually upon her face, waiting for her smile.

"Hilary's killing himself," she said as Morris was removing the tea things, "and nothing I can say affects him. Thank goodness it will soon be Easter. Isn't he thin, Mother?"

"You are, Hilary. Are you sure you're well?"

"Perfectly. Just tired. A late night working, and a full day today. I'll rest up tomorrow."

"He'll rest up," said Lex, "by making six calls, having an unexpected wedding and a funeral or two, reading a paper at the Clerical Club, and supervising something or other in the Parish House half the night. I'm a neglected wife, I tell you. I'm thinking of a divorce."

"Lex! Please don't say such things even in fun."

She was quickly penitent. "Don't be a goose, Hil. My big worry is that you're running yourself ragged. You've got to take a vacation after Easter. Things really are going well, though, with the church, aren't they?" Her voice held an unexpected note of pride.

"I think so. We had amazing congregations at all the services today. Oh, by the way," he added, turning to Old Alex, "you've never got that information I wanted, have you? About the ownership of those flats?"

Old Alex fidgeted. "When things are going well, why do you have to stir up trouble? Why don't you keep your nose out of those flats?"

Hilary glanced around. Lex was bearing her mother off upstairs to display her new suit and had not heard her father's remark. He turned back quickly to Old Alex.

"I've really got to go into that. Did you find out the owner?"

"I did, three months ago. I've been stalling, for I'm warning you it's none of your business. If I tell you it's going to put you on the spot. Now you be sensible and don't ask any more questions."

Hilary's tired face grew whiter.

"I must know," he said quietly. "Please tell me without more delay."

Old Alex made a despairing motion with his cigar.

"All right," he said, "you asked for it. The man who owns those flats is Henry Alvord."

CHAPTER X

HILARY WOULD HAVE confided to no one his method of using the brown scrapbook which was proving his grandfather's most valuable bequest to him. During the first weeks it had been in his possession he had found remembrance too painful as he had glanced at the neat, hauntingly familiar script. Later, when he had read enough to discover what a store-house of wisdom and practical help the volume contained, he had considered two ways in which he might employ it. One was to read it through at once, and then, with a general knowledge of what it contained, return to it from time to time to refresh his memory as to its advice.

The other was a more sentimental and slightly illogical approach, but Hilary chose it. He decided to remain unaware of the full contents of the book, going to it only in times of real need, just as he would have gone to his grandfather, himself, for special counsel. What he then found would seem a more direct contact with the Bishop's own spirit because of the sudden and appropriate timing.

His other reason for this method was that he wanted to make his own way, rely upon his own judgment, and reach his own decisions, without dependence upon any one, even Grandy. Even though he made mistakes, he must shoulder his own responsibilities in his own way. Only in extremities would he consult the book.

On the morning after the alarming disclosure concerning Henry Alvord, Hilary went straight to his study, disregarded the mail, and took down the worn volume. Since it was so carefully—if originally—indexed he could always find quickly what he wanted. He went down the list of V's now, smiling as he read:

vacations	vespers
vanity	vestry
ventilation (church)	

He turned to the page for "vestry." There was detailed information concerning their election, function, general qualifications, and the rector's attitude toward them. Underneath was written:

General Comment

In my years as a rector I was always fortunate in my vestry. In all my parishes they were, with three exceptions, fine men. Capable in managing the temporal affairs of the parish but also good men in the best sense: devoted to the church, honest, chaste, upright, kindly. The type of men needed to build a church (or a world) upon. My deepest friendships through the years were with my vestrymen. But as to the three (not many exceptions over a thirty years' ministry) one was immoral, one dishonest, and one just plain ornery. (By the way, the dictionary definition of that word is: "mean; low." In trying to describe the spiritual state of this man, this is the only term that fits.)

In each case, once I was sure of the facts, I tried to get him to change his ways. When this failed I asked for the man's resignation. And in each case it was a sore, troublesome business, especially since the wife of each was a fine woman. But my strong feeling, increasing during my years as bishop, is that the leaders of any church, while naturally faulty and fallible like all humans, must have as their outstanding characteristic an unquestionable and unswerving *purpose for good* in all the departments of their lives. If they fall short of this, they are a hindrance to the church of God and should not hold office in it.

Here's a story: Back in Maryville in my grandfather's day there was a Presbyterian elder who was supposed to give short measure when he sold his grain. One day when he was out at his corncrib ready to load his wagon, old Dr. McAllister, the preacher, drove up, took off his long-tailed coat, hung it over the fence, and pitched in to help him. On each skimpy bushel the preacher would pile on more ears. " 'Good measure, pressed down, shaken together, and running over,' " he'd say. "That's what the Bible tells us."

The elder was furious but helpless. When the load was finished the old preacher straightened up and looked him in the eye. "A man that serves in the house of the Lord must serve him also at the corncrib," he said, and left. The story went that the elder gave full measure after that. So, try first to convert your man to good ways. If it isn't possible, don't compromise. Oust him.

Hilary replaced the volume, his face grave. He must still proceed slowly, carefully, but proceed he must, eventually.

175

In the mail were many letters concerning what he called now in his own mind, "Solomon's Sermon." One in particular surprised him. It was from Dr. Shane. They had met one way and another frequently during the last months and had advanced to terms of real friendship.

> DEAR LAURENS:
>
> As you know we doctors don't have much time for the luxury of saving our souls but this afternoon I dropped in on your vesper service to see what all the commotion was about. I haven't been so impressed in many a long year. Tell me again what that passage was that you read, will you? It mightn't do me any harm to look it over occasionally.
>
> Do you know what I've recently decided? A man that stays a bachelor all his life is a damn fool.
>
> SHANE

"I wonder," Hilary muttered to himself, "if he might be in love."

Lex's joking description of his Monday holiday had not been far wrong, Hilary wryly admitted to himself as he stacked the mail for Miss Mowbray tomorrow, and then considered what lay before him. There was a funeral at three. A hard one, too. He wondered now if the average layman ever dreamed how much emotional strain a clergyman suffered through his constant association with death. Much more than a doctor, for example, for the latter was concerned chiefly with curing men's ills. When he failed, he was rarely ever present at the end. Then he could forget the case and go on his busy way. The minister was the one who must at that point take over and perform the strange, sad, almost primitive rites of burial. It was he who must consign the body to the earth: *"Thou most worthy Judge eternal, suffer us not, at our last hour, for any pains of death, to fall from Thee . . ."* It was he who must tear from his own heart some comfort for the stricken family. Unless he suffered with them the words of holy consolation did not, somehow, ring true. He wondered if after long years in the ministry he would learn to look calmly, objectively upon this part of his work; if he would ever repeat the Committal at the grave, watch the white faces of grief bent above it, and then go home cheerfully to his own dinner. Perhaps men of God had to learn this in order to save their own health and reason. So far, he had not.

Today's service was a poignant one to him. The young woman, a Mrs. Hartley, wife of a University professor, had sent for him the day before she went to the hospital. He could see her vividly now, her face laughing and apologetic by turns.

"It's really just a simple thing I'm going for. I know I'm silly even to think of any danger in connection with it, but since I have no family near, would you keep this envelope and give it to Hank, my husband, if—if anything should go wrong? Of course nothing will and we'll have a huge laugh over it when I get back. It's a sort of mixture of where to look for the children's summer underwear and how much I love them all! Isn't it idiotic?"

She was delightfully entertaining, and they had been quite gay when he left. On the way back he had smiled over the foolishness of women and the curious commissions intrusted to the clergy. A week later he had handed the letter to Henry Hartley.

"The service will be in the church, of course," Hartley had said with white lips. "Everything just as she would wish. As for myself, perhaps I should tell you that I think there is nothing after death. Nothing."

This lay heavily upon Hilary's heart. For the man's own sake and for the sake of that laughing, eager face that had turned to him that day, he must try to find some help for him. No mere repetition of the usual Scriptural phrases would do in this case, not even the conventional Easter sermon. The man was a scientist. Hilary knit his dark brows. He must find time somehow to do some extra reading along this line, searching for an approach to the whole matter which would seem at least intelligent to Hartley's mind. He made a note of this.

This afternoon at five there was a meeting of the Clerical Club at which Hilary was to speak. (He was planning to skip the dinner which followed because he was determined to take Lex out that night.) The Clerical Club was at once a challenge and an aggravation. It seemed to him it offered a possibility for the development of religious unity and tolerance if representatives not only of various denominations but also of all the major creeds were invited to join. Instead, it resolved itself into a small group of rectors who read erudite papers on the Pauline doctrines and was permeated by a mild exclusiveness. He was determined to set forth his views that night. What about making the club a forum for the discussion of the problems they all, as city ministers, faced? What about inviting Father Connelly of St. Mary's and Rabbi Hershman to join if they would? Probably they wouldn't, but no harm in asking.

Hilary knew this would be a bombshell, and might produce no constructive results but he couldn't go on month after month without at least expressing his honest conviction. He got out his notes for his speech now and was going over them when Hastings stuck his head in the door. On Mondays, with Miss Mowbray off, Hastings gloried in answering the telephone.

"It's that Mrs. Diana Downes," he said in a stage whisper. "She don't give you no peace. What'll I tell her?"

Hilary got up suddenly, shoved his notes in his pocket, and started out.

"I'm not here, Hastings, and there is no possible way of reaching me."

"That's what I thought. Fact is, that's what I thought that first Sunday when she give me the note. I'll take care of her," he added darkly.

At a quarter to seven that night Hilary ran up the stairs in the rectory and found Lex dressing in their room. He caught her to him and circled about the floor.

"Let's go dancing!" he said. "You're right. I've just realized it. I do need diversion. I've got to throw off care and other people's troubles once in a while or I'll go crazy. What do you say, Mrs. Laurens? May I date you up for the evening?"

Lex's eyes shone. "Oh, Hil, this is wonderful! This is just as though you were a regular—just as though you weren't a parson at all! You even look different! Honestly, you don't know how serious you've been lately. A regularly old Jeremiah. And dancing! You know how I love that, and I haven't danced for weeks and weeks. Oh, let's have a lovely time tonight!"

"I don't believe it had better be a night club, darling. I'm sorry, for after all, I'm young myself. I'd like to go out once in a while and kick over the traces and not care a cent who saw me. But can't we go somewhere else very top-drawer and elegant where there's good food and a good orchestra?"

"I know the very place," Lex said. "The Windsor! I've always been keen about it. It costs like murder, though."

Hilary made an expansive gesture. "A fig for the cost! This is our big night. Good heavens, you must have flowers, and the florists will be closed! Do they grow orchids at the Windsor?"

"Yes. Beauties. You're so sweet, Hil! No wonder I married you in spite of everything."

"Let's have a sandwich and coffee up here now while I'm catching my breath, then we'll go out for dinner about eight-thirty. O.K.?"

"Perfect. I'll tell Morris."

She paused in the doorway, turning to look at him mischievously. "I feel quite like a girl again," she said.

The words struck Hilary. Lex had been pretty patient, considering all she had given up. Suddenly he had a glimpse of something so deep and unalterable in her that it was like a revelation. Who, he thought, was he to have won her love?

When they returned that night they stood a moment in the lower hall. Lex dropped her wrap and her bare shoulders gleamed in the soft light. Hilary stooped and pressed his lips to her arms, her throat, her lips.

"Did you have a good time?" he whispered.

She looked up at him soberly.

"I don't believe you realize how handsome you are in evening clothes!

Yes, it's been wonderful tonight." She drew a little sigh. "I needed this, Hil. Let's do it often. Don't forget!"

Before he fell asleep, Hilary thought again of Hartley, whose wife he had buried that afternoon, lying now with his arms empty, his heart void of hope. He turned and drew Lex's warm, fragrant body closer to him. He must get some new books on the subject of immortality and see if he could find a thought, even a hint which might reach the man.

He thought again, too, of his speech at the Clerical Club. As he had feared he hadn't gotten to first base with his suggestion. Well, at least he had made it, and he could keep on trying!

With all the pressure of the Lenten season upon him, Hilary finally decided to postpone taking up the tenement ownership problem until after Easter. His days were so crowded that he often, if Lex was to be out, dashed across to Mrs. Milligan's hole-in-the-wall shop for a quick lunch after the daily noon-time service. These, like Sunday vespers, were now thronged with men and Hilary strove earnestly over the brief ad-dresses. It was becoming increasingly clear that his greatest work was to be that of a preacher. Adams was taking over, more and more, the routine pastoral duties, though of course there were still many weddings and funerals for which Hilary's services were particularly asked. But his fame as a preacher was spreading. He would have been less than human if he had not realized this and humbly rejoiced in it. All his native powers of mind and personality seemed to unite as he mounted the pulpit steps.

> Oft when the word is on me to deliver,
> Lifts the illusion and the truth lies bare!

The lines came often to his mind as he looked down upon a waiting audience and felt the certain power of the words given him; felt the need of the hungry souls and his own longing to serve them; felt, in fleet-ing, exalted moments, in touch with those deep, spiritual reservoirs from which the heart of man must draw. Daily he prayed for guidance and humility in his preaching.

Attractive invitations to speak at this affair or that kept pouring in constantly. Because he loved dealing with ideas and with words, because he possessed that magnetic quality which draws and holds an audience, he still, as from the first, had a half-shamed longing to accept them all. This was, of course, impossible, so he curbed his desire and tried to choose the occasions with increasing discrimination. Miss Mowbray was of the great-est help here. Her knowledge of the city and its featured organizations was extensive. In addition to this she had an uncanny way of discovering the plain and often extremely shaky framework beneath many a highly upholstered "benefit" or "rally." As a rule he followed her advice in the matter of selection, and kept these occasions down to a minimum, but he could not help knowing that there was wide acclaim for him as a speaker.

One day, when Lex had planned to lunch with her mother, Hilary crossed to Mrs. Milligan's when the noon service was finished. The latter eyed him with her usual affectionate interest.

"It's gettin' more and more like ourselves ye are every day," she said to him.

"How so, Mrs. Milligan?"

"The people, the crowds goin' in. Anybody'd think it was a Catholic church to look at it now. I'll tell ye what," she added confidentially. "When the Pope dies I'll vote for you!"

At that moment Miss Mowbray entered, and the quip was repeated for her benefit. She took a stool next to Hilary at the counter and they laughed together as they ate. They were laughing again as they left, over Mrs. Milligan's parting salute. Then, as they crossed the street together they fell to discussing a speaking invitation which had come in the morning's mail.

"I wouldn't go there," Miss Mowbray was saying positively as they reached the opposite curb. "I think it would be a foolish waste of time. I know that set-up."

"All right," said Hilary smiling. "I guess that settles it."

So engrossed had they both been in their conversation that neither had noticed Lex, standing near the entrance to the Parish House. Hilary now saw her first and looked rueful. The only thought in his mind was that he had somehow missed having lunch with her.

"Why, Lex," he said, "how do you come to be here? I thought you were uptown with your mother."

"That was called off at the last minute. I've been wondering where you were."

Her dimpled chin was well up and there was a quizzical look in her eyes.

"Hello, Miss Mowbray," she added.

Miss Mowbray's expression was strange. Even before she spoke, Hilary saw to his amazement and discomfort that she had flushed up to the very roots of her ash-blond hair.

"I'll run on in and get to work," she said now, trying apparently to sound casual. "Goodbye, Mrs. Laurens."

When she was gone Lex stood looking up at her husband.

"So," she said, "I have secretary trouble and didn't know it!"

"Don't be an utter goose! Come on. Let's walk round the block and get some air. I'm terribly sorry I didn't go home to lunch. When I know you're going to be out I often run over here for a snack. It saves time. You know Morris. He makes a ceremony even over a sandwich. And just now I'm so rushed."

Lex slipped her arm through his.

"All right. I really do understand how it is. But what about Miss Mowbray?"

"Well—nothing. She eats there usually because it's convenient. She says Mrs. Milligan always cheers her up. The old woman's funny as a crutch. That's all there is to tell."

"Not quite, Hil."

"What do you mean?"

"Didn't you see her blush?"

"Yes," he admitted hesitatingly, "I did. I don't know what struck her." They walked on for a few minutes in silence, then Lex spoke.

"She's in love with you, Hil."

"Don't!" Hilary said almost angrily. "Don't say such a thing. It's absurd! She's the most poised, sensible girl in the world. I don't want you ever to think that again, let alone speak it."

"Well," Lex said, "don't get so excited about it. I don't like the idea myself, but at least I'm trying to treat it calmly."

"But it's not so! It's perfectly ridiculous. She was just a little flustered now for some reason."

"Don't be a modest ass, Hil. I think it would be more queer if she didn't fall for you. Only I had never thought of it before and I don't feel too comfortable about it, somehow."

"And what about me? You've put this darned idea in my head and I'll be afraid now even to smile at the girl. I wish you'd kept your crazy thoughts to yourself, as you should have done."

It was the nearest to sharp words he had ever come, and suddenly Lex's eyes filled. She dropped his arm and turned back without speaking. Hilary looked at her quickly and then felt wild with anger at himself.

"Darling," he said, "please forgive me! I don't know why on earth I snapped like that. I was upset and embarrassed, I guess, because I have to work with her every day. Lex, let's go home for a minute. I've got to be sure you forgive me. I know I'm edgy these days, for I feel so tired and so driven. But that's no excuse. I could kill myself for making you weep."

They went back to the house and he took her in his arms, protesting his love between his kisses. Lex slowly smiled again and reassured him. But as he returned to his study he was still disturbed, most of all because, for the first time, quick words of his had brought tears to Lex's eyes.

He found Miss Mowbray her usual calm, contained self. She met him before he reached his door.

"You have a caller," she said in a low voice. "I tried to steer him off but he was insistent. He said he would wait till you came. He's in there now." She handed him a card. It read: "Rev. James C. Murdoch, D.D."

Hilary walked in. His guest was a short, stocky man of perhaps fifty with black eyes, an unlined face and dark, thinning hair. His chin was strong, and his lips thin.

They shook hands and sat down, Hilary uneasily conscious of the work awaiting him. He hoped the man would not (in Grandy's parlance) "have his sittin' breeches on."

"Mr. Laurens," the caller began, "I have come to you in the spirit of Christ to see if by some means it might be given me to turn your mind from the heresies you are disseminating. You are young yourself. You may not realize the great harm you are doing to those, especially the young, who come to hear you preach. You are doubtless carried away by a desire for popularity and false adulation. But what you do not realize is that you are selling your own soul to the devil."

Hilary looked back at him blankly, too surprised to speak.

"I am a professor of theology in the Calvin Seminary," the other went on. "One of our most promising young men has left us, largely, I think, due to a recent conversation with you. He finally confessed as much. The weight of that you must bear upon your own conscience."

Hilary recalled at once the troubled young divinity student and felt a sudden pleasure at his release.

"He's not giving up the ministry, is he?" he asked eagerly.

"I believe," the other said stiffly, "that he is changing to another seminary, but the harm already done him is irreparable. How can you, for the sake of a little publicity, a little notoriety, tamper with the word of God and with men's immortal souls? How can you sell for a mess of pottage that faith once delivered to the saints?"

Hilary was still so dumfounded that no words came to his lips. Besides, the other, evidently feeling he was making the impression he wished, rushed on, without waiting.

"I have read extracts of your vesper sermons in the papers; I have talked with some men who have been to your services. Everything gives evidence of the fact that you are unsound. These young men who come to consult you have doubtless been touched by the poison of doubt. Are you establishing their faith or breaking it down? If they question those tenets of the creed against which the higher criticism has been aimed, *what are you answering them?*" His dark eyes pierced Hilary's, as he leaned tensely forward.

"But, my dear sir," Hilary said, "the young men who come here to talk to me aren't even considering the matters you have in mind. You're thinking in terms of a generation ago. These young people now are asking, Is there a God? Does he *care*? Can prayer reach him? Does his hand actually guide the universe? These are the questions that our young people—the ones who really think—are asking today. If any one will listen to them," he added.

The man before him looked stunned. "You mean then that they do not question the usual disputed articles of the creed?"

"No, I don't mean that. Those points simply do not seem important to them. They've gone away beyond that. As I say, it was their fathers who questioned those. This new generation is thinking in different terms, and, I believe, straighter to the mark."

Dr. Murdoch's face was actually pale in his earnestness. His voice had the sternness of doom in it.

"There are no different terms for religion in different generations, Mr. Laurens. There is one plan of salvation and one only, whereby men may be saved and those who reject it will be utterly lost. Lose sight of that at your peril. I have never before heard any minister of the Gospel so desecrate his holy office as you have just now done by your loose words. You say lightly that some people consider certain tenets of the creed unimportant. You evidently concur with this or condone it. The creed! Upon which the whole Christian church rests! Mr. Laurens, I tell you you are an *apostate*. In sackcloth and ashes you should leave your pulpit before you lead any more souls to hell."

Hilary flushed, and pressed down a not unnatural anger.

"Dr. Murdoch, you have certainly not spared my feelings. Now I'm going to tell you how I feel about you. Your conviction that you are absolutely right in all things religious, and your readiness to sit in judgment upon any who differ with you, savors to me not so much of true faith as of spiritual self-conceit. Maybe a little humble uncertainty is good for a soul. Maybe it would be good for yours."

Dr. Murdoch started to retort, but Hilary raised his finger.

"The other thing I want to say is more important. I want you to do something for me. I want you to face a question honestly. If Jesus could suddenly come back to earth, now in March, 1940, do you think he would be concerned over anybody's adherence to a creed? Do you think he would even have the slightest interest in creeds? Do you honestly think he would?"

"I—"

"Or," Hilary went on, "would he preach as he did before, as the compassionate Son of Man, looking out upon a stricken world, beseeching men to love God as their Father and all men as their neighbors, to feed the hungry, clothe the naked, and visit the sick and the poor. Would this not be the burden of his message? I charge you to think of this, for it has great bearing upon our present-day religion, and answer it in your own soul. I have already answered it in mine."

Dr. Murdoch rose slowly, his lips set.

"I can only reply by telling you that I shall pray that somehow your heart may be enlightened and that you may be brought to a knowledge of the truth."

"Thank you," said Hilary courteously. "I shall do the same for you."

Dr. Murdoch looked up, startled and angry, then shook his head and allowed himself to be ushered out without further words. When he had disappeared down the stairs, Hilary remained leaning in the study doorway.

"What is it?" Miss Mowbray asked, from her desk in the outer office. "You look completely done in."

Hilary smiled, forgetting momentarily the complication of Miss Mowbray.

"I don't think I like being consigned to hell even though I don't expect to go," he answered.

Margaret Mowbray's face stiffened.

"I knew that man was here for no good. I should have headed him off. You have enough to think of right now. I'll see to him if he comes again."

"I don't believe he will," Hilary said, "but it's all right. My skin is thick."

He went back into the study hastily and closed the door. There had been in Margaret's voice a certain protective fierceness. This sudden revelation concerning her had hit him hard.

He sat down now, thinking over the conversation with Murdoch. He was glad he had kept his temper and yet said his say. But how comfortable, how immeasurably comfortable to be entirely sure of one's self in all matters of religion! To lean upon a system of theology, and rest one's mind upon it completely! That was the way with Murdoch and his kind. That was the way also with Father Connelly of St. Mary's, of whom Hilary had grown very fond. They were both young men, congenial in most ways except doctrine. Once only to him Hilary had ventured a hesitant question:

"Do you ever think about religious matters as honestly and openly as you would about anything else?"

"I beg your pardon?"

"I mean, do you believe everything your church teaches without question?"

"Of course," Father Connelly answered. "The church is our infallible mother."

184

He was thinking now that consciously or unconsciously both Murdoch and Father Connelly had their feet set upon the easier way. He respected their sincerity; he envied them their unquestioning convictions. And yet—and yet—how easy it would have been for the Master himself, when he began to preach, to accept the rigid theology of his own day! There would then have been no conflict with the Pharisees. But there would also have been no new Gospel.

Slowly upon a sheet of paper before him he lightly traced a line he recalled from college days. Then, strongly, firmly, he wrote it again and propped it in front of him:

Truth is a staff rejected.

He turned to his work. If he were lucky he might get an hour in on his sermon before time for the next caller.

On the Monday before Easter Lex met him at the door as he came in to lunch.

"A letter from Dick!" she announced excitedly. "Hurry up and open it. I've a crazy hunch he's coming."

"It's about the first we've heard since January, isn't it?" Hilary said, eagerly slitting the envelope and reading aloud.

> MOST RIGHTEOUS ONE!
>
> I hope to arrive within the shadow of your sanctuary on Thursday afternoon. Kindly apprise members of your household of my intentions (which toward Muff at least are still strictly honorable). Also, if convenient, please substitute baked ham for the fatted calf which would otherwise be indicated.
>
> Yours, in a continued state of unregenerate contentment,
>
> DICK

When they had finished laughing they began to plan. Already a light mood had fallen upon them. They told Morris; they told Muff; they discussed entertainment over their lunch.

"Why not have some of my crowd Saturday night for an informal buffet?" Lex said. "Just the come-easy, go-easy kind of thing Dick likes? Wouldn't that be fun? I hope I haven't spoiled Sunday dinner for him. I asked Aunt Samantha just today on the impulse if they'd come. Will Dick hate it?"

"I don't think so. He may find Aunt Samantha amusing. Anyway I'm glad you did it. Let's invite Forrest. He's alone. Dick's so crazy about Mrs. Reed, why not ask her, too? She would fit in all right with the Adamses and antidote Aunt Samantha."

"I'll call her up right away," Lex said, "then I'll get things started for Saturday night. Oh, it's good to be planning for something! I could hug Dick!"

"You know what?" Hilary said suddenly. "I'd like to have Shane. Would he fit in for Saturday night? I think he and Dick would take to each other."

Lex considered. "He's older, but that wouldn't matter as long as he's a bachelor. The crowd all know him. He can really be fun when he gets going. Yes, I'll ask him."

"I've a feeling he's gotten interested in a girl. I may be all wrong. Just an idea."

"Well," said Lex, "I'll invite him and tell him to bring a girl along if he wants to. I'm going to tell a lot of the fellows to do that, and the girls to bring men. I can't be bothered matching everybody up for this kind of an affair. It's always more fun this way anyhow, for you never know who's coming. Look at Morris. He's so happy he can't walk straight!"

The old negro was swaying out of the room, executing a fancy step or two as he went.

"Dick's always been his favorite," Hilary said, smiling. "Well, I've got to get back to work. This week's going to be a hard one. If I can just last through Sunday, then I'm going to relax. You're sure you're satisfied to go to Atlantic City next week? It's not a very original idea, but it will be a few days' rest and just us!"

"It will be all right," Lex said. "We both like the ocean. Mother wants us to fly down to Florida and join them for a couple of weeks. She and Dad will pay all expenses. I got the letter this morning, but Dick's sort of knocked that news out of my head. I didn't suppose you'd want to go, anyway."

"You would like to?"

Lex shrugged. "I like to go anywhere any time. If they were at Miami or Palm Beach I'd be crazy to go. But they're at this inland club, you know, because of the golf and it sounds pretty deadly to me. I guess we'd better stick to our first plan."

"I think you'll like our rooms. I haven't told you, but I really blew myself. Second honeymoon, you know. Now, I must be off."

On the way back to his study he took time to rejoice that they were not to accept the McCollys' invitation for Florida. He was already genuinely fond of Old Alex, though by all standards they should have been thoroughly uncongenial. But to Mrs. McColly he could feel no closer than he ever had. The word "Mother" still stuck in his throat. She was always easily friendly, correctly pleasant, but he had an uncomfortable feeling that she resented his profession as shutting Lex out of the spectacular social life she could otherwise have had. All in all, he was glad Lex was her father's own daughter.

The week moved swiftly toward the great climax of the church year. Hilary found every nerve of him taut with the mental and emotional strain. As though the preparation for the great services themselves was not enough, there were constant extra and often tragic demands upon his time and strength: a sick call at midnight from the family of a man who wanted communion before he died; a distraught husband who begged for help with his wife, who was a confirmed alcoholic; the desperate plea for aid and counsel from a woman whose husband was about to leave her—these and other extraneous duties tore his mind and heart to ribbons daily when he most desired complete integration for his sermons.

Dick's arrival Thursday seemed to blow a strong fresh breeze through the rectory. He was still too thin, Hilary thought, and his dark eyes looked bigger than ever in his long pale face, but he was his usual exuberant self. He came tearing downstairs and into the library before dinner, grinning from ear to ear.

"I kissed Muff! Caught her in the upper hall and gave her a red-hot one! Gad, you should have seen her face! Couldn't have looked more shocked if I'd raped her. But I'll bet she liked it. Bet she'd like the other too, only I haven't quite the nerve."

"Dick!" Hilary remonstrated. "You're getting worse!"

"Let him alone," Lex begged through her laughter. "What we need, Dick, in this house is a little more normal depravity. Even mine doesn't quite balance Hil's virtue. It's really a strain, trying to live up to . . ."

"A man of God," Dick ended wickedly. Then as they both saw a shadow on Hilary's face they set about being particularly gay to reassure him that they were only joking. It had hurt a little, however.

Dick had to leave Monday, so they carefully planned the days.

"I have the twelve-to-three services tomorrow, Good Friday, you know," Hilary said.

"Won't Adams take part of it?" Lex asked.

"Of course, but I will be there all the time anyway. Then tomorrow night I'm awfully afraid I'll have to work in the study, for this week has been so broken up I'm not sure enough yet of my sermon. And you know on Easter people really expect something."

"Sure," said Dick, "go right ahead and feed your flock. Lex and I will go into church tomorrow at twelve for a few minutes just to fool the devil and then we'll bum around the city the rest of the day. What say, Lexa?"

"Swell! You won't mind, Hil?"

"Don't be silly. Can't we have a quiet dinner then tomorrow evening—just us—since Saturday night will be full?"

"Lex tells me she's having a blow-out. I was hoping for one, so I brought my duds. I haven't been dressed up for so long I don't suppose I can tie a bow. Who all's coming, Lex?"

"Everybody. I've no idea really. Buffet and grab as grab can. You know the kind. I thought you'd like it better than a set dinner."

"Heavens, yes! What I want is a nice, refined, dressed up brawl."

"That's it," said Lex. "You'll get it. Then Sunday— Should we describe Aunt Samantha to him, Hil, or let him just meet her cold?"

"Cold," said Hilary. "Then, he won't be prejudiced. She's my assistant's wife, but you didn't see her in the holidays. She was sick. She and Adams are to be here to dinner Sunday. Also Forrest, my organist, and of course your girl friend."

"Mrs. Reed!" said Dick. "Now there's the real gal! If I ever marry it will be a woman past seventy. They only begin to mellow then and get interesting. Of course, Lex, you're an exception. Mellow from the start, only Hil here, the old fox, got in ahead of me. Say, when do we eat tonight? I'm starved."

It was a gay meal. They sat at the polished table which had once stood in the Bishop's house, with the candlelight falling on the centerpiece of bright spring flowers—three young people bound closely by mutual love, and for the moment, carefree and happy. With every new burst of laughter, old Morris hovered nearer, his thin brown face wrinkling in delight. Here at the old table, close, so close that he could touch them, were his best beloved Mist' Dick, Mist' Hilary and Miss Lex. Hilary, watching him, knew intuitively what the old man was thinking. If only they could all be here, and he here forever to serve them, that would be heaven. He brought the baked ham back to Dick for the third time.

When they had finished at last Hilary spoke of church that evening.

"It's the Maundy service, you know. I suppose you two wouldn't care to come?"

Lex looked at Dick. He answered promptly.

"We would not. We'll go tomorrow and we'll go Sunday, and for secular souls such as we that's enough. Frankly, I don't want to run the risk of becoming *pew-hardened*. You go along, Hil and do your priestly duty, and Lex and I will do the town. As a matter of fact"—he paused, his keen eyes going from one to the other—"if you're busy too many nights in the week maybe Lex can stand a little diversion. How about it?"

"You're sure you don't mind, Hil?" Lex asked quickly.

"Of course not. Go ahead and have fun. It will do you both good. If you're late I may be in bed when you get back. I'm pretty tired."

Lex came close and touched his cheek softly. "Poor boy! You work too hard. Don't you ever wish you'd picked yourself another job?"

"Never!" Hilary said with sudden vehemence, as he smiled down at her. "Though you two heathen won't believe me, it's the greatest profession in the world! I love it even if I do often feel sunk."

"The guy's completely cuckoo," Dick remarked cheerfully, "but mild and harmless. Shall we doll up tonight, Lex?"

"Oh, let's! I've got a new dress."

"I must hurry," Hilary said suddenly. He kissed Lex, then slapped Dick's shoulder.

"Take good care of my wife, you bum!"

Dick gave his solemn wink. "Pax vobiscum," he said as usual, "and don't trip on your petticoats."

A few minutes later as Hilary crossed the court to the church he knew that he had just spoken deeper truth than he realized. Even with all the burden of work, of discouragement, of emotional strain which his profession entailed, he was in this moment more sure than ever before that he would have chosen no other. Great well-springs of satisfaction constantly sprang up in the very deserts of depression; a sense of strange, hidden and uncomputable accomplishment came often enough to compensate for the dark, ineffectual hours of doubt. And most of all, in those high moments before the white altar, when as the priest of God he dispensed the bread and wine of heaven, assisting, as it were, in channelling divine grace into the weary, troubled hearts of men—he knew that, body and soul, he was bound, enslaved, captivated by the ministry.

He did not hear Lex and Dick come home that night. He only stirred from sleep as he felt Lex's body touch his.

"Did you have a good time?" he asked drowsily, turning to enfold her with his arm.

"Wonderful! Dick was simply a riot. He's more fun than anybody I know. But—I love you, Hil."

"I love you, darling."

These were often their last spoken words before they slept.

The next night as Hilary was putting the last touches to his sermon Dick ambled into the study.

"Well, how's the prophet of the Lord?"

Hilary laughed and stacked his notes.

"Not so bad. Except that an Easter sermon's the hardest one of the year. There before you are the crowds of people—a lot of them never in church except on that one day—all looking up, expectant. What adequate message can a preacher give to them? It's a tremendous responsibility. It frightens me. But, such as it is, my stuff's ready. Sit down. Let's talk."

Dick dropped into a chair and lighted a cigarette as Hilary filled his pipe.

"You know you've got a good voice for this job, Hil. Believe it or not, I was quite impressed today in church. Do you realize that's the first time I've ever heard you preach?"

Hilary smiled. "That wouldn't be called much of a sermon. It was just a little Good Friday talk."

"There was a darned lot in it, though. You set even my wheels going a little. You know—I won't shock you, will I?"

"Hardly," Hilary laughed.

"Well, the plain fact is that all this idea of the *Atonement,* lamb for sinners, and so on—I've never been able to stomach. Sounds so savage, so bloody primitive, like something carried over from the heathen. Well, that remark you made today seemed reasonable to me."

Hilary was watching his brother incredulously. "What was that?" he asked.

"Why, you said that when any man gives his life for his faith or an ideal or out of pure duty he dies for all mankind because all men benefit by such a death. Now that somehow makes sense, even to me. How'd you come to think that one up, Hil?"

Hilary drew slowly upon his pipe. "I don't know," he said. "I guess because it suddenly struck me that the law of sacrifice is implicit in the universe. Sort of a continuous thing which we all have to accept sooner or later if we're going to be much good."

Dick eyed his brother, "I'll probably keep on wise-cracking, but I honestly believe, Hil, you're right for your job. And God knows the world needs saving now if it ever did. What do you think about the war?"

"I'm scared."

"So am I."

"Think it's coming our way?"

"Not a doubt. Just like last time. We'll have to go in. You watch. Gad, I wish I were twenty again! I'd rather fly one of those damned bombers than anything else in the world. It gives me a queer feeling to be 'too old' for anything. Me! Well, it'll be quite a show whenever it starts. Some," he added, lowering his eyelids, "aren't waiting for that."

"I know," Hilary said. "Thornton's grandson has gone to join the Canadian Air Force. In fact several boys from the congregation have." He drew a long breath. "I'm not giving up yet. I think we may not actually get in it. May not need to, I mean."

Dick had risen and was walking restlessly around the study, hands in pockets.

"Well," he began in a brisk voice, "we have now arrived by the devious routes of theology and war at the real purpose of my call. The fact is, Hil, I'm here to strike you for a touch."

Hilary experienced a wretched sinking of his heart.

"Trouble with the mine?" he asked, trying to speak calmly.

"The mine," Dick stated, "is at present nonexistent. It was a phony from the start, but it had everybody fooled. There were plenty besides me, I'm telling you, who put their last shirt into it, so I'm not the only sucker. But it is now time for the old I-told-you-so refrain from you. So go ahead."

"You put Grandy's money in it, too?"

"Every cent." Dick's lighter tone vanished. "I tell you, Hil, this was the most promising-looking thing I've ever seen, and I've seen plenty of mines. It seemed fool-proof, so I sank everything I had. And I know I'd do it again under the same conditions. The only difficulty right now is that I'm cold-broke. You see, I'd ditched my other job to sell stock in this thing."

"You didn't tell me that before."

Dick shrugged. "What was the use? I was sure I was right. You were sure I was wrong. Now, you win. So what? I've got some other work in mind, but I need a little stake to tide me over. I don't want to bleed you. Can you spare something? I'll pay you back as soon as I can."

"Don't be an ass. Of course I can. How much do you need?"

"Oh, I don't know. I'm going back West to straighten up a few affairs. It will take about two or three months, I guess. After that, I ought to be on my feet."

"You've got another job lined up?"

Dick eyed the ceiling. "Yep. If it works out."

"Same sort?"

"A little different," Dick replied and vouchsafed no more.

"Five hundred—a thousand?" Hilary asked. "I can stake you."

"I'll take the grand then," Dick said. "Just a loan, and thanks, old man. I hate this, but I never was so sure of anything as that mine. As a matter of fact I fully expected to be all set for the rest of my life. I've felt a bit dazed ever since the bottom fell out. Hil, you're a good egg."

"What about you? You'd give your eyeteeth away if anybody needed them. Can you tell me more about the new job?"

"Well," Dick said warily, "I'd rather not discuss it just yet. Sort of nebulous at the moment, but I have hopes. I'll tell you as soon as it's settled."

"O.K.," Hilary said. "Good luck! I'll write the check now. And listen, Bib, don't be a fool about money. If you need more be sure to say so. I've got a pretty good salary. Lex, you know, has plenty of her own. And I've got a little of Grandy's still lying idle. It's as much yours as mine."

"Hold on there. Not quite."

"Well, you know what I mean. It's there if you need it, and it's not pinching me for you to use it."

Hilary did not say that he had kept a few thousand uninvested for just such a situation as this. Dick had been broke before. He wrote the check now, and Dick took it lightly, making it easier for them both.

Hilary stood up, stretching his arms above his head.

"I'm dog-tired! We'd better go over home now. I'm glad tomorrow's Saturday, and I'll be gladder yet when Sunday's over. Lent is a terrific strain."

"You certainly work at your job. Don't kill yourself, that's all." At the door Dick stopped.

"Look, Hil, have you thought what you'll do when we get into the war? It sort of puts the clergy on the spot in a way. Will you be a pacifist, or what?"

"I honestly don't know," Hilary answered, his voice deeply troubled. "I'll have to face up to that when it comes, *if* it comes."

"You might as well say 'when,' for it's coming, sure as hell."

The Saturday-night party was an unqualified success from the social point of view. The rooms were filled with pretty girls in dinner dresses and debonair young men in black jackets. There was an inordinate amount of laughter in which Dick's voice seemed to rise above the others. Lex was everywhere at once with an expression of such radiant animation on her face that Hilary watched her anxiously. He had never seen her look quite like that before. This was a glimpse of the old Lex in action then.

Indeed, as the party grew livelier, Hilary had a wretched feeling of being a stranger in his own house. He had never more strongly wanted to be gay and young with the rest of them; he had never more strongly craved the relaxation of lighthearted mirth; but the trouble was that he was too tired, his head ached, and the responsibility of the next day lay too heavily upon him. He tried to be a good host, he laughed with the girls, moved about among the men, speaking to as many as he could; but he realized it must all seem forced. This was not his evening. All he really wanted to do was to sneak off upstairs to bed.

It was nearly nine when he suddenly saw Shane enter with a tall, dark, glowing girl by his side. He took a second to pull himself together before he went over to greet them. The girl was Francine Avery!

Shane was beaming. "Well, this looks like a good party, Laurens. Nice of Lex to ask me. I believe you know Miss Avery. Didn't you say you were one of his flock, Francy?"

The girl looked straight into Hilary's eyes. "I know Mr. Laurens," she said, "but I have not met his wife."

"I'll get her at once. Awfully glad to see you both. Have you had supper?"

"Not that you could notice," Shane said. "I had an emergency, and Francy worked late. Anything left to eat?"

Hilary found Lex and brought her over. It was evident that she took to Francine at once.

"Come on out to the dining room," she said. "You poor things! You must be famished. Some other people came only a few minutes ago. It's just one of those crazy pitch-in affairs, so you're never too late. Where have I seen you, Francine? I'm sure we've met."

"I danced at the Versailles Club last year. You might have seen me there."

"But of course!" Lex said, delighted. "Hil, Francine's the most *beautiful* dancer! I knew I'd seen you! Where are you appearing now? I wouldn't know, for we don't go out often."

"I'm in training at St. Luke's Hospital," she answered with the lure of her unexpected accent. "I find it much more interesting than dancing."

Lex gasped. "Oh, I've got to hear the story of that some time. I'm sure there is one. Come along now and get some food. Eat wherever you wish. Everybody is just milling around. Morris?"

"Yes, Miss Lex," Morris answered, grinning happily. A party sent him into intoxicated delight.

"Please see that Dr. Shane and Miss Avery are served. They're practically starved. Have you some nice hot lobster puffs for them?"

"Yes, Miss Lex, millions of 'em. This way, miss. This way, doctah."

When Morris had taken charge of the guests and a surge of hilarity from a near-by group had swept over and claimed them, Hilary slipped out of the room and stood for a moment in a quiet corner of the hall. He felt stifled. Shane with Francine Avery! There was that unmistakable something in Shane's eyes as he looked at the girl, which told the story. It was natural that they should meet in the hospital. Indeed it had been in Hilary's own mind to ask Shane to be on the lookout for her. That, he now admitted wryly, had not been necessary. They had met; Shane at least had fallen in love. And what would be the outcome? He had developed for Shane not only liking but a profound respect. Where would he, Hilary, fit into this tangled web of human affairs? He hoped not at all, but he felt shaken by his discovery.

The party was growing gayer by the moment. The matter of drinks had been settled in advance; there was to be no liquor served, only some sparkling Burgundy from Old Alex's cellar had been Lex's decision. So now, the mirth could not be imputed to cocktails. It was Dick, Hilary could plainly see, who was leading in all the fun—Dick, his black eyes flashing, his crooked grin at its most engaging, his quips and jokes coming faster and faster. Twelve struck and one. They were all dancing then to Sam Foster's jive. Hilary found Lex, circled the rooms with her once, and then drew her near the stairs.

"Darling, my head's splitting and tomorrow is such a very important day. I'm afraid I'll have to slip off. Will you mind too much?"

Lex did not speak for a second. One wonderful thing about her, Hilary was thinking, was that she could always see both sides of a situation. Her radiant expression faded now, though.

"I hate to have you leave, but I know you're dead-tired. I guess you'd better go, for Heaven knows how long these goons will stay. Can you sleep though, with the noise?"

"I'll go into the Prophet's Chamber."

Lex looked up, troubled. This would be the first time since their marriage that they had slept apart.

"I suppose that will be best," she said slowly.

"Where can I kiss you? Come on up along for a minute."

They went up the stairs together, and Lex began turning on lights and arranging the bed in the small room.

Hilary caught her to him. "I adore you!" he said huskily.

She stood for a minute, her face hidden against his shoulder. He knew she was disappointed over his leaving the party and even a little hurt, perhaps, at his sleeping here. Yet he had no choice.

He raised her head and kissed her.

"Is it all right?" he asked. "I've really got to get some sleep. Tell me you love me."

She kissed him again for answer.

"I'm going to tell Morris to wake me early when he calls you. I'll go to eight o'clock Communion with you, and then we can have breakfast together afterward."

"Oh, Lex, will you?" His face brightened.

She looked at him, and her eyes were very tender.

"Dear Hil," she said, and with that turned quickly and went out.

Hilary undressed and got into bed. At once the austerely bare little room received him restfully. The party was far away. He reached for the Prayer-book on the bedside table and turned to the pages for Easter-even. The whole present world seemed suddenly remote as he read the brief, concise narrative appointed for the day.

When the even was come, there came a rich man of Arimathaea, named Joseph, who also himself was Jesus' disciple: he went to Pilate and begged the body of Jesus.

194

Then Pilate commanded the body to be delivered. And when Joseph had taken the body, he wrapped it in a clean linen cloth, and laid it in his own new tomb, which he had hewn out in the rock: and he rolled a great stone to the door of the sepulchre and departed. And there was Mary Magdalene and the other Mary, sitting over against the sepulchre. Now the next day, that followed the day of the preparation, the chief priests and Pharisees came together unto Pilate, saying, Sir, we remember that that deceiver said, while he was yet alive, After three days I will rise again. Command therefore that the sepulchre be made sure until the third day, lest his disciples come by night and steal him away, and say unto the people, He is risen from the dead: So the last error shall be worse than the first. Pilate said unto them, Ye have a watch: go your way, make it as sure as you can. So they went, and made the sepulchre sure, sealing the stone and setting a watch.

Hilary put out the light and lay very still, thinking of that first Easter-even. Then, with a sigh of weariness he turned upon his pillow and fell asleep.

CHAPTER XI

HENRY ALVORD, wringing Hilary's hand with unaccustomed warmth after the eleven o'clock service, told him, almost with awe, that St. Matthews had never known such an Easter! Such flowers, such music, such overflowing crowds, *such a sermon!*

"I'm very proud, very gratified, very—ah—secure in my hopes for the future," he said.

Hilary thanked him, and wondered. This was the greatest praise he had ever received from Alvord. He had small time to dwell upon it, however, for, as on his first Sunday, people crowded into the chapel to express their appreciation and extend their good wishes. He felt a tremendous uplift, knowing himself that the service had been indeed a great one. It was good to be through at last, however, and cross the court to the rectory, forgetting cares to come or the exhaustion waiting to claim him later, happy in the fulfillment of the present.

The guests were already there when he reached the house. As he was entering the library he saw Aunt Samantha in one of her usual rayon crêpes with prolific machine trimming, staring up, fascinated, into Dick's face.

"But," she was saying in a voice that reechoed through the house, "you don't look anything alike. Are you *full* brothers?"

Dick regarded her solemnly. "I am quite frequently, I regret to say, but Hilary—never! So, set your your mind at rest on that."

Lex came to the rescue at once.

"You have to get used to him, Aunt Samantha. He simply doesn't talk sense. But he and Hil are real brothers. They just happen to take after different sides of the house."

Hilary was close enough then to overhear her saying in an aside to Dick: "You dog! Don't you dare tease her!"

Mrs. Reed, who was busy subduing her mirth, moved over to enjoy Dick and there was general conversation among the rest, chiefly of the service. Forrest's thin face was luminously alight. He, like Hilary, knew that his arduous work had been crowned with success. They all spoke, too, of Adams' reading of the service. His voice, a truly remarkable one, had made every syllable distinct and yet, as Hilary kept thinking, had managed somehow to hold it in that lofty, reverent remoteness which one associates with "the blessed mutter of the Mass," an effect few men could achieve. Yes, Adams, too, had reason for holy satisfaction.

It was near the end of dinner that Mrs. Reed addressed herself to Aunt Samantha.

"Mr. Laurens tells me that you are doing a marvellous work in the slum district around here, Mrs. Adams."

"Well," Aunt Samantha said, "between you and I, I get discouraged sometimes. But, as I always say, what are we in this world for if it isn't to help one another? So I go right ahead and do what I can. I keep finding out little things about those people every week. Things you'd never think of. Now there's mail. You know how to you or I that's a common thing. Well, it isn't to them. Some of those families haven't had a piece of mail in five years!"

Hilary could see that Dick had stopped talking and was watching Aunt Samantha with a shade of interest.

"Where would it come from?" she went on. "Lots of them don't have any folks living at a distance. They don't get bills. They don't get circulars. They don't get anything. Now I'm making lists of the sick and shut-ins and the women who are just downright *blue,* and I'm going to see they get cards in the mail once in a while if I have to write them all myself."

"Send me a list. I'll do some," Mrs. Reed said quickly. "It never occurred to me that everybody didn't get mail. I've often felt at the first of the month as though I'd like to shoot the postman, but if he never came at all I guess I'd welcome even a bill. Yes, send me a list of your names."

"Now that's real nice of you," Aunt Samantha beamed. "Mr. Adams thought this was foolish, but as I always say, 'Despise not the day of small things.'"

"I think you've discovered a good many important small things in the lives of these people," Hilary said, smiling at her.

"And don't forget about the canaries!" Lex put in.

"Now this is something I must hear," Dick said.

"Oh, well," Aunt Samantha began, patently pleased at being the center of interest, "I've been placing canaries where I felt they would do the most good. Something to bring cheer, you know, especially where there's sickness. Mr. Laurens has been very kind giving me money from the Rector's fund to try the experiment; but of course they're expensive and I can't get very many. It's just wonderful, though, what they've done in some cases! One woman said she hadn't heard a bird sing for thirty years.

Think of that! She says now with the canary she can put up with most anything."

Aunt Samantha raised her horn-rimmed glasses and adjusted them on her nose with an habitual gesture.

"Of course I have to be very careful not to show partiality, but one nice thing about a canary is that it can be moved around. The last one I placed was with the understanding that it was to be taken into a sick woman's room for an hour every morning. I can't place one there, for the room has no window—you know that awful tenement, Mr. Laurens. But would you believe it?"

Her resonant voice lowered a trifle. She shook a stubby forefinger to emphasize her remark.

"Every single morning they tell me that canary sings when they take it in there. Now I feel that's the Lord's doing. As I always say, 'Not a sparrow falleth,' you know."

"Nor a canary singeth," Dick added, a curious expression, amused but respectful on his face. "You say you need more birds?"

"Oh, my, yes! I could use any number."

"Well, put me down for two canaries. I would like to aid the Lord's work and yours to that extent."

"I'll match that," Forrest said quietly.

"So will I," Mrs. Reed chimed in.

Aunt Samantha's round, flushed face was beatific. "Six, that'll be, and I know just where to place them. My, I do thank you! There's a woman in one of those old-law flats—"

"And an interesting fact about canaries," Adams broke in, gently but firmly, "is that in their natural, uncultivated state they are very dull and unattractive-looking—no color . . ."

Hilary was annoyed at Adams and yet grateful too. Once Aunt Samantha got started upon details of her work it was practically impossible to stop her. Now the conversation became general again, and in a moment Lex gave the signal to rise. She bore Aunt Samantha off upstairs to show her some dresses already sorted out for her protégées, Forrest and Adams drifted into the library to finish an argument, while Hilary, Dick, and Mrs. Reed sat down in the drawing room.

"She's the most amazing person I've ever met!" the latter was saying. "You had your courage to bring her here, Hilary, but your wisdom has been justified."

" 'The last canary I *placed*'!" Dick quoted. "But the thing is, even I can't laugh at her. Funny, isn't it?"

"She's the despair of all the trained social workers," Hilary told them.

"She does everything wrong according to the books, but she gets results. She goes into these frightful flats, picks up a dirty, howling infant, sits down, and jounces it comfortably on her knee and talks baby talk to it, and before you know it she and the mother are gabbing away like old friends. She's dug up the most astonishing facts about some of those people!"

Hilary began to smile. "For example, one couple were at swords' points. Apparently the woman hated her husband, and her children, too, which no one could figure out. She was a vixen, a regular devil! But Aunt Samantha studied her. She noticed the woman never wore a wedding ring, and finally got the truth out of her that she had never been married. She had been a decent girl, and the shame of the thing kept eating away at her through the years. Aunt Samantha got hold of the man, found there was no real obstacle now, and then read the riot act to him. She talked to me, got a time set for the nuptials, got a little money from our fund, bought the ring herself, and let the woman pick herself a new dress, then, for fear of slip-ups, went after them in a taxi on the day appointed and brought them to the church."

"And you married them?" Mrs. Reed chuckled.

"I did, in my most impressive cope before the altar! You should have seen that woman's face! They'd been living together, mind you, for seventeen years and had five children. When I told the man to kiss her at the end of the ceremony, he did, and she blushed like a virgin. Afterwards Aunt Samantha and I congratulated them with our very best manner, wished them long life and great happiness and dispatched them back home in a taxi. Now, the woman's a changed character. Happy and proud as you please, and a good wife and mother. Well, that's only one case in dozens."

They could hear Aunt Samantha's voice approaching, so they rose to join the others in the library.

"I'm going to see if Mr. Forrest feels like playing for us," Lex called to them.

During the music, Hilary leaned back in his chair and relaxed gratefully. Vespers was yet to come, but his talk was well fixed in his mind. It would be unusually short because of the extra music. Very soon the day would be over, Lent would be over, Easter would be over—his first Easter at St. Matthews. His very limbs ached with weariness and his head felt heavy from the strain, but his heart was momentarily at peace. With a week's rest at the shore he ought to be able to tackle the coming problems. And meanwhile there was the satisfaction over the successful culmination of the church year.

Beneath the thrall of Forrest's music he suddenly became aware of

Dick and Mrs. Reed on the divan near him. Mrs. Reed was looking up at Dick with a strange, white face.

"I've been expecting it," she said almost in a whisper. "When?"

Dick shook his head. "I'll tell you as soon as I get more details."

She held his hand in both of hers, and Hilary was sure there were tears in her eyes. She must know then, he thought, about the failure of the mine.

When they returned from the shore, both Lex and Hilary had the look in their eyes of two people completely in love who had for a space at least, counted the world well lost. Before a week was gone, however, the cares of the parish like engulfing tide had swept Hilary away with them.

In the first place he was more acutely conscious now than he had even been during his curateship of the sudden falling away of the eleven o'clock congregation after Easter Sunday. It seemed, indeed, as though the people, like the priest, had strained up toward that Easter peak, and then they, weary and relaxed, had decided to take a rest from religious observance. The first Sunday after his return, Hilary was shocked at the relatively small congregation at morning service. Vespers, he was happy to note, still seemed to attract an increasing number.

He decided to make more pastoral calls himself, trying to catch up any loose ends before people began leaving for the summer. The short spring social season was, of course, in full swing now. Already he had five large weddings on his calendar. The perpetual conflict between religion on the one hand and the pleasant world and the flesh on the other, seemed to Hilary more pointed in this post-Easter period than in any other.

His mind, taxed sufficiently already, was now constantly harassed by embarrassment in Margaret Mowbray's presence. He tried to retain his open, casual friendliness, but with Lex's revelation it was difficult. He noticed now, what he had not seen before, that a faint flush would often steal over her face as she spoke to him. It had the effect of softening her angular features and giving her a transient prettiness. Hilary hated the situation and, because he had a genuine fondness for Margaret, hated himself for having unconsciously caused it. His problem with the beautiful and unscrupulous Diana Downes was in a way not so troublesome, although he still feared a violent climax. He had only a feeling of repulsion and righteous anger there, while with Margaret he felt both sympathy and responsibility. He pondered upon what his manner should be. Should he turn stern, aloof, critical? He decided not. Whatever developed in her own feelings, he could not quite act the cad in order to check them.

He was amazed one day to receive a letter from Bronson:

My Dear Hilary:

I have just received a note from my good old friend, Henry Alvord, telling me of the great success of your Easter services. I wish to take this opportunity to express my gratification in connection with your year's work at St. Matthews. You have succeeded beyond my most fervent hopes for you. My prayer for you is that with continued zeal, Christian tact, and constantly mounting ability you may become one of this generation's outstanding servants of God.

Yours in Christ,
A. Bronson

Hilary read this several times, muttered, "There's more to this than meets the eye," and then filed it carefully away. The wording was impeccable. No stranger, perusing it, could find the remotest hint of church politics. No bishop certainly would commit himself to their furthering, on paper. Discretion, as Grandy had always said, was the better part of the bishopric. And yet, as clearly as though outlined, Hilary caught the implication of the letter. With *Christian tact* he was supposed to play along with Henry Alvord, deferring to his opinions, doing nothing to disturb the status quo, and in return . . .

Hilary closed his lips tightly. He had to face the fact that he would enjoy the work of the conventions of the church. He would like to be a leader in his denomination. The fact that Henry Alvord had been for years the lay delegate to the National Convention was something to be reckoned with. To go there, under Alvord's enthusiastic sponsorship, to meet the most important clergymen of the country, to be appointed to committees, to help mold the policies of the church in a changing world—Hilary knew that this picture stirred a deep interest within him. Whether the desire was weak or even wrong, he was not sure. As he looked at himself now with objective honesty, he decided that it was compounded partly of natural vanity (for he knew he had ability for this work as well as the speaking engagements) and partly of a sincere desire to serve his day and generation well, to throw the weight of his strength upon the side of organized good; to use what talents he had for the definite furtherance of God's kingdom on earth through the medium of his own denomination. There it was. There he was. And there was the subtle suggestion of Bronson's letter.

He thrust the whole thing from his mind now, with violence. Let time attend to its own crises and he to their solving when they arose.

Upon his calendar for that day was a call from Maudie Dunn. He was keenly interested in seeing her but dreaded what he knew she must be coming to discuss. When she did arrive he was amazed at her appearance and manner. The nervous, twitching, overdressed girl of the abortive sentences was gone. This young woman wore a tailored suit, her haircut was distinctive and becoming, the whole negative face had become suffused with the warmth of an inner joy. Maudie's blossoming had been long delayed but was here at last. She had been working Sundays, so Hilary had not seen her for months.

"Maudie Dunn!" he exclaimed. "You are not the same girl I knew before."

She laughed, pleased at the startled look in his eyes.

"You really see a—difference?"

"A striking one."

"I'm glad it shows outside. I'm completely metamorphosed inside. It's that I've come to talk to you about."

"I'm more than interested."

She paused a moment, only her hands showing her embarrassment as they fingered her bag uneasily.

"Since I was once quite disgustingly frank with you, you can at least understand better what I'm going to say. Of course the work itself at the settlement has been wonderful for me, and my association with Miss Barton. But that is not all."

She leaned forward, Hilary could see, confident that her disclosure would be a complete surprise to him.

"Mr. Laurens, I'm going to be married."

It was the positiveness of her statement that amazed him.

"You see," she went on, "I had never dreamed there was a man in the world like Jerry, and he never knew— Well, he loves me so much, I can't believe it. I'm still afraid sometimes I must be dreaming. And I can't even tell you how much I love him."

"This is wonderful news, Maudie," Hilary said. "Now tell me all about the young man."

"Well," Maudie said slowly, "it's that part that I am worried about. He's so fine, so wonderful, but he's just about everything Father hates. He's an artist, and he has no money, and he's a strong Socialist. I'm afraid to tell Father about him. I thought—that is, I hoped maybe you would do it. I mean—if you could meet Jerry and like him, and then mention him to Father—he is so very fond of you . . ."

Her eyes were beseeching.

Hilary sat thoughtful.

"Your own mind is made up, Maudie?"

"Absolutely. I love him and, you see, he needs me! We can live on what I inherited from my mother while he's getting ahead with his work. It's not much, but we wouldn't care. And, Mr. Laurens, you must know this. He's from the Middle West. Father's name meant nothing to him. He loved me before he knew I had a single penny. He thought I was a paid worker, earning my living. He almost stopped seeing me when he knew about Father. Miss Barton had to intercede. He's proud, and he thinks Capitalism is *terrible*."

She hesitated again, as Hilary smiled.

"He's not very strong yet. He was quite ill for a time because he nearly starved himself. And even yet he gets discouraged easily. So he needs me. I can look out for his health and see that he can go on painting. Miss Barton knows an art dealer, and he's taken two of his pictures already. You see he's a real artist, not just another young man who thinks he can paint. It will be hard going even so, but," she reiterated, "he needs me and I want us to be married soon."

"Now let's get this straight, Maudie. Do I understand that you would like your father's approval, but that you are going to marry your young man anyway?"

"That's it," she said without hesitation. "I want so terribly, though, for Father to agree to it. I'm all he has, and he has always talked so much about the big wedding he'd give me some day and how proud he'd be, going down the aisle with me. It used to nearly drive me insane to hear him, for I never thought it would happen. Now I would like a lovely wedding for his sake and mine too. Jerry's very good-looking," she added naïvely.

Hilary saw it all. First, he knew, Maudie was thinking of her father, but in addition to that there was her very natural desire to show off her young man and prove to all her circle that she was no longer the ugly duckling, destined for embarrassing social failure.

"I must meet Jerry, Maudie," Hilary said slowly, "and form my own opinion before I can promise to commend him to your father. I'll have to be honest with you both, no matter how much I want to help you. You understand that, don't you?"

"Of course. But you can't fail to like Jerry. And, if it's convenient, I'll bring him in right now. He's waiting outside with Miss Mowbray."

Hilary laughed outright. "You certainly move quickly, but it's all right. Bring him in and then . . ."

"Yes," she finished for him, "I'll leave you to yourselves."

In a minute she returned with young Seaton. Even as she made the introduction, Hilary knew he would be on the side of the young people. It was not only the overpowering sweetness of the look which passed between them, and the pride in Maudie's voice as she spoke his name, but as he looked upon the young man he loved him.

He was not at all the frail esthete whom he had expected to see. He was thin, but the great bones were there, waiting to be filled out again. He had good features, honest eyes, and a smile made the more disarming by his extreme shyness. He told his story hesitantly but without apology. He had nothing to offer Maudie but his love and an increasing confidence in his art. His father, a farmer in Indiana, had been outraged that a son of his should try to paint pictures for a living and, after a sharp quarrel, had refused him any help whatsoever unless he returned to the farm where three generations of his people had lived before him. It was an ordinary story enough, but the young man who told it was not. Each time he mentioned Maudie's name, Hilary was convinced that the feeling between them was love at its best, not to be trifled with. He knew, even as his own heart sank a bit, that he was already committed to wrestle with J. V.

When Maudie came back he told them that, come what might, they could count upon him. Their gratitude was touching, and they left him, surrounded by an aureole of hope. One thing was clear enough. Maudie had emerged from her former narrow and heavily dominated existence as a free person. Love had performed this miracle. It must now follow its continuing course, and he must aid it if he could.

He sat thinking, then looked at his watch. It was three-thirty. If he went at once he might catch J. V. in his office and have the preliminary over with. He had enough disagreeable problems ahead of him without delaying this one. He picked up his hat and went out.

On the way he planned his attack. J. V. was not a man to be caught by delicate indirection. Hilary decided the best method would be complete candor, with all cards on the table. Perhaps a slight show of firmness and strength might surprise the man into some sort of compliance. But he felt himself growing more and more nervous as he reached the office and gave his card to the secretary.

"If you can wait for ten minutes Mr. Dunn will see you," she reported.

During the interval, Hilary went over and over in his mind different approaches, each one of which seemed upon examination unsuitable. He felt almost as frightened as Maudie herself might have done when he was finally ushered into J. V.'s sanctum.

"Well, well, well!" J. V. said with more than his usual cordiality. "This is a pleasant surprise! Sit down. What can I do for you?"

"I've come on really a very happy errand, Mr. Dunn," Hilary began bravely, his feeling belying his words. "It's a matter concerning Maudie."

J. V.'s frostbitten countenance glowed in so far as that was possible.

"Mr. Laurens," he replied, "I have no words to express my gratitude to you for getting Maudie into that settlement work. She's a changed girl. I don't think I've made too many mistakes in my life, but one was in shielding her too much. She needed responsibility. It's been the making of her! Why, it's even improved her appearance! I feel now she's ready for—"

"That's it, Mr. Dunn. I want to tell you—"

J. V. waved his hand with finality. "I have made my plans. She's been at this job long enough now. It's done enough for her. I've decided to stop it the first of June. The fact is, I've a young man just lately come into my organization who is"—he lowered his voice—"the most suitable possible husband for my daughter whom I've ever run across. And he's very anxious to meet her. He's seen her picture."

J. V. proudly turned a photograph toward Hilary. It was, indeed, the new Maudie with the smile on her face which Jerry had brought there.

"I'm not saying a word yet to Maudie. I'm just waiting till June, then I'll bring them together up in the country. I have great respect for the way the French handle these affairs, Mr. Laurens. If more marriages were arranged by parents here we'd have fewer divorces."

"Mr. Dunn, I really must insist upon explaining the purpose of my call." Hilary knew that he was going to blurt out the truth now without finesse. "The fact is that there's a young man already interested in Maudie."

J. V. leaned forward, a look of incredulous pleasure on his face.

"There is?"

"Yes. A young man she met down at the settlement. He's completely in love with her and wants to marry her. And he is no fortune hunter. He comes from the Middle West and had never heard of you."

Still J. V. looked fatuously happy.

"You don't say! And he's really been paying her attention?"

"Very much so. He's a fine young fellow. I've met him, and I like him thoroughly."

J. V. rubbed his hands and beamed.

"Splendid! Couldn't be better! That's what she's needed, Mr. Laurens. Attention from young men. Young chaps falling in love with her. Gives a girl confidence in herself. Yes, sir. She's always been too shy with boys, too nervous. Now—what does this fellow work at?"

"He's an artist. He has real ability."

Almost to Hilary's horror, J. V. threw back his head and laughed heartily. He slapped the top of his desk.

"An artist! By Jove, that's the way with young girls. Sentimental over artists and poets and musicians. You know Maudie's never mentioned a word of this to me, the sly little puss. Well, we'll get it all straightened out in short order. But I'm very grateful to you for telling me."

Hilary felt desperate. "I haven't made this clear to you yet. Not only does the young man love Maudie, but she loves him. They want to get married."

J. V. smiled more broadly.

"These things happen," he said almost with pride. "I'll have a talk with Maudie. She's easily managed. But this episode, you see, will make her feel more—well—shall we say—ah!—*desirable*. Gives a girl confidence. Just what Maudie needed. It's been very good of you to tell me, though. The thing's probably gone on now long enough. Wants to marry her, eh?"

"But she is in earnest, Mr. Dunn. Her mind is made up. She intends to marry this young man and I consider him entirely worthy of her. He's a fine fellow."

J. V. looked upon him as upon a child. Hilary could see that already, in his mind, Maudie had become a beautiful, popular young woman, beset with suitors.

"I know. I know. But we'll smooth things out. Divert her mind. Have her meet other young men. I'll handle it. And thanks again for your kindness in telling me, Mr. Laurens."

He pressed the buzzer, rose, and still smiling broadly, extended his hand. The interview was over.

Hilary walked out, feeling as though he had mustered all his strength to smite a rock and had struck a down pillow instead. The reaction was almost nauseating. He had never felt more futile, more inadequate than before J. V.'s consummate confidence in his own power to mold Maudie's life to his will. And might he not do it even yet? Had Maudie's metamorphosis been complete? In a struggle with her father, might she even now succumb to his wishes?

When he returned to the rectory late in the afternoon, however, there awaited him a letter from Dick which drove everything else from his mind.

MY SAINTED BROTHER:

The job I mentioned vaguely to you has suddenly come to a head. I've been accepted by one of our American units as an ambulance driver for overseas. I've been itching to get into this thing and since I'm a bit on thirtyish side for the bombers I've decided this will be best and quickest. At least, as you know, I can take any damn car apart and put it together again and this native gift seemed to impress the powers. I'm supposed to leave sometime in June. No one knows of this yet except Mrs. Reed. She guessed it when I was there last. Psychic, the old gal is. I'll stop on my way of course to burn up the town with Lex and receive your holy blessing. I'm quite excited about the whole thing. Think somehow Grandy would have cottoned to the idea.

Love to the both of you,

Dick

Hilary was shaken by this more than he would admit even to Lex, though they talked it over from all angles that evening.

"It will be a great adventure for him," Lex kept saying, "and you know how he loves excitement. Maybe this is just the chance he's been waiting for all his life. Don't worry too much, Hil."

"It brings the whole thing pretty close, that's sure. Queer how Mrs. Reed guessed what was on his mind. I should have from one or two hints he let fall, but I was so concerned over the mine project's going under that I didn't notice. He's always had a charmed life, though. When we were kids I was the one to break bones and get stoved up in our escapades. Dick always came up smiling and sound as a dollar."

"He will now," Lex kept cheering him. "He's born for this sort of thing, and it isn't as though he were fighting. The morale of the army ought to go up several points when Dick gets on the scene. Father's glum over the whole war business. I was talking to him today. He says England's crazy to keep Chamberlain in. He's all for Churchill. He says he's the only one can stand up to Hitler. Hil, do you think we'll ever have to go in?"

Hilary hesitated. "This Norway situation looks bad. I'm ashamed that my own thinking isn't more clear. I'm so absorbed in the church problems I keep pushing the war back in my mind. I do admit, though, that I'm scared and not too optimistic."

Suddenly Lex threw her arms about him and held him close.

"For the first time, I'm glad you're a preacher," she said. "I think I'd die if you had to go."

They stood long at the window before they went to bed. Even in the city there were signs of the year's incredible miracle. The trees in front of the rectory now bore a soft, hesitant, lacy green, and rising above the never quite stilled sounds of traffic and the stale city smells, there was a fresh breath, a portent, a stirring at once of the air and of the senses. Somewhere, one knew, there were dewy meadows with little running brooks, sweet with penny-royal; somewhere dark boughs were burgeoning into white; somewhere there were young voices harmonizing beneath a country moon, for May had come.

A tragic May, however, a ghastly May. On the tenth, the Germans, without warning, invaded the Low Countries by land, sea and air. On the eleventh Chamberlain resigned in Great Britain and Winston Churchill succeeded him. On the thirteenth the new Prime Minister's words, brutally frank, magnificently brave, rang round the world. Hilary read them in his study, and felt as though a bullet had struck his heart. By the twenty-eighth the King of the Belgians had surrendered. By the thirtieth it was Dunkerque! So swiftly, so devastatingly moved the events beyond the sea.

In the parish of St. Matthews, May had been notable for its own happenings. The largest wedding ever held in the church took place with the attendant fee larger than Hilary had ever received before. He discussed it with Lex.

"It's yours, darling. Sometimes I wish you weren't rich."

"Why ever?"

"Because I'd like to make your eyes shine over a whopper like this. I'd like to feel you were dependent upon me for every single penny. Selfish cuss, I am."

Lex fingered the bills and then slipped them back into the envelope.

"Why not send some of this to Cousin Mattie? Every time I look at the quilt I feel we owe her something. She probably doesn't have too much."

Hilary was touched. "I believe you've got a real idea there. I'll send the gift as from Grandy. You're sweet to suggest it, Lex."

"As for my money," she went on, "you know it doesn't matter between us. It's just an accident. From now on, though, I'll make a point of nagging you for some every day or two. Just to make you sure you have a wife. If you don't know what to do with the rest of this fee, there's always the canary fund for Aunt Samantha!"

Hilary smiled and smoothed her hair.

"Some day I feel I should go out to see Cousin Mattie. Sort of a debt-of-love visit. Would you like to come along?"

Lex wrinkled her nose.

"Do you want an honest answer?"

He laughed. "You and Dick both. All right, you needn't. But you won't mind if I go for a few days?"

"When?"

"Oh, perhaps this summer when you are away. I'd really like to see the old town again and the scenes of Grandy's boyhood. I can mention the idea when I send the money. Lex, you really were an angel to think of this! I feel ashamed that I didn't myself."

When Cousin Mattie wrote in her fine, shaky script to thank him she told him that even more than the money she would appreciate a visit from him whenever he could come.

"And please don't put it off too long. I'm very well but I have been living on borrowed time now for a good many years," she added in a post-script.

The matter of Hastings' dislike of Adams had grown steadily more obvious. One day Hilary felt the matter must be brought into the open. He called the old man into the study.

"I am greatly worried about something, Hastings, and it has to do with you. I think you can guess what it is."

Hastings' solemn, undertaker face showed no sign of intelligence.

"If it's them tiles in the chancel, I've told you before they've got stains won't come off."

"I'm not concerned over the tiles. It's your attitude toward Mr. Adams. It's getting on his nerves. I can see it."

"He gets on my nerves."

"In what way?"

Hastings stiffened. "I don't like a sneak. I don't like a pretender. I don't like no wolves in sheep's clothing. Goes again me."

"Just what are you driving at?"

"I'm makin' no accusations, mind. But I know a man who's got a niece by marriage, a widow woman, livin' up where the Adamses come from. Murder will out. But my lips are sealed, mind you."

Hilary suddenly saw daylight.

"Perhaps you have heard of Mr. Adams' struggles occasionally with drink."

Hastings' jaw dropped.

"You knowed that?"

"Certainly. I knew it before I asked him to come. He refused at first because he thought I didn't know. There's a saying we should all remember, Hastings. 'Judge not another till thou standest in his place.' Mr. Adams is a good man. He's so interested now in his work here that I don't think the—shall we call it illness?—will ever overtake him again."

Instead of being apologetic, Hastings showed righteous anger.

"An' how was I to know all this if people don't take me into their confidence? How do you expect me to run things smooth here if there's information held back from me? I've been here goin' on thirty-five years, and it seems to me I could be trusted."

Hilary called forth all his powers of tact and persuasion.

"It was not my own secret, so I've told no one. But I'm glad now that you have the facts. Make things as pleasant as you can for Mr. Adams, and always be a friend to him. I am greatly relieved, Hastings, that this has finally come up. You know how I always count on your assistance."

Hastings, somewhat mollified, finally retreated with his duster high, and Hilary turned to his desk with a sigh of relief. Hastings could make or break a rector, and he well knew it. Thank Heaven he would not now break Adams.

It seemed to Hilary that during May there was an unusual number of sorrows in the parish. There was the constant problem of the old and the lonely; there were the ever recurring cases of alcoholism, both men and women; there were those who suddenly knew they were appointed to die; there were those bent under desperate grief.

In between, Hilary came to grips with one keen disappointment of his own. He had at last decided that his cherished plan for a gallery congregation made up of the humble from the slum district near the church simply would not work. Aunt Samantha put it all in a nutshell.

"Oil and water won't mix, not in this church anyway, and you can't make 'em. These women I work with won't come here in the kind of clothes they have, not even to sit in the gallery. Besides, they can't make head or tail of the service. What they need is a nice cozy little chapel of their own where they can sing 'What a Friend We Have in Jesus,' and 'I Need Thee Every Hour.' *I* know. You see"—she lowered her voice for once—"although I never mention it, I was a Methodist before I married Mr. Adams."

"You may be right," Hilary admitted sadly. "Perhaps we can work something out for them in our chapel here. A song service or some such thing, though I don't know when we could get it in or whether they'd come if we did."

He felt that there was something deeper, something more fundamental in connection with the failure of St. Matthews to attract these people living in its very shadow, than he had yet been able to put his finger upon. At St. Mary's, for example, only three blocks away, he knew that Father Connelly looked down each Sunday upon a church packed to the doors with both rich and poor, kneeling together as the Lord had made them. Why did Catholics of all classes go unfailingly to church while Protestants did not? What was the great secret at the heart of Rome? Was it fear that moved its people? Was it compulsion? Was it the iron grip of early-formed habit? Was it that the human soul, brought up from birth upon them, thrived upon miracle and mystery and drew spiritual nourishment from them?

He pondered this carefully, setting over against each other the two great divisions of the Christian Church. On the one hand the Catholic, the ancient mother, rooted in antiquity, entrenched in absolutism, never compromising, never giving ground, the great autocrat, secure in its central authority and the regimentation of all its devotional practices.

On the other hand the still relatively young, but strong, growing, changing spiritual democracy of Protestantism with its various forms of worship, its freedom of observance and complete liberty of soul under God. There they stood, unalterably opposed in certain principles but united in their common service to men, each possessing a secret power to hold its own kind to itself.

And yet, Hilary thought suddenly, how little individual volition was concerned after all, in this matter of religion! He himself was a Protestant because his ancestors had once long ago shed their Covenanting blood upon a Scottish moor; Father Connelly was a Catholic because for two hundred years his forebears had told their beads by an Irish peat fire. Why should either of them ever be dogmatic about his faith? They had made no choice. Each had been born to it, had inherited it as unconsciously and completely as men inherit their physical features. The point now was to make the most of what had been begotten, fiber and sinew, into each of their beings; and in his own immediate case to see if anything in the way of a congenial service could be arranged for the Protestants near by who had no interest in St. Matthews.

Meanwhile the season of Confirmation approached and the problem of Francine Avery was much on his mind, for she was one of those to be confirmed. Lex had reported that Shane was seen with her everywhere.

"She's darling," Lex said. "An absolute doll! I'm crazy about her. I wish I had an accent. It's funny about Hal Shane. Nobody thought he'd ever marry. He's always liked to philander around, but this is different. He's completely mad over her. Everybody bets they'll finish it up this summer. Don't you think it's a perfect match, Hil?"

"There is only one perfect match—that's ours," Hilary evaded, but he was anxious.

On an afternoon in early June, as beautiful as the day of their first interview had been stormy, Francine came to his study. He had known she would come, known and dreaded it. While no one but Lex could stir his senses he was fully conscious of Francine's charm. The subtle grace of her movements, the slow, sweet surprise of her smile, the enchantment of her voice—all these he had noted on that other day when she had come in, distraught, out of the rain, evidently looking her worst. Today, they were all enhanced by the artistry of her clothes and make-up.

"I have come," she said gravely, "once again upon a hard errand because I have no one to turn to whom I can fully trust but you. Your friend Dr. Shane wishes to marry me. I have for him a strong affection. It is nothing like that first love for Stephen. Nothing can be to me like that ever again. This is an older, a different kind of feeling. Not so beautiful, but also very real. I know I could make him happy. I want to marry him. I want to build a good and beautiful home with him. I want children, with my whole life centered upon them and my husband. I want this, oh, so much!"

She paused, looking searchingly at Hilary.

"I have come to ask what I must do. Shall I tell him everything as I told Steve? Shall I marry him and say nothing? It is you must decide. I cannot, myself. I am all confused. I will do as you say."

"But, Miss Avery! I cannot possibly take this responsibility!" Hilary's tone was aghast. Her affected calmness, he could see, covered a tremulous fright and excitement. His own heart reflected it. It was monstrous of her to ask this of him.

"Who am I," he went on a shade angrily, "to arrange the destiny of two lives? I can't do this, Miss Avery. You must make your own decisions."

She did not waver.

"I once did that, and you know what happened. I must now have help. You are the only one who knows all. You are also Dr. Shane's friend. It is you who must tell me what to do. I will have it no other way. I will bear whatever comes. I want to do the right," she added.

Hilary felt the sweat break upon his forehead. He saw that the girl meant exactly what she said and would stand up to it unflinchingly. He honored her for it, but he felt something like terror over the weight of the thing thrust upon him.

They talked then with a desperate earnestness. They both agreed that even if full confession were made to Shane he would probably still marry Francine. He was a bachelor in his thirties, and a man of the world. He would perhaps understand even as Hilary had done, that the girl's essential integrity had not been impaired by the strange experiences of her young girlhood. But it would not be a pleasant revelation.

"And it might never be again as it is now between us," she said, raising her clear eyes to Hilary. "He might even feel always a doubt, always a cloud across his happiness. And he now is so very full of joy. I cannot tell what is right to do. You are wise and good. You are a priest. You must decide."

Hilary felt sick. He could see that she would not allow him to refuse. She left at last, thanking him gently. He was to let her know his decision the next day. At the doorway, she turned to him. Her face was pale and inexpressibly sad.

"If I had only been more wisely taught . . ."

That night Hilary did not sleep. He walked the study floor until one o'clock, allowing Lex to think he was at work on his sermon. He thought, he reasoned, he prayed. Shane, as Francine kept pointing out, was his friend. He must consider his happiness, his honor, even as his own. What in such a case, would he want for himself? Suppose again, it were Dick who was involved. What would he do if it were Dick?

He went home at last and to bed, where he tossed until morning. He got up, heavy and red-eyed, with his decision still unmade. He had wondered during the night if the Brown Book might have any help for him, but decided not. Not even the wide diversity of counsel there could possibly include any light for this strange problem. He must somehow work his way out alone.

In response to Lex's questioning he told her he had a wretched headache and let it go at that. Still weighted with the desperation of uncertainty, he got the car and drove uptown. He felt he must get away from the study and draw a breath of different air, or the mental stalemate would never pass.

At the Park, he got out and walked slowly along a path. The grass and trees were fresh with dew and the first light morning shadows accentuated the sun's brightness. He dropped wearily down on a bench, determined to go over the evidence for the last time.

Suddenly he saw sitting upon another bench facing him a short distance down the path, a young man with a little girl of perhaps five in the curve of his arm. His head was bent toward her, and a tender, humorous smile played upon his lips as he kept up a steady conversation. The little girl leaned against him, her chin resting on her hand as she listened intently, sometimes chuckling with quiet delight. No sound of voices came to Hilary. The two, absorbed in their own pleasure, were entirely unaware of his presence.

A stab of jealous longing pierced his heart as he watched the gentle picture. "I want children," Francine Avery had said. And she and Shane would have them. Beautiful children, with Shane's dark, distinguished features and Francine's delicate grace. With sudden and complete certainty he felt that nothing else mattered except that new life should be born of those two; of Shane's passionate love and Francine's steady devotion. The clarity of his viewpoint and the intensity of his conviction amazed him.

He looked for a long moment at the little girl whose slim fingers now pulled absently at one short brown braid as with lips parted in a smile she leaned still closer to catch the man's low words.

Hilary got up, drove back to the study, and put in a call for St. Luke's Hospital. When Francine was at last on the wire, he was brief.

"I have given your problem the deepest thought," he said. "My best advice to you is to say nothing and go ahead with your plans. Do you understand?"

There was no reply for a long second. Then her voice came almost in a whisper.

"Thank you. Thank you. I cannot speak now. I am weeping."

It was on a still, heavy June day, when the city smothered under unseasonable and oppressive heat that Hilary knew he could no longer delay action concerning the old-law tenements and keep peace with his own soul. His time had been so engaged with affairs necessary and important to the parish that it had been all too easy to postpone this unpleasant task from week to week. He had even had periods of doubt as to whether he should challenge Henry Alvord's worldly affairs at all. Reasonable arguments pressed him in on every side. There were plenty of rich men in the congregation. Could he ferret out the secular policies and practices of them all? Could he sit in judgment upon the involved intricacies of every business represented by the wealth even of his twelve vestrymen? And if not, what right had he to single out Henry Alvord for a rebuke? Dare he pillory one man, not knowing whether or not a dozen other men were equally culpable in the manner of their earnings?

He tugged and tore mentally at this problem, now and then deciding to have nothing more to do with it; to concern himself only with those immediate spiritual responsibilities of his office, of which there were enough, heaven knew, to keep him busy. And then, swiftly, there would come to him a clear-eyed view of the whole matter in which there was demanded of him absolute moral courage. Under his very eye a great evil existed to which his most important vestryman was a party. He could not refuse to recognize this merely because he did not see other possibly existing evils in the business dealings of other men. No matter how logical the arguments against action which rose in his mind, there was a steady inner voice in his own soul which he could not ignore.

The thing which precipitated his action was a morning call from Aunt Samantha. This in itself was unusual, for she had been too long a clergyman's wife to intrude needlessly upon a precious forenoon. She came into the study about eleven o'clock looking, Hilary noted, white and discouraged. Her usual air of complacent efficiency was absent. Instead of sitting bolt upright in her chair, she sagged, her dark-rimmed glasses resting unheeded halfway down her nose.

"What's the matter, Aunt Samantha?" Hilary asked with concern.

"It's that back tenement at 55 Ash Street," she said. "I don't know what I'm going to do with my folks there this summer. We've got to get the children all off to camps for a week or two. We've *got* to manage that. But the older girls and boys! And the women! I have two bedfast now with no windows, no air. I'm about at my wit's end. I went down early today to see Mrs. Grusak. I could hardly stay in the room for half an hour. Suppose I had to lie there for twenty-four? or you had? The canary died," she added despondently.

Hilary sat regarding Aunt Samantha's white face. He knew she never spared herself, but he suddenly realized now how utterly sacrificial her life was. She herself needed rest, change, diversion, and he must speak to Adams about it, and also to Lex. For outward reply to her now, he got up.

"I'm going down to Ash Street myself, Aunt Samantha. Right away. I think the time has come for us to act. Maybe we can't do anything constructive, but maybe we can. I'll let you know later. And now I want you to go over to the rectory and get something to eat. You look completely fagged."

He smiled at her as he helped her up. "Go over and have a chat with Lex. She's in, and she always likes to see you. Forget about Ash Street for the time being. Let me do the worrying for a while."

He saw her to the rectory door, gave her into Morris' hands, with his orders, and then swung off down the street. It was not too long a walk from the church to the tenement, which made the situation somehow seem all the worse. Ash Street itself reeked now in the humid heat of stale, unpleasant smells. All the buildings across the narrow thoroughfare looked rotten at the heart. At 55, Hilary stopped. The unkempt red brick reared four stories from the sidewalk, its windows open futilely as though gasping for air. Here and there bedclothing drooped from them; here and there a child or a woman leaned languidly out, contemplating with deadly lethargy the dirty, fly-bitten shops opposite.

This was one of the buildings Hilary had canvassed that fatal day of the Pettigrew wedding. Here the sights he had seen had been bad enough. What he did not know then was that another tenement stood directly behind this one, separated from it only by a small, filthy courtyard, and reached by a narrow alleyway at the side. The discovery of this had so shocked him that he had at once discussed it with both Miss Mowbray and Celeste Barton. They told the same story. In former days there had been many of these in the city, so foul and dark that at last even the civic conscience had been pricked concerning them. A law had been passed condemning their use. In spite of the struggles and evasions of owners, the pernicious dwellings, known now as old-law tenements, had gradually been torn down or used for other purposes. A few had remained, protected by quiet graft in the right places. The worst of these was the one on Ash Street. This was the story.

Hilary walked now through the alleyway and came out in the small dirty courtyard. A few feet across it the other tenement stood in the dank heat. While the windows of the front building looked out upon a scene sordid enough, these of the back faced upon blank and utter hopelessness. His eyes moved slowly up the brick walls which now caught the reflected heat from the ones opposite. From a few of the opened windows tattered curtains drooped, but most of them gaped emptily. There was little sound, and Hilary understood why. The young children played on the streets, the men and older boys and girls were off at work or wandering about in search of anything better than the hot stifling air of the flats, the women were listless and beaten down with life. The sick . . . He took out his handkerchief and wiped his face. He must now go on and see the worst. His clerical vest was always its own introduction. Besides this, he was now known here.

He entered the door and walked very slowly through the long, narrow hall. It was unlighted even at night. This, too, was against the law, but Alvord had evaded that also. Hilary had not been inside this building before in the summer, but he knew that while the pitiless sun was the dwellers' enemy now, in winter their fight was against cold, for there was no means of warmth in the whole building except the kitchen stoves. Hilary stood, looking at the battered gloomy walls, reviewing the situation; then he climbed to the second floor to see Mrs. Grusak. Her daughter, a pale woman in her thirties, let him into the kitchen. It was literally steaming, for two tubs of washing stood before the back windows. There were the uncleared remains of breakfast on the table, dirty clothes on the chairs, and an unpleasant disorder everywhere. Hilary had grown used to this, just as to the fact that the bathtub against the side wall by the stove contained coal under its wooden lid.

"I dropped in to see your mother," he said. "Mrs. Adams told me she was very sick, and I stopped by to see if there was anything more we could do to help."

"You can see her," the woman said heavily. "I do the best I can, but I ain't got the strength to do no more, an' that's God's truth, especially with another comin' in two months. Sometimes I'd like to jump off the roof an' just forget it all. But I ain't goin' to do that," she added hastily. "I just gotta stand it. Ain't this heat somethin' awful?"

As Hilary talked to her he looked again keenly at the layout of the flat, which was the same as all the others in the building. There were four rooms in a line, one opening into another. The front one (if front it could be called) had two windows looking out upon the small court over which he had just come. The two middle rooms, each just big enough to hold a double bed and a cot, had no windows at all. The kitchen, as he had just noted, had two, facing a junk yard in the rear. In one of the middle rooms, which had neither light nor air except what came through the doors of the adjoining rooms, lay Mrs. Grusak. He went in, stunned as Aunt Samantha had been at the sight. She lay high upon the soiled pillows, stifled with the heat, breathing hard, her face resigned to despair, and yet giving the squalid spot dignity. For there were stamped upon her the strong peasant features of a far-away country. Fresh winds and temperate sunshine and the peace of green fields had gone into the molding of those inherited bones. They showed now, cleanly alien to her surroundings. Hilary talked with her a little, made a note of a few comforts which could be sent, offered a prayer, and returned to the kitchen.

"Could you possibly put your mother in the front room, near the windows?" he asked.

The woman's haggard face grew more troubled. She shook her head.

"I gotta think of Jake too," she said. "He ain't too strong, an' he works so hard. We tried sleepin', him an' me, in Mum's room; but Jake couldn't get his breath at all. It's sort of like asthma he's got. He coughed all night somethin' awful, so I moved Mum back and we went into the front room again. I've done my best. I put Joe and Bill and Harry back here next the kitchen. That's the worst place for heat. I give Mum that room all to herself next the front. It's the best I can do. When there's a breeze, onct in a while, there's a little air goes right through. Course like these last days an' nights it's awful anywhere."

"How many of you sleep in the front room?" Hilary asked.

"Just Jake an' me an' the girls. They'd ought to be by themselves now they're older. They want Mum's room, and I don't think she'll last long now."

Her voice was not heartless. It merely had the toneless quality of one who had ceased to feel either joy or sorrow. As though to soften her words, she added: "Mum's life ain't no good to her now. She might as well be dead. I often wisht I was."

As Hilary walked back toward St. Matthews his lips were tightly set. Through his brain ran one of Stephen Foster's songs which Grandy used often to sing. Now his feet moved to the rhythm of it.

> Let us pause in life's pleasures and count its many tears,
> While we all sup sorrow with the poor.

He felt as though the comfort of his own home would smite him. The only thing he could honestly share with the people in the old-law tenement was the oppressive city heat. But how different even that was in the beautiful blue and white bedroom which he shared with Lex!

> Hard times, hard times,
> Come again no more!

Before he crossed to the rectory for lunch he went to his study and called Henry Alvord's office. He was in.

"Mr. Alvord," he began, "when could I see you to have a talk? I have something very important on my mind."

The older man's tone sounded flattered and unusually cordial.

"I'll be very happy to meet you, I'm sure. Would four this afternoon be convenient, either at my office or yours? I'm leaving town next week for a month."

"Four will be fine for me. Would it be asking too much to have you come to the study? We will be entirely uninterrupted there."

"Not at all. I'll be glad to come. I'll see you there, then, at four."

For Hilary the intervening hours were close to anguish. He knew well that there was nothing worse for a rector than to have real dissension with his vestry. He knew Henry Alvord's position in the church, his dominant personality, his wide circle of influence. He knew that things were now running smoothly, that his own work had been so far successful beyond his dreams, that the future would normally hold for him increasing opportunity and advancement. What the selfish inner man of him desired to do was to make a close ally of Henry Alvord. Then, who could tell what preferment the years would bring? Had not Bronson even hinted at that?

As a matter of fact, Hilary had not been prepared for the bitter struggle now going on again within him. It was not yet too late, he knew, to alter his plan. When Alvord appeared he could consult him about any one of a dozen questions relating to the affairs of the parish, and the older man would never know the original purpose of his call. Perhaps he, Hilary, was being quixotic, unwise, needlessly imprudent. Was not the peace and concord of his church worth more even than the lives of the dwellers in one tenement?

Then he recalled Grandy's old story of the elder at the corncrib. He saw clearly the strong, spare features of the Bishop's face. He knew with a clear certainty what Grandy would have done in a like situation. There must be no more hesitation, then, no more cowardice. He sat down at his desk and waited, trying to calm his mind.

Henry Alvord was a gentleman by birth and a perfectionist by practice. His suits gave the effect of a more distinguished tailoring than those of other men; his tiny waxed mustache looked as though established once for all upon his lip by nature herself, entirely above need of tonsorial ministrations; his hands were slender and immaculately kept, a neat diamond ring showing on one little finger; his accent was Exeter and Harvard, and as he seated himself in the study after the first greetings his tall figure fell at once into lines of ease and grace. As Hilary looked across at his caller he felt himself hot, untidy, young, and gauche.

"Mr. Alvord," he began, the words coming stumblingly to his lips, "I have asked you to come so that we might discuss a matter . . ."

He paused, annoyed at his own embarrassment.

"I visited a near-by old-law tenement this morning, and I'm considerably shaken by what I saw there. As you doubtless know, the building at the back not only has its air shut off by the one just in front of it but gets all the reflected heat also. There is a woman dying there in a room with no windows. There are children living there like rats among garbage pails. There are young people . . ."

Henry Alvord flicked the ash delicately from his cigarette. "I think I know conditions in the city fairly well, Mr. Laurens. But just what has this to do with me?"

"I was at 55 Ash Street. You are the owner of it, I believe."

Alvord's eyes narrowed and became hard.

"You were at some pains to get that information?"

"I felt I had to know."

"I think I see the touch of Alex McColly's Machiavellian hand in this. He's about the only one who could have ferreted this out for you, and frankly, Mr. Laurens, I don't like it. My business affairs are my own, and I consider it rank impertinence for you or anyone else to question them."

"You know this building is being used in direct violation of the law?"

"That," said Alvord crisply, "is my own lookout. I will attend to the law. And you, if you are wise, will attend to the spiritual concerns of this parish and not meddle in real estate. I warned you in the beginning," he added, "that your youth might run away with you. I warn you again now that it is dangerous for you to pry into what is outside the realm of your legitimate activities. I repeat, I'm *warning you.*"

The threat of the tone angered Hilary, but he held himself in leash.

"It is not so far outside my province as you think, Mr. Alvord. Some of the young people who come to the Parish House live in that building. I have gone there to see their families. Mrs. Adams goes there constantly to visit the sick. I know I am a young man and you are an older one. I know it sounds presumptuous for me to question your actions, but I am supposed to be the spiritual adviser of my people. I feel that it is wrong for any man, let alone a church vestryman, to flout the law, and to derive revenue from the needless suffering of the poor. I am compelled by my very office to say this to you, though it is very hard for me to do it."

Alvord's face was inscrutable, but his tone was ironic. Actually or by intent he misunderstood Hilary's words.

"Well, now you can consider your conscience clear. You have done what you conceive to be your duty in rebuking me and attempting to save my soul from the lions. I believe that is as far as your clerical prerogative goes, is it not?"

Hilary was for a moment baffled. Was this not true? Had he not done as much as the prophets of old in bringing the evil to light? Could he not now go on his own way, leaving the rest to Alvord's own conscience?

And then he heard himself saying quietly: "I will not consider my conscience clear, Mr. Alvord, until yours is also. I do beg of you to think this over. I'm sure you will find a way to relieve the situation. I can easily see how you could be unaware of the seriousness of it. You have probably never been to the tenement yourself. Your agent collects the rents, and you are entirely removed from all that I saw with my own eyes today. Won't you go and see for yourself? If you once go there you will know why I am disturbed. Will you come with me, now? I'll go along. It's not far."

Hilary leaned forward impulsively, trying to compel the other man by his own eagerness. But for answer Alvord only looked coldly back at him.

"My suggestion to you, Mr. Laurens, is that you forget this entire conversation. I will brook no advice from any man upon my personal affairs. I intend to forgive your presumption upon grounds of your youth. If you recall our first conversation here in this room you will remember that I foresaw the possibility of your being diverted from your main function by the—ah—shall we say, socialistic tendencies of the times? You are the rector of this parish and responsible for it and to it. You are not responsible for all the riffraff of the city, and neither, incidentally, am I."

He rose with icy dignity.

"We will consider this matter closed, and I shall thank you never to reopen it. When are you taking your vacation?"

"In August," Hilary said absently. Then he added: "I'm sorry to have offended you, Mr. Alvord. Won't you please believe me that my position is not an easy one, and that I'm more constrained than other men to do the thing I believe to be right. How can I stand up in the pulpit to preach unless I do?"

He held Alvord's eyes to his beseechingly, but the other man's features did not soften.

"Let us merely say then that your good intentions were somewhat misguided."

When he was gone, Hilary wilted in his chair. He had accomplished nothing except to estrange Alvord more than ever. Was he to drop the whole matter now or renew the attack at a later date?

Suddenly he reached for his hat and started for the settlement house. He craved a talk with Celeste Barton.

When he reached the big rambling brick building he sauntered around now as he often did, looking upon its manifold activities. The work of the Parish House was small in comparison, but he often picked up ideas for it here. When he faced Celeste at last, seated before the window which always caught the faintest breeze, he felt a release of tension. Their friendship had taken on depth in the last months. They had in a measure become necessary to each other. Behind her outward gaiety and social charm he now saw constantly revealed the woman who knelt at early communion, her life as dedicated as that of a nun. On her side she found in him a soul, completely honest, completely consecrated to a purpose. Mentally, too, they were congenial. Their common language was suffused with that lively play of spirit known only to the cultivated few whose meeting is an intellectual sacrament.

Hilary poured out to her now for the first time the whole story, omitting only Alvord's name. As she listened, Celeste's face grew strained.

"What must I do? What ought I to do now?" Hilary was asking, his voice hoarse with his earnestness.

She rose and walked back and forth across the room.

"This is dreadful, Hilary! This is a ghastly problem. If I weren't so fond of you, it wouldn't be so hard to advise you. I can't bear to see you stir up trouble for yourself when you're on the highroad to being the most successful minister in the city. I don't mean that in a secular sense. You're really influencing people for righteousness. This whole business could actually lead up to an enforced resignation, you know. Or have you thought of that?"

Hilary nodded. "I've thought of that, and much more."

She resumed her pacing. When she finally sank down beside him, she was pale.

"The trouble is, I know 55 Ash Street only too well. As soul to soul, Hilary, I think you are right, though I doubt if many ministers would consider it their duty to go into the matter at all. It is like you to go straight to the heart of it, though, and I can't tell you how I honor you for it. As to your next move, you'll have a little time to think it over, for the summer will intervene."

They sat silent for a few minutes, then Celeste spoke again.

"You've had your Forty Days in the Wilderness over this, I suppose?"

Hilary nodded. "I have. You see there are so many logical arguments why I should stay away from the thing altogether. But my conscience keeps egging me on."

"Follow it, then," she said quietly, "and God bless you. Are you going to talk it over with any one else?"

"I've been wondering about that. I believe I'll take Stephen Cole and Judge Ball into my confidence. Feel them out a little. They are two of the best men I've ever known, and the Judge especially is a very wise one. I don't want to blunder more than I have to. Oh, by the way," he added suddenly, "what about Maudie Dunn's romance? Is it still on? I haven't heard anything since I gave her the report of my visit to her father."

Celeste laughed and looked gay again. "You will, very soon. They're going to be married the first of next month. I'm as excited as though I were the bride."

"But—what about J. V.?"

"No change. Refuses to take it seriously. Pooh-poohs the whole thing. Maudie took Jerry up to meet him, and J. V. all but laughed in his face. Told him in effect to run along like a nice little boy and play with his paints! Maudie was more furious, I believe, than she would have been if he'd stormed. She's actually become a strong-minded person. She has to be, for when Jerry saw her home and met J. V. he was ready to give up everything for fear of being unfair to her. So she's got to take hold, and she's doing it. There's really a little of J. V. himself in her make-up. You'll be hearing from her soon."

"If she asks me to marry them I suppose I'll have to do it," Hilary said slowly.

"Oh, you couldn't refuse! Maudie's heart is set on having the ceremony in St. Matthews. She has decided to telephone her friends who may still be in town and drop notes to those in the country a few days before. All very informal. I'll have the party here afterwards. You can really squeeze a lot of people into this room. We'll use the reception room outside, too, for an overflow. I'll simply love doing it. Aren't you pleased?" she questioned him suddenly.

"For Maudie, yes. But I'm still worried about J. V. I'll probably make an enemy of him, too, if I perform the ceremony."

"Good heavens!" Celeste said irritably. "He couldn't be as mean as that, could he? It isn't as though Maudie were a child. Well, anyway, I've never nursed a love affair along to its consummation which gave me the satisfaction this one has. It's as though I'd watched the birth of two souls. They're going to make a marvellous pair, those two, if only the next few years don't sweep them into the maelstrom."

They fell then into talk of the war. Seriously, tragically, their faces darkened, their voices fell. Celeste switched on the radio and they listened to a broadcast. German troops had captured Brest, their cavalry had taken possession of Lyons. Daladier with his ministers had fled from Bordeaux to French Morocco. Would France stand? Would she fall? And if France fell, then what of England?

"My brother," Hilary said heavily, "has enlisted in an ambulance unit. He expects to go overseas next month. If I let it, the whole pressure of the war would unfit me for work completely. It's like a black cloud, at first no bigger than a man's hand, now covering all the sky. The doom of it smothers me."

When the broadcast was ended, they turned to look at each other as for comfort.

"Have you any theory, Hilary, as to where God fits into this whole ghastly mess? For the life of me, I don't know what to believe. Is it the case of an omnipotent Father taking his children through the fire for the ultimate good of the world, or is it just poor, blind, blundering mankind running to his own destruction under a heedless 'inverted bowl'? I've never felt so insecure in my own thinking."

Hilary pondered. "I ran into a passage by William James the other day which my grandfather had copied," he said slowly. "I think I can remember it. If you give me a bit of paper I'll write it down for you. It's rather a startling thought but it's bolstered me up."

Celeste brought a sheet of paper from the desk, and Hilary wrote carefully, making sure of each word:

> God himself, in short, may draw vital strength and increase of very being from our fidelity. For my own part, I do not know what the sweat and blood and tragedy of this life mean, if they mean anything short of this.

He handed it to her and she read it slowly over and over, then their eyes met.

"I like that," she said simply. "Maybe we're each important in the whole scheme after all. I'll read it often and keep it near in case of darker days ahead. Do you think they will come?"

A far-away, fixed look fell upon Hilary's face. His answer startled even himself.

"I'm afraid they will," he said huskily.

CHAPTER XII

AND FRANCE FELL. Incredible catastrophe! When Hilary heard the final news he was in Mrs. Reed's little sitting room. They listened, their faces paling, then the old lady suddenly switched off the radio.

"That's our own death warrant," she said. "Even if there were no moral weight compelling us, we daren't let England fall."

"You can't convince the whole nation of that," Hilary said. "At least not yet."

"There will be a way. All too surely there will be a way." She sighed heavily and picked up her knitting again. "What's the word from Dick?"

"There isn't any. I wish he'd write. We have no idea when he may drop in, and of course when he does, he'll be starting over soon. I'm a frightful coward at the thought of it."

"So am I. I love the crazy fool. When he does come I want you all to dinner. Tell Lex I won't let you off." Then she eyed him sharply. "Any parish troubles on your mind?"

"Plenty. But the one I want to ask you about is this." He produced a letter and handed it over. "It's from Miss Hettie Breckenridge and it came only this morning. I don't want to show it to Lex unless I have to, but it's really a blow."

Mrs. Reed reached for it and read it aloud:

"DEAR RECTOR:
"Ever since your regrettable marriage to my great-niece I have felt that St. Matthews, to which I have given a lifelong devotion and support, was less congenial to me than heretofore. It is inevitable that your character, which I have greatly respected, should suffer from the union with a headstrong girl who has no interest in religious things. I have tried to be patient but, having recently come into possession of certain facts indicating that her worldliness and flippancy have reached the point of indiscretion, I have reluctantly de-

cided to withdraw my membership and that of my brother
from St. Matthews.

> "Respectfully yours,
> "HETTIE BRECKENRIDGE"

Mrs. Reed laid the letter down, her gray eyes shooting sparks.

"I've been expecting this. The old harpy! What's Lex been up to lately, anyhow?"

"Nothing, except that when Dick was here before Easter they made the rounds of the night clubs. Some one who didn't know who Dick was probably saw them, and the thing got around to her. But I wouldn't stoop to explain it to her."

"Certainly *not*," Mrs. Reed snapped. "Indiscretion, indeed! Do you suppose Tommy Tatler put something in his column about it? But no, he's too smart for that. He'd find out first who Dick was. He's always sure of his ground before he prints anything. That's why his stuff is so devilishly interesting."

"He'd just better not put in anything more about Lex," Hilary said angrily. "He did once, and I wanted to go to the mat with him about it, only Lex wouldn't let me. He's a dangerous person, I think."

"He's all of that," Mrs. Reed returned, "but I must admit I smuggle in the *Courier* sometimes to read his stuff. I knew his grandparents. Fine people. Early settlers, blue blood and all that. Tommy's just a decadent offshoot of good old stock. But he's got a great racket with this gossip business. He lives in style at the Colston. You know, that new apartment hotel? All the ultra-sophisticates are moving in, I hear. They tell me he can pick up enough scandal right there day and night to fill his column. But I'm sure he didn't put in a note about Lex and Dick. A brother-in-law would be too tame for him. No, Hettie got it some other way. And Hilary, I'm going to attend to her!"

"Do you think you can?"

A complacent air of mystery spread over the old lady's countenance.

"You wait and see. Write her a nice, mild little note. Tell her you hope very much she will reconsider her decision and remain in St. Matthews."

"I can say that with all my heart. The thing has me worried. I would hate the general unpleasantness of her leaving, and I know the vestry would be upset over the loss from a financial standpoint. And then, worst of all, if she broadcasts the reason for her move it would be dreadful for Lex and me both."

"Don't even mention Lex when you write, and stop worrying over the whole thing. I think you'll hear from her soon with a different tune."

Hilary studied the alert old face opposite him with interest. There was a definite look of pleased expectancy upon it.

"I don't entirely trust you," he said laughing, "but I'm going to give you my blessing anyhow."

"Good boy! And look, Hilary. Don't take to heart what she said about Lex. The girl is headstrong, of course, and she's completely of her own generation with all their points, good and bad, but she's as true as steel, as you very well know, and every time I see her she's prettier than the last time! After all, even if you are a parson, you had a right to marry a *woman* and not a Prayer-book! Just give Lex a few years."

"If she only doesn't find life boring in the interim."

Mrs. Reed eyed him with a sly grin. "I don't believe a girl would find it too boring to be married to you."

"Thanks," Hilary said, flushing a little. "You always lift my spirits. And good luck in the name of the Lord with Aunt Hettie!"

Lex had planned to leave the city the first of July but at the news of Maudie Dunn's approaching nuptials decided to wait over for the wedding, which was now set for the sixth.

"I've got to see that man of hers," she told Hilary, "if it's the last thing I do. Is he cute looking?"

Hilary laughed. "If a huge, shy, amiable animal could be called 'cute.'"

"You know what I mean. Would I think he was cute?"

"Yes, I think you might. He's really rather handsome, though he's very thin now from an illness, and he has a good smile."

"And Maudie got him! Everybody's staying over or coming back for the wedding. It's a riot. All the girls are simply mad with curiosity and the fellows aren't much better. They can't wait. Clarissa Ball met Maudie on the street last week and didn't even know her! Has she changed as much as that, Hil?"

"She's changed a lot. Mostly in her manner and the way she dresses."

"Poor Maudie! We were dreadful, I suppose, for we all made fun of her behind her back. She was older than our crowd, but J. V. would throw these marvellous big parties and keep inviting the younger sets as they came along. We all called her the perennial debutante and Bill Bostwick used to say every fall, 'Well, now we've got to bring Maudie out again.' And, poor soul, she was always so namby-pamby and sputtery and ruffly! Her aunt picked her clothes, and they were always too-too."

"I think she's on the right track now."

"That's what Clarissa said—that she looked positively smart. By the way, I sent a pretty swell wedding present. I thought I owed it to her."

"That's right. I'm glad you did."

"What do you think old J. V. will do when he finds out?"

"I wish I knew. I'm nervous."

"He couldn't walk in and stop the show, could he? You know where you say, 'If any man can show just cause' and so on?"

"Hardly. He has no just cause. Maudie told me she'd tried last week again to tell him all about it and he refused to listen. He merely forbade her absolutely to marry the fellow and wanted to hear no more nonsense about it. So she says she's done her best and is going ahead with a clear conscience. But I wish the set-up were different."

"It's not *your* fault. Will J. V. hate you for marrying them?"

"I imagine so."

"And be a real enemy?"

"Could be."

She smoothed back his hair.

"You're getting little worry wrinkles, darling, across your forehead and around your eyes. Can't you stop carrying everybody else's troubles? Why did you ever pick this job?"

Hilary smiled into her eyes. "You're forgetting the other side of this affair. I wouldn't go around boasting about it, but the truth is, if it hadn't been for me, all this happiness would never have come to Maudie. I got her the place at the settlement. I definitely set out to help her, after I heard her story, and I did. I'm personally responsible in a sense, and I'm pleased as Punch. So even if J. V. tries to get my skin for this, the satisfaction will outweigh the unpleasantness. See?"

"Yes. And I think you're wonderful!" She leaned against him. "Then you feel the whole job pays?" She asked it slowly, fingering a button on his coat.

"Oh, infinitely! It's a tough one, but I honestly feel I'm doing a lot of good. More than if I were—well, in business, for example. But how is it with you?" He cupped her face in his hand and raised it. "Are you growing more adjusted yourself?"

He had not meant to say it but the words came, in spite of him.

"Darling, are you happy? Is everything all right?"

Her eyes fell, and for one moment his heart stood still.

"I love you, Hil," she said softly. "Isn't that enough?"

But he knew she had not answered his question.

Maudie Dunn's wedding, while simple and informal in the extreme, was reckoned by all one of the prettiest and certainly the most gossip-provoking of the season. At noon of that day Hilary, still anxious about J. V., made one last attempt. When he called the house the butler, whom he knew, answered the phone. Miss Dunn was already in the country, opening the place there, he reported, and Mr. Dunn was in Chicago on business. He would return the last of the week, the old man added, and would then take Miss Maudie with him to the country for the summer.

So that was that, Hilary thought, surrendering himself then to the enjoyment of the occasion. The matter of the giving away of the bride had been solved by Jerry himself. He and Maudie would walk up the aisle together, he said, and the usual question could be omitted from the service. So it came about that at four o'clock, Celeste Barton, having just taken her place, *in loco parentis,* in the front pew, Forrest swung into the wedding march, and Maudie and Jerry, unattended, started slowly up the long aisle.

To Hilary's surprise the central block of the church was half filled! And as the bride and groom advanced there was a general turning of heads and intaking of breaths. Celeste's infallible taste had aided in the choice of Maudie's beautiful gown and hat, but it was her own consuming love that touched her face now with light and made her old acquaintances stare. She moved down the aisle on the arm of her amazingly good-looking young man, in her day of triumph at last.

As Hilary watched them draw near he had a fleeting picture of the Maudie who on that night he had first had dinner with the Dunns had poured out her strange story to him with tears. What a transformation! And he himself had helped bring it about.

He could remember no marriage service which had given him deeper satisfaction to perform unless it had been his first one at St. Matthews when he had married Joe and Mary McComb. Even the thought of J. V.'s sharp features did not rise to darken the words.

The party at the settlement was all gay and young and infused with that undercurrent of excitement which accompanies the unusual and dramatic.

"It really was a lovely wedding," Lex remarked as they left for home in a taxi. "And Maudie! Never would I have believed it if I hadn't seen her with my own eyes! I wish my wedding had added that much to my good looks."

"I couldn't have borne the sight, then," Hilary said laughing. "It's all I can do now to look at you in public and keep from kissing you. What about right now? The taxi driver won't care."

Lex raised a brow in pretended shock. "Mr. Laurens, how vulgar! How low! In a public taxi! And you a gentleman of the cloth!"

She was wearing pale green, a color Hilary loved. A small flower hat was perched upon her curls, which fluffed upon her shoulders as though she were still eighteen. There was in her beauty that vitality, the dynamic charm which quickened Hilary's pulse each time he looked at her just as it had enslaved him at their first meeting.

"You should have heard Bill Bostwick at the reception," she was saying now. "I certainly got a bang out of him. He couldn't get over the change in Maudie. He said to me: 'Have we fellows missed the boat? All that, and

J. V.'s millions too!' And the thing that simply slayed the girls was how good-looking Maudie's man is. He's really cute, Hil, though he doesn't look too strong. I like him. Do you suppose J. V. will cut them off?"

"I'm wondering. At least they aren't expecting anything. They've got three rooms and a kitchenette down near the settlement, and they're going to live very simply on Maudie's own little income and whatever he can make with his painting. They can't splurge much but they can get by."

"Well, I think you and Celeste Barton between you did a good day's work. One thing I just thought of is that Maudie will be spared having Tommy Tatler paw over her romance in his column. He can't make wise cracks about the daughter of the big boss."

"Oh, that's right. J. V. owns the *Courier,* doesn't he? They've tried to keep it from all the papers, but some reporter will probably nose it out. It will be a shock to J. V. if he reads it in Chicago. I'll go to see him as soon as he's back and dangle an olive branch. Lex, when do you think you'll leave?"

His eyes were pleading. "I don't want to be selfish, and you ought to be out of the heat."

"I'll stay another week," she said. "We may hear from Dick by then. Can't you come up before August?"

Hilary shook his head. "I'm afraid not. I have a lot to do here, and besides I feel I should go out to see Cousin Mattie when I've promised. That had better be the last of this month. But I'll still have four good weeks with you in the country. I'll try to exist in the meanwhile after you leave, but it'll be tough. Well, here we are. Hurry. I want to kiss you before you take off that hat!"

Hilary's plan had been to keep in touch with the Dunn house and as soon as J. V. returned, to see him. But he was spared that trouble. Two days after the wedding J. V. appeared in his study one morning with a face so terrible in its anger and shock that Hilary was afraid the man might drop dead in the room. He did not rave or rant. The voice that came between his blue lips was scarcely more than a whisper—more frightening by far than a shout.

"Mr. Dunn," Hilary began quickly, "I meant to go to you as soon as you were home. I know this is a—"

"I have been betrayed," Dunn hissed. "Betrayed by the child of my bosom and by you whom I'd begun to love as a son. I've been *betrayed!* You—you—*Judas!*"

"Mr. Dunn, sit down. Let me explain—"

"There is nothing you can explain. Behind my back you aided and abetted my daughter to do this unspeakable thing which I'd forbidden. Forbidden, do you hear? Here in this church, which I help support, you did this thing to me!"

"But, Mr. Dunn, I did nothing wrong. Neither did Maudie. I tried to tell you. She tried to tell you. You wouldn't listen. Maudie is twenty-eight years old. She has a right to marry whom she chooses and she asked me to—"

"Don't speak to me. You knew well enough what my plans were for Maudie. And yet you sanctioned this marriage to a cheap, penniless, fortune-hunting Communist!"

"He's not a Communist, Mr. Dunn. He's a Socialist."

"What's the difference? They're all the same. He's nothing but a—"

"Listen, Mr. Dunn. I investigated this young man. If he hadn't been all right I would have refused to perform the ceremony. But he's a fine fellow and Maudie's happier than she's ever been in her life. I think you ought to see your daughter and—"

J. V. came closer, and his bloodshot eyes looked crazed.

"She's no longer a daughter of mine. Never will she enter my house. Never will she have a cent of my money. She's made her bed, and she can lie in it. Lie down in the slums with her Communist till she rots. And as for you—the man I trusted—before I set foot in your church again I'll see you damned in hell."

With that he swayed toward the door and started down the stairs. Hilary followed quickly to be sure he hadn't fallen, then slowly and with a feeling of weakness in the pit of his stomach went over to the rectory and gave Lex an expurgated report of the conversation.

"Why, the old Dodo!" Lex sputtered. "He must think he's living in the eighteenth century. I hope he has a stroke before he has time to change his will!"

Hilary was too disturbed by his encounter to expostulate.

"He looks as if he might have, at that. But I rather fancy he'll live on in his ire till he's a hundred. There was something I always liked in the old fellow, too. Well, I guess I'm off his list now, the same as Maudie. It's a nasty mess. I suppose he'll turn in his pew. If many more people resign their membership I'll have to look for a new job."

"Why, who else?" Lex asked, interested.

Hilary turned the question aside. "Nothing," he said. "Just one of my quips. But in any church people get offended occasionally and leave. I'm truly sorry about J. V. I really pity the man. He's pretty well shot. You should have seen him!"

"I'd have wanted to smack him right on his old beak if I had. I've no patience with him. He's a selfish, bossy old tyrant and Maudie's darned lucky to get away from him. The marvel is she had the guts to do it."

"Lex, really!"

"O.K. Gumption, spunk, fortitude, then. But anyway I won't have you all broken up over this business. Forget J. V. and drive me out somewhere for lunch. You need a day off. If he hates you, he hates you. The really important thing is that—"

"That you don't hate me!"

"What a delicate little understatement! Come on, darling. Let's go."

A letter came from Dick before Lex left. He was in Nevada fussing around with a mine there at the moment. There had been a hold-up in the other plans but he still hoped to get overseas by fall. Meanwhile he loved them both and hoped they were the same.

After Lex left, taking Muff and Morris up with her, Hilary plunged into work to dull the awful ache of missing her. The rectory seemed unspeakably empty and forlorn. Lex had insisted upon Muff's staying behind to look after him, and then taking the train up when Hilary left for Maryville, but he had vetoed this and started them all off in Lex's own car. Adams and Aunt Samantha were having their vacation during July, so he did not have their society. Miss Mowbray asked him out to dinner one night, and he went, feeling oddly guilty of he didn't quite know what. The evening was easy, however, casual and to outward appearances entirely normal. Nothing in the girl's behavior then or during their hours in the office alone gave any further indication of a hidden tenderness on her part—nothing except that sudden blush that rose often to her cheeks when he was accidentally near her. Perhaps, he tried to reassure himself, she flushed if any man came close. She was so fine, so entirely lovable a girl, it was a great pity some nice chap did not recognize her worth and try to win her. He wished he could put her in as advantageous a position toward that end as he had Maudie Dunn. Then he took himself to task for such an idea. Margaret Mowbray was not the sort of person whose personal affairs one tampered with. As his secretary she was invaluable. Never a day passed but her quiet efficiency and wisdom did not ease his burdens. He must simply appreciate her and try to forget the uncomfortable suspicion that so easily now leaped to his mind.

He dined during these weeks with a number of his men parishioners who either were bachelors or whose wives and families were out of the city for the summer. He had a good evening with Forrest whose companionship he greatly prized. Shane called him up also and they dined together at the club. It was the first real talk they had had since the engagement had been announced. Shane was radiant, exuberant as a youth. He could talk of nothing but his love. Hilary had a few bad moments but in the end went home satisfied.

"Funny about me," Shane said. "I never could even picture myself before as a family man. Now, I can't wait to be hog-tied completely. Francy wants a big family, so you'd better begin filling up your font."

"I'll do that," said Hilary. "Have you set a date for the wedding?"

"Not yet. Some time in September, I fancy. It will be very quiet though. Francy wants it like that, and any way at all suits me, just so she doesn't change her mind."

"I know the feeling, old man," Hilary laughed. "But I'm sure you're safe!"

The two evenings which were most important to him, however, were those spent with Stephen Cole and Judge Ball, for they gave him the opportunity he wanted for discussing in secret his problem with Henry Alvord. In each case the men sat far into the night, smoking, talking, weighing with tremendous seriousness the issues involved. To Hilary's surprise, Stephen Cole advised him to take no further action in the matter. He had done his duty, perhaps even now to the point of estranging Alvord and making working conditions within the vestry difficult. Why not forget it for the present and see if harmony could not be restored? He seemed anxious and concerned over Hilary's own position.

Judge Ball's reaction was quite different.

"I don't like Alvord," he wheezed as he settled his huge bulk more comfortably in his chair. "I never did like him. I have a profound distrust for any man whose clothes match up as well as Alvord's do. He was on the vestry when I was elected, and I've tried not to lock horns with him since, but I don't like him. Now let's get this all straight. Just what is it you want to do?"

"There are two angles," Hilary said. "I want to get that old-law apartment condemned. I want to prevail upon Alvord to do the right thing of his own accord. If he is obdurate and continues to operate it and draw income from it, then I feel he should not be on the vestry. That's the amount of it. Am I queer? Am I quixotic? Am I making a straw man and shooting at it? I declare I've thought around this matter so much that sometimes I'm not sure whether I'm a fool or not."

Judge Ball did not reply for a long minute. Then he spoke.

"I'm going to tell you something which I've known for some years. Henry Alvord owns at least two apartment houses used for immoral purposes. He's a corporation lawyer by profession, but he's made his big money in real estate. He owns more buildings in this city than you'd ever dream. And two or three are what I've just said."

Hilary's face looked stricken.

"No!" he said. "I can't believe that."

"True, just the same. To be fair to the man, I'm sure he didn't ever set out to own that type of thing. These apartments probably just came to him in various deals. But he does own them now. And they're valuable."

Hilary could not speak and the Judge went on.

"Odd what can happen to a man in the course of his life! Friend of mine has known Alvord from the time he was a young fellow. Says in his early years he was positively idealistic. Sensitive type, you know. Then he made a lot of money too fast—I've seen it happen to lots of them—and he got all involved with success. Got to the place where ideals sometimes cost hard cash. So he ditched the ideals. Now, you've got Alvord as he is."

Hilary groaned.

"If he were simply a parishioner and I knew these facts, I could only point out to him what I felt was his duty as a churchman, and a Christian and let it go at that. But Alvord is the Senior Warden. Every Sunday, in the face of the congregation he walks up the aisle and stands before the altar. I can't go on, knowing all this, unless Alvord either changes his practices or gets out. That's the sum of it."

The Judge drew steadily upon his pipe.

"I've always been pretty much live-and-let-live, myself," he said at last. "I know only too well that in real estate as in politics a man can get some pretty queer pigs by the tail before he knows it. He doesn't have to hold on to them, however. If you are really in this thing to a finish with Alvord, I'll back you. But my advice is, don't go too fast. You've already fired the opening round. Now give the smoke time to settle before you go at it again. It's barely possible he may have a change of heart. And also I'm bound to remind you that you are playing with dynamite as far as your own career goes to meddle with this."

"I know it," Hilary said soberly.

"You still intend to go on?"

"I think so," Hilary replied.

This new and revolting information in connection with Alvord's real-estate holdings sent Hilary back to the rectory in a black and bitter mood. He was sleeping since Lex went away in the Prophet's Chamber, since he missed her less there; he went directly to it now, but not to bed. Instead he paced back and forth in the small room, reviewing Judge Ball's disclosure. It seemed incredible that Alvord should actually be linked up with organized iniquity! It seemed that the most unspeakable irony, the more unforgivable hypocrisy, that Hilary, as rector of St. Matthews, should in his "Solomon's Sermon" have warned his congregation of young men against the houses of evil women, while some of these very houses were owned by the church's Senior Warden!

"No!" Hilary shouted the word. "I won't tolerate this situation. Something's got to be done!"

He realized that he could do nothing more now, this summer, with Alvord gone from the city, but the first thing in the fall he must go to him and lay this all before him. Surely, *surely* the man could not fail to see the deadly incongruity between his business and his professed religion. Surely, when confronted by this new evidence against him he would not dare to hold out, but would capitulate then on both points.

Hilary walked over to the window and stood looking out across the court at the church, its spire and buttresses now wrapped in shadow. He loved it. Each day it was becoming more vitally a part of him. He realized that he wanted to serve here for years to come; that he longed to see his labors take root and finally flower into consummation. He knew also, without Judge Ball's keen reminder, that he was indeed playing with dynamite as far as his own career was concerned, in continuing to raise the issue with Alvord. Stephen Cole's advice was to do nothing more. Judge Ball's own partisanship had been more or less grudgingly given. All the old arguments against proceeding rose in his mind once more and had to be fought again. But while his face fell into haggard lines as he wrestled, he came out at the same place. I can't compromise on this and keep my own integrity, he thought. I can't sidestep a situation like this. But I somehow feel that I can still win Alvord over!

Another and quite different anxiety struck him the following day, when he caught a glimpse of Diana Downes getting into her car in front of a downtown restaurant. He passed on rapidly, hoping she had not seen him. The beautiful widow—Mrs. Potiphar, as Lex still referred to her— had indeed become to him a thorn in the flesh, for certain stretches unfelt and ignored, but with recurrent stabs to disturb and render him uneasy. With incredible persistence the woman kept on calling him up, and writing to him, begging him to come to see her on this pretext or that. He had stopped talking to Lex about her, for once she had looked strangely at him as she had done that day when she had met him and Margaret Mowbray together.

"Is that Potiphar woman still after you, Hil? It seems to me you're always mentioning her."

He had felt embarrassed.

"She bothers me."

"Well, for heaven's sake! Can't you flatten her out, once for all? And just remember you don't handle her kind with kid gloves. You surely don't still believe that *lonesome* line she gave you."

"No."

"Well then. Get rid of her."

But this was more easily said than done. In his normal, rested moments he looked at the whole matter sensibly. The woman was a fool and a nuisance, but she could do him no actual harm. How could she? He was certainly capable of handling any situation which might arise. Her persistence had worked upon his nerves, that was all.

Then, at a time when he was very tired and generally discouraged, she would catch him on the telephone, write him a letter of veiled allusions, turn up in church looking so stunningly beautiful that all eyes followed her, come after service into the chapel to speak to him with indecently melting glances—and he was once again disturbed.

In spite of himself he thought of the ministers, from Beecher down, who had had trouble with women. Every city clergyman had to recognize this menace. A few to his own knowledge through the years, in spite of their utter innocence, had yet escaped scandal by a hair's breadth. A few here and there had not even escaped. There were always the neurotic women who flocked not only to the psychiatrists but also in almost equal numbers to ministers, pouring out their heart confessions and their fancied ills; there were those pitiable ones in whose minds religion and sex had become confused and intermingled; there were those who quite starkly fell in love with a clergyman and wanted love from him in return. Yes, a man of God had to be constantly on his guard in connection with this problem of women.

In his own case he had already run into all the unpleasant types. He had received confidences that both distressed and revolted him and which he tried to forget; he had watched helplessly as he saw that thin veil between the normal and the abnormal being rent in the name of religion; he had himself gone down into the valley of bitterness with those unfortunate ones who must be forever lonely and apart due to a mistake of nature. *And* he had had the long and annoying acquaintance with Diana Downes.

Ever since his first conversation with Lex concerning her he had steadily refused to go again to her apartment. She had invited him over and over, using every possible excuse. He had as persistently declined. In fact when either Miss Mowbray or Hastings answered her phone calls the matter ended there, for Hilary had advised them both upon the subject. Recently, however, she had, with diabolically clever timing, called up at certain odd times when he was alone in the study. He wondered if she might actually have him "covered."

The Monday of his last week in the city was hot and sultry. Hilary decided after dinner to go over to the study and clear up some work at his desk.

He removed his coat and necktie, rolled up his sleeves and settled down to his job. The Adamses would be back the next day from their vacation and Miss Mowbray would start her own the following week. Hilary felt that after this night's work he would have his house well in order, so that he could spend the next day in making a few last calls, keeping one or two last engagements, then leave for Maryville on Wednesday. He worked now doggedly, trying to forget the heat.

At eight-thirty the phone rang. He had an odd premonition. His strong inclination was not to answer at all. But the phone kept ringing. Suppose it should be Lex who had called the rectory first. He took the receiver in his hand at once.

"Hello."

"Mr. Laurens! So I did catch you at work on a hot night like this!"

It was Diana. But this time her tactics appeared to be different. She was not the lonely widow; she was not the spiritual novice, craving counsel; she was the easy, friendly, assured woman of the world, and parishioner of St. Matthews.

"I'm back in town just for a few days. I've been wanting to make a contribution to our Fresh Air Fund, and since I happen to be free this evening I suddenly wondered if you would care to drop in and pick it up. I'd really like to hear more details about the work. I'm very much interested in it. And I can promise you a nice cold drink while we talk. Completely innocuous, of course," she added with a charming little laugh.

Hilary's dark brows were frowning.

"That is very kind of you, Mrs. Downes, but I'm afraid I'll have to stick to my desk all this evening. I do appreciate your gift to the fund, though. We always need more money. Could you mail me the check?"

Her voice when it came was very low, husky and tender.

"You work much too hard. Is it fair to yourself or to St. Matthews? Can't you finish now by ten o'clock? Or eleven? I stay up late these summer nights. There is actually a breeze now coming through the windows. I'm so high up here, you know. Come over later on, whenever you wish. I'd really like to talk to you before I make out the check. I want it to be in line with the needs."

Devil, Hilary thought to himself. This really was temptation, for he desperately wanted more money for the Fresh Air work. Through his brain the thought went swiftly that by refusing to comply with her request he might be depriving a dozen children of their chance of a summer outing. But he knew he could not, must not go to her apartment.

"I can tell you in a second about the need," he said. "It is most pressing. There are a hundred children of whom we know right now who simply must be gotten out of the city. We need all the money we can get. Do make your check as generous as you possibly can. I'll be so very grateful. And certainly the children will."

"I'll expect you later, then?"

"I'm afraid I must go on with my work, Mrs. Downes. But thank you, and I'll look forward eagerly to receiving your contribution. Just mail it here to the church office."

There was a brief silence.

236

"You're a very strange and obdurate young man," she said.

To Hilary's discomfort there was, instead of annoyance, a hint of laughter in her voice. "Go ahead then and work hard. Goodbye."

She knows Lex is away, Hilary thought angrily as he replaced the receiver, and she was all ready to take advantage of it! He lighted his pipe and settled again to his desk. It was nearly eleven when he stretched his cramped arm, rose and went over to the window for air. He stayed for a moment, considering how plainly the light from the study could be seen from the street. At a faint sound behind him he turned quickly. Diana Downes stood in the doorway! She was dressed in a thin form-fitting black dress, her dark, shining hair brushed high as usual. She wore no color except the scarlet of her lips, and no one would have questioned the seductive quality of her beauty.

"I brought the check myself," she said smiling, advancing toward him, "since you would not come."

She opened her bag and held out the slip of paper to Hilary. He scanned it hastily and saw that it was for two hundred dollars!

"This is most generous of you, Mrs. Downes. This is really very kind. You've no idea how much good this will do. Thank you. I had just finished my work here and was about to leave. Can I show you down to your car? You shouldn't have troubled to come."

He felt that he sounded like a fool or a boor but he disliked the situation intensely.

She smiled provocatively and came close to him, looking up. The line of her white throat was exquisite.

"Yes, we'll go down to the car, and then we'll both go back to my apartment. You've no idea how cool it is there. I have our drinks all ready, iced and waiting." She hesitated and then looked compellingly into his eyes. "In fact, there will be everything for you there that a man could desire. Come, Hilary. You can't refuse, and I know you really want to come, don't you?"

There was in her face and tone the assurance that comes of fully tested power. She caught his arm and leaned slightly against him, somehow conveying in the gesture a complete physical surrender.

Hilary freed himself and moved back toward the door.

"Mrs. Downes," he said, "I cannot pretend to misunderstand your meaning, so that gives me the chance to make my position unmistakably plain. I have no slightest interest in you as a woman, only as a member of St. Matthews. First of all, I am a clergyman and your own rector. Besides that, I am a married man completely in love with my wife. Have I made myself clear?"

The expression of her lips did not change. He wondered at her self-control. Her eyes seemed to grow suddenly smaller and darker, however.

"All right," she said, "let's be honest with each other. I care nothing about St. Matthews and all its workings. I was lying when I told you I was lonely and when I said I wanted spiritual counsel. But I am not lying when I tell you now that I've been mad about you since that first Sunday I saw you in the pulpit. I only went that day because I was insufferably bored and I heard there was a handsome new rector."

She paused for breath, then went on rapidly.

"I'm not a patient woman, but in this case I see the obstacles in your way. I'm not at all convinced that you are indifferent to me. You naturally have to appear so. I understand that. I'm not in the habit of asking for love, either. Au contraire. But I'm so mad about you that I can wait until you come to me. As I know you will come eventually."

"Mrs. Downes!" Hilary began angrily.

She made a light gesture. "Don't worry. I'm going." Then she stood looking at him, a hot wave of color passing over her face. "At last you look like a real man, not a priest. I love you without a tie. Well, goodbye for now. And don't forget I'll still be waiting."

She started for the door. Hilary made no move to follow. He was too stunned by the woman's colossal assurance. There was also in her eyes the hint of something like a threat which made him literally tremble. "Hell hath no fury . . ." he muttered miserably to himself. Just what would her next move be? She was completely unscrupulous and therefore doubly dangerous. Even this evening's encounter would be embarrassing to explain if any one had seen her coming out of his study alone at this hour of the night. It might have been better if he had done the normal thing and accompanied her to her car, talking in good strong ordinary tones about her gift to the Fresh Air Fund.

Oh, well, it was too late now and probably no one had seen her. He got into his coat quickly, put out the lights and went over to the rectory, a feeling of revulsion overcoming him. It was so strong that he found he could not settle himself either to read or to sleep. Unlike last night he could not even fall back upon the concentration involved in a great decision. After midnight he started out to walk off the unhappy restlessness that possessed him. He walked for miles thinking in widening circles around his problem. He thought of all the fine, good women he knew. His congregation was full of them; the city was full of them. Yet he seldom stopped to consider their virtue. It was as casually accepted as the air and as unobtrusive. Now, one woman's aberration had power to throw his whole consciousness into chaos, and make him feel physically and spiritually soiled. There was deep injustice in this, somehow—a cosmic unfairness. Why should goodness always pass unnoted and the evil be dramatized? Even in his own sane, well balanced mind, he knew that Diana had suddenly become Lilith, Circe, Cleopatra, in short, the eternal temptress—*The Woman!*

But as he returned home at last, walking wearily through the quiet streets, his forehead bathed by the cool night air, he saw it all in its true light. There was no reason to arraign the high-lighting of evil. It only proved what he had always honestly believed, that in human-kind decency was, after all, the norm.

He wrote a long letter to Lex before he slept, a sweet letter, full of love and whimsy and intimacies. It eased his heart so to write. Of his evening's encounter with Mrs. Potiphar he said nothing. He was able to thrust it aside because he knew now that it had not besmirched his natural reactions to life and to women in general. Certainly—here he smiled to himself —certainly not to the one woman who filled his heart completely.

He left for Maryville in his car early on Wednesday morning. He could make the trip easily in a day, pay his duty visit to Cousin Mattie and be headed up toward Maine by Friday. Indeed, as he left the city he had a feeling of frustration and irritability that he was going to Maryville at all. It had probably been a foolish and overconscientious notion on his part in the first place. Grandy was gone, Cousin Mattie merely a name, and he himself was dead tired and eager only to get to Lex and start his real vacation.

By late afternoon, however, his mood had changed. There was something about the rolling farm land through which he was passing that reached out and took him to itself. He watched the ripe wheat and the windrows of hay, drank in the good rich summer smells of fields and woods and felt his worries slipping from him. He forgot Henry Alvord and Diana Downes. The war itself seemed incredibly remote. He was conscious only that it was nearing evening when the sun would set behind the hills and men, their day's work done, would eat and sleep and question nothing. He drew a deep breath and thought that after all he had done well to come.

In the little village itself, he drew up, after some inquiry, in front of a white frame house on a side street. The shutters were a faded green and the iron fence around the front yard was shabby, but there was an air of neat comfort about the place. Hilary noted the details with pleasure as he waited a moment in the car: there were hollyhocks in bloom along the fence, a bed of myrtle underneath the windows and a gravel path leading to the front porch, bordered by whitewashed stones. He got out, unlatched the iron gate and went in, still looking curiously about him. All his life had been spent in cities and more or less conventional vacation places. He had known the sea and the woods, but never a country village, except for that one brief, all but forgotten visit in his boyhood. He rang the bell, eyed the woven willow porch rockers with their Turkey red cushions, and smiled to himself.

"It likes me well," he murmured.

Cousin Mattie hurried through the hall straightening her white apron nervously as she came. Hilary saw that she was tall and spare with white hair and fine, beautifully shaped bones showing under the aged wrinkles of her face.

"Well, well," she greeted him, looking eagerly into his eyes, "so this is Hilary. Your grandfather wrote about you often enough, so I almost think I know you. You're like him, too."

"I am?" Hilary asked, delighted. "Nobody has ever told me that before."

"Well, you are. Come on in now. I'm really a little flustered to think you'd come all this length to see me. I never believed you'd do it!"

She led him into the big square sitting room, saw him seated in a sloping-backed rocker and sat down herself on a small horsehair sofa. She was "flustered," Hilary could see, so he began talking easily to relieve her embarrassment. He talked of Lex and of Dick, and of his day's trip, all the time feeling a peculiar sense of repose stealing over him. Strange, he kept thinking as Cousin Mattie's self-consciousness vanished and she began to chat on naturally—strange how this room with its marble-topped tables, straight chairs, narrow sofa and wooden rockers seemed more restful than the soft, downy luxury of the ones he knew best! This put forth no highly decorative effort to please, certainly. It seemed, indeed, a trifle aloof. Those who entered it would sense its calm, its reticence, but they would never dominate it. Its essential integrity, established by the years, would be beyond their reach. That must be the reason, Hilary decided. Perhaps modern rooms were too much the slaves of their masters; too easily moved by caprices of taste, so that their very subservience was a temptation not to rest within them but to agitate the more. He was rather pleased with himself over this idea. I must tell that to Lex, he thought. She'll probably laugh at me, but still . . .

"And so," Cousin Mattie was saying, "if you'd like to go upstairs now and wash up after your trip, I'll be dishing up the supper. I must explain that there's no bathroom. Some folks have them here, but I never bothered. I filled the pitcher on your washstand and I'll give you some hot water to take up with you. And betimes when—well, betimes, we just have to take a little walk through the garden. It will seem pretty old-fashioned to you, I'm afraid."

Hilary laughed. "I'm going to like everything about this place, including the walks through the garden," he said.

He went up the ingrain-carpeted stairs, carrying his bag in one hand and a small bucket of hot water in the other, wishing that Lex could see him!

He wished the more for her when he entered the "spare" room with its great walnut double bed, high bureau, and washstand covered with flowered china. He must bring her some time. She would love it, once she was here.

He found himself outrageously hungry for supper. For weeks he had had little appetite; now at the simply set table he wolfed the fried ham and potatoes and apple sauce, and begged for more bread and jam to Cousin Mattie's innocent delight.

"I don't usually eat like this," he kept saying. "I'm ashamed, really."

"It's just plain country fare," she said, "but it's the supper your grandfather always liked best."

"You loved Grandy, didn't you?" he asked lightly, using the word as he would have done to any of the Bishop's devoted admirers, forgetting in the moment his passing suspicion as to their feeling for each other.

Cousin Mattie did not reply at once. Then she said quietly, "We were first cousins, you know, and we lived on adjoining farms, so we just about grew up together. Yes, we were always very fond of each other."

That was all. Perhaps the relationship had been the barrier, Hilary thought. People felt strongly about it in the old days. He wished he could know the secret if there was one, but he knew that the past should be allowed to bury its dead loves undisturbed.

"Eat up your pie, now," Cousin Mattie said. "It's made of wild blackberries picked right back here on the hill. This time of year there's hardly a day goes by but what there's some boy or other at the back door to sell them. It's sassafras and horse-radish roots in the spring and berries in the summer. It's good for boys, though, to get out in the fields and woods. It's wholesome for them and it's nice for us in town to have things brought to the door. Hand me your plate and I'll give you another piece."

Later on, they sat out on the porch while the dusk fell. They talked much of Grandy, Cousin Mattie telling of his youth and Hilary of the ripe, distinguished years. Each listened eagerly to the other. She wanted to hear all about St. Matthews too, and Hilary found it easy to tell her. The distance, the contrast in surroundings, threw a new perspective upon the city scene. He found himself pouring out to her not the acute and dramatic problems of the last weeks, but rather his long range plans, his half-formed, hidden hopes. It seemed natural here to speak with confidence.

"I have to go slowly, of course, for I'm pretty new yet, but some day I want the pew rental system abolished. Most churches have got rid of it already. I want free pews in St. Matthews, and the present chapel all done over and the Parish House enlarged, and perhaps some time a new chapel built and financed by St. Matthews, a simple little building to which the tenement people—the Protestants—might be willing to go—"

He laughed. "You see I have big plans for the future. Right now," he added thoughtfully, beginning to put into words for the first time a concern that had been growing upon him, "I've got to find some way before another summer to give our Parish House young folks a breath of country air. The children we do take care of after a fashion at the summer camps, but the young fellows and girls in their late teens and early twenties who have jobs—they weigh upon my heart.

"You see," he went on, "when they do get any sort of vacation they've no place to go. Naturally, they can't afford resorts or hotels. Most of them are giving their earnings to help their families, anyway. So when they have any time off they just loaf around their usual haunts. And how they need a change! Good God, if you could just see where some of them live!"

"That's pitiful!" Cousin Mattie's voice all but broke upon the words. "Poor young things! Never to get to the country and feel the grass under their feet! You need a nice farm where they could get out and roam around and gather berries and pick apples and ride in on a load of hay. Just the city streets! Oh, that's pitiful!"

When the night began to grow cool they went inside and Cousin Mattie got out the old family albums. While in prospect Hilary would have considered this boring fare enough, he was surprised now to find himself interested. As he regarded the faces of his forebears and especially those of Grandy in his youth, a new feeling of soundness, of wholeness, of integration of spirit possessed him. In this plain, quiet house, in these old pictures, most of all in the person of Cousin Mattie herself, he and the past had met and something in the encounter was refreshing.

Later as he lay in the big walnut bed upstairs, the air of the room sweet from the porch honeysuckle, he decided to analyze this feeling. Instead, he sank immediately to sleep and woke to strong sunshine and a tapping on his door.

"I brought you some hot water to shave with," Cousin Mattie called. "Can I set it in? It's after nine o'clock."

She smiled tenderly at him, as she turned from the washstand, and Hilary returned it with tenderness. There was a binding force in consanguinity, no matter what any one said to the contrary, he thought.

He threw his arms above his head, stretching luxuriously.

"What a sleep I had! There must be something in the air here. And, of course, the quiet. I'll be ready now in a jiffy, though. I hope I haven't kept you waiting."

"Not a bit," said Cousin Mattie. "I can fix breakfast any time. I'm glad you had a good rest. I hope you'll be satisfied with the plans I've made for the day."

"Sure to be," Hilary told her.

"You see, Dave and Lizzie are on the old farm, that is, Uncle Will's place where your grandfather grew up. I didn't say a word to them about you till I was sure you'd really get here; but I phoned them early this morning and they want us to get out there for dinner by twelve o'clock and spend the day."

"Fine!" said Hilary. "I intended to go out to the old place. Did I tell you Grandy had planned to make a visit back here himself, the summer he died? And wanted me to come with him? So I'm just in a sense carrying out his wish now."

"I know," she said briefly. "He wrote me about it. Well, I'll get along and give you a chance to dress."

They drove slowly into the country, Cousin Mattie pointing out landmarks as they went. At the farm itself a host of poignant associations met Hilary under her guidance. In this room of the old red-brick house, the Bishop had been born; this was the secretary where he had done his lessons as a boy; from this doorstep he had left for college. Cousin Mattie had been there to see him off. He had turned to wave again to them, she recalled, when the buggy passed that big walnut tree there in the lane. It was long-lived, that tree.

She insisted upon going with him down to the spring though the steps now had fallen into disuse. The water still trickled into the stone basin, however, and lay there clear and cool under the shade of the willows.

"It was here," she said, "that he told me he had decided to enter the ministry. We'd come down to get fresh water for supper, I mind, and you could see the sunset right behind those trees. Nobody else knew about his plan till he'd finished college. But he told me right here. I thought you might like to know."

David was a big fellow with the same heavy brows Hilary had himself, and a quick smile. His whole family, Lizzie, his plump wife and the four children, made in Hilary's mind a blurred composite of inquiring eyes and tanned, healthy faces. He did his best to be entertaining during dinner while they all listened and watched him shyly. It was afterwards as Dave was showing him over the farm that Hilary suddenly stopped short, struck by the force of a new idea. It was so potent and withal so logical that he did not pause to weigh it but accepted it instantly and completely with a sort of holy wonder. He did not speak of it to Dave but followed him about with a lively interest, pouring out questions as he went, about acreage, taxes, fruit trees, the hay crop and prices of animals.

David answered them all, laughing good-naturedly.

"Anybody'd think you were going to turn farmer," he said.

An elation filled Hilary as he said goodbye to them all and drove Cousin Mattie back to town. It remained with him that evening, though he did not reveal his secret. He would write Cousin Mattie later if anything came of it, for it was she herself, he recalled now, who had suggested it.

He parted with her next morning with real affection, promising to come back and bring Lex with him. Then, still with a strong inner excitement, he headed for Maine. The idea which had struck him as he walked through his ancestral fields was at once daring and simple. Why could not the parish of St. Matthews own a farm? A smallish one within possible reach of the city. A farm upon which a resident couple might earn a living from chickens, a couple of cows and a big garden, subsidized perhaps by a small salary, but which would be primarily the St. Matthews Church Farm for the use of the Parish House people in summer.

Swiftly his imagination ran on. A barn could easily be converted into a dormitory for the girls with the big barn floor left for a recreation center. There could be simple barracks built for the boys, perhaps old sheds already on the place could be converted. The young folks could come out on Saturday afternoons, have a picnic supper, a dance in the barn that night and on Sunday get a taste of the open air and the country, pick berries, wade in the brook—there must be a brook—watch a cow being milked, help get the dinner, play games in the sunshine.

Hilary's face was flushed with happiness as he thought of it. It was all practical, it was possible, it was perfect. And on Sunday afternoons he would make it a rule that they must all assemble at four in the—in the *orchard!* That's where he would hold the service! They would have Evensong in the orchard.

And wouldn't Aunt Samantha take to the whole plan like a duck to water? She would be the perfect chaperon for the young folks and she could have her "mothers" and older women out through the week for picnics. Adams, he believed, would approve. Perhaps he and Aunt Samantha might even stay there during the summer with himself and—he wondered about Lex. It might all sound crazy to her. For the first time, his elation left him. He doubted if Lex would really be interested in the idea at all.

When he reached his destination at last he felt a new thrill of anticipation as he drove through the stately tree-lined avenue and saw the great house still lighted in every window though the hour was late. They were all on the porch as he reached it. Evidently they had been anxious about him. Lex flew down the steps and hurled herself into his arms, regardless of onlookers. Old Alex greeted him with hearty affection and Mrs. McColly kissed him and called him "dear boy." Muff came forward to wring his hand and say solemnly that she was glad he'd been spared to reach there in safety, and Morris, grabbing his bag, grinned from ear to ear, his eyes wet as always when he was particularly happy.

"What a welcome!" Hilary kept exclaiming. "It would be worth going round the world for one like this. Nobody knows how glad I am to be here. I don't think I could have stayed away a single day longer!"

As soon as they decently could, he and Lex went to their own quarters, prepared for bed, put out the lights and then sat down in the deep window seat which had always been Lex's haven from a child, to catch up on all their news. He held her close as they talked, his lips often touching her hair, her neck, her arms, while the sweet night air blew in upon them.

"Listen, darling, what do you think? I had a run-in with Mrs. Potiphar."

"Oh, Hil, really? What did she do?"

"Tried to seduce me. Went all out this time."

"That's terrible," Lex wailed. "And she's so damned beautiful."

"Not to me. She's a viper. I hate the very sight of her, and I told her plainly where I stood. If I hadn't been a clergyman I'd have told her where to go."

"Well, believe me, I'll tell her if I ever run into her. I've got no inhibitions as far as language goes. Oh, Hil, you haven't any business being so attractive. I told you women would fall in love with you!"

He laughed and gave her a long kiss.

"Who's jealous? Go ahead, it tickles my vanity. It sets me all up. Lex, you must go out along to Maryville sometime. You'd really love it. Cousin Mattie is a dear. Must have been a beauty in her youth. I'm sure there was something between her and Grandy but she didn't mention it. And the house!"

"What's it like?"

"Oh, old-fashioned, quaint—I can't describe it. The bedroom has a bed a mile wide and you wash in a big flowered bowl at a washstand and carry the hot water up in a little bucket. There's no bathroom. And out in the garden—"

Hilary began to laugh. "There's what Cousin Mattie calls 'the little house,' only it's really rather spacious, considering. It's painted white and has a climbing rose over it and inside the walls have uplifting clippings tacked all over them. You could sit there for hours improving your mind."

"I'll go next time," Lex said. "I've got to see *that!* There's something else you haven't told me yet, though. I know you. You're excited about something. I could see it the minute you came. What is it?"

He drew her closer and laid his cheek against hers. He suddenly felt afraid to trust his plan to words.

"There is something else. It's all rather queer. I went to Maryville out of a sense of duty, a debt I owed Grandy, that sort of thing. Then when

I got there I found a curious refreshment of soul and I got an idea. It seemed almost as though I'd been sent there for it, though I know that's probably stretching a point. If I tell you—sweet, you won't laugh it down, will you?"

"Do you want me to pretend I like it if I don't?"

"No, of course not. Just don't treat it lightly. I'm so full of the thing."

He told her about the farm, the *St. Matthews Church Farm* that he wanted to bring into being. He poured it all out swiftly, half frightened at his own vehemence. When he stopped, his heart seemed to stop, waiting.

For a second Lex sat silent, weaving her fingers around his own.

"Hil," she said slowly, "I do believe you've got something! There hasn't been anything about the church work that I can honestly say I've ever been interested in before, but I *am* interested in this. I'll give you some money toward it and I know Dad will if I ask him. And when we really get the place, I could help with the reconditioning. You know, supervise fixing up the barn—we'll have it like camp, rustic but attractive —oh, I can think of a million things I'd like to do—and we could even furnish one bedroom in the house for ourselves and go out often in the summer for week-ends before your vacation and help chaperon the kids. Adams could take the St. Matthews services. Why Hil, I *love* the whole idea!"

Her enthusiasm was so unexpected that the joy of it left him trembling. His love rose within him like a flame.

"Darling!" he said huskily. "Oh, my darling!"

He lifted her in his arms and, as he often did, carried her gently over to where at last they would sleep.

CHAPTER XIII

THAT MONTH of August, 1940, was to Hilary the happiest holiday he had ever known. Old Alex was taking his vacation then also, and he and Hilary golfed and fished and talked with growing comradeship. While the older man was uncultivated in the conventional sense, his strong opinions, vivid language and shrewd wisdom more than made up for the lack. One day as they were getting their tackle together, he spoke of the Bishop.

"Ever tell you how I met your grandfather?" he asked.

"I don't believe so," said Hilary.

"Well, years ago, it was. I was up here fishin' one summer and I'd set my heart on catchin' a ouananiche. Been after one for years. One day I got a beauty. On the hook, that is. I was more excited than if I'd been puttin' over a million-dollar deal. Just when I thought he was safe, the damned thing got away from me. I can swear pretty good most any time but that day I sort of outdid myself. I just opened up and let 'er rip. Well, when I'd run out of breath I heard some one chucklin' behind me. I turned round and there was a man in the bushes not far away, eatin' his lunch. Fisherman too. He says, 'Very soul satisfyin',' he says. 'I missed a ouananiche yesterday and I couldn't find the right words to fit the situation. Now I feel better. Come on,' he says, 'I owe you a lunch for that. I've got plenty.' So we struck up a friendship. Never dreamed he was a bishop, then. Great man, your granddad. Great fisherman, too."

While Hilary still did not feel as close to Mrs. McColly as to her husband, there was always a pleasant give and take between him and his mother-in-law. In short, he felt at ease in his wife's home, so there was nothing to mar his happiness with Lex, herself. For during that month, while with studied determination he shook off the worries of his office, they were completely happy. They swam, they golfed, they danced, they sat long hours planning the Church Farm; if possible, and perhaps because of this new common interest, they fell more deeply in love. As he lounged in the sunshine or drank the bracing air, an unreasoning optimism concerning his work possessed Hilary.

The news of the war was harder to shake off. He and old Alex listened at the radio and felt the lengthening shadow. For Lex's sake, though, Hilary did not talk too much about it.

"Let's have one month free," she had pleaded. "One beautiful month in which we'll shut out the world, but keep just enough of the flesh and the devil to make it interesting. Please, darling, let's!"

So when he did talk of the war in her presence it was in more or less academic terms; the sand storms in the Libyan desert; Churchill's masterly use of the English language; the bombing of St. Giles in London where Oliver Cromwell had been married and John Milton buried.

The lovely days flowed on, and the sweet nights of love. Never had time passed so swiftly. Before they deemed it possible they were back in the rectory which now in spite of its comfort and modern furnishings, seemed by contrast, dark and hemmed in and overshadowed by St. Matthews itself.

When they went over the mail awaiting them, Lex gave a gasp of astonishment.

"No! It can't be! Look at this, Hil, and tell me whether you see what I see."

Hilary took the note:

> MY DEAR ALEXA:
> Could you and your husband take dinner with us the evening of the twenty-first at half after seven o'clock? I have begun to feel that it is wrong to allow old quarrels to affect our relationship with you, especially since you are now the wife of our beloved rector. May we hope to see you both on the date I have mentioned. It will be quite an informal, family dinner.
>
> Your affectionate aunt,
> HETTIE BRECKENRIDGE

"Now what do you suppose the old girl is up to?" Lex queried. "I can't imagine anything more deadly than spending an evening with her and the White Rabbit. And what are you looking so pleased about?"

Hilary was smiling broadly. "I'm delighted. We will certainly go. I've always felt distressed over the family feud, and I'm greatly relieved that she's dropping it as far as you are concerned. It will make things easier for me in the church. And you can stand a Victorian evening for once."

Lex rumpled her curls.

"I *would* like to see the house. I've never been in it, you know. Mother says the silver's gorgeous. It's all marked with the family coat of arms. Why, Hil, maybe if I mind my p's and q's she'll will me some! I begin to see possibilities. I'll accept this and when we go I'll be so sweet and demure she'll realize what she's been missing all these years. Wait till I tell Mother!"

When Hilary went over to the study he found a brief note to him from Aunt Hettie. It stated that she was sorry that a mistaken rumor had prompted her former letter. She deeply regretted her impulsiveness, thanked him for his forbearance and would of course continue to remain a member of St. Matthews.

Hilary whistled. There was work piled up all around him, but he couldn't resist the impulse to see Mrs. Reed that afternoon and find out what had happened. He found her as usual in her sitting room knitting one of her endless army socks. She had aged that summer, he thought, but her eyes were as bright as ever. She received him warmly and then fell upon the matter in hand.

"Any word from Hettie?" she demanded.

He told her what had come, quoting as accurately as he could. She chuckled delightedly.

"That's wonderful! That's marvellous! Making up to Lex, too. That's even better than I expected. Hilary, maybe I'm an old devil but I've had the time of my life!"

"I've come to hear about it," Hilary answered. "And remember, I want to be told *all!*"

"You will," she said. "I'd have told you before only I was afraid you'd stop me. And don't you ever say it was blackmail, for it was no such thing!"

"Good heavens, I should hope not!"

She eyed him with the faintest embarrassment, then the complacence returned to her countenance.

"Well, it was like this. Hettie and I were in love with the same man when we were young. Even when he asked me to marry him Hettie wouldn't give him up. Not she! She was determined to get him no matter how, and she wrote him two letters stating that pretty plainly."

"So?" said Hilary, his brows rising.

"Now, don't you look like that! Of course they should have been destroyed, but my husband was always careless with papers. That's how I happened to know what was in them," she added with a sly little grin.

"So you threatened her?" Hilary asked uncomfortably.

"I did nothing of the kind! I went to call, dressed up in my best, and dripped sweetness and light all over the place. She nearly had a stroke when she came into the room and saw me! Wish Lex could have been along! I told her I'd heard a rumor that she was thinking of leaving St. Matthews. Was so pained to hear it. Liar that I am! Wouldn't she reconsider? She would not. She made that very definite. Then I began to sound the nostalgic note. The dear dead days beyond recall! Did she remember them? I had come across the letters she had written my husband before our marriage. How vividly they brought back the past. Ah, dear, *dear* me! I swear she turned scarlet even at her age."

The old lady paused, with an irrepressible giggle. "Hilary, I was wonderful! I never knew before I could act. I took my leave then, still cooing like a turtle dove, telling her how much I thought of you and of Lex and just tossing out the little suggestion that perhaps after all she would decide to stay in St. Matthews. She was so upset she followed me clear to the door, sputtering. She said of course leaving the church would be a wrench! I knew then I'd clinched it. Oh, I haven't had as much fun for forty years. And I crave praise, now. Don't you dare scold me!"

"You certainly brought her around," Hilary said, laughing, "but it still smells a little to me like—"

"It does not. Anyway the results are worth it. And listen. When I got back I burned those letters. So that's off my conscience. I've wanted to shake them under her nose often before this when she was mulish about the Orphanage affairs, but somehow I didn't. Glad now I saved them for this, for with you and Lex threatened, I felt justified. Righteously so. Now, say 'thank you'!"

He had to praise her, for she was so inordinately pleased with herself. Besides, his own relief was great. He went home, pondering on the strange secrets housed in human hearts.

The whole work of the parish got off to a good start that fall. Adams was rested and full of enthusiasm and Aunt Samantha brisk and busy as usual. Forrest had vacationed in his own way by composing a new Te Deum which Hilary took time to hear at once. It was magnificent. They made plans for a special service for its first rendering. Even Hastings' undertaker face relaxed as he patted Hilary's arm. "Not bad to get back in the harness, eh? Hope things go smooth for us this year. There's a few little improvements I think we'd better make. Tell you later when I get it all decided."

Only Miss Mowbray looked thin and rather pale, Hilary thought.

"Did you have a good vacation?" he asked with real solicitude.

Margaret gave a small shrug.

"When you are at a loss for something to do, you might write a treatise on the social problem of the unmarried young woman of thirty."

There was an irony in the tone, unusual for her.

"I'm sorry," Hilary said seriously. "I'm truly sorry. I wish I could . . ."

Then he stopped. Anything he could say would sound both crass and rude. She covered his discomfiture by changing the subject promptly. The small flush, however, had risen again to her face.

"Here is an invitation to speak which I really think you should accept if you can find the time . . ."

In a moment they were plunged into the accumulated mail.

In October, certain events stood out sharply upon the world horizon. London was evacuating mothers and children at the rate of two thousand a day; the air raids continued on both sides of the Channel; Hitler and Mussolini met at the Brenner Pass; President Roosevelt announced American policy to be total defense of this hemisphere, continued aid to Britain and no appeasement of the dictators; and the first peacetime compulsory military service in the United States was inaugurated when the Secretary of War in Washington drew a number, blindfolded, from a glass bowl.

Toward the end of the month Dick suddenly arrived one evening unannounced, gay, excited and nervous as a cat. He was to drive an ambulance for the American Field Service and would sail on the thirty-first. He swaggered through the house, displaying his uniform to Morris and to Muff, then back to Lex and Hilary.

"It's mine, too, I'd have you know. We have to outfit ourselves and pay all expenses except passage over. I've a hunch we'll be sent to Libya. Gad, I can't wait! How do you like me, Lexa? Pretty snappy, eh? Off to the wars, that's me!"

There was so little time. Perhaps, Hilary reflected, it was better so, for his heart was heavy. He could not have kept up the usual banter for long. Lex, too, he noticed, was practicing a forced gaiety. Only Dick himself was completely at ease, completely debonair as usual.

It was after Lex had gone to bed on the last night and the two brothers had had a long talk before the charring logs which Morris had lighted after dinner " 'cause Mist' Dick do so admire a fire," that Dick turned partially serious. He pulled from his pocket the gold watch Grandy had given him on his twenty-first birthday. It was an unusual one which, upon the pressure of a spring, struck the hours and the quarters with a sweet, quick chime.

"I'm leaving this here," he said. "I might happen to trip over a monkey wrench and stub my toe. These little accidents happen over there, I'm told, so you keep this. I'll hand it on someday to your oldest son, anyhow, if you and Lex ever get busy and have one. All my other so-called personal effects will come along soon in a trunk. Just put it in the attic and forget it. It does seem as though I haven't collected much gear after thirty years of living. Rolling stone, I guess."

"I hate to see you go, Bib. For God's sake don't run any more risks than you have to. You're such a rash fool."

"Nothing over and above the line of duty, eh? My sainted brother, I'm surprised at you. Don't you want a hero in the family?"

"Can't say that I do."

"Pish tish! That's no way to talk. I expect to come back with a special citation: Richard Laurens, after all hands had failed to make a motor turn over, did, by dint of caressing, cursing, and kicking it, put the damn thing into action and drove on victorious! You know I always did want to work in a garage. Good mechanic spoiled when I went to college. Of course I wouldn't have stayed long in any one place, though, so the mining suited me better at that, I suppose. Everything all right with you, Hil?"

"Professional or personal?"

"Well—personal."

"Yes. Very much so."

"Lex content with the holy life?"

"I think so, in the main."

"Don't forget she's young and needs diversion."

"I'll try not to. There are difficulties of course. My time isn't my own."

"But your wife is. And you're a lucky guy to have her. She may not go hard for the religious business but she's a girl in ten thousand. One you can trust as far as hell and back. So—just keep her happy, old man."

Hilary's face was grave. "I'll do my best, you may be sure."

Dick laughed. "It's turning the tables for me to be giving you advice! Sheer presumption and all that, but I do happen to be pretty fond of the two of you. Well, we'd better have a little shut-eye at this point. Come on, you look done in. And listen, Hil. Don't have me on your mind. I'm going to have the time of my life on this spree. Can't wait to get into it. I'll keep you posted how things go, but don't stew around thinking something's going to clip me. Nothing will, actually. I'm the kind that always lives on to cumber the earth."

At the top of the stairs, they knew it was the real good-bye. They stood a moment looking into each other's eyes, then Dick cocked his head.

"Well, pax vobiscum," he said jauntily.

"Good luck, Bib," Hilary returned, trying hard to smile.

After Dick had gone the next day, it was Lex who sobbed uncontrollably while Morris wept quietly in the kitchen and Muff wiped her eyes as she tidied up the room he had slept in. It was Hilary who had to make the fatuous expostulations. Dick wasn't going into real combat! He bore a charmed life! He'd come through without a scratch! They must not worry. Then when he had comforted the others, he went over to the church and knelt for a long time at the altar.

At the first fall vestry meeting, Hilary felt he had his important matters well in hand. First of all he presented his plans for the Church Farm. Perhaps it was his own enthusiasm, perhaps it was the practicality of the suggestion, but in any case to his surprise and intense pleasure the vestry to a man showed interest in the idea. Even Alvord made no adverse comment. After full discussions of the possibilities, a committee of three was appointed to work upon the project, with a view to purchasing a suitable farm if possible by the next spring. The appointees were Hartley, Powers and Weston, three of the younger men (all in their forties) whom Hilary definitely wanted to see taking more active part in the work of the vestry. For one reason or another he did not feel as close to them as their relative nearness of age would warrant. Hartley was a broker, blond, suave, stout and generous with money. Powers was owner and president of the Powers Iron Works, having succeeded his father in that capacity as he had done on the vestry. He was lean, dark and nervously active, with an ability for getting things done. Weston was with the Alpha Insurance Company and had intimated that they had a number of farms on their own list which they wanted to get rid of. Hilary felt he had done well in intrusting his pet dream to these three and hoped that along with its realization would come a closer bond with the men themselves.

When all the farm business had been finished, Hilary stated that one more important matter remained for him to speak of. (After weeks of thought he had come to what seemed to him a reasonable, fair, and tactful approach to his problem.)

"I have something lying upon my heart," he began, "which I want to present to you with all the earnestness of which I am capable. You, as the vestry of this church, are chosen to represent what is best in the personnel of the parish. You are leaders, picked men in a religious organization. I have every reason to believe that in your private lives you are blameless and upright."

A chill silence had fallen upon the group. The men's faces had taken on that mask of withdrawal which falls on a countenance when unwarranted intimacy encroaches upon ordinary conversation. Hilary realized this, but he went on.

"You are also men of affairs, of large business and professional interests. I want to point out to you that there lies upon you the peculiar obligation to see to it that there is no discrepancy between your business dealings and your religious profession. If, after searching your hearts, any one of you feels that there is in his secular affairs a situation which is not in line with Christian standards, I beg of you, with all the power that I have, to clear up that situation between now and the New Year even at financial loss to yourself."

Then he told them Grandy's story of the Elder at the corn crib. There was a deep chuckle from Judge Ball and a few smiles here and there, but general silence.

Hilary turned quickly then to the suggestion of a dinner for Forrest to celebrate the composition of his new Te Deum, and the men unbent and talked as usual. Though Alvord gave him a cold stare as the meeting broke up and Avison whispered, "We're all rather in the 'Is it I?' position after your talk," Hilary felt highly pleased with the way he had handled the matter. He had made the strongest public appeal to Alvord of which he was capable and yet had done it without embarrassment to him. Indeed, if any of the other men were in any like sense culpable, he had saved himself from unfairness by including them all in his exhortation. Yes, he had done well and his mind was relieved.

Judge Ball called him up that evening.

"Very cleverly and impressively said," he wheezed. "I've decided to go over all my recent decisions with a fine-tooth comb. I don't know whether you'll get any results from Alvord, though."

"Somehow I feel that we will," Hilary answered hopefully.

The wedding of Shane and Francine Avery was to take place early in November. It had been delayed because Shane had a number of serious operations which he wanted to see through before he took any time off. When the day was finally set, Hilary sent for Francine to come to his study for a last talk. One matter still rose to trouble him. He wanted to clear it up before performing the ceremony.

"I have advised you according to my best judgment, Francine," he said soberly. "I believe that you will make a wonderful wife and mother. That part of the past which has been a burden to you will probably always remain buried. There is just one thing I feel in duty bound to say to you. If at any future time Shane should hear some fragment of it and question you, tell him then the complete and absolute truth."

"Of course," the girl said. "Do you think I would do otherwise?"

"No," Hilary said, "I don't, but I felt obligated to hear your promise. Also I want you to keep this statement which I have written so that if you should ever need it you will have it. Here it is. I have dated it last June."

He handed her an envelope. She drew the paper out and read it in a low voice:

> "DEAR FRANCINE:
> After our talk together, my advice to you as your rector is to marry my friend Dr. Shane, and make him happy. Keep those memories which you wish to forget locked within your own heart. May God bless you both."

The girl raised her beautiful eyes to his, her whole face alight.

"You have done the last thing to make me at peace. Now I feel happy and safe. How can I ever thank you? When I came to you that first time I had planned to end my life. I felt so wicked, so lost, so desperate. You remember the little paper you sent me after that day? Always I read that until I grew strong again and knew I would go on living and maybe even some time have happiness again. You know that little precious paper?"

Hilary wrinkled his brow. For the life of him, he could not remember what she was talking about.

She laughed gently. "So many good deeds you do that you forget them! I will tell you. I so well know the words. You must give them to others like me who need them."

She quoted them slowly: *"For he who rises quickly and continues his race is as if he had never fallen."*

"Oh, of course," Hilary said, glancing unconsciously toward the brown scrapbook on the shelf. "That line from Molinos. I'd forgotten about sending it. I'm glad it was of help."

The girl came close to him and her face was tender.

"You sometimes, too, feel troubled? So many sad stories, so many sorrows for other people make you feel discouraged, yes?"

"Very often, indeed."

"Then you must think about me, that you saved my life and showed me how still to know happiness and be, I hope, a good woman always."

When she was gone Hilary walked up and down the study, his hands in his pockets, a mood of vast well-being possessing him. What a satisfying room this was! He eyed the books, the pictures, the rugs, the mullioned windows overlooking the fountain. What a delightful place in which to work! And the church itself! One of the most beautiful in the country! And the parish! Where could you find more charming, more cultured, more *good* people? And the opportunities for service? Endless, boundless! Stretching years ahead!

As Hastings came to the door Hilary caught him and waltzed him into the room.

"Do you know, my good friend, what I've just decided? If I were asked to name the one position in the whole world which I would most like to have it would be—the rectorship of St. Matthews!"

"Well, you've got it, ain't you?" the old man returned calmly. "You'd better get on over to the house and take an aspirin. You look feverish to me."

The mood of exaltation remained with Hilary over the next day when he married Shane and Francine in a quiet ceremony and watched them leave the church with the glow of happiness upon their faces. Then, because of the strange facts which he alone knew, he went to call upon Mrs. Cole. She gave him tea in the library where he had stood on that terrible night when he had learned of the tragedy. The woman's face, like the room itself, now had the appearance only of warm hospitality. The Coles, Hilary thought as he had often before, accepted their bitter grief quietly and carried their burden with the courage of heroes.

They chatted easily for a time and then Hilary began to pour out his plan for the Church Farm. Mrs. Cole had not heard of it.

"Stephen is so terribly busy just now," she said, "that he probably forgot to mention it. Please tell me more. I'm interested for a special reason."

"Only a symptom of interest and sometimes not even that, is enough to start me going on this," Hilary laughed.

He went on rapturously, giving details as he and Lex had worked them out that summer. As he talked he saw a great tenderness envelop the woman's face.

"Perhaps you have wondered," she said at last, "why we have given no gift of remembrance for Steve. It has been because I insisted upon a *living* memorial and we haven't been able as yet to decide what it should be. I believe the answer to our search may be in this plan for the Farm. What, for instance, will you be needing most?"

"A sort of barracks-dormitory for the young men, for one thing. Another will be a portable altar. I want something simple and yet beautiful which we can set up outdoors, or, in case of rain, in the barn. We'll need furnishings for the sleeping quarters, we'll hope for a swimming pool eventually, and of course we'll need just plain hard cash to buy the place and keep it up. So, think it all over. I don't know anything that would make me happier, personally, than a memorial for Steve at the farm."

"I'll talk to Stephen. And meanwhile, won't you keep me informed about developments? I promise you, we'll do something to help and I hope a great deal."

He told Lex that night in a happy mood. She passed over the good news lightly for the moment.

"Hil, you know what Clarissa Ball told me today? She said Steve Cole used to take Francine out when she danced at the Versailles Club. I began to wonder. He shot himself. She stopped dancing. I don't know—it just seemed to sort of add up. Do you know anything?"

Her eyes looked straight into his. Hilary thought fast. He hated less than complete candor with Lex, and yet there was too much involved in Francine's story to tell the secret to any living soul.

"I don't think Francine ever really liked the dancing job," he said calmly. "Shane told me that. As to her going out with Steve, I imagine she went out with dozens of young men. She's attractive, and she was in a good place to meet them. The Coles still have no idea what happened to Steve and, for myself, it was such a bad night for me, I try to forget it. But I am tremendously interested in this memorial idea. If they go on with it, what should we suggest to them? The boys' barracks or the altar?"

Lex seemed satisfied. She turned the question over in her mind.

"Why not the barracks, if they would. The boys who will be sleeping there probably never had a good bed in their lives. It could be rustic and still awfully comfortable and beautiful in its own way. Like a big hunting cabin. It could be called the Stephen Cole Memorial Lodge."

"I believe you have it!" Hilary said with elation. "I can see it, already. Only we'll have to be careful that the girls fare as well."

"I'm taking care of that," Lex said quickly. "I've got Mrs. Reed all excited over the idea, and you know what? I'm going to work on Aunt Hettie! Ever since we were there to dinner she's been practically eating out of my hand. And she *is* so lousy with money. I've just been wondering . . ."

He drew her close to him on the sofa. "What, darling?"

"About this Christmas. Last year it was all so perfect. Now, with Dick away, it will be different. Had we better just go to Mother and Dad's?"

"Whatever you want, sweet."

"I like it here at home best. But—I've been thinking a lot about Mother. She's acted so funny about my getting friendly with Hettie and the Rabbit. Almost jealous. I believe she'd love it if they would make up with her too. I had a wild idea of trying to get them all together for a love feast around the Christmas board. At Mother's."

"I think that would be marvellous. But would your father be willing?"

Lex laughed. "Oh, Dad! He'd entertain the devil himself if Mother suddenly took a fancy to him. Hil?"

"Yes."

"I wonder sometimes about Dad and Mother. They're completely devoted of course and happy, only—I've just begun to realize that Mother has missed her own family all these years. And Dad's always kept working so hard to make it up to her. I don't believe," she added slowly, "that it's good in a marriage for one person to have given up too much."

There was a wistfulness in her voice that went to Hilary's heart. He felt consuming tenderness and a great fear also. He bent his head until his cheek was against hers. His heart was beating uncomfortably.

"Everything's all right with your father and mother. A blind man could see that. I think your idea, though, of getting Hettie and Edward there for Christmas is perfect. If anyone can do it, you can and it will make the day exciting for all concerned. So let's hope. At the moment, though, I'm interested in dating you up for tomorrow night. I've got a whole evening at your disposal. Dinner and dancing somewhere? Or a show? Or all three? How about it?"

It was his sudden and immediate reaction to her little sentence, which had hung strangely in the air between them. Even with Dick's pointed advice he realized that he had not taken Lex out for an evening's fun for weeks. Their social engagements had been with the older people of the parish. She looked up at him now, incredulously, then she laughed.

"Without even consulting my calendar I shall accept for tomorrow night! And I have no suggestion whatever about flowers except that I do prefer orchids!"

They hugged each other like two children, and laid their plans gaily. Lex was all at once her bright and glowing self.

"I'm so darned sick of dining with all these old stuffed shirts and tabby cats, the way we've had to do this fall. One more evening like that and I'd take me to a nunnery or get high as a kite, I don't know which. Oh, well, we won't go into that now. We'll make up for it all tomorrow night. Hil, you're psychic! I never wanted so much to go out with you and have a really good time. You know, in spite of everything I still do sort of like you!"

Christmas came swiftly and missed this year the complete joy of the one before. They all, including Muff and Morris, had dinner at the McCollys'. In spite of Lex's efforts, Hettie and Ed Breckenridge did not come. Although there had been at first a tentative acceptance, Hettie had doubtless decided at the last that she could not quite bring herself as yet to sit at Old Alex's table. So she begged to be excused because of a cold but proffered a counter invitation for Lex *and her mother* to have tea with her soon. This in itself was sufficient to add an undercurrent of excitement to the day and Hilary noted that Mrs. McColly's ordinarily pale cheeks were flushed with a hidden pleasure. Lex had been right then as she usually was in her perceptions.

In the afternoon they went on to an open house at Judge Ball's which Clarissa was having. Lex was particularly delighted over this occasion for, as she pointed out, it was at last a party of her own old crowd which Hilary could attend without fear of criticism since it was at the house of one of his vestrymen.

"But listen, Hil," she said seriously before they left the McCollys'. "I don't want you to get off in a corner with the Judge and talk church business. If you do, I'll never forgive you. This is once we're going out together when you're just *my husband,* nothing else. I want you to stick to me like a leech!"

Hilary looked down at her. She was wearing a fur-trimmed suit with a small muff and hat to match. She looked like an adorable little girl on an old time Christmas card.

"I don't think that will be too hard an assignment," he said, stooping swiftly to kiss her.

But once at the Balls', where the great rooms, garlanded and candle-lit, were filled with boisterous young people, it was not so easy after all. In the first place the Judge waylaid Hilary at once.

"Come into the library," he said, "where we can at least hear ourselves think. This is the worst gang of hoodlums we've had here yet. They're completely crazy. Not one of them can utter a sensible word, and Clarissa's the worst of the lot. Come on in here and sit down. I'm worn out now and the thing's hardly started."

Even as he was refusing, Hilary saw a young man descend upon Lex as he shouted to the others.

"It's Lex! Our long-lost Lex! Our little Eremite! Our cloistered nun, returning to the world! Alexa, my only love!"

He swooped down upon her as though to kiss her, but Lex pushed him playfully away.

"Call him off, someone," she was saying. "I'm an old married woman now."

"All of sixteen she looks," another young man proclaimed with mock tears. "Ah, the ravages of time!"

In a second the crowd, screaming with delight, had hemmed her in. He had a glimpse of Lex, giving back banter for banter, the center of all the hilarious group.

He edged his way determinedly through until he was beside her.

"Remember me?" he said in her ear. "I'm the man you came with."

She caught his arm. Her face was radiant. "Oh, Hil, isn't it *fun!* They're all so crazy and so sweet. This time I want you to meet everybody."

She did her best, and so did he. After an hour, however, Hilary saw that it was useless to try to stay together. Some one was continually dashing up to Lex to renew old acquaintance, or sweeping her off to a new group. Hilary marvelled at the flying conversations. If, as the Judge had remarked, there was spoken no profundity or even what he termed *sense,* there was certainly a wit, a sharp, quick cleverness, a brilliance even, which Hilary could not match. I simply haven't got the coin, he thought uncomfortably to himself, and repaired to a less crowded spot in the drawing room to rest up a little. From his vantage point he could see more clearly what he had already noticed. That was, that the men eyed Lex with unconcealed admiration and flocked in numbers around her. He had just decided to go back to rejoin the fray, when he saw a young man entering the room. He was tall and thin with full, pasty cheeks and sleek black hair. He sauntered slowly forward, his hands in his pocket, an almost insolent ease in his whole bearing.

"Oh, my gosh!" Hilary heard a young chap beside him say. "Here comes Tommy. Now watch all the black sheep scamper to cover."

Hilary knew suddenly who it must be. It was Tommy Tatler whom, until this moment, he had never laid eyes upon. As if in answer to his thought, Tommy looked across at him, stared, gave a faint smile, and came directly over.

"Well, Mr. Laurens," he began, "I wasn't expecting to find you among the fleshpots. I am Tom Worthington," he added, "though I believe I am better known by my trade soubriquet."

"How do you do?" Hilary said stiffly.

Tommy stood, glancing swiftly over the room. His black eyes, Hilary was sure, missed nothing, and his nostrils seemed to dilate delicately as though picking up the scent of scandal. A servant paused before them with a tray of cocktails, and to Hilary's surprise Tommy waved them aside even as he himself did. He found himself hating the thought of sharing even a virtue with this man.

"Unfortunately in my work," Tommy drawled, "I have to remain sober most of the time. The only real drawback to it," he added.

He picked up a tidbit from the table behind him and savored it with the air of a connoisseur.

"Excellent caviar," he pronounced. Then in the same breath: "You have a very beautiful wife, Mr. Laurens. If her upper lip had been the thousandth of an inch shorter, I should have said *pretty*. Interesting how it's the narrow margins one has to look out for in this world. But in Alexa's case, I say she is beautiful."

"Thank you," said Hilary curtly.

Tommy turned, and looked at him intently.

"Very good," he stated. "Very clever. Just 'Thank you.' That's all. Most men would have fumbled around with sentences—comments, agreements, or deprecations. Unwise. Give me then all the advantage. You merely say, 'Thank you,' and that throws the ball right back to me. The conversational game interests me greatly. At this point you score."

Even as he spoke, the crowd in the next room parted to admit a newcomer, and they could see Lex, flushed, radiant, laughing perhaps a bit too loudly, but dynamically the center of the admiring group. Hilary felt his own cheeks grow warm as Tommy stared and smiled.

"I presume you know, Mr. Laurens, that Alexa's marriage with you set the whole town by the ears?"

"I was certainly not aware of it," Hilary answered.

Tommy turned to look at him again. "Ah," he said, "not so good. Your first error. What you should have said, with a raised, supercilious eyebrow, was, 'Really?' Just that. Deny nothing. Admit nothing. Throw the burden of proof right back on me. Now you've made a statement of questionable sincerity, and the advantage is mine. So . . ."

He paused to select another tidbit from the tray behind him.

"So, I shall proceed. For Alexa McColly to wed a parson was as unthinkable in her circle as for—well, let us say for me to join the Trappists."

"Mr. Worthington, if you don't mind, I would—"

"Right," said Tommy. "We shall say no more. We shall mention Lex no further, greatly as I esteem and admire her. I do want to tell you before we part, however, that I attended one of your Sunday vespers."

"You did?" The words were shocked out of him.

"Quite so. I noted in the paper that you were preaching on the interesting subject of morality, and I decided to hear what you had to say. As a matter of fact, you didn't preach at all. You simply read a most extraordinary passage purporting to be from the Bible. Was it, actually?"

"It was. From Proverbs."

"Remarkable wording. Very—ah—frank. Odd that the book hasn't been banned in Boston, isn't it? Well, as I was about to remark, there was to my mind only one thing the matter with your performance. That was that you sounded just a little too damned sure of yourself."

"What do you mean?" Once again Hilary spoke in sheer surprise.

Tommy's smile at the moment was particularly offensive.

"Well," he said calmly, "take the matter of murder. I don't expect to commit murder, you don't expect to. And yet I knew a little meek mouse of a man who just suddenly one morning at breakfast killed his wife. He called the police, pleaded guilty, and never opened his mouth at the trial. They pronounced him insane. Now, what I think really happened was that for forty years that woman had burnt his toast or cooked his eggs too hard, or made him eat cereal when he didn't like it, and when the last point of his endurance was reached he just up and bopped her."

"I don't quite see the connection," Hilary said icily, feeling at the moment that he would like to try a good left to the jaw of Tommy's pasty countenance.

"Oh, merely illustrative of a general truth," he went on. "You are a young man yourself. When you preach morality to other young men, if I were you I wouldn't sound so virtuously smug, that's all. Idols sometimes develop foot trouble, you know. Now I must leave you and look over the party. At these little affairs there are always a few men who have accidentally wrapped up the wrong wives to bring along. Most interesting to have met you . . ."

He sauntered off, leaving Hilary in a state of bottled-up fury. The man was viciously rude and diabolically clever. He was more hateful and also more dangerous than Hilary had imagined. His last insinuations were particularly alarming. Were they meant merely as clever effrontery or could it be that he had learned of Diana Downes' visit to the study that night and drawn his own evil conclusions? Hilary's whole body felt hot with an impotent rage.

When he had pulled himself together, he made his way straight to Lex. She always had a glass in her hand, he noted, and it disturbed him greatly.

"Listen, dear," he said, bending his head, so she could hear him. "I think it's time we left."

"Left?" Lex cried. "Why, the party's just getting exciting! Oh, Hil, not yet. Aren't you having fun?"

"I should speak to the Judge," he said. "Could you be ready to leave in half an hour? I'd really like to go then. Could you?"

She looked at him unlaughing, with her clear, straight glance.

"O.K.," she said. "In half an hour."

He found the Judge in the library, listening to the radio. He motioned Hilary to a chair.

"Those English!" he said. "You can't beat their spirit. Just heard now that they've got signs all over downtown London that read: 'Christmas is 1940 years old, and Hitler is only fifty-one. He can't spoil our Christmas.' I tell you, Laurens, I'm afraid before too long we'll have to go in. It looks bad to me. But, let's not darken the day. How's the party going? Generally madhouse?"

"Everybody seems to be having a gay time. We must leave soon, so I just came in for a moment. I suppose you haven't run into Alvord in any connection?"

"No, I never see him except at church and vestry meetings. What's your next move?"

"I'm going to talk to him again privately, and then if he's still obdurate I'll have to take the bull by the horns."

"Well, just watch how you grab it. By the way, this farm idea of yours has sort of caught my fancy. Queer no preacher has ever thought of it before. I don't believe we'll have any difficulty raising money for it. You see, it's a concrete venture that every contributor can watch for himself. The committee hasn't found a place yet?"

"Not yet. It may take time, for our requirements are pretty rigid but I think we'll locate something by spring. We're going to have some memorial gifts too and that's a good thing."

"Yes," said the Judge, gently for him. "I may add a little to that. For my wife and Clarissa's mother."

Hilary felt a sudden sharp regret that he had not spent more time with the Judge that afternoon. He drew his chair now nearer to the fire and exerted all his powers of conversation in telling of the farm plans in detail. The Judge was delighted with all of it.

"Scratch the skin of nearly every business and professional man in the city and you'll find a farm boy underneath. That's why this thing has caught hold so well. That's why I think it's going to be a big success. Four o'clock vespers out in the orchard, eh?"

"And everybody on the place will have to attend," Hilary laughed. "Even visiting vestrymen."

"You've got a great idea here, my boy, if only . . ."

"If only what?"

"Nothing," said the Judge. "Here's your wife."

Lex came in, in hat and coat, but the Judge made her sit down.

"You can't deny an old man the chance to look at you, Lex," he pleaded. She had always been one of his favorites.

"It's been the most perfect, the most utterly divine party, Judge! I've seen everybody. I've talked myself hoarse. Nobody's even thinking of leaving yet. Hilary looked tired, though, so I hurled myself on the sacrifice. He's always wearing himself out over something or somebody. What can I do with him, Judge?"

Instead of answering her, the older man looked from one to the other, studying them with a pleased smile.

"I still give it as my considered judgment," he wheezed, "that you two made the best marital deal of any young couple I've met. Come on, Lex, and lead me to the mistletoe, then you can run along if you must."

They went out into the darkness and found their car. Once inside, Lex leaned against her husband.

"Were you bored, Hil? What did you do when you went into the drawing room?"

"I visited with the Arch Serpent, Tommy Tattler."

"You did? Honestly? What do you think of him?"

"I couldn't say it in front of a lady."

Lex giggled. "Oh, don't be too hard on him. He is a snake, of course, but it doesn't pay to hate him. He always has to put on a show, so he probably laid himself out to shock you. He can say the most awful things in the smoothest way. Hil?"

"Yes, darling."

"Do we have to go home now? I don't want to. I'm restless. I keep thinking about Dick. I wonder if he got our cable. It's odd we heard nothing from him. Jack Haverstraw was awfully subdued for him tonight. You know, he's the one who usually does the crazy tricks at parties. He's

263

off next week to join the Canadian air force. He says he thinks it's time this country pitched in. Hil, are you a pacifist? You never say."

"I should be, I suppose, theoretically, but I find I'm not. I would do anything in the world to help *prevent* a war. But once it's started, it seems to me it's got to be fought out."

"I just wondered," Lex said in a flat voice. "Let's eat supper out somewhere. Anywhere. How about Nick's?"

"Where's that?"

"Oh, I forgot you'd never been there. It's just a dive, but we often drop in for a snack."

"How do you mean, you 'often drop in'?"

"Oh, some nights when you're busy, Clarissa and a few of the crowd pick me up. I needn't assure you, I suppose, that I never have an escort! I just tag along as an extra. But it saves my life when I'm lonesome too many nights in a row."

"I never knew this," Hilary said in a strange voice. "Why didn't you tell me?"

"Well," Lex stated with her usual honesty, "I suppose primarily because I was afraid you wouldn't like it. But it really *is* a help to me. Usually we just go to a movie and maybe Nick's afterward. I'm never out late and yet it's something to do. Do you really mind?"

"I suppose not," Hilary said slowly.

"You see," Lex said with a sweet catch in her voice, "they all know I'm crazy about you, that I do it just to fill the time when you're busy. Doesn't that make it all right? I'll stop doing it if it truly bothers you."

"It's all right," Hilary said. "Man is just naturally a jealous and selfish critter, that's all. But be careful, dear, never to do anything that would look in the least as though you were leading a double life. Tommy might take a gibe at you. I certainly wouldn't want that for many reasons."

"Oh, I'll be careful," Lex said, "and I'll tell you from now on if and when I go out."

When they finally reached the rectory, they found Morris had lighted a fire in their bedroom. After the chill, misty night it warmed both their bodies and their hearts. They sat before it, in each other's arms, and talked tenderly of last Christmas.

"I'm so glad we had it, just as it was, all happy and perfect," Lex said. "I know Dick's thinking of it today, too. I suddenly feel safer about him. I know we'll hear soon. Hil, what do you suppose this next year will bring?"

"I'm sure I don't know."

"One happy thing we can count on is the Church Farm! I can't wait to get at that. And you should see Aunt Samantha when she talks about it. Really, just the idea of it seems to have made her ten years younger. She'll be in her element there managing suppers and picnics. She's telling the women in the slums about it already. She says the anticipation will help them over the winter."

"I hadn't intended for her to mention it until we at least have the place."

"Oh, let her. She says if people have a little hope to live on, they can stand anything. And we'll get the farm if I have to buy it myself. Poor Aunt Samantha!"

"Why do you say that?"

"Oh, I don't know. She's so good, and she tries so hard; but she and Adams are as far apart as the poles. They're so wrong for each other. You can see him cringe when she shouts out her 'As I always say' proverbs, and her 'between she and I' speeches. And yet I think she's the better of the two. I love Aunt Samantha, but I'm awfully sorry for her."

"Oh, I think she's happy enough. As you say, the work at the Farm will give her just the outlet she needs."

Lex suddenly threw her arms around his neck. "Hil, you're not sorry you married me?"

He did not answer in words.

On the third day of the New Year Hilary with a quick-beating heart approached the office of Henry Alvord and was finally ushered into his presence. Alvord's greeting was outwardly cordial enough but there was a certain cool reticence in his manner which chilled the air. When the first amenities were over, Hilary began upon his difficult errand.

"Mr. Alvord, I have not spoken to you in private since I made my general appeal to the whole vestry at the October meeting on the subject of . . ."

"I recall your speech quite distinctly."

The next move was hard to make.

"I hope, Mr. Alvord, that you have considered again the matter of the tenements . . ."

He was unprepared for the hot anger in Alvord's face as the man rose to his feet.

"Mr. Laurens, for the last time I'm going to tell you that I will brook no interference from you about my business affairs. And I want no more veiled allusions in front of the vestry either. This is final."

Hilary rose too. "In addition to the old-law tenement you own two apartments which are used for immoral purposes. Can you deny that?"

"I deny nothing," Alvord shouted, shaking his fist. "I simply say to you to mind your own business, or there will be trouble and plenty of it. I brought you here and I can damned well get rid of you if I want to. And I will if you ever dare to reopen this subject again. Take your choice."

His face was crimson as he walked to the door and opened it.

"Miss Hay will show you out," he snapped.

On the way home Hilary was surprised at the quiet in his own soul. "This is it," he kept repeating to himself. After all the long delaying, the struggle, the consultations, the prayers for guidance, the hoping against hope— "This is it," he kept saying now over and over. Happy New Year, oh, happy New Year! Lex had done well to ask what it might bring. It might now bring the ruin of all their hopes, the downfall of all he had striven to build. It might bring sharp and terrible disaster to their personal happiness itself, for it had been only because he was rector of St. Matthews that Lex had been willing to consider marriage.

And yet, curiously, almost miraculously, Hilary's heart was quiet. There would, he knew, be no further struggle, no more anguished temptation in the wilderness. That had been fought through already. He was like a soldier, shaking with dread up to the moment of attack and then, in a steely calm, feeling the reality upon him. He would speak now at this stage with no one, for no one could help him. He must go ahead swiftly to do his duty as he saw it. The issue was in the hands of God.

He called a special meeting of the vestry for the following Monday night. He notified every man except Alvord. They would meet in his study at nine.

He awaited them there in the room which he loved more with each passing week. He had come to feel that this place belonged to him. In it he had lived through exaltation and despair, and the steady, daily satisfaction of his chosen work. The sermons he had written here out of his heart's blood, the strange confidences heard, the counsel given, the consultations with Adams and Forrest and Miss Mowbray and Hastings— the essence of all these surrounded him now, blent with the fond familiarity of the furnishings themselves. In a short time, he realized, still with a deadly calmness, this room might be his no longer.

The desk light fell upon the Bishop's face. He met the eyes in the frame steadily, then with a smile, rose to greet the first comers.

It was a full meeting. Only Alvord was missing. When the men were all seated, Hilary began. The pallor and drawn lines of his face showed at once that this was to be no ordinary message from rector to vestry. He spoke slowly and with complete simplicity, allowing the facts to stand for themselves.

"I have talked as often as I dare to Mr. Alvord, urging him to make some change in his business policies. He refuses almost with violence. If the matter of the old-law tenement were the only thing involved I might

266

persuade myself that I had done all I could, and let the matter rest. But I cannot continue my work of serving the young men of our parish and the University group, advising them often as I am asked to do on matters of morality and decent living, while my Senior Warden owns two buildings used as brothels and draws income therefrom."

There was a heavy silence. Then Avison spoke.

"How did you discover that he owns those buildings?"

"These things leak out," Hilary said slowly.

"I told him," Judge Ball wheezed. "I've known it for years, but I hadn't the guts to do anything about it. Didn't feel I should, as a matter of fact."

"May I ask," Powers inquired with a thin edge to his voice, "just what you wish the vestry to do with the information you have given us?"

"Yes," Hilary said very slowly, "I must come to that. As matters stand I feel it must be either Mr. Alvord's resignation or my own."

There was one split second when no one seemed to breathe and then the confusion of many voices raised at once in question and expostulation. Hilary faced them quietly as they shouted to each other and to him.

"This is the most outrageously quixotic thing I've ever heard of," Thornton said when he could break in. "We can't afford to lose Alvord. He's our biggest single contributor. We couldn't pick up anyone on a minute's notice to pay his pew rent alone. But we certainly aren't going to let you go, Mr. Laurens. You just calm down now and remember that some compromises have to be made even in running a church."

"That's right," Weston echoed. "You can't help what a man does in his own business affairs. I'll admit this thing of the apartment houses has a pretty bad odor, but who's going to know? The Judge hasn't spilled it all these years. None of us will. Certainly Alvord won't. Can't you see, Laurens, that the thing to do is for all of us to forget this and keep our mouths shut? Where's the harm? We're not running the city's real estate. We're running a church."

"And let's have no more talk of anybody's resigning," Avison added.

Hilary and the Judge were the only two who seemed almost uninterested in the storm of discussion as it raged. The Judge smoked his cigar and looked down at his shoes. Hilary toyed with a paper knife and looked at Grandy's picture. He listened anxiously the while for Stephen Cole's voice. When it came at last, the words startled him, considering their previous conversation. Very quietly as was his wont, very briefly, Cole spoke.

"I believe our rector is entirely right. I move that we ask for Henry Alvord's resignation as vestryman."

"I second," said Judge Ball.

It was a half-hour before the question could even be put to vote. When it came the noes had it.

Hilary rose to his feet. He must get out, get away, he thought, before he broke down. The strain at this point was growing unbearable.

"Gentlemen," he said, "you have, then, my resignation as your rector. It will be mailed to the secretary in proper form tomorrow. I suggest that you call another meeting soon with Alvord present and act upon it, as promptly as possible. I find I can't talk any more just now, so if you will excuse me, I'll leave you here. Good night."

He bolted swiftly out and down the stairs before anyone could follow him. He went into the rectory and on to the library in search of Lex. A note was propped against the vase on the piano.

> Darling, I've gone out with Clarissa. I won't be too late,
> but if you're tired, don't wait up.
>
> LEX

He crumpled the bit of paper in his hand and threw it into the fire. A mist stung his eyes. Where had she gone? She must have known she would be late when she worded the note in that way. Always before she had been home before him. That was why he had never known of her evenings out. He sank down in a chair and spread his hands to the flame. He was shivering—nerves, of course. In spite of the calmness with which he had met the crisis, he realized now that he was frightened to the core. He wanted Lex desperately. He had decided before to tell her nothing until the issue was settled, but if she had been here now, his need of her would have triumphed.

When Morris came in to look after the fire Hilary's teeth were chattering.

"Mist' Hilary, you havin' a chill sure 'nough! You get you up to bed quick an' I'll fetch a hot drink."

"I'd rather stay by the fire, Morris," Hilary managed to say.

The old man hurried out, and almost at once Muff was beside him.

"It's just nerves, Muff. Don't worry. I haven't a cold. I'll be over this in a minute."

He was docile, though, accepted the blanket, the aspirin and the hot cocoa without demur, and in a short time was relaxed again, but limp and weary. Muff stood there, regarding him. Her presence in the house had been far from disturbing as he had at first feared. She lived on the third floor, performed a thousand tasks that kept the household machinery running smoothly, even lent a helpful hand to Morris when needed and advised and watched over her child as always. She was the most efficient and at the same time the most self-effacing person he had ever known. Her strong features were now set in anxious lines. She looked again to be sure Morris was no longer in earshot.

"Mr. Laurens," she began, "I do not approve of Miss Lexa's going out in the evenings except in your company. I've been meaning to speak to you about it for some time. It's perfectly true that she's always in a group, but I still feel there is a slight indiscretion connected with it."

Her Scottish accent was always richer the more serious she was.

Hilary did not reply at once.

"I just thought I'd mention it," Muff added a trifle stiffly. "No offense, of course."

"Thanks, Muff. I'm certainly not offended. I'd like to be free to go out with my wife whenever she wishes. Since I'm not, I've tried to be as fair as I can about her diversions. Suppose we just let it rest there for the present, shall we?"

Muff bowed, though he could see she was not satisfied.

"You run along to bed," he added. "I'm quite all right now. I'll be reading here for a while."

It was after two when Lex got home. There was the sound of a man's voice in the hall and Lex's, speaking her thanks, then the front door closed and Lex started for the stairs, was caught by the library light and looked cautiously in.

"Why, Hil!" she exclaimed, coming toward him. "I thought it must be a burglar. What are you doing up at this hour?"

"It must be rather obvious," he said. "I'm waiting for you."

The blanket was still around his knees and he did not rise.

"What are you wrapped up for? Are you sick?"

"Just a bit of nerves. I started chattering like a fool and Muff and Morris took me over. Lex, who was that man at the door?"

He knew his voice was sharp but he could not control it.

Lex looked at him anxiously.

"I believe you *are* sick. I'll get you to bed at once. What did you wait up for, anyway?"

"Who was the man?"

"Oh, Hil, you make me mad. Who *would* it be? It was Clarissa's Bill, and he walked me from the car to our front door. All of that. If you keep on sounding like an injured husband I won't tell you anything. What made you chatter? Was it a nervous chill?"

"I guess so. I've had sort of an upset with my vestry. I thought I was very calm and controlled, but I guess I wasn't. I'm all right now. Where were you?"

"What about?" Lex said. "What's up with the vestry?"

"Where were you?"

269

"Oh, for heaven's sake, why do you keep asking me in that tone? It sounds as though you didn't trust me, and I resent it. Clarissa's cousin Jane was coming down from Boston and Bill had tickets for tonight to take them to that new show, 'Over the Moon.' Jane wired that she couldn't get here till tomorrow and Clarissa called me up just after you'd gone. Bill found he couldn't change the tickets. The show is a riot. We went to the Fontaine Club after for supper and ran into some of the crowd there. So we stuck around for a while. Hil, what's the trouble with the vestry? I thought they were all eating from your hand."

He found he couldn't tell all the story. This was no time for that. All he could clearly see was Lex at the Fontaine Club, dancing probably. All the men would be attentive, and while they laughed and joked they would be watching her beauty. She had thrown aside her fur jacket and stood now before him in a slim black evening gown which emphasized every lovely line of her body. His face grew hot. He hated the thought of her in other men's arms when he was not there.

"Did you dance?" he asked abruptly, ignoring her own question.

Lexa's face changed. The warmth of it faded as though a chill wind had crossed it.

"I did. Since when has that become an immoral act? I believe I'll go on up."

She caught up her jacket and started toward the door. With a bound he overtook her and caught her in his arms.

"Wait," he said, "till I put the lights out and fix the fire screen. Then we'll go up together. I know I'm a dog in the manger. I'm ashamed. I'm sorry. Forgive me, sweet. I'm really not myself tonight. I'll tell you about the church business again. It's Henry Alvord. He and I don't see eye to eye."

"Father doesn't like him. Is he making real trouble for you?"

"I still hope we can settle it. Do you forgive me, Lex?"

She put her arms up to his neck.

"I shouldn't, but I do. You look so pathetic. But remember I don't want an inquisition each time I go out. That's not like you, Hil. How *can* you be jealous or suspicious? You know I'm all yours."

He looked into her clear, sweet eyes.

"It's just that it still seems too incredible to believe," he said.

They climbed the stairs, their arms around each other.

Hilary learned from the Judge the next day that the vestry meeting with Alvord present had been called for Monday night two weeks hence.

"My dear boy, I'm scared. After you left the study there was almost a free for all. I don't honestly know how this thing will end. Cole of course is with us, and in the long run Avison and Thornton, in spite of what they said. Every man of them is a friend of yours, don't misunderstand, but one or two are also old friends of Alvord's and most of them feel we can't do without him, financially. So when the real show down comes, I'm afraid the vote may be close. I'm being honest with you. And I wish to heaven I'd never let you start this thing in the first place."

Hilary smiled faintly at the Judge's assumption that he could have altered the course of events.

"Just sit tight now," he went on. "I can't believe they'll really let you go and I don't want to sound ominous, it's only . . ."

"That I should be prepared for the worst."

"That's about it. I've got a man working to see if there's anything more we can dig up on Alvord. It's only fair to have all the facts if there *are* any more. My boy, I needn't tell you I'll fight for you to the last ditch."

"I know. Words can't thank you. I'm not saying anything to anyone. I'm going to go on my usual way. All I ask is, will you call me at once after the meeting and tell me the result?"

The Judge's voice sounded unusually husky.

"I will. And don't worry."

"One thing I do not want, is to make any breach in the congregation. I would rather let the vestry decide, even if it means my leaving."

The days wore on. The arrival of a letter from Dick was an event of the first water. He wrote, however, a bit too blithely. It was not hard to read between the lines that the great adventure was different from his expectations. Lex summed it up at once.

"He's trying too hard to be funny," she said anxiously. "I wish he'd write plain facts."

They read the letter over and over again and were not comforted.

Another disquieting missive reached Hilary at his study. It was a note from Bronson. Once again it would have conveyed nothing to a casual reader. It was quite clear to Hilary:

> Now and then, certain bits of advice occur to me which, due to my close association with your grandfather, I feel constrained to pass on to you. Pray forgive the presumption and accept the motive as one of friendship. There are times in the career of every young clergyman when he will be tempted to pronounce hasty judgment upon men and upon situations. Guard, I beg you, against sudden and arbitrary decisions. Let time and tact do their work. Remember always that the priest should confine himself to matters of the spirit, leaving temporal affairs to those in secular walks of life.

So ran Bronson's letter. Alvord had reported the matter then, and by now it was quite possible that he was fortified by the ecclesiastical blessing. Hilary tore the paper up slowly and dropped it into the waste basket. The advice was, on the face of it, excellent. He wondered, once again with a troubled mind, whether he himself was being merely a young, rash, meddlesome fool. True to his nature he was capable of judging himself honestly. But after long thought, he decided that the course he had taken was the only one possible for him, let others do what they might.

On the Sunday before the fatal Monday the congregation was large, and the music magnificent. As Hilary went up into the pulpit and gazed over the congregation he felt for a moment as though his legs would not bear him up, as though his voice would fail and his memory forsake him. But the feeling passed and he preached, he knew, with his full power. Never had the faces before him looked so familiar, so dear! Never had St. Matthews itself so encompassed him with its beauty.

By Monday evening Hilary found he could not eat dinner. He tried to reassure both Lex and Morris, though Lex was greatly concerned.

"Is it still the vestry business that's upsetting you, Hil? Can't you put them all in their place? Aren't you the boss?"

He smiled. "It's not as simple as that."

He wanted to tell her everything and yet he hesitated. If he actually had to leave St. Matthews he was fairly confident that he could secure another good church. Where he went, Lex would naturally go too, but the wrench for her would be greater than for him and for quite different reasons. He decided again not to tell her until he had to. When the call from the Judge came, it would be time enough.

He wondered how to put in the evening. Should it be fasting and prayer? Should he concentrate upon a book? Should he take Lex out?

"Listen, darling, I'm not sick, just jumpy. What do you say we take in an early movie? I'm expecting an important phone call later from the Judge but we could see a picture first, couldn't we?"

"I'd love it!" Lex agreed instantly, "and it will do you good. You get yourself so tied up in knots over these everlasting church problems. There's a good show, they say, at the Palace. I'll get my coat and we'll go right away."

He hardly saw the picture but he sat close to Lex, holding her hand like a schoolboy, watching her face in the half-light, lovely, mobile, absorbed in the story. His own throat was tight and there was a queer heaviness like lead in his breast.

When the picture was over they sauntered along the street, Lex chatting, window shopping, laughing, teasing, trying, he knew, to bring back his spirits. Strange prayers had been ascending from his heart all evening,

the strangest he had ever formed. They were, indeed, not so much petitions as a sort of humble justification of his action to the Almighty:

. . . How *could* I go on with Alvord remaining Senior Warden when
I know what I do about him? How *could* I face my congregation? How
could I talk to my young men? Haven't I done the only honest and
righteous thing? . . .

At eleven there was yet no call. Lex knitted a while, played the piano,
turning to Hilary's favorites. At half past, she suggested they go on to bed.

"The Judge certainly isn't going to call at this hour. Come on, Hil. You
ought to get your rest."

"I'll wait a little longer," he said. "No need for you to stay, though.
Run along to bed and I'll be there soon. Please!"

She looked at him questioningly but went on up.

It was after midnight when the phone rang. The fact that the meeting
had been so protracted had made Hilary fear the worst. He cleared his
throat carefully before taking down the receiver. He must sound strong
and controlled.

"Hello."

"Well, we've had a night of it!" The Judge fairly panted the words.
"But I've been asked to tell you that Henry Alvord's resignation from the
vestry has been tendered and accepted. Yours is in the wastebasket where
it ought to be. And just between ourselves I've more faith in the whole
state of Christ's church militant and her humble servants than I've ever
had before in my life. I'm so damn proud of the fight we had tonight I'm
like to burst my buttons. And let me tell you if you had sidestepped or
compromised or pussyfooted, that dirty stench would have remained in St.
Matthews for a long time to come. Now, God help us, we've let some clean
air blow through."

Hilary tried to speak but he couldn't stop the Judge.

"I'm proud I'm on that vestry! I know all those men better tonight than
I've ever done before and I want to tell you they're *good* men! And here's
what's going to please you the most. At the last every man jack of them
voted to oust Alvord, and hold on to you. So, now, you can relax."

"How did Alvord take it?" Hilary asked breathlessly.

"First, cool and assured as the devil, then surprised, then frightened,
and finally violent. I had a few other unpleasant facts to present to him.
In the end he showed his hand so completely that even his own friends
were disgusted. When he finally, in a rage, offered his resignation there
wasn't a dissenting vote about accepting it. Well, now, you have the story.
I'm going to bed and I've an idea you're ready for yours, too. See you
soon."

"Thank you, Judge, more than I can ever tell you."

But the Judge had characteristically hung up already.

Hilary climbed the stairs and went softly into the room. He sat down on the edge of Lex's bed and bent to kiss her. She had already fallen asleep like a child.

"Did you get your call?" she asked drowsily. "Is everything all right?"

He laid his cheek against hers.

"Everything is wonderful. I'm so happy I don't know what to do!"

Still half asleep, she murmured against his ear.

"Let's always be happy, Hil. It's so nice just to be happy!"

CHAPTER XIV

THE WORK OF the church flowed on smoothly that winter with a new and marked respect in the attitude of the vestry toward their rector. The backdrop of the war, however, grew darker. Dick's letters changed in tone. He no longer tried to be funny. He wrote brief notes in his old style but with a new vein of seriousness, and what he did not say shouted between the lines. Hilary was convinced now that Dick's life was not only constantly in danger but that with his native recklessness he was performing all sorts of minor miracles in the rescue of the wounded. Both he and Lex began to feel the daily weight of constant anxiety. They knew what it was to blanch at sight of a telegram.

> . . . Now don't get scared and decide this is an omen or something [Dick wrote once to Hilary], but I often think, when I have any time for cerebration, of that Good Friday talk of yours last year. Remember? I hope that was the real McCoy. If it wasn't, there's been a damned big mistake made in the running of this universe. If you have any more cosmic ideas, you might try them out on me. I could use several over here. Don't ever think, though, that I'm not having a whale of a time in this mess, for I am . . .

This was as close to a call for help as Dick had ever come. Hilary sent him at once the William James quotation he had once copied for Celeste Barton, and a small Prayer-book which he had been afraid to offer him before. He wrote him, too, a letter from the depths of his heart.

One day Old Alex asked him to stop in at his office. Hilary was always delighted to have a chance for a chat with his father-in-law, but he wondered a bit anxiously if this visit might be connected with Lex's evenings out. When he arrived, however, one afternoon, Old Alex was in fine fettle. He lighted a fresh cigar and looked fondly at Hilary under his shaggy brows.

"Well, how are you making out without Alvord? Church of the Lord still running, eh?"

"Still intact," Hilary grinned, "though I must admit we're having to recast our budget a little."

"Of course," Old Alex said with his customary candor, "I think you were a damn fool to stir that thing up at all. I warned you well of it. Too dangerous. What if the vestry had stuck by Alvord? Where would you have been? Where would Lex have been? But now you've done it and Alvord's out and I'd say, good riddance. He's a stinker. And as far as the loss of his contribution goes, I've got a little suggestion."

"You have?"

"Yep. If there's no objection I'll take up Alvord's pew myself. Eunice has never been happy in Christ church. Everybody she knows is in St. Matthews. Now, since that old she-devil of a Hettie has drawn in her horns there's no real reason why we can't come back. What do you say?"

Hilary drew a full breath.

"You know the rental?"

"Sure, I can afford it. I might say I'd still do it whether I could afford it or not, though, for the sake of the family. I sort of think this will please Lex."

"And I sort of think it will please me," Hilary said, wringing the older man's hand.

As he stepped out of the elevator in the lobby of the office building, smiling and elated over Old Alex's news, he all but ran into a woman who moved suddenly in front of him. She raised her head as he began his apology. It was Diana Downes, beautiful as ever, still diabolically sure of herself.

"Hilary!" she said in sugared tones. "How nice running into you here of all places! Are you driving?"

Hilary admitted it, reluctantly.

"Then, would you mind running me home? I've been to my lawyers and that always uses me up for the day. I have a splitting headache and was just wondering how I could ever cope with the taxi situation. It's my chauffeur's day off," she added.

Hilary hated his honest tongue and his slow-moving brain. What excuse could he give? It seemed so insufferably rude to refuse.

"I'll call a cab for you," he said quickly. "I know they're hard to get at this hour."

She did not reply to this, but walked out with him to the curb, where he looked both ways and signalled frantically. Once upon the sidewalk, Diana moved very close and began to talk animatedly, smiling up at him, giving to any who might see, the appearance of intimate familiarity. When Hilary saw a car pass them with two of his parishioners in the front seat, looking straight at him—and her—he felt his face grow hot.

At last a cab stopped and he turned to help her in. She was smiling as she had smiled that night in the study. "So you really are afraid of me!" she said. "I've made a dent in your armor then, and that's all I ask for the present. Don't imagine, though, that I'll ever give up. I always know what I want and I *always* get it!"

Hilary drove home, angry and miserable. He certainly was afraid of her, though not for the reason she vainly supposed. He hated the thought that the two men in the car had seen them together on the sidewalk, apparently preparing to get into a cab together! It would have been better, probably, to have taken her directly home in his own car, as she had requested. The woman was poison to him no matter what he did. Each time when he succeeded in forgetting her, she popped up more dangerously troublesome than before.

In addition to the discomfort of his new encounter with Diana, Hilary had a peculiar fear with regard to Margaret Mowbray. Ever since fall she had not looked well. She laughed less often and the little flush he had noted rose now in her cheeks each time he spoke to her. Her easy charm of manner was gone, also. She was self-conscious and sometimes extremely nervous. Besides all this, he had caught her straightening up the files, clearing out drawers, and rearranging the bookcases. He was worried.

"Is this spring housecleaning, or pre-Lenten discipline, or what?" Hilary asked one morning as he entered his study to find Margaret on her knees, carefully straightening up the lowest bookshelves.

She tried to laugh as she rose, but it sounded strained.

"I'm putting my house in order," she said, "or rather your house. You see, I've been meaning to tell you that I may be going away for a little trip. Mother and I are thinking of Florida for a few weeks."

She stood there, fingering a book nervously, her eyes not meeting his. He noted again the light on her smooth blonde hair, and the soft immaculate folds of her white silk blouse.

"You mean during Lent?" he asked with consternation.

"I'm afraid so," she said. "I—I tried to plan it differently, but it seems, I can't. I've found a really wonderful young woman, though, who can take hold right away if you are willing to try her. I won't leave until she is thoroughly familiar with the place and the work. She's secretary to Dr. Marsden at Central Presbyterian but she wants to get into an Episcopal parish."

"She shouldn't leave where she is just for a temporary job here," Hilary objected.

Miss Mowbray still did not meet his eyes. "That's what I've really been getting up my courage to say. I won't—be—coming back!"

"Margaret!" he burst out. "What is the matter? Why are you leaving? I simply can't run this church without you!"

To his utter dismay he saw her eyes overflow.

"Sit down," he said, going to her and leading her gently to the big chair reserved for callers, the one she herself had dubbed "the confessional."

She sank into it, a strange smile on her face even as the tears still flowed. "So many confidences have come from this chair," she said, "and now I'm sitting in it myself. Who knows? Even I may break down and confess."

"You'd better!" Hilary said, trying to make his voice light. "This has knocked the pins from under me. I can't get along without you. What you've done for me while I've been feeling my way can never be told. I know you're tired. Go to Florida. Rest and get built up and then come back. I'll get you an assistant. You need more help badly. I've been selfish and blind not to realize this before. It's only that you are so efficient. Please forgive me for not seeing that you were working too hard. I'll . . ."

She stopped his nervous, anxious speech. She looked at him now, and her eyes were tender.

"I haven't been at all oppressed. I've enjoyed it. Every minute of it. I think, though, that you will need two in the office from now on. Mr. Adams could use a secretary of his own. But please don't think I was ever over worked. That isn't my trouble."

She sat very still for a moment, as though striving for calmness, and then said quite simply, "The ill from which I suffer is a common enough malady, only mine is incurable. I'm hopelessly in love with a married man who is so fine that he would not dream of suspecting this nor of admitting it if he did. I'm not ashamed. Certainly I'm not sorry. I've always felt that perhaps I was an odd, cold sort of girl, for I never could become really interested in a man. Now, I know I'm perfectly normal and I rather glory in it. I do need, though, to have a change. New scenes for a while, then a new job. I'm sure you will understand."

She had given her confession in such a way as to preclude any awkward baring of souls. Indeed, Hilary was thinking, from her wording, the man she loved could be someone else entirely. He wished that he could believe this was the case.

"You are probably right," he answered very slowly, keeping his eyes on the desk before him. "The trip, the Florida sunshine, then a new job when you come back will refresh you in body and spirit. As to the confidence you have given me I can only say that any man in the world should be deeply honored by your interest whether he can return it or not."

She had brushed the tears aside and now stood up abruptly.

"There!" she said, "I feel better now that you know I'm leaving. The business of telling you has been hanging over me for weeks. Don't worry about the work. You are no longer feeling your way, as you say. You have the whole parish and the city, too, at your finger tips. Mr. Adams is almost as familiar now with the congregation as you are and Mrs. Adams knows every man, woman and child who have anything to do with the Parish House. All you really need is an excellent stenographer and you'll find Mrs. Watson that and more. Perhaps she can suggest her own assistant. Anyway," she added brightly, "you'll probably never miss me!"

"I'll miss you more than I can tell you," Hilary returned, and then was awkwardly unable to say anything more.

He felt shaken after the interview. He made the excuse of an errand, left the study hurriedly and went on over to the house. When he entered the hall he saw Lex standing rigidly at the table there, her face stone white, one hand gripping a yellow envelope.

The telegram, then, had come.

In the days following, Hilary learned that there are many gradations of grief. The long continued, lonely ache after Grandy's death was completely unlike this knife-like anguish which followed the news of Dick. This was beyond acceptance, beyond consolation. Everyone was kind, but their words meant no more than rain falling on the roof. Few of the parish had even met Dick, so their sympathy seemed, at best, perfunctory. When he could not be with Lex he went in his few moments of leisure to Mrs. Reed or to Celeste Barton. The former did not go about much this winter. She sat in her little sitting room, reading and knitting, and receiving callers, confessing that the spirit had somehow gone out of her. To her, Hilary talked endlessly of Dick. Because they both had loved him, they could even laugh together over his jokes, his pranks, his unquenchable *diablerie*. Then when Hilary rose to go, the old lady would draw his head down and kiss him with the tears streaming over her cheeks.

His visits with Celeste were different. She was the one person with whom he could be mentally frank. To no one else of his acquaintance could he have told the torture of his present doubts concerning a future life. He, the priest, the spiritual leader of his people, he who must by virtue of his office be *sure* of everything—how could he confess that now in the dark sleepless hours the old despairing cry of Job, himself, wracked him?

But Celeste was not shocked. The beauty of her thin face, wrought partially at least by her sacrificial dealings with human misery, was lightened by her usual quick smile. She stirred the fire to a blaze in her lovely room, she gave him hot tea, she accepted without question his sudden, broken sentences. Her brilliant mind, eager as her smile, had travelled this way before, so they talked freely.

"I have never felt like this," Hilary said one afternoon, early in Lent. "It

279

seems as though all my foundations were crumbling. I can't get hold of myself. Now about immortality—all at once the old religious clichés are not enough. What I have said so often to others in sorrow suddenly doesn't comfort me at all. I keep groping for something like proof, like a logical hope. And all I come up against is the damning fact that spirit is dependent on matter, and it looks as though it must perish with it. This thought completely sinks me in connection with Dick."

Celeste saw the misery of his face and spoke quickly.

"Listen. I'm not so sure but that the interdependence of body and soul may give us our best hope for a life after this one!"

"How do you make that out?"

She gestured toward the radio beside her.

"I'm certainly not among the scientists, but I'm always fascinated reading about their discoveries. At least we know now that there *is* a substance called 'ether' which fills all space and penetrates all matter and is the medium through which light and electricity and the radio waves travel. You admit that, don't you?"

"Of course."

"Well, the big point to me is that the scientists themselves say that when they get down to the atoms and the electrons and so on, they have actually touched the borderland where matter and energy seem to merge into one another."

"There might be a thought there," Hilary said slowly.

"I think there's a mighty big one. It looks as though the physicists and the psychologists have followed their quests along converging lines so that at their meeting point they find that matter and spirit are practically the same. Each in its ultimate form may be either. Don't you see? This idea has given me more 'reasonable, religious and holy hope' about an afterlife than anything I've ever heard in church. Or maybe I should say it's bolstered up what I've heard there. Anyway, you think it over. And don't worry, Hilary. Remember, every person who really *thinks* must go down into the depths to bring up his faith. Don't despair."

She changed the subject after a while and succeeded in bringing a smile to his face, but as he was walking home he knew there still was despair in his soul coupled with his grief. A blackness lay across all his thinking. The horror of the war, the death of the countless young men like Dick, the cruelty, the barbarism, the whole titanic avalanche of the present disaster overwhelmed him. As in the darkness of a pit he kept questioning his stricken soul. Was there really a *caring* God? Was there even a moral order in the universe? All that saved him in these days from complete wreck was the echo of Grandy's words that afternoon as he had stood by the Bishop's bedside.

"Hang on, my boy. Even when you feel there's No One or Nothing there, hang on anyway."

Hilary hung on. As he went and came in the busy round of his duties the sympathy which he had at first thought perfunctory began to reach him. The Coles' quiet thoughtfulness, Judge Ball's wrenching handclasp, the solicitude of dozens of others to whom he had brought strength in their own dark hours. He realized that he was being initiated into the Fellowship of the Bereaved. In the office, too, he felt the kindness. Hastings hovered continually around him, Adams insisted on carrying extra work, Aunt Samantha mothered him in homely ways, Forrest played for him, as David to Saul, and Miss Mowbray told him gently that her plans were changed and that she was staying on until after Easter.

Still, the light that had been within him was darkness. One day in the late afternoon his bitter uncertainties seemed more than he could bear. He took down the brown scrapbook and read over again the Bishop's notes upon immortality. They had seemed strangely unsatisfying to him each time he had read them before. As a matter of fact he had felt an added hurt that there was not more comfort in them. He couldn't quite see what Grandy had been driving at.

Now, as he read slowly again, he saw that the Bishop's mind had been thinking along the very lines which Celeste Barton had pointed out. The sentences took pattern, the meaning became suddenly clear until, at the very end, the page seemed positively illumined!

To sum up [Grandy wrote], I find my hope for an embodied future life—and a disembodied consciousness is unthinkable—in the inexhaustible resources of this universe, of which we know so little and glimpse so much. Curiously enough, this whole idea was set forth plainly nineteen centuries ago. St. Paul wrote with an almost scientific precision (see Moffatt's Translation): "Some one will ask how do the dead rise? What kind of body do they have when they come? Foolish man: What you saw is not the body that is to be: it is a mere grain of wheat or some other grain. God gives it a body as he pleases, gives to each kind of seed a body of its own. There is an animate body. There is also a spiritual body. Thus, as we have borne the likeness of the material man so we are to bear the likeness of the heavenly man. For this perishing body must be invested with the imperishable, and this mortal body invested with immortality."

Hilary, holding this last sentence to his heart, went swiftly down to the quiet church and sat in a pew with folded arms, as he often did, to meditate. And as he sat in the silence a strange picture came into his mind. He thought suddenly of this planet itself. He seemed to see it struck off as a spark into the great void. He watched the little sphere, tortured by its birth of fire, learning first obedience to an ordered path, then cooling and contracting until there came upon it the gradual, laving waters and the stable land. He saw at length the miracle of bounteous life with all its beauty and diversity. He saw finally the new young race of men bearing somehow deep within them the potential import of God himself.

And he knew that there was law here, and order; there was purpose and design. There was now and ever had been *The Guiding Hand*. He raised his head. Slowly within him he felt the foundations of his faith gather, re-assemble, strengthen, and become impregnable.

Dick, himself, seemed close. He saw again the tall, lean body with its quick, graceful movements; the dark arresting eyes in the long, pale face; the all-conquering, crooked smile. He could hear his voice.

"Well, how's the man of God today? . . . How fares it with the Prophet of the Lord? . . . You know what you said on Good Friday, Hil, makes sense, even to me. . . . *I hope it was the real McCoy. . . .*"

And Hilary knew that it was; and as such, the sacrifice was not wasted. He squared his shoulders and stood up. He could bear his grief now and carry his burden. "Pax vobiscum," he could hear Dick saying in his old jaunty farewell. And from the depths of his own heart he answered, "Et cum spiritu tuo."

They agreed, he and Lex, as the days passed on, that any outward show of mourning even between themselves would have been distasteful to Dick, so they tried hard to act in every way as usual. Only covered by the darkness of night they often lay in each other's arms and let their full grief possess them. It was Morris they had both feared for most when the news came.

"This will kill Morris," Hilary had said stonily.

But with his pathetic racial aptitude for sorrow, the old man had rallied after the first shock. He sang sad songs about the "rolling Jurdon" continually to himself now, in the kitchen; the tears came quickly whenever he mentioned Mist' Dick, but his health was not visibly impaired. One day he spoke soberly to Lex.

"I just been thinkin', Miss Lexa, all at once I feel safe 'bout Mist' Dick. You know he always gettin' into trouble someway. Now he with the Bishop an' the Bishop be lookin' after him."

It was two weeks after Easter when Weston of the Alpha Insurance Company, one of the committee to arrange for the farm, called up in great excitement.

"Well, Laurens, we've had a lucky break. The company's just taken over a farm which I think is made to order for us! Could you come out along this afternoon to look it over?"

"I certainly could!" Hilary rejoined. "And I'd like to bring my wife. She's interested in this thing up to the hilt. Where is the farm?"

"Out by Newgate, right near the bus line. If you and Mrs. Laurens want to go out and be looking around, go ahead. I can't get away from here until three o'clock. Drive out the West End Pike until you come to Newgate. Stop at the Inn and ask for directions to the Rogers place and pick up the key. I left it there for convenience. Don't let my enthusiasm influence you, but I really believe we've got something!"

Hilary and Lex drove out in the bright April weather. "If the farm itself is suitable," he kept saying eagerly, "the location is perfect. Not too far from the city and near the bus line. Those requirements are not easy to fill."

Lex scanned the passing fields, her face brighter than it had been for weeks. "I hope we get it. Somehow I'm terribly excited about the whole thing. We need this just now, Hil, don't we?"

They got the key, followed directions and in a short time were driving up a locust-bordered lane. They parked the car on the front lawn under a big maple tree, got out and began looking about them. They spoke little at first, eyeing each other cautiously now and then as if to judge reactions. Then suddenly they both broke out at once.

"Why, this place has everything!" Hilary said, almost with awe. "Look at that old stone house! Look at that barn! Look at that orchard!"

"This is it," Lex said in the same breath, "and I love it! It's just been sitting here waiting for us. We've got to buy it! Let's go over every inch of it now all by ourselves while we have the chance."

With each step they grew more jubilant. They shouted to each other like children over each new find. There was a brook running through a meadow; there was a space just made for a baseball diamond; there was a berry patch; there was a clover field; there was a long chicken house with dormitory possibilities; there was the huge, sound, and altogether perfect barn!

Before Weston arrived they had planned the initial improvements. First of all, a well designed sign over the lane, reading "The St. Matthews Church Farm"; then plumbing for the house and the renovated barn; and a huge outdoor fireplace where picnic meals could be cooked.

"Morris will come in handy for that," Hilary said. "He's been hinting ever since he heard about the project. It will give him a lift, too, to get out here and have something new to do."

283

When Weston arrived they went over the place again, discussing the practical details. There was nothing, it seemed, to dull their enthusiasm. Even the price was right. It was agreed that the Committee should close negotiations immediately. Enough general interest had already been shown to warrant the purchase; then they would start raising money in earnest for the improvements.

After Weston had left, Hilary and Lex walked again through the orchard. The grass was showing fresh green and very soon a cloud of scented blossoms would cover the trees. After this would come summer's calm and happy shade.

"Right here," Hilary said, pausing, "would be the perfect spot for vespers, wouldn't it? That particular part of the farm idea means a great deal to me. I want it to be the high light of the week ends."

The sunset was rosy above the distant woods. The spring air blew sweetly upon their faces. Lex moved closer to her husband and they stood hand in hand under the old trees.

"Somehow I think we're going to have luck with all this, Hil," she said.

And she was right. During the next two months the plans went forward steadily, the first and most important renovations were begun and the new Church Farm became a fact. The most brilliant coup of all, according to Hilary, was the securing of Joe and Mary McComb, country bred across the sea, city-bound here by circumstances, to be the resident couple in the old stone house. This idea had struck him violently one morning during church and he had had difficulty in restraining himself until the end of the service. The McCombs, almost stunned by their good fortune, moved out in May and at once gave the place an atmosphere of permanent homelikeness. A cow and two horses moved into the barn shortly after. Joe would do a little farming and gardening and keep the place in order, while Mary would lend a hand with the week-end meals when the young people came out. Nothing could have given Hilary a greater feeling of satisfaction than having the McCombs there.

As Judge Ball had foreseen, something in the Farm idea caught the imagination of the people of St. Matthews. Men and women drove out of a Sunday to look the place over. Tired business executives who had once been barefoot boys, roamed the fields nostalgically, and decided to add a bit more to their contributions. Middle-aged city women smelled the clover, walked beside the brook, inspected the barn floor where the dances would be held and the converted chickenhouse which was to be a temporary boys' dormitory, and suddenly began to offer suggestions and the contents of their attics.

"I don't know whether we're running this Farm for the pleasure of the poor or the rich," Hilary remarked whimsically one day to Lex as they checked new lists of gifts. "I believe we'd better launch the thing with a picnic for the vestry and their wives!"

"It would probably do them good," Lex laughed. Then she sobered. "I hope Aunt Samantha doesn't kill herself over this. She doesn't look well to me."

"She's got all the Parish House young folks so excited there's no holding them. Did I tell you Jim Dolton and a few of his pals are going out next Sunday to paint the inside of the chickenhouse themselves? It's the only day they have and they're so pleased over the prospect I hadn't the heart to suggest it was rather an unsabbatical performance. I've stipulated, though, that they must come to the eight o'clock service first and I think they will. Do you realize that that whole group has now been confirmed? I'm pretty proud of that. In fact I'm so pleased over the way everything is going right now, I have to hold myself down a little. And listen, darling, I've got to hold you down, too. It's too much for you to drive out to the Farm every day the way you're doing. You mustn't work so hard. Though I must admit," he added admiringly, "that I never saw you look better or more beautiful."

"Flatterer! Just you try to stop me! I'm having the time of my life."

By early July enough had been completed to warrant actual use. The Cole Lodge and one or two other memorial projects were only now in the architects' hands. These must wait for a later season. But the big outdoor fireplace was built, the chickenhouse painted inside and out, the water piped, the electricity installed, and the barn partially transformed. Here Lex had worked magic. The central upper floor was clean and shining, with one end, furnished from donations, turned into what would seem a luxurious living-room to the young people who would frequent it. The remainder of the floor was to be kept free for dancing. There had been left a portion of the hay mow, now properly partitioned off, but the rest of that side and all of the other had been converted into sleeping quarters for the girls, with one real room for a chaperon at the end.

"Some night," Jim had confided to Lex, "us fellows are goin' to come out here just by ourselves and sleep in that hay. By God, I never thought—I mean, excuse me—I mean I never thought I'd get a chance like this. You know what? Some nights when it's been too hot to sleep I used to just lie there steamin' an' try to picture what it would be like to be in the country. An' now, by God—I mean, excuse me—I mean, here we're all goin' to get out here every week end. I tell you, we can't never thank you folks for doin' this for us. An' there's one thing I can tell you. If any of the fellows don't behave themselves right or start messin' up the plans or gettin' fresh or anything, they'll get the hell out of here so fast you won't see their dust. I'll 'tend to that myself, by God, I will."

It was Jim Dolton whom both Hilary and Aunt Samantha had always counted upon in the Parish House work—six feet of muscle and iron, tender-hearted, cheerful, kind, incurably profane—no responsibility was too large, no favor too small for him to discharge. He was a leader and the others followed him like sheep. He had been the first from the Parish House to agree to attend Confirmation classes; he was the one who always spotted an undesirable in the dance hall and quietly but firmly evicted him; he was the one who had come awkwardly to Hilary to suggest that one young pair ought to get married right away and by God he'd see they got there in a hurry if Hilary would tie the knot, not meanin' to be hard on them or anything for sometimes young kids get fresh and these here kind of accidents happened.

So now, with a tremendous joy in his gray eyes, Jim worked to prepare the farm for its big opening week end. He and his particular gang of helpers had continued to go out each Sunday, when they painted, cleared away debris, rustled furniture about, cut the grass, and, as Hilary learned, followed Joe McComb about his small farm duties with faces awed and beatific by turns. Several of them, Jim for one, had never been on a real farm before in their lives.

"That tallest one," Joe told Hilary, "that boy, Jim. He went to the barn along that first Sunday they was out and just leaned up against the side of the stall while I was milking Daisy and he kept saying over and over, 'A cow! By God, a cow!'" Joe lowered his voice and made sure no one was within hearing. "I didn't even tell this to Mary but it really looked to me like as if his eyes were sort of—'course I could 'a been mistaken."

Lex and Aunt Samantha, with Muff sitting in on the conferences, arranged the practical details for the opening week end. The young people were to bring their own picnic lunch Saturday afternoon. This would give them a feeling of independence and there would be supplies on hand to add to it if there was not enough. Sunday morning Morris would cook a breakfast of flap-jacks and bacon on the outdoor fireplace, and for dinner hamburgers and vegetables. Upon one point Hilary had been adamant. There must be homemade ice cream.

"I've dug up two big freezers and I think they'll work. The farmer up the road has an icehouse. If that isn't luck! Morris knows how to do it, for we always used to have it on vacations. And just watch those boys churn it! They'll be fighting for turns. There's just something about *making* ice cream—"

Lex suddenly kissed him. "What a little boy it is! I don't believe the others will even get a chance with you around. Oh, I hope we have fine weather!"

It proved perfect, in that the stifling heat of the city seemed sent to contrast with the shade of the farm trees; and in the evening Providence had even decreed a full moon. The young people, having eaten to repletion under the big maples in the yard, danced to the tunes of a country fiddler in the barn, sang songs under the bright night sky, and lay down at last to sleep on clean, comfortable cots, with the fresh country air blowing over them, the girls in the barn, chaperoned by Muff and Aunt Samantha, the boys in the erstwhile chickenhouse.

Lex sat down in the farmhouse bedroom when the evening was all over, and proceeded to weep.

"You're as bad as Jim when he looked at the cow," Hilary said tenderly, but his own eyes were a trifle moist.

"And wait till tomorrow!" he added eagerly. "Wait till they have a chance to roam over the place and—"

"And make the ice cream," Lex interjected, wiping her eyes. "We've got to make room for more here, that's all. Oh Hil, I never knew until tonight how much we take for granted. That one girl acted as though she'd never seen a full moon before!"

"She probably hasn't had a chance to notice it much. These kids have been stuck in city tenements all their lives."

"Aunt Samantha's so happy," Lex went on. "She's going to have a mothers' picnic once a week if she can manage it. And isn't Muff funny? They all shock her to death but she likes it. She's crazy over Jim Dolton, you can see. Of course I suppose you know why she's been so keen about the farm idea all along?"

"No," Hilary said innocently, "why?"

"Because I've been interested in it. She feels I've been a dud as a rector's wife. She thinks I ought to be running the Girls' Friendly and the Altar Guild and the Women's League for Missions and heaven knows what else. She says she knew a *meenister's* wife in Scotland who always hunted up the texts for her husband's sermons and even helped him write them!"

"God forbid," Hilary laughed.

He put out the light and they stood looking out the window. Lex touched his arm and pointed to the edge of the lane.

"Would it be a prowler?" she whispered anxiously.

A man's figure could be seen walking there, pausing, looking this way and that, but coming on slowly toward the house. They stood, watching, until he reached the lawn itself, then they recognized him.

"It's Jim," they said in one breath.

He kept looking now up at the moon, now across the hills, at the barn, at the house, as though he could not fix it all firmly enough in his mind. Occasionally he stretched his arms above his head and drew a long breath. At last he started off, whistling softly, toward the chickenhouse.

Sunday dawned fair, and the young folks, having lost their first shyness, began to take over the place. With shouting and laughter they picked berries, waded in the brook, played baseball, took the animals to pasture, set the tables under the trees, churned the ice cream, and watched Morris cook on the stone fireplace. Never, they all said, had a day gone so fast! At four o'clock they gathered in the orchard. There were camp chairs and a temporary altar which the boys set up, and a small portable organ, which Aunt Samantha had found in a secondhand store. Jim passed out the books as Hilary, in his vestments, took his place.

It was the gentlest time of the day. An occasional note from a songbird sounded from the trees above and now and then the far-off call of a crow. A light breeze had arisen and brought to them the scent from the near-by clover field. The sun was dropping toward the crest of the hill as they knelt on the grass for the prayers, and stood to sing, "Sun of My Soul" and "Now the Day Is Over." A lump rose in Hilary's throat as he watched the young faces before him, and caused his voice to break once as he pronounced the benediction. It was all going to "work," even as he had dreamed it would.

Through the rest of the summer the Farm and its activities filled the minds of both Hilary and Lex. With indefatigable zeal, the latter still pressed the workmen on so that by August the old wagon shed was ready to house more boys and the accommodations in the barn were nearly doubled for the girls.

Contributions, too, continued to come in steadily.

"Enclosed please find one hundred dollars for the Farm. The story you told us about the young chap looking at the cow really got under my skin."

"I'm sending a little something to help with the meals at the farm. What we saw the day we were out moved me deeply. Call on me if you run short."

So it went. The hearts of the people of St. Matthews, it seemed, were touched by the new venture as by no other feature of parish activities. Of all this, Hilary wrote often to Cousin Mattie, insisting gratefully that he was indebted to her for the original idea. He found himself clinging to her, too, as the last family link, for his grief for Dick was constantly with him even though he had learned to surmount it. To this end the tremendous new interest of the Farm had served him well.

There were two anxieties, however, in Hilary's mind, as the autumn approached and the time for closing the Farm season drew near. One was that, apparently, Aunt Samantha had worked too hard. She was white, she had lost weight and something of her breezy complacence seemed to have deserted her. She had stayed out at the Farm most of the time, while Adams, himself, had stuck by the city work all summer. This had, he admitted, been most congenial to him. He had enjoyed the Sunday preaching, had done an excellent job in breaking in the two new secretaries, and had had a pleasant social life with Forrest and many of the men of the parish who were alone much of the summer. While evincing courteous general interest in the Farm he had never seemed eager to go out. Lex was annoyed.

"I know Aunt Samantha isn't right for Adams but I hate to see him so openly enjoying her absence. And you can't smooth it over! He's made all sorts of excuses to keep him here all week as well as over Sundays. I've been furious at him."

Hilary had a deep respect for his assistant. The man had ability, a charming personality and an unfailing tact which had often been to Hilary as salve to a wound. If, for example, Adams had had his own suspicions as to the cause of Margaret Mowbray's leaving, he had never by look or tone revealed it. Yes, all in all, Adams had been the right man for the place and Hilary took pains often to tell him so. The older man's gratitude was touching. While he did not share Lex's violent criticism of Adams as a husband he did venture to speak to him of Aunt Samantha's health.

"I'm a little concerned about Mrs. Adams," he said, one day in September. "I'm afraid she's done more than she was able for, this summer. I want you to know that my wife and I both tried to hold her back but there was no stopping her. Did she tell you about the day she and Mary McComb baked a dozen cherry pies between them?"

Adams smiled. "I'm sure she has enjoyed the summer. I have noticed that she looks a bit tired but she'll soon pick up. She's never been ill a day in her life to my knowledge. This week is the wind-up out there, isn't it?"

"Yes and a big one, we hope. We're having a corn roast Saturday night. Why don't you come out for it?"

Adams gave a short laugh. "I hoed so much corn when I was a boy that the very thought of a cornfield now makes me ill. Just let me remain urban the rest of my life. That's all I ask."

Hilary's other and much larger anxiety after the last big week end was over, had to do with Lex. What would happen now when they settled to the usual winter routine, when there was suddenly ended all the enthralling work and excitement of the Farm into which she had thrown herself completely? Would she grow restless? Would she begin again to go out evenings with the crowd? He had heavy moments of foreboding.

"Well," Lex remarked one night as they drank their coffee before the library fire, "I was at a party today, so I am now prepared to give you all the latest dirt."

Something in her expression, Hilary thought, was not quite right.

"Go ahead," he said, "I guess I can take it."

"First, Maudie Dunn is going to have a baby! One of the girls who used to go to Miss Hewitt's classes with her was down to see her the other day and she says their flat is darling! It's near the Settlement in an awful location and they have only three rooms and a little studio place where Jerry works, but she says they've managed to make it really attractive, and that Maudie is so cute about everything and so happy, you'd never know her!"

"Good," said Hilary. "I haven't been down to the Settlement for a while or I suppose I'd have heard the news. Did she say how Jerry is making out?"

"All right, I guess. He has this job with an advertising firm which keeps them going. Then he paints evenings. He hopes to do nothing but portraits later on. Hasn't Maudie the courage, though? You know J. V. has cut her off completely."

Hilary nodded thoughtfully. "What else did you hear?"

"As a matter of fact, I didn't like the other tidbit. Clarissa told me that this summer up at Watch Hill she ran into Mrs. Potiphar."

"She did?" Hilary's eyes narrowed.

"Yes. Clarissa was visiting the Watsons, and it seems they know Diana and had her to the house one evening to some sort of fancy brawl. When it was over, Bess Watson told Clarissa that Diana had told *her,* brazenly, that there was only one man in the world she wanted, and that was you. And that she was going to get you if it was the last thing she ever did. Those were her very words. And I can't say they sound particularly pleasing to me."

"Nor to me. She's got a tongue like an adder."

"Do you think," Lex asked slowly, "that you should say something about this to the vestry? Just take them into your confidence about the whole situation. So that if they should ever hear anything . . ."

Hilary shook his head. "I'd feel like a fool to do that. Besides"—his face colored—"while the Potiphar woman is far and away the most troublesome, there are others of course."

"You mean other women—all the time?"

Hilary nodded, and Lex gave a small wail.

"Oh, Hil, that's dreadful! What kind of women? Do they come to your study?"

"Yes. I always make sure the secretary is in her office, but sometimes it's pretty messy at that. I mean, their confessions. They're mostly neurotics, a few alcoholics and then some others that really give me a shock. I mean the type I would not have expected."

"And you never tell me about all this?" Lex's voice was distinctly hurt.

Hilary was at once desperately earnest.

"But darling, wouldn't it sound pretty conceited and sloppy if I were to tell you every week or so that some woman or other would like me to make love to her? You haven't ever told me about all the men who wanted to make love to you, have you? Well, it's the same sort of thing that holds me back. Besides, I wouldn't even repeat to you most of the stuff I hear. I'd be ashamed. I just try to forget it. It's certainly not that I'm being secretive. You do believe that, don't you?"

He looked so anxious that Lex smiled at him. "Yes, I believe you, but I hate it all just the same. What are you going to do, though, about Mrs. Potiphar?"

"Just keep out of her way. That's all I can do."

The announcement of Clarissa Ball's engagement started the fall social season off with unusual gaiety. Lex herself was hostess at a luncheon and a large tea and was out most days, attending parties given by others of the crowd. Then, as Hilary had feared, she began again to go out at night. He chafed and worried and felt impotent because his own evenings just then were so frequently full; a speech here, a committee meeting there, a session with the vestry, his regular conferences with the University men, a night when he absolutely had to work on his sermons, and the dinner engagements within the parish so important that he and Lex could not disregard them! What it all added up to was that there was very little time left for the sort of social life which Lex enjoyed unless she took part in it alone.

There were two events in quick succession which led up to that tragic gray afternoon in November. The first was an unusually stuffy dinner with an elderly couple, where the time had dragged, and Lex, Hilary could see, kept growing more and more restive. When she finally rose to leave, the small bag on her knee fell sharply upon the wide marble hearth, scattering its contents of cigarette case, lighter, and cosmetics.

"Oh, damn it!" she said with quick vehemence.

There was a shocked second of silence, then Hilary hastily collected his wife's property, made what pleasant adieux he could muster, and they finally got away. Once in the car he spoke sharply to Lex, who every now and then gave vent to wild giggles.

"It is not funny," he said. "Not at all. That old man probably doesn't even say 'damn,' himself, in front of a woman. What would they ever think of you?"

"Oh, Hil, relax! It will give them something to talk about. Heaven knows they need it. I was so bored all evening I thought I'd scream."

"But after all, Lex, you do have a position to maintain. You are the rector's wife." There was still a distinct edge to his tone.

"Do you really need to remind me?" she returned icily.

Not even before they slept was the constraint lifted. Hilary lay troubled and hurt, for Lex had shown none of the warm, quick penitence which was part of her nature. Even as he had kissed her good night, she had remained silent and aloof.

It was only three days later that Muff appeared at his study door. This, Hilary knew, was ominous. Although he tried to make some joke in connection with her coming, her Caledonian features remained fixed and stony. She laid a paper on the desk before him. It was J. V. Dunn's yellow *Courier,* and she was pointing to the column of Tommy Tatler.

Hilary felt cold. He followed Muff's finger and read:

> One of the most beautiful young women in the city (as I have always contended) who eschewed society some time past in order to wed a young man of God, has now, it would seem, decided to relinquish the ascetic life and return to the pavilions of Babylon. Her own sparkling vivacity and the heavy male admiration which surrounds her now frequent appearances in the hot night spots makes one wonder if perhaps— Well, at least one will watch the situation with interest.

Hilary thanked Muff curtly, gripped the paper and went down the stairs and over to the rectory. This was the last unbearable straw. This was what he had feared all along. This was what he had definitely warned Lex against, a warning to which she had apparently paid no heed.

He found her in the library and confronted her with a set face. They had regained their usual manner since the dinner episode; holding each other close, Lex had confessed to real regret for her unlucky "damn" and Hilary to his sharp tone. All had been right again, until now.

"So you've seen it," Lex said, trying to smile. "Tommy never misses making a mountain out of a molehill."

"You told me yourself, once, that his greatest threat lay in the fact that he always told the truth."

"Just what do you mean by that?" she asked quickly.

"Oh darling, I know exactly what you did and why you did it. I sympathize with you. I know how much you miss your own crowd. I know how much you like a good time and how helpless I am to give it to you. But Lex, your going out without me has to stop. After this blast of Tommy's you can't take any chances again. You do see that, don't you?"

Her face was suddenly pale. She moved over to the piano and stood with her back to him, touching one key and then another. The sound seemed eerie in the silence. Hilary went to her and put his arms about her.

"Darling, if I could see any other way out, I wouldn't ask this of you. But there is no other way. We can't have Tommy's ugly mouthings touch us and start rumors. You do see that, sweet, don't you?"

She nodded slowly, but did not turn to him.

"If I could just go and punch him on the nose," Hilary gritted between his teeth.

She turned quickly then.

"You mustn't do that, Hil. Promise me you won't go near him. That's fatal. I know people who have tried it, and he made their lives miserable. The only thing to do is to ignore it completely. I thought," she added, and her tone was pitiful, "that we'd make quite a joke of this."

He drew her close. "That last innuendo of his is beyond a joke. I've had a feeling ever since my encounter with him at the Balls' that he's lying in wait for us. That he'd really relish doing us harm if he could. We don't dare give him the chance, darling, that's all." Then as she still said nothing, he burst out, "Oh, I could shoot myself if it would do any good. I hate to have you give up so much because of me."

She put her hand gently over his lips. "Don't say such things. It's all right. I'll get my second wind in a minute. It's just that now, on account of the wedding parties, it comes hard. But don't worry . . ."

She straightened and tried to smile into his distressed face.

"It's all right, really," she repeated. "Tommy ought to be run out of town but we'll have to let somebody else do that. And don't look so bleak, Hil. I see the situation just as you do." She smiled. "We'll—we'll make up for it all, somehow."

He had never loved her as much as in that moment.

But the next day Judge Ball called him up, and so did Mrs. McColly. They were both agitated. Lex had dropped out of the wedding party and she was to have been matron of honor! Her reasons were vague. What on earth was the matter? He tried to calm them both and promised to do all he could to make her change her mind. But when he broached the matter to her, he found her quite set.

"It's no good, Hil. I've decided. I will not be in the party and be out of everything. I'd rather not be in it at all. It won't spoil the plans for Clarissa. She wanted to get one more girl in as a bridesmaid anyhow. Now she can jump one up for maid of honor and it will work out perfectly."

"But—but you," Hilary stammered, "this is a big disappointment for you, and I still can't see why you can't go ahead . . ."

"Please don't make me argue," she said. "I know all about the parties leading up to the wedding. Better than you do. It's going to be a very gay time indeed. I can't go to them. Even after rehearsal, you and I would probably come on home. I will either be in the whole thing or I'll be out of it. So, I'm going to be out of it. And don't worry about Mother and the Judge. I'll handle them."

So October ended and November began. For the most part there were crisp, bright days and above, a rich blue sky, but to Hilary as to many more, there was a cloud across the sun, a pall across the world. Europe lay buried and beaten, Britain fought on with her back to the wall, and Russia was apparently struggling against death blows. The war was the only subject of conversation wherever men met, while the newspapers and the radio told of little else. Hilary pored over maps each night before he went to bed, while he listened to the last commentator. He did a few editorials for one of the newspapers, he wrote articles for the *Churchman,* he spoke at various dinners, he preached, he prayed, and with it all he felt utterly futile. He thought deeply of Dick. It had been so like him to go swiftly on a purely volunteer mission, and fling his life away in one grand, careless gesture of bestowing. Oh, happy dead, he thought sometimes, to have done their full part and now to lie in peace! For the struggle tore at him. The whole ghastly question of war had now gone far and away beyond academic consideration, even for men of God. It had to be faced in all its present, agonizing reality.

That November afternoon, that heart-breaking afternoon, was in itself gray. A chill rain had been falling and the streets looked dank and dreary. Hilary had been out on a sick call and returned to the study, tired, cold, and sobered by the scene he had left. He had just gone through the afternoon mail when there was a tap on his door and, to his surprise, Aunt Samantha entered. Her appearance shocked him and he hurried to help her to a chair.

"I'm all right," she said, "I just stopped to rest a little before I went on home and I find Sammy's gone, so I came in here . . ."

"You're worn out!" Hilary said swiftly. "And it's a beastly day. I know what we'll do. Lex will give us tea to cheer us up! When you've caught your breath, you go on over, and I'll follow soon. I want to get a couple of letters off."

Aunt Samantha smiled. "That would be nice. It always does me good to talk to Lexa. I believe I will go over for a little while if you think she's in."

"I'm sure she is. A day like this. Tell her we want a big tea, for I'm starved. I'll be over in a few minutes."

When Aunt Samantha was gone, Hilary turned again to his desk. A half-dozen brief letters needed to be done by hand and he attacked them swiftly. When they were finished, he stacked them for mailing and went down the stairs and across the court. He opened the side door and went toward the library where he heard the odd sound of a voice. At the doorway, he stopped, rooted to the spot. Lex sat huddled on the couch behind a low table on which stood a glass and an almost empty cocktail shaker. Her guest sat beside her, stricken.

"We're all wrong, Aunt S-Samantha," Lex was saying in the strange voice. "You and I are both all wrong for our men. I'll t-tell you why. You aren't s-socially ac-*cept*-able, because you're still countrified, so you don't get to any parties. I'm *too* s-socially ac-*cept*-able so *I* can't go to any parties. So we're both lonesome. So we shouldn't ever have married p-parsons. That's our trouble. Both of us. Now, you say 'between you and I,' and that's bad grammar and that made Adams take to drink. And I say 'd-damn it,' and Hilary gets mad and that makes *me* take to drink and it's all so f-funny about us, Aunt S-Samantha, only it's so s-sad, I'm going to cry . . ."

She crumpled up, weeping, and Aunt Samantha, her face marble, put her arms around her as Hilary, until then incapable of speech or motion, rushed toward them. He lifted Lex forcibly and half carried her into the hall.

"Muff!" he called, and his voice brought the Scotch woman running from the second floor. "Get Miss Lex to bed at once."

He came back to Aunt Samantha. She was leaning against the sofa, her head thrown back, her eyes closed.

"I don't know how—" he began, but she stopped him.

"All through the years," she said, "I thought I was bolstering Sammy up, and helping him, and covering things for him. Now I can see it all the way it really was. I've never been the one for Sammy. She's right. I am still countrified. Mebbe it was even because of me—"

The agony of her voice tore Hilary's heart in two.

"Don't," he cried, "Oh Aunt Samantha, you mustn't think of this again. Lex was not herself. When people are that way they say anything. You know they do. Please, please promise me you'll never pay the slightest attention to it."

But she had not even heard him. "Yes, she's right. I can see it now. Sammy's been kind, but—I guess it hasn't been the way I thought it was between us. I loved him so I just didn't notice. I tried so hard. I thought I was such a helpmeet but—I just wasn't good enough for Sammy. Mebbe now, though, it won't be so hard to leave him."

"What do you mean?" Hilary asked in fright. "You're not going to leave him."

She looked at him. Since she had lost weight her face had taken on some of the lines of her youth. Her voice no longer boomed. It was, indeed, very weak.

"Yes. I'd have had to tell you soon. I only found out last week. I haven't long to live."

"No," Hilary cried. "No! You're just tired. We let you work too hard. You and Adams must go off on a long vacation, and you'll forget all these foolish ideas! I insist upon this. I'll arrange for it!"

She tried to smile at him and patted his hand. "No, dear," she said gently. "It wouldn't do any good. The doctor told me the truth. I felt I just couldn't tell Sammy but now—I guess it won't matter, not the way I thought it would."

Hilary was beside himself then, with anger, with anguish. The words poured from him with no volition of his own. But Aunt Samantha's eyes were far away. He saw at last she was not listening.

"I must go," she said. "Sammy's dinner . . ."

Hilary took her home in the car. She would not let him come in. "I'll take care of everything," she said, "and don't be hard on Lexa. She was lonesome, I guess. That's why she did it, or discouraged over something mebbe. That's the way it always was with—don't be hard on her. Nobody'll ever know." Her voice pleaded with him.

When he returned the rectory was quiet. Morris, who had seen nothing and yet sensed calamity, silently served the dinner which Hilary could not touch. When he went upstairs at last Lex was asleep and Muff, doubtless humiliated to the depths for her child, was nowhere in sight. Hilary moved about the bedroom, collecting his things. When he had done so, he went into the Prophet's Chamber and shut the door. His heart was in such bitter tumult that he did not even think of going to bed. He sat by the table, his head in his hands: *To be wroth with one we love, Doth work like madness in the brain.*

The words kept ringing in his ears, for this that racked him was like a madness. Lex, his own wife, had that afternoon, been—yes, say the ugly word. Why should he try to euphemize? Why should he try to gloss it over, to excuse, to spare her, or ever, ever to forgive her? Why should he? He groaned. Her drinking had been horrible enough, but in her maunderings she had broken Aunt Samantha's heart, the heart of her who was appointed to die. It was of less importance that she had rent his own heart also. But above all this pain rose his anger, hot and dominant, swollen by the very passion of his love. He sat there all night, nursing it. Only with the dusky, breaking day did he throw himself, still dressed, upon the bed.

The house was still quiet in the morning. He did not go near Lexa's room. He ate breakfast alone and went on over to the study. He knew he would have to confront Adams, who would now be aware of the impending fate. When he came in, at last, he was pale but controlled.

"My wife said she told you last night. I'll have to be out a good deal these next days. I'm taking her to see Dr. Shane this afternoon."

Hilary wrung his hand. "Call on me for anything," he said huskily.

"I should have noticed—I should have seen before this. Now, I'll leave nothing untried—nothing undone—but . . ."

There was no more to be said. Hilary turned fiercely to his work. Shane would know. Shane's word would be final. He telephoned Morris he would not be home to lunch and ate at Mrs. Milligan's across the street. Her sallies today brought him no cheer.

"It's missin' the nice young lady, I am," she said at last, "that Miss Mowbray." She leaned confidentially over the counter. "An' I'll bet I could tell you why she left if you don't know already. I could see it in her face plain as a pikestaff when the two of you would be together. Ah, well! Women are always gettin' the worst of it in this world. The men they get ain't fit for them an' the ones they want they can't have. There's no justice for women in this life an' I'll bet it'll be just as bad in the next. Will you have the apple pie today? It'll melt in your mouth."

There was no word from Lex all afternoon and Hilary did not call. At five Adams came in, his face drawn. He simply shook his head and sank down in a chair. When he could speak at last, his voice trembled.

"Nothing," he said. "Nothing can be done. Shane says it's only a matter of weeks. He says only the most incredible effort of will has kept her going at all. She's given up now, and gone to bed. I've got a nurse. She's so different, so unlike herself, so quiet. All in a day's time she has completely collapsed."

Hilary's throat was full. He tried to say something but the sentences stuck.

"I'll get pulled together," Adams said as he got up. "It's the suddenness of it all that has unnerved me. I—I must be going back home."

Hilary went down with him to the car. His silence spoke more eloquently than many words.

When he went over to the rectory he found Lex in the library, sitting by the fire, staring pensively into the flames. She looked up quickly when she saw him, but neither of them spoke. He came over and stood, leaning against the mantel. His eyes were stern and hers were questioning.

"Well," she said at last, trying to smile, "am I going to be forgiven? I know it was utterly dreadful. I've never had too much to drink before in my life. In fact I've prided myself on keeping a level head under all circumstances. But yesterday I felt so low, so completely sunk, that I mixed up some Manhattans and sat down here in a black mood. I honestly didn't know I'd had too many until Aunt Samantha came in and I found I couldn't stand up. I'm terribly ashamed, Hil. I've had a wretched day. You kept away from me, Muff never once stopped scolding me and my head aches like murder. What did I say to Aunt Samantha? I can't remember a thing."

"Do you want to know?"

"Of course I want to know. What makes you look like that? Did I say something awful?"

Hilary's voice was sharp. He knew he was cruel, but his anger was still hot.

"You told her the whole truth about her life with Adams. You told her she had driven him to drink because she was countrified, used bad grammar and was not socially acceptable. You told her she should never have married him."

Lex had sprung from her chair at his first sentence and now stood before him, her eyes wild with horror.

"No!" she cried. "Oh, no! I couldn't have! Oh, Hil, I *couldn't* have said that to Aunt Samantha!"

"But you did. That much I heard with my own ears. What else you told her before I came in, I do not know. I might add that you also said your own marriage was a mistake, even as hers was."

Lex sank back into the chair as though he had struck her. Her head dropped in her hands and her whole body shook with sobs.

"There is one thing more," Hilary went on, mercilessly. "You will have to know it soon. It might as well be now. Aunt Samantha has only a short time to live. Adams took her today to see Shane. He says it's only a matter of weeks."

Lex raised her tear-stained face. Despair was in her eyes. She reached out her arms to him.

"Oh Hil," she begged brokenly, "I can't bear this!"

But he did not move. His heart felt like a stone in his breast.

"I can't help you, Lex. I'm too hurt myself, too broken up over everything . . ."

He stopped and for one long moment their eyes met. Then Lex rose slowly. Even her lips were white.

"I—I see," she whispered and walked out of the room and on up the stairs. When Hilary heard her door close he realized that the house had never been so still.

CHAPTER XV

THE FUNERAL of Samantha Adams was like none other that St. Matthews had ever known. True, many notable people through the years had lain in state in the shadow of the white altar, and crowds had assembled to do them honor. But never before had the church been packed to capacity and the sidewalk filled with men and women who stood quietly, with heads bowed, during the service. Now, Hilary realized with ironic pain, there was fulfilled his impetuous early dream of a congregation where the rich and the poor would meet together, for on this day the regular membership of St. Matthews came out of respect to Adams, and the whole slums behind the church came out of love for Aunt Samantha.

Even Hilary, himself, was unprepared for this latter outpouring. But they came, in their poor and shabby best to do honor to her who had been their friend. And in so far as the church would hold them, they were seated next to the broadcloth and furs of the regular pew holders, for Jim Dolton and his boys were doing the ushering.

Just before the service Hilary had been seized with a fear amounting to panic, that he could not go through it without breaking. He had even cast wildly about in his mind for assistance. Then, with an effort, he mastered himself. Not only for Aunt Samantha's sake but for those who sat for the first time in St. Matthews he must make the ritual beautiful, unmarred by his own emotion. Later, he said to himself, as he looked down upon the massed faces before him, later I'll give way, I'll let myself go, but not now, God help me, not now.

And so, as though his cry had been answered, his voice had never been more controlled. No syllable was blurred or lost; but strong, crystal clear and tender, the ancient words fell upon the waiting hearts even up to that last great moment when before the altar he uttered the final prayer for Aunt Samantha:

"And may light perpetual shine upon her soul."

On the way back from the cemetery Hilary spoke to Adams, who sat, gray and haggard, beside him.

"Won't you reconsider and come home with me for tonight? Or go to Forrest if you'd rather?"

But Adams shook his head.

"If you don't mind, I'd rather be alone."

So Hilary returned to the rectory without him. He and Lex had been living in strange, tense misery since that fateful afternoon three weeks before. She looked wretched but she made no outward moan. She had gone daily to sit with Aunt Samantha, taking with her every comfort of which she could conceive. What might have been spoken between the two women in those poignant hours, Hilary had no way of knowing, for, with a dignity he had not dreamed she possessed, Lex kept her own counsel, talking to him only when necessary and upon general topics.

Her eyes, often red in spite of the careful make-up, pleaded with him, but Hilary could not yield. Something of the first angry hurt and condemnation still remained within him. And saddest of all, the image of Aunt Samantha, herself, seemed to rise between them and keep them apart.

On this evening after the funeral, the tension between them was harder to bear than it had ever been. Neither of them could form the painful comments relating to the service nor could they bring themselves to talk of anything else. Hilary realized the remorse which lay upon Lex, the infinitely greater sorrow than his own, which showed in her eyes and her white face; but he felt powerless to comfort her. So they sat almost in silence until she rose at ten o'clock and went upstairs.

It was nearly eleven when Hilary heard the bell ring and answered it himself. To his amazement he found Hastings at the door. The old man came inside quickly, putting his finger on his lips as he did so.

"Anyone else round?" he whispered.

"No," Hilary assured him. "What's wrong, Hastings?"

"I just kep' thinkin' all evening about Mr. Adams. About—you know what. I kep' thinkin' if I was him tonight what would I most likely do? I called up his apartment an' there was no answer, so I came in to the church 'bout eight. I found his study door locked. I opened it with my key and there he was." The old man's face worked. "He—he wasn't so well. I got a cab an' took him home with me. My wife took care of him. He's to bed now. Jest thought I'd let you know. Face to face, that is."

"Why didn't you call me at once, Hastings, when you got to his study?" Hilary was quick to feel his own remissness. He was the one who should have foreseen this if his own heart had not been so heavy.

"Thought better not," Hastings said with finality. "You don't know anything, understand? Don't make any difference about me. He'll be all right by morning. We'll—we'll have to make allowances."

Hilary took the old man's gnarled hand in both his own. "God bless you, Hastings," he said. "Let me know if you need me."

The next day was Sunday, the seventh of December. Hilary woke early in the Prophet's Chamber, and lay thinking. Of Aunt Samantha, of Adams, of Dick, of the war, of Lex—most of all of Lex and himself. She had looked so white last night, but it had made the beauty of her features more pronounced.

O so white, O so soft, O so sweet is she! The old line rang in his mind. He wondered miserably if their love would ever be complete again after this bitter interlude. Would some great joy of reunion sweep this nightmare away as though it had never been? Perhaps, he thought, when time had wrought its patient work. Perhaps, but oh, the weary, wretched days between!

He picked up his watch from the night table. It was seven and he must get up. When he had bathed and dressed he stood for a moment outside Lexa's door. There was no sound, so he went quietly down the stairs and over to the church. More and more people had been coming lately to the eight o'clock communion, a sign of the spiritual life of the parish for which he gave thanks. This morning as he turned to face the congregation, the words all but froze upon his lips. Adams knelt in the front pew.

During the service he found his voice unsteady, for he was speaking from his own heart to the man before him. "Ye who do truly and earnestly repent you of your sins . . ." Then in the General Confession that followed he could detect Adams' low, broken tones as if in direct reply:

"'. . . The remembrance of them is grievous unto us; The burden of them is intolerable. Have mercy upon us, Have mercy upon us . . .'"

They met at the close and Hilary insisted upon bearing him back to the rectory for breakfast. Lex was not down, so the two men, ignoring, for each other's sake, all that lay behind, looked at the paper, discussed the war and drank Morris' good coffee with thankfulness.

"I'm sorry about dinner, today, Adams," Hilary said. "We're invited to the McCollys'. But you must come in soon."

"Thanks for the thought but I'm going to Forrest's. It may be that he and I will join forces permanently. He spoke of it a week ago when we knew . . ."

"Splendid!" Hilary said with enthusiasm, feeling as though one weight, at least, was lifted from his heart by the news. "Forrest has plenty of room and it would probably be a godsend to him to have your company. You are old friends, congenial and both alone—it sounds a perfect plan to me."

Adams nodded gravely. "I've practically decided to go. We could help each other, I think."

Hilary took the last words at more than their face value, as he felt Adams intended.

"I'm sure you could," he answered, with feeling.

Dinner at the McCollys' was quieter than usual in spite of Lexa's efforts to make everything seem normal. Old Alex and his wife evidently suspected nothing amiss maritally, being convinced that Aunt Samantha's illness and death was the sole cause of their daughter's altered appearance. They were anxious about her, however.

"I was tellin' Lex," Old Alex said to Hilary when they were back in the living room, "that she's got to snap out of this now and get some color in her cheeks. What about her and her mother taking a week at the shore? A little change, you know. Do her good. By George, I never knew she cared so much about this Adams woman. Great person she must have been, though. Never saw such a funeral in my life! What about Atlantic City, Lex? Can you leave this big lug of yours for a few days?"

Lex looked over at Hilary, a question in her eyes.

"Would you like to go?" he asked. To himself he was thinking—it might help us to be apart for a little. It might ease the strain.

Old Alex had turned on the radio. Suddenly, before Lex could reply, the excited voice of the announcer filled the room. *The Japanese had bombed the United States fleet in Pearl Harbor.*

When they could speak, Old Alex, standing with his cigar half smoked and dead in his hand, said hoarsely, "This is war! Great God, we'll be in it ourselves!"

Hilary's face looked graven.

"Yes," he echoed, "we'll all be in it, now."

When he had to leave for Vespers, Old Alex, his cheeks scarlet, his curly hair rumpled and rampant, stopped shouting his vilifications and looked anxiously at his daughter.

"What about Atlantic City? This won't make any difference. I'll get hotel reservations at once. Your mother and I have talked this over and we think . . ."

Lex walked across and kissed him.

"Thanks a lot, Dad, but I'm not going. Don't worry about me, I'm fine. It was a wonderful dinner, Mother! I'll be over tomorrow."

On the way back they talked wildly of the news. Astonished and shaken to the core, they repeated to each other over and over all they had heard. Their words ran forward, took fright and retreated before the awful implications of the disaster. They spoke, however, with a sudden fluent, eager release about all that was farthest from themselves.

When Hilary came in for tea, he found the Judge there.

"Couldn't stay alone tonight! Had to be with somebody, so I called Lex and she took me in. Well, Hilary, this comes heavy but it looks as though we'll have to take it. See if you can get WEAF, Lex. They've got a good man on at five-thirty. We may get more details." All at once he sank back in his chair and his whole body sagged. "My God, I only now thought of it! Clarissa's Bill will get into this. He's just the kind to enlist at once."

Neither Hilary nor Lex answered, for they were looking at each other.

They all hung upon the radio throughout the evening. When Lex rose at last, she dropped a kiss on the Judge's cheek, glanced toward Hilary and turned to the door.

"I'm going soon, Lex," the Judge called after her. "I won't keep him up long."

But Hilary, listening, heard the door closing, above.

America was at war. Swift as a weaver's shuttle, the dread fact worked into the fabric of the nation. The great country, over night, acknowledged it and began to prepare for the worst. Would New York be bombed? Was the whole East Coast in danger? Men with grim faces discussed the probability as organization of civilians began at once. Keen eyes started their watches by day and by night, wings overhead kept ward, the lights went out and the whole machinery of defense was set in motion.

But this was but the least of it. America, stretching three thousand miles from ocean to ocean, happy in the peace and the fruitfulness which had been bought and dearly paid for by the blood of her pioneers, must now call her youth from California and Maine, from Texas and Michigan, from Delaware and Oregon, from the mountains, the plains and the cities to drop the plough, the hammer, the pencil, and the book, and prepare to fight unknown foes in the uttermost parts of the earth.

And the young men came, mystified, incredulous, pawns of a fate they could not explain, but warm with life and a heart-breaking readiness to accept the thing which had been thrust upon them.

It was the University men, Hilary found, who were the first to enlist. On Thursday evenings they came in numbers to see him, sometimes for counsel, but more often now to say good-bye. In a few weeks' time a hundred had left, and the Sunday Vesper services began to thin out. Then the young men of the parish itself began to go. He tried to see them all and send them off to camp with a special farewell. He arranged for Corporate communion services for young men only; he had small, khaki-covered Prayer-books made to give them as parting gifts; he wore himself to the bone in his effort to be at trains and places of departure; he followed them when he could to the nearest camp.

One day Jim Dolton entered his study. At sight of him a pang went through Hilary's heart. He loved this boy. Until this moment he had not known how greatly he loved him.

"Hello, Jim," he tried to say brightly. "How's everything?"

"Why, not so bad. I just thought I'd drop in an' say good-bye. Me an' the other fellahs we just been talkin' it over. We've all got to go sometime an' I says to them we might as well make the break an' get goin'."

He grinned. "Not that I'm anxious to fight anybody but since they've started it I guess we'll just have to go an' beat hell out of them."

"When do you leave?" Hilary asked, his mouth feeling suddenly dry.

"I guess mebbe on Thursday. I just want to say, Mr. Laurens, that you've done us fellahs a lot of good an' we won't ever forget it. By God, we won't." He swallowed. "An' I want to tell you I never had as good a time in all my life as I had this summer at the Farm. Them days will be something to keep thinkin' about when I'm away. Guess there won't be many of us fellahs to go out next summer but the girls can run it. An' it'll be something for us to come back to."

They had a long talk. When he left he all but crushed Hilary's hand. "An' say good-bye to Mrs. Laurens," he said. "She was swell to us out at the Farm." Then he added, "Seems funny not to be seein' *her*. I keep feelin' kinda lonesome, somehow. She was always round."

After he had gone, Hilary sat down at his desk and stared into the Bishop's eyes. Steadily closing in upon him was the necessity of making a decision. Day and night he faced it—had faced it now for weeks. With this going of Jim Dolton he knew he could delay no longer. Slowly, logically, he went over all the arguments again. As he thought of Lex and their present estrangement a sweat broke out upon his forehead. But he kept on looking into the Bishop's calm, strong face. At last he drew a long sigh and stood up. He knew what the ultimate answer to his own soul would be.

He went out into the winter afternoon, wondering which calls were the most pressing for that day. He craved companionship at the moment and weighed the choice between Celeste Barton and Mrs. Reed. Finally, he set off for the home of the latter. He had been to see Celeste two weeks before. She had told him again of Maudie Dunn's approaching joy, jokingly referring to herself as a prospective grandmother, trying, evidently, to lift his spirits. For she had seen that all was not essentially right with him. She always read him too well. And while they settled soon into a discussion of the war and its effect on their respective work, Hilary knew that he had not deceived her. She guessed that there was a deeper fear even than that of the war in his heart. He felt he could not go back until he and Lex were reconciled.

But he could go to Mrs. Reed. He found her lying on the sofa, buried in newspapers, with the radio going close to her ear. She looked shrunken and frail.

"It's about time you showed up," she greeted him. "I need holy consolation if anybody ever did. I'm scared stiff. I want to take to the back-woods, but I'm not going to let those Germans run me out. So I'm staying. The worst of it is, I can't knit any more. My hands shake. It's utterly damnable to be old, Hilary, Mr. Browning to the contrary. Come over here and sit down. Kiss me or scold me or pray for me—I don't care which just so long as you make a fuss over me. I'm lonesome."

He laughed in spite of himself. He sat close to her, and began at once to tell about Hastings' preparing a small cache in the basement where he placed the altar ornaments every night, bringing them up again early each morning.

"He seems to feel that he and the Lord between them can take care of things in the daylight, but at night it's best to take no chances," he laughed.

He racked his brain for other bits of lighter news to amuse her, as he held her trembling old hand in his strong ones.

"How's Lex?" she asked suddenly.

"She's pretty well."

"What do you mean, 'pretty well,'" the old lady said quickly. "Has she been ill?"

"No, just upset. Aunt Samantha's death, the war, everything."

"And Dick."

"Yes, always that, with both of us."

"With all three of us," she amended. Then she changed the subject quickly.

"What's the latest about Hettie?"

"Completely docile. She's promised Lex the family silver and the hatchet's really buried apparently, between her and Mrs. McColly. It's an enormous relief all around."

Mrs. Reed chuckled. "I did a good job that day! I only wish I'd had a bigger audience! I've been thinking. I may ask Hettie in to tea. She looks a lot older than I do and that might cheer me up."

When he announced that he must be going, she smiled at him, whimsically.

"I don't believe a prayer would do me any harm. I haven't been to church all winter. Or have you noticed?" she finished with asperity.

Hilary only smiled his reply, but he dropped to his knees beside the couch, still holding her hand.

"Support us all the day long," he began, thinking of the day he had uttered the same words for Grandy, "until the shadows lengthen, and the evening comes and the busy world is hushed, and the fever of life is over, and our work is done. Then in Thy mercy give us a safe lodging and a holy rest and peace at the last. Amen."

He felt strangely better as he went home. The words Mrs. Reed had once uttered in praise of Lex kept returning to him. At dinner that night he knew that the pain in his heart was lifting. He looked across into Lexa's eyes and a wave of tenderness swept over him. For the first time, instead of anger he felt compunction. He saw again that gray, cheerless November afternoon. It had been the day following Clarissa's beautiful wedding when Lex had been only an onlooker instead of being in the center of all the bright excitement. She had been, then, lonely, disappointed and discouraged. Not, he hastened to tell himself, that any of these facts could be construed to excuse what she had done, but they explained it.

It was something else, however, which now that the breach in his resistance had been made, came flooding into his heart. It was the strangest of all feelings, considering the harsh finality of his previous judgment; strange, too, in that it and it alone could steal away the bitterness and bring healing. This feeling was respect. For suddenly he realized that from that sad afternoon on, Lex's behavior had been better than his own. She had borne herself with dignity, but with gentleness. She had not pleaded with him after that first beseeching cry for help. She had made no more excuses for herself, shown no resentment at his aloofness, asked nothing of anyone; but alone had shouldered her guilt and carried the burden of her unhappiness. She had waited in silence, was still waiting.

When they went into the library he stood close to her before the fire. He even touched her hair softly. She looked up quickly, eagerly.

"I wish I didn't have to go out," he said. "It's the Men's Club night and I have to speak—but I wish I could stay."

"I do too," she said.

His heart leaped within him. "I won't be late," he said, as he got his coat.

When he returned, he hurried up the stairs, but the light in the blue room was out. Lex, then, would make no slightest move toward reconciliation. This attitude was inherent in her dignity and he admired her for it. He must go all the way. And tomorrow he would! How could he wait for the day to come? Only a brief span of hours away, and yet to his heart, an eternity. For the stone in his breast was now once more flesh—warm, eager, palpitating flesh. His love came surging tempestuously over him, even as great waters, freed from restraint, rush in headlong flood.

He started to go to her, then he checked himself. The hour was very late—the meeting had been much longer than he had expected and he had been detained afterwards. She was doubtless asleep. He would wait until tomorrow and then with the first light of the new day, go in and break her dreams with his kiss.

He lay wakeful, resolutely putting aside the thought of the war and the darkening shadows that lay ahead, dedicating this night to his regained happiness. *Love watcheth, and sleeping, slumbereth not.* The words from *The Imitation* ran through his mind. It would be so, he felt, this night with him.

But he must have slept, for he woke in the darkness with the ringing of the telephone on the desk. He switched on the lamp at the bedside table, seeing the hour on his watch as he did so. It was two o'clock.

He got to the phone and grasped it nervously.

"Hello."

"Mr. Laurens, I want. Mr. Hilary Laurens."

It was a woman's voice with a French accent and it sounded extremely agitated.

"This is Hilary Laurens."

"Mr. Laurens, could you please come quickly? I am speaking for someone who is very ill and wants a clergyman at once. She has been in your church and seen you. She prays you to come as fast as you can. I will give you the address. Will you come now, quickly?"

"Of course," Hilary answered. "Tell me the address."

"The Colston, at 259 Le Monde Avenue. When you come in go straight to the elevator. Get off at the tenth floor and turn to your right. It is Apartment E."

Hilary repeated the directions carefully.

"I'll come as fast as I can," he said.

He dressed swiftly, putting on his clerical vest, slipped his Prayer-book into his pocket and called a cab. That would be easier, he thought, than getting his own car. He went softly down the stairs, hoping not to disturb Lex, or Morris, who always slept with one ear open. The cab came promptly and he repeated the address to the driver. It was that of a new and very smart apartment hotel. Who was it—he tried hazily to recall—of some notoriety who lived there? He could not remember. He had never had occasion before to visit the building but he had often passed it by. He wondered suddenly if he should have brought with him his small portable communion set. He had had a number of cases, strangers, and High Church, who had wished the Sacrament before death. He watched the deserted streets now as he rode along, thinking of the strange, sad errands upon which the priests of God must go.

He paid the driver, telling him not to wait, entered the quiet lobby and walked to the elevator.

"Tenth," he said to the operator.

When he got out, he turned right in the long, wide, elegantly furnished corridor. He found Apartment E at the end of the hall and rang the bell, feeling the same nervousness he always did at an unexpected sick call.

In a second the door was opened by a woman in maid's uniform who silently led him through the foyer, through a large living room, and into a small hallway with several doors leading from it. Opening one of these she showed him inside, then closed it behind her. A swift feeling of unease possessed Hilary. The room he had entered was very dimly lighted. He approached the bed slowly, in the semi-darkness, his sense of foreboding growing stronger. As he reached it, a hand switched on a light, a soft light, but sufficient to reveal what he saw with horror before him. Reclining against the satin pillows in a filmy negligee was Diana Downes!

In the first shock and revulsion of the moment, Hilary stood speechless.

"Don't look so startled," Diana said in a low, caressing voice. "It's all right. You came honestly on a sick call, not even knowing I had moved here. Don't you see? Now, you don't need to think of anything except that at last we're really together—like this." She stretched a hand toward him, smiling.

Hilary flung himself back, his face on fire. "You lied! You tricked me here!"

He was scarcely conscious of the foul name he spat from his lips for a fear like death was upon him. He had been trapped, *framed!* His one thought was to get out, to get away as fast as possible. He made a rush for the door, opened it, and stood for a second confused in the inner hallway, uncertain of his direction. In the moment of his delay he could hear Diana spring from the bed and cross the floor behind him. She was talking hysterically, half in rage, half in pleading.

He gained the living room and then the foyer. As he put his hand to the outer door, Diana had caught up with him. She came close.

"You fool!" she said furiously. "You crazy, pious fool!"

He opened the door into the corridor. As he stepped out he was conscious that Diana was looking past him.

"Good night, darling," she said distinctly with a quick change of tone; and then shut the door.

The suddenness of his release left Hilary stunned. He drew a shuddering breath of relief, raised his eyes and started for the elevator. Then he stopped, his hair rising upon his head. Down the hall, watching him, stood a tall young man in evening clothes. His hair was black, his full cheeks pasty and his look one of sardonic amusement.

"Well, well, well!" said Tommy Tatler, and disappeared into an apartment as though the earth had opened and swallowed him.

Hilary stood there, trying to grasp the full import of the situation. In a flash he remembered that it was Tommy who, he had once heard, lived here, along with some of the city's smartest society set. The man must have just now gotten off the elevator. From where he stood, he could look straight through the opened door into Diana's foyer. She, glancing up, had seen him, and her revenge upon Hilary had been swift and complete. As of old, Mrs. Potiphar had triumphed even in her defeat. Alas, poor Joseph!

His first fully coherent thought was to rush after Tommy, proclaim his own innocence and demand his protection. But even in the thinking he realized the futility of this. Not only Lexa's repeated warnings but his own common sense told him that to a man of Tommy's type what he had seen was so utterly damning that no words could explain it away. No protestation upon Hilary's part would make Tommy believe him. Would *any* man believe him, Hilary thought with anguish, after witnessing such a scene?

In a daze he moved toward the elevator and went down. He crossed the empty lobby and went out into the night. Heedlessly, blindly, he walked along the street. In these last months he had known discouragement, bitter grief and estrangement from Lex, but all this seemed at the moment less than the blackness of the pit into which he had now fallen. For this was ruin.

No one knew better than he that no breath of scandal must touch a man of God. His usefulness, his value, then, as a clergyman was over. He clenched his hands until the nails cut, as he thought of his young men! Upon them he had poured out the best of his own ideals and counsel. To them, in season and out of season, he had preached morality and the clean life. Now, disillusioning, devastating, there would come to them, even perhaps in faraway army camps, the echoes of Tommy's malicious report of tonight's happening. And he, Hilary, would be helpless to prevent it.

He thought of his people, his congregation. He could call a meeting of the vestry at once and tell them the truth! He could even, if necessary, send out some sort of statement to all the members of the parish, humiliating as that would be! But still, still there would be the ugly rumor passing from lip to lip. Still there would be those who would say, "I wonder?"

He could sue for libel! But could he? All Tommy would report was the scene he had witnessed with his own eyes and which Hilary could not deny. Who ever said that men were secure in their strength? Who ever said it was a man's world? They were the most helpless, the most vulnerable of mortals, for a word, an unholy gesture could destroy them! No, he was ruined. *Lost!* His precious work, his career, his reputation, fallen like the wreckage of Babel.

He felt faint and leaned for a few minutes against a doorway. At last he straightened. I must get home, he thought, I must get to Lex. If I am with her, at least I will not lose my mind.

He hailed a wandering taxi, and before long was back at the rectory. He went in, climbed the stairs heavily and opened the door of Lexa's room. Her regular breathing told him she was asleep. He crossed to the bed and bent over her. How different from his planned intent to wake her at the first light of day with his kiss!

"Lex!" he said urgently. "Lex!"

She roused, sensed his nearness and turned toward him.

"Oh Hil, is it you? I waited so long last night," she said drowsily.

He sank down on the bed beside her.

"Lex, I'm in trouble. Terrible, ghastly trouble."

She woke thoroughly then, sat up, shook back her curls and snapped on the light.

"What is it?" she cried at sight of his face.

"Something unspeakable has happened to me. I'm ruined."

He told her, watching as her face took on the horror of his own. Then he sat with his head in his hands, the tears, which a man dreads, searing his eyeballs.

"It's completely hopeless. I can do nothing. I'm lost," he repeated. "Everything is lost."

For several minutes Lex did not move nor utter a sound. Then he felt her spring from the bed and hurry about the room. He looked up and saw that she was flinging herself into her clothes.

"Listen, Hil," she said, and her voice was resolute, "we have only one chance and we're going to take it. Pull yourself together. We're going to see J. V. Dunn and we're going at once."

"Lex, you're completely mad!"

"No, I'm not. J. V. owns the *Courier.* He's the only person on earth who can stop Tommy and we're going to face him."

"But darling, we *can't.* The man hates me. The very sight of me would send him into a rage. If anything could make matters worse than they are already, it would be to drive J. V. to fury again at me. Please stop, dear. We'll bear this somehow but we *can't . . .*"

Lex had her coat on now and was jamming a beret wildly upon her head. The line of her lips was like that of Old Alex.

"We've got to, Hil. It's our one chance. If you won't come with me, I'll go alone."

And he knew she would. He rose slowly and came over to her. With indescribable tenderness he looked into her face.

"You believe that all was just as I told you?"

Her clear, beautiful eyes looked back into his.

"It would never even occur to me to doubt you."

Then she caught his arm. "We must hurry. I've no idea when Tommy does his dirty work or sends in his copy. We don't know about newspapers. So we've got to get to J. V. as fast as we can."

Hilary got the car since he feared they might have to leave swiftly. He felt much worse than hopeless about the outcome of the visit; he felt actually afraid. It was Lex who was strong. As they drove along the empty streets she kept telling him what he must say, how he must combat J. V.'s rage, how he must compel him to action. Hilary marveled at her.

"And if you can't stand up to him, I will," she finished grimly. "I only hope we can wake him up."

When they drew to the curb in front of the house, however, they were surprised to see lights. They rang the bell and stood on the step, gripping each other's hands. The great door swung open and J. V. himself, fully dressed, stood before them. For a second he looked at them, incredulously, then with a smile warming his whole bleak countenance, he drew them in.

"You have come," he said, "at this hour to rejoice with me! In spite of all that is past, you have still come! I'll never forget this, my boy," patting Hilary upon the back, "never forget this kindness. And you, my dear! This is most gracious of you! Come in! Come in here to the library. Well, this is the greatest day of my life!"

Lex drew near her husband. "He's gone crazy, Hil," she whispered in fright. "What will we do?"

"How did you hear the news?" J. V. was asking, without waiting for an answer. "A nine pound boy! A *boy* in the Dunn family. After all the years I longed for a son. Sit down, Mrs. Laurens, sit down, my boy! We'll have to have a little port, eh? I'm opposed to alcohol in any form, you understand, but an occasion like this calls for a little something, eh? And I've got someone now to drink a toast with me. My sister's out of town and if you two hadn't come I'd have been all alone. At a time like this!"

He poured the glasses with a shaking hand.

"To my grandson!" he said, proudly, beaming upon them. "To Maudie's boy!"

They managed to drink the port and to make some sort of rejoinder. Fortunately they had no need for many words, for J. V. was too intent upon pouring out his story. He hadn't known a child was expected until the day before! Then Jerry had phoned him. There were complications about Maudie at the end and he felt her father should know, should even be at the hospital in case— J. V. had gone, had waited with Jerry through the hours of torture. Then at midnight, "A strong, healthy boy," he told them. "A regular Dunn, and Maudie herself safe and doing well!"

When at last he paused for breath, Lex looked at Hilary and saw the hesitation on his face.

"Mr. Dunn," she said swiftly and her voice was steady, "we are so happy for you and for Maudie and Jerry. It's wonderful about the baby and we're glad we are here to celebrate with you. But we came for another reason. My husband is in terrible trouble and you are the only person who can save him. Tell him, Hil."

J. V.'s countenance looked startled and puzzled.

"You say you came here, for my help?"

"Tell him, dear," Lex repeated. "Tell him everything."

As Hilary spoke, he could see J. V.'s face sharpen. His eyes narrowed to two shrewd slits of concentration; his vulture beak grew thin.

Hilary finished and wiped the sweat from his forehead. At the end his voice had been unsteady, for he knew Dunn would not believe him. He keyed himself now for the sharp questions he was sure would come. Instead J. V. sat silent, his face inscrutable as though reviewing what he had heard. Then he spoke deliberately.

"I credit your story, Mr. Laurens, about this woman, this *Jezebel!* I know you to be a man of truth, so I do not distrust the facts you have presented. As to Tom Worthington, Tommy Tatler, as we call him on the paper, I must explain that he is an important man to us. You might not believe it, but his column has increased our circulation tremendously. We couldn't afford to lose him. I hope you understand his ah—value to us."

A chill crept up Hilary's spine.

"But," J. V. went on, "he has been getting too careless lately. Too damned cocky. Won't listen to advice. I've warned him before. Twice we've been too close for comfort to libel suits. Now, he'll have to learn who's boss. I'll fix this."

He walked to the desk, picked up the telephone and gave a number.

"Managing editor," he snapped. "J. V. Dunn speaking."

In a half dozen clipped sentences he had wiped out the danger.

By the time Lex and Hilary left, J. V. had apparently forgotten the real purpose of their visit. His mind, completely bemused by his new joy, had reverted to his original assumption. He wrung their hands, giving them no chance to speak.

"I'll never forget this! You were the first to drink the health of my grandson. In spite of all that was past you came anyway. That was fine of you both. Very fine. I'll remember your kindness!"

He even waved them off from the top step, the wind fanning his thin, gray hair.

The reaction was so great that once in the car they could not speak coherently. The relief, the joy, overwhelmed them.

When they reached home they went on up to their room. It seemed chill and Hilary busied himself nervously, lighting the fire. A hesitancy hung over them both as though they were alone here for the first time. Then, at last, they were in each other's embrace—closer, far closer than they had ever been before.

The morning came on gently and it was a new day. Muff stirred above them and Morris' soft, punctual steps went through the hall below, but Lex and Hilary did not hear.

"I've grown up, Hil," she whispered against his breast. "I've done so much thinking these last awful weeks when I've been alone in this room. I know now what I want from life. I know what doesn't matter and what does. I won't ever fail you again. If only we could start from here and go on safe and happy together. If only there was no—*war*."

The last word was choked.

"You know then? You guessed?" he asked in amazement.

"Yes. I knew that first Sunday night after the news came. I saw it in your eyes. I've tried to tell myself a chaplain would be in no danger, but I know better. You'll be in the thick of it with the rest of them. I think it will all but kill me to let you go but Hil, I'm proud of you. I know if I were you, I'd do the same thing. And I'll try to carry on here as well as I can. I'll bolster Adams up. I'll see to the Farm . . ."

After a little she asked, very low, "When, Hil? How long will we have?"

"I don't know. I haven't offered myself yet but I don't think there's much doubt of my being accepted. Now that you know, I'll tell the vestry at once. It will all take a little time."

She laid her cheek against his.

"I want a child, now, terribly. I've been selfish to put that off. Now, it matters more than anything else in the world. You see, I have grown up, at last."

His arms crushed her. "My dearest! My own beloved!"

In spite of his weariness, Hilary found that his mind would not let him rest. When Lex, worn out from the excitement, had at last dropped off again to sleep, he rose softly, dressed and went down stairs and out into the court. In a moment he had entered the familiar door. He went slowly into the chancel and knelt at the altar, looking up at the fair white and gold of its adornment. He thought of all the times he had stood before it as the priest: the weddings, the funerals, the eucharists. He thought of what he must soon say to the vestry. By what words could he explain to them this thing he was about to do?

"I hate war," he would say, "with every fiber of my being. All the rest of my life, if it is spared to me, I will work for peace on the earth. But right now we are in war. The young men of this church are going. The young men of the Parish House are going. The young men from the University are going. I, too, am a young man. If I am to preach to them in years to come I must go along with them, now. I am enlisting as a chaplain. I will be leaving . . ."

The words he could not say, even to his vestry, tore at his heart.

"I will be leaving the woman I passionately love—my wife, whose spirit has only now, this night, been truly joined to mine. I will be leaving, it may be, my unborn child. I will be leaving my work, all that I've just begun to build. I will be leaving it all for months, for years—perhaps . . ."

He raised his eyes to the white sculptured form above him. He looked long until a change came over his face. The sadness, the strain and the fear went out of it. It was as though he had arrived at peace.

Slowly he bowed his head upon the altar rail.